THE
WELLS

The Hope Trilogy
Book One

Patrick Gooch

KNOX ROBINSON
PUBLISHING
LONDON • New York

KNOX ROBINSON
PUBLISHING

3rd Floor, 36 Langham Street
Westminster, London W1W 7AP
&
244 5th Avenue, Suite 1861
New York, New York 10001

Knox Robinson Publishing is a specialist, international publisher of historical fiction, historical romance and medieval fantasy.

First published in Great Britain in 2012 by Knox Robinson Publishing
First published in the United States in 2013 by Knox Robinson Publishing

A CIP catalogue record for this book is available from the British Library.

ISBN HC 978-1-908483-41-6

ISBN PB 978-1-908483-42-3

Typeset in Bembo by Susan Veach
info@susanveach.com

Printed in the United States of America and the United Kingdom.

Download the KRP App in iTunes and Google Play to receive free historical fiction, historical romance and fantasy eBooks delivered directly to your mobile or tablet.

Watch our historical documentaries and book trailers on our channel on YouTube and subscribe to our podcasts in iTunes.

www.knoxrobinsonpublishing.com

To Gwen, whose research of the period was invaluable

CHAPTER ONE

Hastings 1736

It had cost him sixpence merely for a soft-spoken word. The rest he had painstakingly fashioned piece by piece. Covertly watching the owlers, Heath, Morrison and Piker John over a mug of ale in Bulverhythe; heeding the gossip of the fishermen on the Stade as they hauled their boats up the shingle; catching whispered conversations between known batmen and tub carriers. At dusk, standing in the shadows to pick up a chance remark, the hint of an assembly. The Riding Officer had slowly gleaned the details until, finally, he had the place, the time and the day.

It was a still night, just the slow, rhythmic wash running up the shore. The gravelly ebb and flow muffling the voices on the beach. Safely hidden amongst a crippled, wind-bent line of trees above Toot Rock, the Officer took out his pipe. He was a cautious man, it went unlit. His horse's muzzle was wrapped in cloth to suppress a chance snicker.

Although moonlit, whispy cloud made it difficult to see all that was happening. Instead, his gaze fastened on the lookout man facing landwards, his back to the sea. Ready in an instant to shout the arrival of the Preventative Men, to fire off a shot alerting the incoming vessel.

He had counted twenty five men and an equal number of packhorses making their way down the path. Although a small shipment, it was one Mr Collier would soon learn about. When questioned, he would explain it had been too late to advise the Surveyor-General, for a force to be raised.

The ship would be letting go anchor. He heard the splash of oars, and dimly perceived four bobbing shapes making their way into the bay. Fifteen minutes passed, then the first, low and sluggish in the water, slithered up the beach. There was feverish movement, unloading, burdening the horses. It was pushed back into the surf, another took its place.

An hour later it was done. The laden horses picked their way up the slope accompanied by the tub carriers brandishing cudgels and muskets – likely stolen from the Blockade Men.

The Riding Officer let them by. What else could he do? Each man in the convoy would earn ten shillings for this night's work, making them more than ready to defend their dues, to avoid the clutches of the law.

In Hastings, the contraband would be secreted in unknown recesses: below floors, under eaves, in the caves that riddled the hillside above the town. The wine, brandy, tea, lace and silks would never be found. Not that it mattered. The Riding Officer already knew where the consignment was destined. Soon it would be on its way to The Wells, to gratify the pleasures of those taking the waters.

CHAPTER TWO

London 1736

He hurried across the marble-floored hall. The warden moved quickly to open one side of the ornate double doors. On the steps the lamps were being tended by a porter, who murmured a courteous goodnight.

Damnation! He'd been looking forward to this evening. The Beechams would be sure to make it a splendid affair, arriving at this hour would be thought unseemly. Why, of all times, had they raised the subject? It had not been urgent. It should have been held over to the next meeting.

He turned in the direction of London Bridge.

Earlier in the day, a backlog of ships had been cleared for discharge and his passage had been blocked by an endless stream of wharfmen clambering up and down gangplanks; a confusion of carts and horses; harassed clerks, desperate to keep tally of all the packages, bales and packets. No way through the mêlée, his carriage had come to a halt by the fish market.

Now the quays were closed he would have to walk to the monument where his driver would be waiting. No great distance, but at night the waterfront took on a different mantle. During daylight hours the shouts and cries of the traders, tellers and porters, the flow of goods in and out the cavernous warehouses, made it a scene of bustling liveliness. All that had long since drained away. Now it was sombre and forbidding. The buildings were cast in bold shadows, ever-changing in the flickering moonlight. Images were created that pricked the imagination.

As he passed Ralph's Quay his step became more pressing. The fall of his shoes, kicking at the cobbles, echoed in the stillness. Why should I be nervous, he thought. No one wishes me ill.

He was misguided.

They had been ever-present since he had left the house. He had not been difficult to follow, the congested streets had slowed his progress. They had observed his arrival, and waited patiently for his reappearance.

When he finally emerged, the task had been that much easier.

They kept him in sight as he walked upstream. The sheds, passageways, and overhangs of the warehouses giving them every advantage. His footsteps on the cobbles hiding the faint sounds of their pursuit.

A canvassed load on the quayside forced him closer to one of the buildings. The moon, momentarily obscured, cast its frontage in deepest gloom. Was it his fancy? Had he heard a snatched breath, the scuff of a shoe? His pace quickened into a stumbling shuffle. Unaccustomed to exertion, his chest heaved, a sheen of perspiration glistened on his brow.

He stopped briefly, leaning against a pillar. How can I entertain such fears he questioned, gasping for air.

An involuntary movement, his head lifting for a deeper breath. A hand snaked out clamping over his mouth. Even in that moment of terror, he was aware of its roughness, the calloused skin, a strange, earthy smell.

The knife moved in an arc sawing into flesh. He hardly felt it. Cold air whistled in his throat, blood flooded the side of his face, splashing across a moonlit pillar.

Slowly, he sank to his knees. His vision dimmed. It was hard to focus on the two figures emerging from the shadows. The taller holding the weapon of his destruction. He mouthed words that never came. Toppling forward, he fell his length on the cold, damp stones.

Without comment, each assassin took a leg. It was the work of a moment to drag the still-warm corpse across the wharf. Dropping their burden at the edge, they rolled the body, almost disdainfully, into the dark waters lapping the wooden piles of Dice Quay.

CHAPTER THREE

"I'm right am I not?"

Deep in thought, Marius Hope was oblivious to the conversation around him, yet the question was directed at him. Turning his gaze from the coach window, he stared at the man opposite.

"I was saying to our companions . . . consider the evidence. The black frock coat, grey breeches, white chemise and cravat . . . a silver-topped cane. As obvious as the Caduceus of Hermes! He must be a doctor of physick . . . I'm right sir, am I not?"

Marius gave the briefest of nods, and resumed his unseeing study of the passing countryside.

The fellow was undaunted. Tapping Marius on the knee, he continued. "You could say we have similar occupations, you and me. I too practise as a physician, though not of humankind. I treat horses. Allow me to introduce myself . . . Nathaniel Jordan, farrier."

Once more Marius nodded, declining to be drawn.

The two women resumed their conversation. He learned their husbands had journeyed ahead to acquire suitable lodgings. Mrs Fielding said little about her spouse. Mrs Johnson, next to Marius, readily declared that hers was a man of property. He travelled widely, and had a considerable number of clients for whom he purchased land and all manner of buildings. Marius allowed himself the briefest glance. The lady's background seemed at odds with her wardrobe. She had a pleasing face, and was amply figured. Yet neither her dress nor bonnet appeared to match her status. If they were comfortably off, Marius thought idly, why was she not dressed in keeping.

In addition to the farrier there were two other men on the opposite bench.

In the far corner sat a slightly-built, young fellow. Thin-faced, staring eyes of the palest hue. He wore a wispy moustache, which lay bedraggled on his top lip. Brightly dressed in a green topcoat, yellow chemise and a green cravat, the cut and colour of his breeches were obscured by a large, grey cloth bag held firmly on his knee.

In the middle of the trio was a portly gentleman. He was clearly unable to contain himself.

"I hear that if you drink the spa waters, it makes a new man of you."

The leather bench squealed in protest as he turned his bulk in the younger man's direction. "Are you travelling to The Wells for your health, sir?"

Mumbling he was a musician, he added in a firmer note, "I'm joining a musical ensemble in The Wells."

The gentleman straightened, and cleared his throat. "Augustus Brown," he said portentously. "Trader in comestibles."

Still taking in the passing scene, Marius was aware of an ill-concealed smugness in the tone. He angled his gaze to take in the gentleman's appearance. Elegantly bewigged, and wearing clothes of obvious quality, his self-importance was palpable.

"I am about to open a food emporium in The Wells," he declaimed, his several chins rippling in the wash of words. A man who weighed each phrase for its effect.

"I have a wholesale business in Tooley Street in Southwark, and several shops in Bermondsey and Walworth."

Pause.

"I shall sell foodstuffs firstly in The Wells, and thereafter take premises in Tonbridge."

The farrier next to him shifted in his seat. "Tonbridge is a much larger town, why not start your business there?"

Augustus Brown deliberated on his answer. Almost shamefacedly, he sighed. "My wife is joining me later in the season, and I must ensure she is provided with the items we enjoy at home." He added lamely, "It will still be a worthwhile venture, you understand."

Marius glanced at the farrier from time to time. Nathaniel Jordan had not removed his hat. Despite the growing heat of the midsummer day, his dark frock coat was still buttoned. On one occasion, when their eyes met, they held an unwavering, mocking gaze. His swarthy features were dominated by a large, bulbous nose. Although tall, he carried little excess weight. An air of controlled aggression emanated from his presence.

The man sat stiffly on the facing bench, hands thrust awkwardly into his pockets. As the coach rolled, his knees hit against Marius' with unwelcome regularity. Occasionally, the farrier would cross his legs, and an ornate, well-polished shoe would catch his shin. Small wonder, he thought, that this had been the only unoccupied seat when he had boarded the coach.

The decision had been made on a whim, prompted by the comment of the hospital's chief physician. "Until you rid yourself of your bad humours, sir, you'll be no use to me here!"

Well, if I am suffering any maladies, he had decided, what better than a visit to a spa town. Whereupon, he had gone to the coaching inn at Southwark and bought a passage to The Wells, paying eight shillings for an inside seat.

That morning, he had been unprepared for the tumult in the coaching yard. Baggage boys struggling with their loads, dragging the heavier items across grimy cobbles. Serving girls dispensing jugs of ale. Many of the passengers and early drinkers at the tavern standing in the yard, taking their ease in the thin, early morning sun. Opposite the alehouse, a first floor balcony was lined with spectators, waving their ale mugs, shouting encouragement to the industrious below.

In the middle of the yard was the coach. The grooms steadying the horses as they were backed to harness. Hooves clattering in short, staccato steps as the team reversed either side of the shaft. All the while, the vehicle was swaying and creaking on its leathers as the outside passengers clambered into the high seats. An assortment of luggage was being tossed and stowed beside them in the roof net.

Marius identified the passengers travelling within. They were standing to one side in a silent group. The innkeeper checked his right of passage. A boy was called to take his valise, which was placed with the heavier baggage on the accompanying wagon. Taking Marius' carrying bag, the innkeeper squeezed it into the basket at the rear of the coach.

As ten of the clock approached, the inside passengers were called forward. Finishing his mug of ale, Marius climbed the short steps, and eased himself onto the end of the narrow, leather-covered bench. The worse for wear from the impression of countless breeches.

Doors slammed, steps were removed, the coachmen climbed to their seats on the high box. Then, as the hour tolled, the coach jerked forward, pulling slowly out the yard into the Borough Road to the sound of the horn trumpeting its departure.

CHAPTER FOUR

The Wells

As the final peal declaring the hour resonated over The Wells, Adam Loveday made his cautious way along the Lower Walk. The uneven surface a ready trap for the unwary. He was not prepared to sacrifice a week of his family's labours for one careless step.

Clutching the bulky parcel he concentrated on his footing, ignoring the sounds of the Walks readying for another day. Shop front shutters noisily being thrown open; handcarts rattling over the flags; the mounting chatter of vendors as they set out their wares. The frequent muffled curse when an item was found unsellable, or something was dropped.

Stallholders were erecting their trestles and boards. Covering them with brightly-coloured cloths as an enticing backdrop to the goods on offer. Others pulling canvases over high wooden frames to protect their merchandise from sunlight or a passing shower.

The fish market was already busy as early morning shoppers sought the best of the catch. The smell of fresh and salted herrings was heavy in the air as Loveday mounted the steps to the raised concourse of the Upper Walk. Unsighted by his load, his feet searched for each new level. He leaned against the handrail to steady his progress.

When set firmly on the evenly-laid pantiles, he turned in the direction of the Well. Away from the coffee houses and the Assemby Rooms, by Bond's Long Room and the Flat House, and on past the well-stocked shops set back beneath the white-pillared colonnade. At this hour their doors were firmly shut. They would open later to tempt those taking their leisure along the Upper Walk. With a more measured stride, Loveday moved on towards the Dial and the wide flank of steps.

A tall, spare-framed man, seemingly with an intensity of purpose. His eyes, set above a thrusting, hooked nose enforced the image of someone rarely bested in argument, seldom deflected from his aims.

Walking more easily on the even ground, his mind turned to the farrier. He continued to refuse the fellow's demands, but he was aggressively persistent. A smithy close to the Walks would certainly be more practical. The nearest blacksmith's yard was almost a mile away at the top of Mount Pleasant. What the farrier did not appreciate was selling him a parcel of land would also entail the surrender of a freeholder's rights to a share in the Walks.

Giving up income from the rents, or a proportion of the land value if it were sold, would not be a wise move now the lease had expired. Any new arrangement would surely be more profitable. The trouble is, Loveday thought wryly, the lease had ended four years ago, and still matters were unresolved. He and the other freeholders were still seeking an accommodation with the Lord of The Manor.

As their spokesman he felt concern that their future lay in his hands. On more occasions than he could recall he had presented their views to Maurice Conyers, the present Lord of The Manor of Rusthall. Each time, Conyers had been tight-lipped and unyielding. Now his fellow freeholders were becoming restless. Loveday did not agree with threatening tactics. He had declared if they wished someone else to represent their interests, he would gladly step aside. But at their meetings in the chapel in Frog Lane, his suggestion had always been shouted down. Eventually it would be resolved. It had to be for everyone's sake. He wanted some measure of security to pass to his children.

Carefully descending the steps near the Well, Loveday had an uninterrupted path to the church. Using his back to force open the heavy double doors, he edged into the nave. At this hour, the tall, narrow windows set high on the walls, provided little light. He stood for a moment in the dim interior, allowing his eyes to adjust to the gloom.

"Adam!" came the inviting call from close to the pulpit. A slight figure appeared dressed in a dark cassock. "Have you got them?"

Loveday set down the parcel on a nearby pew, and hastily removed his wide-brimmed hat. "Not as many as I would have wished, Reverend. But, they will do for the present."

"Bring them forward! Bring them forward!"

He scooped up the bundle, and walked slowly up the central aisle to the altar rail. The cleric, his sparse, white hair falling around his collar, opened the gate and taking the parcel laid it carefully on the topmost step. Unwrapping it, twelve votive candles were exposed.

"Splendid! These are even better than you've made previously," declared the Reverend Julius, bending closer to examine them.

"I used the best beeswax and the new tin moulds," Loveday said proudly. "Mind you, they took a while to cool. Then I had to hang them for a few days in the fresh air to whiten."

A half of the hour later, Loveday emerged from the church. As the mood caught him, he turned towards the Gloster Tavern. Hitherto, he had made the church candles by repeated dipping and rolling. This new method, using moulds, was no quicker but it was easier to produce the tall, thick-stemmed candles.

Taking a mug of cider he found a quiet corner. He had been told Jordan, the farrier, had returned to London; but, instinctively, he sought the shadows. Loveday was aware that he was not the only one who had been approached to sell his title deeds. The fellow was forcing his attentions on others.

What was more concerning, Jordan was also trying to persuade those freeholders with pitches in the Lower Walk to sell illicit goods. Although he had not yet attempted to coerce Loveday. Yet some had succumbed, and were now offering tea, wine and silks from beneath the skirts surrounding their stalls.

Emptying his mug, he peered cautiously from the doorway before hurrying towards the family stall. His wife would have already set out the candles: the tapers, pillars and containers neatly tied in bundles, in readiness for another day's trade. Loveday was a member of the Tallow Chandlers' Guild. Although, when summer visitors occupied the town, the majority favoured beeswax candles. They burnt with a brighter light and a more agreeable odour. The cheaper tallow candles, mostly of animal fat, gave off an acrid smoke. Even in their manufacture the smell was unpleasant. The hot oil an especial hazard. His eldest son was learning the art, but Loveday or his wife were always close at hand when the lad was dipping.

The Lovedays' younger children were also employed in the family business. With their nimble fingers they plaited the cotton rovings into burning wicks. Essential if the flame were to burn brightly without stutter.

As Loveday strolled across the market square, a number of his fellow freeholders nodded in his direction. He could see from their faces they were in little mood for banter. There was discontent in their manner, irritation evident in the clipped words of conversation. He judged it would not take much to ignite open hostility. Then, where would it lead?

CHAPTER FIVE

The Outskirts of London

The coach rumbled on. With the city behind them, workers could be seen working in the fields. Marius caught the glimpse of a sail on the distant River Thames. After a while, the drumming of the wheels, the creaking and swaying of the coach, the fall of the hooves retreated into the background, leaving him even more alone with his thoughts.

They passed by the church of St Nicholas on the way through the village of Deptford. Shortly afterwards they reached their first stop, an inn in a hamlet close by the ford across the Ravensbourne. A brief delay whilst the horses were changed. The passengers seated on the roof scrambled down causing the coach to rock alarmingly. Some carrying victuals they had brought to eat on their journey.

Inside the inn, a table was set with ale and cider. But Marius was not inclined to sit with his fellow passengers. He strolled towards the stream, watching the small urchins from the bankside houses playing at the water's edge.

Their excitement evoked memories of his own childhood. Hearing again the sharp cries of his brothers and sisters as they revelled in the brook bordering the Chelsea family home. He remembered vividly how they had run in and out the stream, splashing one another, intent on catching anything that moved in their tiny nets. That age, he recalled, held few presentiments of the future.

As he and his siblings had grown into young adults, inevitably their pursuits had changed. Gradually the others began leaving their childhood sanctuary. His sisters had married. Marius' father, as generations before him, ran the family shipping business and his two elder brothers took to working for the company. As a consequence, they had moved to lodgings close to the offices on the quay by London Bridge.

Marius remembered when the topic of his career had been raised. Sitting in his father's study on that fateful day, he had been adamant shipping held little appeal.

"Then, what about acting as an agent for us abroad?" his father had suggested. "Travel is very rewarding, Marius, and such experiences would be an asset."

But, he had held firm against the proposal.

"Well, I suppose I could procure a suitable rank for you in one of the regiments," his father mused. "Or, if you are of a mind," he had said amiably, "you could train as a physician under my old friend Robert Mellors at St Bartholomew's Hospital."

At the time Marius had few insights into the world of medicine. However, in the early years of the eighteenth century, there had been a growing regard for doctors of physick. He had blithely agreed to this choice of profession. A decision lightly taken on the moment that would return to haunt him in the coming years.

"Dr Hope … Dr Hope!"

Slowly the words registered. One of his fellow travellers was calling him.

"Dr Hope, we are about to depart!" It was shouted by the farrier, who must have obtained his name from the coachman's manifest. Retracing his steps, Marius took his seat. It was even more cramped. Mrs Fielding had brought with her a travelling bag from the storage net.

"The next stage," declared Brown, with an exaggerated lift of the head causing a light dusting of powder to erupt from his wig. "Let us hope it is uneventful. I have heard there are scoundrels abroad who prey on passing coaches."

Shortly after the journey had resumed, replete with ale, the three men slumbered. The women were still conversing, but now in desultory tones. The light breeze through the open windows failed to temper the rising noonday heat.

Marius could not settle. Once more, he stared out at the passing landscape, seeing little other than past memories. He still remembered vividly the moment his education had begun at St Bartholomew's Hospital in 1728. Almost eight years ago to the day.

He had taken rooms in Saffron Hill, the other side of the Fleet River, before presenting himself to Dr Robert Mellors, the venerable physician. He had outlined his expectations of Marius and the other young men present.

"It will involve six long years of diligence, endeavour and patience," he had intoned. "You will learn anatomy, zoology, and biology. To qualify as a doctor of physick, you will need to identify the causes and symptoms of illness, be conversant with the means of treatment, and, at all times, keep abreast of medical advances."

Marius' memory of the rest of the introduction was faint. What had struck hard was the declaration he would remain at his studies for six years. This was not what he had envisaged. At that moment he was sorely tempted to take up another career. Suddenly, a military life, even the church, held greater appeal. But, even as such thoughts arose, so they were dismissed. He had stated his choice of career, and could not now lightly set it aside.

The first major obstacle, which almost made him reverse that decision, had been the classes in anatomy. Marius could not come easily to terms with dissecting cadavers. Whilst his compatriots opened and inspected bodies with equanimity, all too often he had been forced to excuse himself from the room.

With family and friends, Marius would enthusiastically declare all was progressing well. Yet, he knew dissection was becoming an increasingly burdensome part of his training. Prior to a class he rarely ate, and drank very sparingly. As this aversion became apparent, often he would be singled out by the chief anatomist, Dr Curtis, to perform in front of his fellow students.

"If you cannot look into a man's innards," Dr Curtis had lectured, in a high-pitched voice that echoed around the tall, joyless anatomy room, "you will not make a physician." His prophetic words would follow Marius on the many occasions he had been obliged to make a hasty exit.

It was during the third year at the hospital that a severe outbreak of typhoid fever occurred. For some time Marius' interest in the spread and containment of diseases had been growing. He held to a passionate belief they were often the result of people living in unsanitary conditions.

"I won't deny, sir," Dr Mellors had commented on one occasion, "that what you say may have a strong influence on the eruption of certain diseases. But, how do you account for their presence in many of our patients, who live in quite congenial surroundings?"

Marius had opined that airborne diseases were no respecters of boundaries.

"Are you making an assumption, sir?" Mellors had queried. "Or is it based on evidence of which I am not aware? Are you suggesting, for example, that noxious vapours such as from the excreta of horses, could be the culprit?"

His fellow students had been amused by Mellors' irony, and Marius had lapsed into silence. However, his leanings towards the treatment of communicable diseases continued to occupy him. When a body exhibiting symptoms of fever appeared in the anatomy room, he had been instructed to dissect it.

"In this instance, you must take precautions, Hope. Or are you not staying with us for long?" Dr Curtis had enquired with biting cynicism.

Vapour burners had been placed around the table, and a wet cloth covered much of his head. However, preoccupied with the effects of the disease upon the organs and tissues of the body, he had been engrossed in the whole procedure. The task had been completed to his tutor's surprise and satisfaction.

From that moment, Marius had become an inspired pupil. After his initial unease, he had become an avid learner. Anatomy classes no longer held any terrors for him. The work was suddenly stimulating, and his interest quickened as each remaining stage of the course was encountered.

Time passed rapidly. In the spring of 1734, at the age of twenty six, Marius Hope was judged by his peers to have qualified as a doctor of physick with distinction.

CHAPTER SIX

Rusthall

Before being called for dinner at one of the hour, it was his practice to deal with matters relating to the estate. Having spent several hours dealing with its administration, he turned to the letters which lay on his desk. One in particular, caught his eye. The flap bore the seal of The Houses of Parliament. Opening it, Conyers glanced to the foot of the single sheet of paper. His eyebrows rose when he noted the signature.

Lord of The Manor
Maurice Conyers
Rusthall Manor
Kent
12th day of July 1736

My Dear Conyers,

I Feel it Necessary to Advise You of a Chance Conversation with Henry Fox. He had Returned to The House Following a Dinner at Downing Street, Arranged to Celebrate Walpole's Installation in His Official Residence.

Seemingly In His Cups, Fox Revealed that The Principal Minister was Taking a Much Closer Interest in The Affairs of The Wells. It would Appear Walpole has been The Receiver of Much Unwelcome Comment. Visitors to The Spa Town, Including Mrs Skerritt, have Complained that the Reception Accorded Them was Less than Gracious. It would Seem Many of The Residents are Displaying Boorishness and Ill-Manners, Loitering in Groups Uncaring and Disdainful of The People of Worth.

In the Principal Minister's Opinion, This Attitude could Well have A Damaging Effect on the Popularity of the Town, Thought by Many to be A Growing Rival to The Spa at Bath.

He Strongly Believes the Problem is Attributable to the Discord that Exists Between Yourself and These Other Holders of Title to The Walks.

He Avows that Something must be Done to Avoid Unpleasantness to Those Seeking Medicinal Benefit from The Waters. If Apportionment of the Land Among the Ownership is not Soon Resolved, Fox declares Walpole Will Take the Matter to The House.

I Would Urge You to Agree Terms with The Other Titleholders with All Speed.

Your Cordial Friend
William Pitt

Maurice Conyers sat at his desk deep in thought. Somewhere, in the recesses of the house came the sonorous chiming of a clock. Mr Pitt was hardly a friend. What was his game?

Though they were not well-acquainted, Conyers knew much about him. Pitt suffered from gout and a haughty temper, and was not disposed to the finer points of politics. Yet, it was widely put about that he had been awarded a soft seat in The Commons, and had been taken under Baron Cobham's wing. A discontented Whig vehemently opposed to Sir Robert Walpole's policies, and keen to see him ousted from his position of Principal Minister …

Was it a ploy to create rancour, to cause upset during The Principal Minister's visit to The Wells? To set Conyers at odds with Walpole? It might well signal a more devious approach than being openly critical in the House. Having been disparaging of the ministry in his maiden speech, Pitt had been beside himself when the Principal Minister had deprived him of his military commission.

Conyers rose to his feet, and stared at the letter. A knock at the door interrupted his reverie. He was being called. As he strode across the hall to join his family, Conyers realised it might be well to heed the warning. If Walpole were exasperated enough to resolve the dispute through Parliament, Conyers could suffer as a result. It clearly called for action, and perhaps a little more discretion.

CHAPTER SEVEN

The horses were changed at a coaching inn in Chelsfield, a hamlet situated on the rolling ridges of the North Downs. Thereafter, good time was made over the next leg to the Grange Inn at Riverhead. In a shady courtyard, the favoured passengers were offered beef, ale, port wine, and cheese from a laden table. Not having eaten since breakfast, Marius devoured a full platter with relish. The horses were replaced, and they boarded to continue their journey. However, no more than minutes passed before the coach came to a rocking halt below the town of Sevenoaks.

"It's too much fer the 'orses," the coachman called. "Yer'll 'ave to take yer baggage, and walk to the top o'' the "ill."

Not a welcome command. Walking off a heavy meal by carrying baggage uphill on a warm summer's day was not what the passengers had envisaged. With ill grace, the coach seats slowly emptied, baggage was retrieved, and in ones and twos, they wearily commenced their upward journey. Marius found himself handed down both his own and Mrs Johnson's voluminous carpet bag.

"How far is it to the top, driver?" asked Brown, adjusting his frock coat and squaring his hat and wig over a reddening face.

"No more 'an three-quarters o' a mile, sir. Yer'll find us by the 'orse trough and pump in the middle o'' the town."

With a click of the tongue, a flick of the reins, the coachman encouraged the team forward, and the now unburdened coach climbed slowly from view.

The pace varied. The column of walkers lengthened as it wound its way up the hillside. Carrying Mrs Johnson's bag, Marius was obliged to walk beside her. Not given to exercise, the gentlewoman's progress was slow and they were soon bringing up the rear, stopping frequently on the incline.

"I wish I could pretend I was taken by the view," Mrs Johnson said breathlessly. "But I'm afraid, sir, the heat is conspiring against me."

On one occasion Mrs Johnson rested on a convenient milestone. "I am not sure what I would have done if I had needed to carry my bag as well," she said in a relieved tone.

"Dr Hope, if I may be so bold," she said, leaning forward and touching his arm with her fan. "I have the strongest impression all is not well. Is something disturbing you?"

Marius smiled ruefully. He would have preferred to keep his private concerns from fellow-passengers.

"If I appear preoccupied, madam, it has nothing to do with present company. More a reflection of my work. In fact, the reason I am making this journey is to distance myself from it. Mr Jordan was right, I am a physician, but not a contented one."

Mrs Johnson was silent for several minutes. Marius thought the conversation was done. Then she enquired. "What does your family advise?"

"I have never seen fit to raise such matters with them, madam," he replied stiffly.

They continued their upward journey. Marius knew he had responded harshly. Yet Mrs Johnson had not been overly inquisitive. When in company, was it not natural to converse in such a manner? Need he have been so cutting in his reply?

As he trudged beside the gentlewoman, Marius realised that this was how he had always reacted. He thought back to earlier times with the family. Whilst the others would discuss their troubles openly, invariably he would leave the room if conversations took a serious turn. He had always revelled in his brothers' and sisters' triumphs, given sympathy when setbacks arose. More than any member of the family, Marius had been anxious to retain the idyll of home life. If there were moments causing upset, so they were hidden away, repressed, until the threat went away.

In childhood, they were rarely of lasting concern. Gradually, it became his way of dealing with personal agonies. Put them out of mind. Allowing them to intrude was to acknowledge their existence.

However, Marius was slowly coming to accept that as one became older, so it became difficult to isolate yourself from the world. Problems dismissed do not melt away. On the contrary, they grow in magnitude. The situation now facing him at the hospital was one such example. Was this visit to The Wells another occasion when he was fleeing from an issue?

As the roadway levelled out on the approaches to the town, Mrs Johnson was able to catch her breath.

"I'm sorry if you thought I was prying into your affairs, " she murmured.

Marius immediately regretted his sharpness of tone.

"Madam, please accept my apologies. Making that untimely remark was more a condemnation of myself."

Hesitating for a moment, he then said something foreign to his nature.

"May I confide something to you, Mrs Johnson?"

"I may appear a chatty soul, Dr Hope," she replied with a faint smile. "However, it is not in my nature to reveal a confidence."

Thus it was, as they walked towards the pump in Sevenoaks, Marius found himself recounting the setbacks facing him at the hospital.

"I am a physician in charge of one of the wards at St Bartholomew's Hospital," he said reflectively. "I treat ailments such as smallpox, typhoid fever, and even periodic outbreaks of bubonic plague."

He hesitated, a flicker of irony crossed his face. "I take satisfaction from my work. But more and more, I am of the opinion that whilst some branches of medicine are progressing in leaps and bounds, many of the treatments we employ are still largely guesswork."

For a moment he wondered if he should unburden himself upon the woman.

"Carry on, Dr Hope."

"Increasingly, I have felt I was treating the symptoms not the causes. Whenever, I have broached the subject with the chief physician, he has declared I was not employed as a medical evangelist. I was there to alleviate pain and suffering, to cure the patients in my charge . . . and I was not doing a particularly good job."

He stopped to change round the baggage he was carrying.

"We practise blood letting of course, use cold compresses and vapour burners. I try to keep patients with the same disease apart from others. But I am convinced there is more we could be doing.

"Even as a student, when assessing contagions I was convinced crowded, unsanitary conditions encouraged the spread of disease. At first, I thought my tutors considered the idea misdirected. I realise now though they might accept the premise, to them it was inconsequential. The majority of patients receiving attention at St Bartholomew's do not come from deprived backgrounds."

They stopped once more some way short of the coach. There was little need to hurry, the coachmen were reloading the baggage, the passengers slaking their thirsts at the pump.

"In many respects, the chief physician was right," Marius observed. "I was not curing many people. I tried numerous remedies of my own devising, but to no great avail. We do little, other than make patients comfortable, and hope their maladies subside."

Marius glanced at his companion. "Forgive me, Mrs Johnson, may I provide you with some water?"

Mrs Johnson smiled her acceptance, and he walked over to the fountain and returned with a metal cup.

"I came to realise," he continued, "that I was not only casting doubt on the chief physician's judgement, but also his attitude to the prevention of disease. Perhaps, the last was a more sensitive issue," reflected Marius. "For the past year I know I have been an irritation in my repeated requests for change. I wanted the hospital authorities to search for ways to eradicate a number of diseases rather than provide ineffectual treatments.

"Matters came to a head ten days ago, during St Bartholomew's Fair. This is held just outside the hospital gates, and attracts a wondrous array of stalls and visitors. There are fortune-tellers, sideshows, strolling musicians, shies, trinket sellers, dancers. The whole square is decorated with coloured garlands."

He stopped for a moment, vividly recalling the welcome diversion from the demands of the hospital. But as the glimmer of past thoughts died, his mouth took on a firmer set.

"After the fair, a gentleman was admitted to my ward suffering a high fever. His companions, who brought him to the hospital, were unable to give an explanation of his condition."

Marius made to pick up their bags, stooping to take hold of the handles.

"On examination, I noticed a small area of broken skin on his left side. Looking at his chemise and waistcoat, there were matching marks on both garments. I spoke with his friends asking if he had been near an animal. Immediately several of them muttered, "St Bartholomew's Fair"."

They neared the coach, which was making ready to continue its journey.

"Strolling around the fair, they had happened upon a musician with a performing monkey. They had teased the animal, much to the annoyance of the owner. It would appear he had snatched up his instrument, and at the first notes, the monkey had leapt at the victim. His name was Doughty, Francis Doughty. The animal had clung briefly to his chest before returning to its perch. At the time, no one realised it had bitten him."

Marius remembered clearly the day Francis Doughty had been placed in one of the beds.

"I was at a loss to recommend the appropriate treatment. His pulse rate and temperature soared. His skin turned yellow, and open sores appeared all over his body. I applied our usual regimens. Alas, after three days of agony, Mr Doughty died," he mumbled, lost in his thoughts.

"Perhaps it was for the best. I have never seen a disease of such virulence."

Their footsteps slowed. Marius was absorbed in his recollections.

"This may sound gruesome, Mrs Johnson, but in severe causes of death, I often remove and dispose of those organs which are diseased. Mr Doughty was so consumed with an attack of unknown origin, frankly, I thought it best to be rid of the whole body," Marius said in a troubled voice.

"In my concern, perhaps I was less than considerate in my handling of the incident. When his family came to the hospital, I put my recommendation to them. They were appalled, and adamant in their refusal. What is more, despite my protestations, the hospital authorities sided with their decision."

As the memories returned, a pained expression crossed his face.

"They even wanted a night-time funeral. I know it's fashionable these days. Many believe it adds to the occasion, with blazing torches, candles, prayers and hymns offered up in the half-light. Burial arrangers say it allows for mourners more easily to express their grief."

Marius recalled he had washed his hands of the whole affair. At least, so he had thought.

"Two days later I happened to be passing the students' quarters, and paid a visit to the anatomy room. To my horror, there was Mr Doughty stretched out on the dissection table, with the anatomist, Dr Curtis, in full flow."

He glanced anxiously at Mrs Johnson. Common sights to him could be upsetting to others. " Forgive me, I often forget how macabre it must sound."

"Go on, Dr Hope," Mrs Johnson said in a quiet voice.

He looked at her uncertainly.

"Well, I accept that Curtis might not have known the provenance of the body. Cadavers usually acquired by hospitals are those of criminals. However, there are times when they are procured from other sources. I am well aware that bodies snatched from graveyards often reappear in mortuaries. It's an abominable practice, hospital authorities should be more diligent."

He stopped for a moment, again glancing sideways to see if he had disturbed her.

"What happened, Dr Hope?" she prompted.

The memory came flooding back.

Marius had stood in the doorway. Unseen, as Curtis, in that keening whine of a voice, had lectured. "This cadaver appears to have suffered from an unknown malady, so we must take precautions."

In outrage, Marius had called out. "Pray, what precautions do you recommend, Dr Curtis?"

"Ah, Dr Hope, welcome to the room from which you so often excused yourself in the past," Curtis had answered bitingly. "I cannot be expected to know all the facts of this body's ailments. But, we shall employ vapour burners and the students in the front row will wear cloths dampened with vinegar over their mouths."

"I tell you now that is not sufficient!" Marius had shouted. "Less than two days ago, this man died in terrible agony from an unknown cause. His body should not even have been interred, it should have been incinerated. You are jeopardising everyone in the whole building by your flagrant disregard!"

"I did not suffer your irrational ideas as a student, and I certainly do not intend to take notice of them now. Leave immediately!" Curtis had cried, beside himself in anger.

After that, events had moved swiftly. The hospital governors had interviewed Marius the next day. For his part, he had despaired of ever making them see the obvious. He was advised to adjust to the methods set for the good of the hospital or seek employment elsewhere. The chief physician had insisted he come to his senses.

He recounted this to the woman who had stopped and was now looking up into his face. The last words had been said in such a dispirited voice, that Mrs Johnson reached out to touch his arm. They stood together for several minutes, each silent with their thoughts.

Then Mrs Johnson remarked, "We must give the matter serious consideration, Doctor. I can appreciate the attitude of the hospital, not that I agree with it mind. What you have done is confuse them. You have asked them to choose between the observance of good medicine and their more practical interests."

She smiled. "I believe you did the right thing in leaving. It will allow for a fresh view of the situation. If you would permit, I would welcome discussing the matter further."

With that she plucked her carpet bag from his hand.

"Come, sir," she declared. "Now we must repair with the others to The Wells."

Marius was preoccupied all the way to the Rose and Crown Inn at Tonbridge. Hardly aware of the coach leaving the town of Sevenoakes, crossing the High Weald, and passing through the borough of Hilden.

What surprised him was the manner of the woman sitting beside him. Of similar age to his mother, yet blessed with a warmth to which one unconsciously responded. Marius had revealed much to her, yet there was contentment in so doing. Perhaps, for the very reason she was a stranger. He felt more at ease with himself, more able to think clearly about his future, and whether or not it lay at St Bartholomew's.

Suddenly, the coach was turning in through an archway into an inn yard. Familiar with the procedure, the passengers inside awaited their moment to alight. When the coach stopped its fearsome rocking, steps were dragged to the doors.

Cool drinks were provided. A number of the passengers strolled the gardens. The weary horses were unhitched, a fresh team brought from the stables. The temperature of the late afternoon sun was bearable. Nevertheless, Marius' fellow travellers stayed in a group, sitting in the shade of a chestnut tree. Marius joined them after stretching his legs by walking the length of the yard. The musician was still carrying his sack, but he now saw the fellow's breeches were rust-coloured. The horse doctor had removed his hat, and had a very full head of dark hair. Brown, the comestibles trader, limped slightly when he rose to place a mug on a nearby table. Mrs Johnson looked up at Marius, and returned his smile.

Once more, the coachman called to take their seats. As they made themselves comfortable, the coach drove out the inn yard and turned onto the Hastings road for the last leg of the journey.

There were two demanding inclines: on both occasions the horses coming close to a standstill. However, they continued steadily in the direction of Woodsgate, before turning towards The Wells.

The last mile into the town was down a steep hill, with both coachmen holding tightly to the long brake arms as the horses' shoes slipped on the rutted descent. Finally, at just past six of the clock, without mishap or hindrance, the coach came to a rocking halt in front of the Angel Inn.

CHAPTER EIGHT

The Wells

The ornate French clock daintily chimed the hour, breaking the silence.

"I believe that concludes what I expect of you. Please attend to my needs with despatch. I bid you good-day, sir."

With those parting words, the gentleman rose: leaving the room through the French windows, he made his way across the lawn and through a little-used doorway set in the surrounding wall. All the while the other man sat rigidly in his chair, fighting indignation at the peremptory manner of his caller. Even when reviewing his involvement with the fellow, he had not expected such cavalier treatment.

He thought back to his movements earlier in the day. Rising early, as was his custom, he had dressed with deliberation. His manservant had prepared a favoured chemise, and set out a matching grey brocade waistcoat and frock coat. It was when staring at his reflection in the mirror he had finally committed himself to the scheme. It should have been a defining moment. No more wavering, no more second thoughts. But, even as he donned his wig, anxieties surged. He had scooped up a freshly-smoothed handkerchief from a chest and mopped his brow.

As was his custom, he had breakfasted at the Clarence Tavern. However, a nervous stomach precluded the indulgence of a full meal. He had tarried over a mug of camomile, his mind a jumble of disconnected thoughts.

The weather in The Wells, as it had been for the past week, promised to be warm. Dust was rising from passing carriages and wagons when he had mingled with those making their way to the Walks. Others having taken the waters, were returning to their hotels and lodging houses to prepare for the day ahead.

The meeting had been arranged for the mid-afternoon. Once again, he had felt the need to revisit aspects of the scheme. Crossing the road to Bishops Down Common, he had turned towards the racecourse. Finding a quiet spot, a much-folded sheet of paper had been withdrawn from a pocket and studied with purpose. Particularly, the annotations scrawled in the margins.

Stowing it away, the gentleman had strolled towards The Walks, and the distant sounds of the company stirring for the day's entertainments.

As with breakfast, dinner had held little invitation. Seating himself in the shade of the lime trees dividing the Upper and Lower Walks, his closed expression forbade conversation. Those wishing him good day were dissuaded from stopping at his table. He had stared, sightlessly, at those around him. Blinded to the scene as emotions again took grip of his imagination. Blankly, he gazed upon the carriages and chairs lining the lower end of the Walks. The owners taking refreshment. Their maids and menservants purchasing the foodstuffs for their meals. Seeing, yet not seeing the overdressed, bright-voiced promenaders strolling by. The hubbub of conversation, the frequent, high laughter.

With a start, the gentleman had gathered his wits. Finishing a cordial, collecting hat and cane, buttoning his waistcoat, he had walked, almost aimlessly, the length of the Upper Walk.

The role of coordinator was one he could comfortably perform. He knew he had the cover to give adequate disguise to the role. Yet, as the day unfolded, so his agitation had grown. Unable to set his mind even to trivial matters, he could recall little of how the time had been spent before the brief, one-sided conversation. When the fellow had so imperiously stated his demands.

Now, as the clock struck four of the hour, apprehension was threatening to break the set of his features. Perspiration flowed freely. If all did not run to plan, he would be finished.

CHAPTER NINE

The baggage wagon had arrived earlier. Its contents, stacked in a pile by the inn door, were now being picked over by the passengers. Marius waited for them to disperse. It had been a relief to stretch one's limbs, to ease the aches of the journey. Other than the few turnpikes between Sevenoakes and The Wells, much of the route had been pitted and uneven. Equally unpleasant had been the dust on the carriageway; at times threatening to choke those seated outside.

Standing in the last rays of the sun, Marius took stock of the people milling around the coach. It was then he noticed a solitary figure standing in the doorway of an adjacent building. The fellow seemed most watchful, noting the new arrivals with interest.

Nathaniel Jordan took up a well-used bag and strode away with purpose, suggesting a knowledge of the town. The musician collected his baggage, and stood for a moment by the coach before a tall, slightly stooped man, dressed in equally bright clothing, came through the crowd to greet him. Mrs Fielding looked hesitantly about her, until a well-attired gentleman came forward. Augustus Brown had obviously corresponded with the inn, for Marius heard a porter advise that everything was in readiness. No doubt the comestibles trader has one of the better rooms, he thought longingly.

Taking up his own valise, he suddenly realised accommodation would be hard to come by at this hour. Marius followed Brown into the Angel Inn, and waited anxiously while one of the serving maids fetched the landlord.

A well-figured man, with a half smile of welcome on his face appeared, wiping his hands on his apron. He was apologetic, but all that was available was a small room located at the top of the building. Marius gratefully accepted.

He manoeuvred his baggage up the winding staircase and the narrow steps leading to the uppermost floor. The heat of the day still lingered uncomfortably when he set down his possessions in the cramped, tiny room under the eaves. Removing coat, waistcoat and cravat he fell onto the narrow bed and thought back to their arrival.

Wearied by the day's journey, everyone had been in a quiet mood, mumbling the briefest of farewells. As she moved to the coach door, Mrs Johnson had said in a low voice that she would look for him in the Walks. Following her, Marius noticed she was greeted by a man, presumably her husband, and a tall, attractive young woman. Heartened by their earlier conversation, he felt a hint of disappointment that the journey was over, that the gentlewoman was now occupied with her family.

Less tortured by memories, and tired from the journey, Marius should have slumbered easily. But, the closeness of the room, the small, narrow window which failed to open fully, made sleep almost impossible. By the time a maidservant brought the morning water, Marius felt wretched. Spending another night in the bedroom, he knew, would be an impossibility.

Washing slowly, Marius attired himself in clean linen, and donned a waistcoat and frock coat. He enjoyed a leisurely breakfast in an uncrowded room. Through a nearby window Marius could see that the fine weather was attracting numerous passers-by, and he decided upon a brisk walk to put much-needed vigour in mind and limbs.

Coming out the main door, he was unprepared for what he beheld. Men and women were strolling by, oblivious to all the normal conventions. They were in animated conversation, talking freely in a mix of company. What disturbed him more, many were in *dishabillé* – attired more for the intimacy of the bedroom. Never had he encountered such a liberal attitude to camaraderie or dress.

Though a doctor of physick, colour suffused his cheeks. He stood back to regain his composure. Then, with as much aplomb as he could muster, hurried across to the open land beyond.

On the pathways others were more soberly dressed. Marius hesitated, looking back over his shoulder, uncertain of what he had just witnessed. Then setting off at a good pace he crossed the undulating slopes, passing a well-ordered clump of trees, before taking his ease on a bench.

With the town spread before him, he surveyed the scene. Identifying the inn in which he had passed an uncomfortable night, a modest church spire, and houses rising up the slopes above the town. Over his shoulder, he noted a number of fine mansions stretching along the ridge. Though finding suitable accommodation was a pressing need, he was loath to move. He found pleasure in breathing the sweet air of the countryside. Shutting his eyes, he turned his face to the sun, ridding his lungs of the last vestiges of the odours of the hospital.

After an hour, he began an unhurried descent towards the distant church. On the downward path a gentleman pointed out the Walks, a collection of buildings on the southern edge of the town. Marius set off with purpose, hopeful of encountering Mrs Johnson. Across a track signposted to Eridge, Marius entered a short passageway to emerge under a colonnade where people were seated at tables taking refreshment. Spying a vacant chair, he sought pardon for joining a table presently occupied.

"My dear fellow," commented a young man. "You must be new. It's the done thing to sit where you fancy, and converse with whom you please."

Marius murmured his thanks. Ordering coffee from a passing serving girl, he turned to those around him. A woman regarded him with interest. "When did you come?" she asked. He mentioned his arrival the previous evening and that this was his first visit.

"Well," she responded cordially, "Bath is very similar, but then I suppose it's because Mr Nash organises both towns in like fashion."

She paused, then in a high, precise voice. "Have you visited Bath? It is much more congenial than The Wells, and the society and entertainment are superior. But I must declare, The Wells has charm, and being closer to London, could soon become its rival. Don't you agree?"

Marius had little to add to her observation, and reached for the coffee now set before him. Another fellow at the table asked, "Are you here for the waters? I hear they have a most wondrous medicinal effect. Apparently the taste is not to everyone's liking, so they must do good."

"I'm not sure," Marius said doubtfully. "I've come down from London for a few weeks to relax. I hadn't thought to take the waters."

"I'm not certain either," said another grinning hugely. "I've been here a week, and managed to avoid it so far. It may have curative powers, but frankly I dislike anything foul-tasting."

Those around the table were amused at their companion's reluctance. As they rose to depart, one of them leaned towards Marius. "Don't let Ruth Porter hear you are not going to drink her magic potion."

As he thought upon the remark, wondering who Ruth Porter might be, a figure slipped into an empty seat. He was not dressed in the latest fashion, but his coat was of good quality. He wore a trim periwig which set off intelligent, finely drawn features. His eyes brimmed with humour, and when he spoke, there was laughter in his voice.

"For your information, Mrs Porter collects the fees for Beau Nash, our Master of Ceremonies. She strenuously encourages all to partake the waters," he said with a chuckle. "Allow me to introduce myself . . . Roger Dashwood. I can tell you, sir, once Mrs Porter identifies a newcomer, she is like a dog with a bone. She will be after you at every turn until you settle your dues."

"As far as I know, I've not incurred any dues," Marius replied hesitantly.

"My dear fellow, you may have missed the chapel bell welcoming newcomers, but the fact is you are here, in The Wells. If you are likely to remain, even for a few days, she'll be on to you. Particularly, if you are attending the balls or the gaming tables."

Marius noted the gentleman was of a similar age to himself.

"As yet, I have no idea what I shall be doing, Mr Dashwood."

"One of the things you will quickly come to terms with is the emphasis on informality," his companion continued. "You will find it is a far cry from the manners of London. Mr Nash demands two things of his company. You converse with any person, regardless of rank or privilege, and he positively insists everyone does the same thing at the same hour."

"How do you accomplish the first if you haven't been introduced? And what does the second entail?" Marius enquired apprehensively.

"You'll soon get the hang of talking to one and all. As for everyone doing the same thing, well, there is a set time for everything, we all follow the programme," Dashwood said brightly.

He ordered coffee, and went on seemingly without pause.

"This means the waters are taken early in the morning. Thereafter, everyone returns to break their fast and dress for the day ahead. We meet in the Walks before dinner, which is taken between one and three of the clock. Tea is in the late afternoon. In the evening the programme is either dancing or gambling. It's quite simple."

"What surprised me this morning," Marius commented, again with a slight heightening of colour, "was the attire of those presumably taking the waters. Is that part of the programme as well? I have never come across so many women, or men, dressed so … informally."

"I must admit the state of dress can be somewhat scandalous," replied Dashwood. "I know the constable thinks it beyond the bounds of decency, and the town fathers are concerned for its reputation. But Beau Nash sees it as one of the freedoms to be allowed …and his word overrides all dissenting voices. As it all adds to the town coffers the protests are muted."

"Well, I was quite unprepared for the sight this morning. Still, I suppose it is a welcome diversion if you have to drink the spa water, which I am told is not to everyone's liking."

"I believe you should try it, if only to have an informed opinion," said Dashwood. "Would you believe that some years ago a certain Doctor Rowzee declared that to be cured of all known maladies, you must drink fifteen pints of the stuff each day. I'm sure he didn't take his own medicine. The good doctor also declared that the waters were best taken early in the day, before the sun reduced their potency."

"By the way," Marius asked casually, "how did you know I came from London? Were you, by chance, observing the coach when it arrived yesterday evening?"

"I sometimes take note of its arrival," Dashwood declared, his voice carefully neutral. "Any road, my dear fellow, do you want to know what you have let yourself in for coming to The Wells?"

"At the moment, I am more concerned with getting a decent bed to sleep in."

"Where are you lodging?"

Marius told him of his room at the Angel. It was nothing more than a garret and unbearable in the summer heat.

"I'm sure there are rooms where I am lodging," Dashwood remarked. His face stilled for a moment as he thought around the problem. "Join me for dinner there. We can enquire about the vacancy. I do recall someone left on Friday on the returning coach to London."

"That would be most welcome. I don't relish another night under the eaves."

"Well, that's settled." Dashwood was animated once more. "Now, whilst on our way to the lodging house, I'll point out some of the more interesting features of the town."

Marius paid for the coffee and they strolled along the Upper Walk.

"Do you know much about The Wells?"

"Only from a maiden aunt who used to visit, purely for medicinal reasons you understand. I am sure she would not have been as immodest as they are today. She rode to the Well in a sedan chair."

"I must admit, the waters have acquired a certain reputation," commented Dashwood. "People often refer to them as, *les eaux de scandale*. They may have health-giving properties, but drinking a good measure each day also promotes the libido . . . so I'm told."

"You have not tested those particular powers?"

"I have only ever drunk half the prescribed dosage before the quantity and the taste got the better of me," grinned Dashwood. "Now, where we met is Smith's Coffee House. Though, Uptons, next door is probably the better known of the two."

He turned slightly, and pointed through the trees. "On the far side of that avenue of limes is the Lower Walk. Both promenades converge on the Well, at the far end. Over there is the pipe shop. You can hire one for two shillings and sixpence and smoke it for the season."

They walked a short distance before Dashwood enquired. "By the way, do you cook?"

"I can't say I've ever tried."

"In which case, this part of the Lower Walk will be of little interest to you. Down there is a variety of shops and stalls, and where the local farmers sell their produce. Many of the company buy their food in the Lower Walk to take back to their lodgings."

"The shops under the colonnade don't sell food?" asked Marius.

"No, they are more genteel. They offer fabrics, china, ornaments and artefacts for the gentry." He took Marius' arm. "In addition to the tea and coffee houses on the Upper Walk, there are the Assembly Rooms. According to which night of the week it is, everyone comes to the Rooms to dance or to gamble. Balls take place on two nights, and we take our chances at the gaming tables four nights of the week."

"How big is the town?" Marius enquired. "I have not yet gauged its size, is there much else to see?"

Dashwood thought for a moment. "Actually, The Wells is quite compact. All the amenities are either in the Walks, or within a short distance of them. For example, there's a bath house near the Sussex tavern, just behind the Lower Walk. There are some shops, houses and a few official buildings on the lane to Southborough. We also have several bowling greens. One at Mount Sion, close to my lodgings in Ashenhurst House, and another at Mount Ephraim. Really, the Walks are the centre of activity for the company."

He noted Marius' quizzical expression.

"I should explain. The people who gather in The Wells during the season, usually from mid-summer to Michaelmas, are known as Mr Nash's Company. I suppose it's another of the terms created by our Master of Ceremonies to bring about compliance and order."

Approaching the end of the Upper Walk, in front of them was a large sundial on a majestic plinth. Beyond were two sandstone pillars, which led to an ornate garden surrounded by a low picket fence. Between the garden and the pillars was a paved area with seats surrounding the Well. By the wellhead was an elderly woman, busily ladling water into small bowls.

"So we arrive at the reason for everyone's presence," said Dashwood in a sardonic tone. "North's Folly. The parliamentarian who happened upon the waters over a century ago. The founder of the magical cure-all who forever changed the lives of the good people in this part of Kent."

"How can you be so scornful if the waters ease people's ailments?"

Marius heard the tightness in his voice.

"Forgive me," Dashwood replied with a shrug, and a hint of a smile. "Unwelcome cynicism on my part."

Marius said nothing, realising he had briefly reverted to type. He hurriedly asked. "The woman at the Well, is that her job to fill the bowls?"

"She is the official dipper. Appointed by the freeholders. Usually one of their wives or relatives."

"Who are the freeholders?"

"They, and the Lord of the Manor of Rusthall, own the land on which the Walks now stand. Long before the buildings were erected, the freeholders and his lordship used this area, as well as the adjacent land on Bishops Down Common, to graze their sheep and cattle.

'In 1682, the freeholders leased their titles to the then Lord of the Manor, Thomas Neale, for ten shillings a year. He, in turn contracted the rights to erect shops, houses and salons in the vicinity of the Well to a London building company. As you can imagine, there were all sorts of stipulations. One of them being the choice of dipper."

"How is it you know so much about it?" enquired Marius, noting the curious tone in Dashwood's voice.

"Because, sir, my uncles were the Lords of The Manor of Rusthall for some years. There was always an uneasy relationship with the freeholders. So they were well acquainted with the fine print of the agreement."

He was quiet for a moment, standing by the Well staring into the waters.

"I lived here for ten years with my relatives." He sighed. "But fortunes change."

He lifted his head. "There is now open confrontation between the freeholders and the present Lord of the Manor, a fellow called Maurice Conyers. The original contract was for fifty years, which expired four years ago. Since then neither party has been able to resolve the allotment of titles," said Dashwood, an unreadable expression on his face.

"It's complicated. Everyone wants something different. Some freeholders want more buildings erected. Others want to preserve the freedom of the surrounding open land. I'm not sure what Conyers wants. Anyway, at the moment, the division between the freeholders and The Lord of The Manor is a matter of great excitement and no little debate."

Marius tactfully let the subject rest, and they walked on towards the church. Crossing a narrow bridge, they entered a short lane which opened onto Mount Sion.

"It's uphill I'm afraid," said Dashwood. "However, the beds are comfortable, there's grazing for horses, and the food is most agreeable."

Dashwood's enthusiasm was justified. The recently vacated room was not only available, but airy and pleasant. Marius wasted little time in retrieving his belongings from the Angel Inn and installing himself at Ashenhurst House.

Placing his clothes in the hanging cupboard, Marius caught sight of himself in the cheval mirror. His reflection stared back at him. Tall, dark hair tied back with a ribbon, the angular face smiled in an inviting, slightly crooked way. The green eyes looked more relaxed. Fast disappearing was the haunted look which had visited his features for the past few years. Perhaps, he mused, I should have taken more time away from the hospital.

That evening, Roger Dashwood suggested they visit the Assembly Rooms.

"I believe a turn on the tables may provide a most pleasing diversion," he said in the doorway, whilst Marius chose a frock coat to wear over a silk green waistcoat.

They walked down the hill and took the narrow track behind the Angel Inn. As they crossed the lane leading to Frant village, a carriage with three passengers came to a halt by the church. The driver had trouble reining in the mettlesome pair. Fresh from the stables, they had not yet settled to their work. As the last occupant stepped down, a figure appeared from the shadows. A short woman of middling years, she wore a smock cap, and a dark, nondescript dress. Her face was unremarkable, except for the piercing eyes – so intense, prey might be locked in their gaze. The other extraordinary aspect of her appearance was the large book she carried. It moved with her, as though an extension of her body.

Turning from the carriage, the gentleman suddenly found himself confronted. In the gathering dusk he was clearly startled. Raising his arms in alarm, the book was knocked from the woman's hands. Off balance, she pitched to the ground. The horses started, the carriage jerked forward, a nearside wheel tumbled her roughly aside.

Marius and Roger Dashwood ran towards the incident. The woman was lying still when Marius dropped to his knees beside her. The three men from the carriage stood in shocked silence staring at her prostrate form whilst he carefully straightened the woman's limbs, searching for signs of injury.

With a low moan, her eyelids fluttered. Slowly she regained consciousness. Doing so, she clutched at her wrist. She appeared to have suffered no other damage, and Marius helped the woman to her feet.

"Do you have a handkerchief, Roger?"

He nodded.

"Take mine, and dip them both in the Well."

He turned to the men in the small group. "Gentlemen, do you have spare handkerchiefs with you?"

Two were quickly proffered, which Marius knotted together. When Roger returned, Marius wrapped the dampened handkerchiefs around the wrist. The others he quickly fashioned into a rudimentary sling. Making a knot behind her neck, he gently placed the woman's arm in its fold.

"As far as I can tell, madam, you have suffered no damage other than to your arm. I don't think the wrist is broken, but it is difficult to judge for it is swelling rapidly. We shall not know for a few days until the swelling subsides. Just keep it rested in that position. When you can, consult with a physician."

The woman spoke in a gentle tone, thanking him for his help. Then her voice took on a harder edge, castigating roundly the man who had caused her accident.

"My dear Mrs Porter, you appeared from nowhere and I was taken aback. It was an unfortunate accident," he responded lamely.

She was not easily mollified. Eventually, it was decided the carriage would take her to her lodgings. Helped into a seat, her parting remark to the agitated gentleman was that he would pay even higher dues when next they met.

"I am grateful for your actions, sir," he said, turning to Marius. "Are you a doctor, by chance?"

Marius said that he was, but did not practise in The Wells.

When they went their separate ways, Roger commented. "Well, what a to-do. Fortunately, nothing serious. Fancy Mrs Porter being on the receiving end for a change."

CHAPTER TEN

His name was Adam Squires. His family had been freeholders long before the ferruginous waters were discovered in 1606 by Dudley, the third Baron North.

Ever since he could remember the entitlements had been a source of discontent. On the death of his father, some twenty years earlier, he had been quite prepared to rid himself of his inheritance. Whilst his fellow freeholders would endlessly debate ways to improve their lot, Squires had been more than ready to accept a reasonable price.

Sitting with the stranger in the Sussex Tavern, he now had visions of achieving that end. The man had been plying him with drinks much of the morning. Come to the point, thought Squires, tell me how much you are willing to pay. He probably thinks if I am in my cups, I shall be more easily influenced. He did but know it, Squires needed no persuasion to sell. All he wanted was a substantial sum of money.

Finally, in exasperation, Squires demanded, "How much are you offering?"

Taken aback, the stranger sat there for a minute, before replying.

"Fifty guineas."

"Not enough," snarled Squires. "Double it and we have an agreement. If that is your final offer, I will bid you good day."

Eventually they settled on the sum of ninety guineas.

CHAPTER ELEVEN

He heard his name called. "Dr Hope, how are you today?"

Mrs Johnson made her way through the tables, followed exuberantly by her niece, circumspectly by her husband.

"Mrs Johnson, how delightful to see you," exclaimed Marius, standing to welcome her. "Let me present Mr Dashwood, who is kindly introducing me to the sights of The Wells."

Roger got to his feet and bowed in greeting.

"May I introduce my husband, Mr Johnson, and my niece, Miss Emily Roper. I believe I mentioned they came ahead to arrange our accommodation," said Mrs Johnson, a smile touching her lips.

Mr Johnson merely nodded. He was of similar vintage to his wife, with good bearing. Tall, he wore a double-breasted waistcoat and despite the rising temperature, a heavy, embroidered frock coat. He had strong features, with sharp, calculating eyes beneath a well-powdered wig. Leaning on his cane, he stood back exhibiting reserve.

Mrs Johnson's niece was far more engaging. She spoke in the breathless tone of one excited by each moment of her day. Attractive, with a full, mobile mouth, which she used to emphasise every mood and comment. She was wearing a short-sleeved yellow bodice and a brown, hooped skirt in the current fashion. A matching parasol hung from a delicate wrist.

"Did you both arrive on the coach with my Aunt?" purred Emily Roper. Dashwood explained he had been in The Wells for much of the season, Marius had been her aunt's travelling companion.

"I presume you are both coming to the ball this evening," she cried. "I shall certainly want to dance with you Mr Dashwood, and you, Dr Hope."

Mr Johnson continued to survey the Walks, ignoring the exchanges.

"Are you attending the ball, Mrs Johnson?" asked Marius.

"We shall all be there, Doctor," she said with a quick smile. "Perhaps, you might grant me a minuet?"

Marius declared it would be his pleasure. With that brief exchange, the Johnsons and their niece bade them farewell.

"I must say I'm not much taken with Mrs Johnson's husband," said Dashwood. It was also Marius' opinion, but he left it unsaid.

"By the by, are you interested in horse racing?" he asked cheerily. "There's a meeting on Bishop's Down next week. It's not top class, but highly entertaining. A worthy diversion to the gaming tables."

"I'd enjoy a day at the races," declared Marius enthusiastically. "When I was young my family would often go to Epsom Downs. Unfortunately, as a medical student I never had time for such pursuits."

"Excellent," Roger said, rubbing his hands together. "We shall make a day of it. I shall organise a picnic and fetch some wine."

"If you are going to do that, then I shall buy you dinner at the Angel."

Roger nodded. "First, I need to visit the Lower Walk. After last night's little adventure, I must buy more handkerchiefs."

In the Lower Walk, in front of the shops were stalls selling a variety of wares. To Marius' surprise, Roger stopped frequently to pick up and peer at items on offer.

After a while, Marius wandered towards the shops under the colonnade. He was looking in a window when his eye caught the reflection of a still figure by one of the lime trees. It was the portly presence of the comestibles trader. Crossing at an oblique angle, Marius caught him unawares.

"Good morning, Mr Brown."

Engrossed in surveying the shops from his vantage point, Brown was taken aback, showing even greater agitation when Marius continued, "Are your enquiries about suitable premises progressing well?"

Flustered, his jowls fluttering, Brown glanced anxiously around.

"Thank you," he replied, in a confidential whisper. "I believe I might be successful in that direction. However, I must move on. I bid you good day, sir."

"Who was that, Marius?" enquired Roger, joining him by the steps.

"A fellow passenger on the coach from London. He is looking to open a business here. I obviously disconcerted him."

At the dinner table Marius enquired about places of interest in the area which might merit a visit.

"Groombridge, which is five miles distant, is a pleasant little hamlet. And Mayfield is a charming village. Though you should visit Tonbridge, a most attractive town on the River Medway, about ten miles to the north. You would have passed through it on your journey from London."

"It did not register with me, Roger. Perhaps, I'll visit there first."

They sat in the inn in leisurely conversation until late in the afternoon.

The gaming tables were gone from the Assembly Rooms. In their place, musicians were playing a gavotte. Couples were making their way to the dance floor as Marius and Roger entered the salon.

"I shall meet with you shortly, Marius," his companion said, a twinkle in his eye. "I see a charming lady bereft of a partner."

He stood alone watching the dancers.

"I saw you arrive, Dr Hope," murmured Mrs Johnson, materialising at his side. "My, you look much more carefree than when we were travelling on the coach. What has happened to lift your spirits?"

He looked round at the gentlewoman, and smiled.

"For one thing, madam, I have forgotten about St Bartholomew's Hospital."

"Ah…The first step, and probably the most important."

"If it were not for you, I confess it would be much occupying my thoughts, Mrs Johnson." The bitterness of truth in his voice.

"Are you attending the race meeting next Saturday?" she enquired.

"Yes, Dashwood is arranging a picnic."

He told her of his lodgings at Ashenhurst House, and was fast learning about the town and what was expected of the company.

"One thing I have found difficult to accept is the mode of dress in the early morning," he added. "However, I am told that this is The Wells, things are done differently here."

"I've seen how they attire themselves on previous occasions."

She was amused at Marius' bewilderment.

"I'm not sure I approve, but there again, my opinions could be thought old-fashioned. Anyway, the gavotte is all but finished, are you to partner me in the minuet which follows?"

When the music struck up they took to the floor. As they danced, he had the impression all was not well beneath Mrs Johnson's show of enjoyment. Something appeared to be troubling her.

"You seem preoccupied, Mrs Johnson," Marius whispered. "Is something amiss?"

She looked up at him. "I wonder if we might meet tomorrow, Dr Hope? I shall be by myself, and could be at the Well at eleven of the clock. Would you be free at that time?"

"My dear lady, I shall be there."

The minuet ended. Marius escorted Mrs Johnson to where her husband and niece were seated.

"Dr Hope, how nice to see you!" cried Emily, rising to her feet. On this occasion, she was dressed in a crimson wrapping gown which had a low, rounded décolletage and lace ruffled sleeves which emphasised her pale complexion. It was evident she had applied a white lead cosmetic, and her lips had been reddened as the current high fashion dictated. Marius greeted her warmly, then courteously asked if she were free for the next dance.

"I have been waiting for you and Mr Dashwood to arrive," she said in that breathless manner of which she was clearly fond. "Now you can take it in turns to dance with me."

There was little conversation. Once on the floor, Emily Roper applied all her energies to the dance and to those around her. Her aim, it seemed, was to draw maximum attention to herself.

So the evening passed. Roger appeared, and both he and Marius danced frequently with Miss Roper and Mrs Johnson. Mrs Johnson's husband continued to exhibit a remote manner, rarely engaging in any of the dances.

Over breakfast, Marius mentioned that he had a meeting in the Walks. Perhaps they could meet later for coffee.

"Who is the fortunate woman?" Roger asked keenly. "Surely not Miss Roper?"

Marius coloured slightly, and his denial was swept aside in Roger's amusement.

Arriving before the appointed hour, Marius took a seat near where the company was taking the waters. He sat idly contemplating the scene, his mind turning to Mrs Johnson. Something was clearly disturbing her. Deep in thought, some time passed before he realised it was much past the hour they had agreed to meet. Rising to his feet, he was walking slowly towards the coffee houses when Mrs Johnson touched his arm.

"Forgive my lateness, Dr Hope. It was more difficult than I thought to slip away, and my niece, Emily, will soon be joining me."

Any slight irritation Marius harboured was immediately dispelled.

"Do you mind if we go to the Lower Walk," she said, as they strolled side by side. "I must buy food for dinner."

They took the steps, Mrs Johnson heading for a meat stall where several animal carcasses were hanging. She quickly procured her needs, and then turned towards a farmer selling vegetables from a row of wicker baskets.

"I did not appreciate how difficult it would be to have a private conversation," he murmured.

Mrs Johnson smiled. "What if we meet on Sunday, directly after church? I shall not be accompanied, and it would seem the most natural arrangement to take coffee together after the service."

"An excellent suggestion. I'll occupy a table at Smith's, and await your company."

"By the bye, Doctor, I have had further thoughts on your dilemma. We shall talk more about a possible solution."

They stopped in front of a fruit seller. Marius, on the point of making his farewell, ventured, "Mrs Johnson, you seem a little distracted. I've been telling you of my concerns, and not enquired if something were amiss."

She turned, a frown appeared on her brow which might have come from her close inspection of the produce.

"Dr Hope, there is something that perturbs me. It might be my imagination, a silliness on my part. It's of no real account. I shall tell you more when we meet."

Marius bowed slightly. "Until then, Mrs Johnson."

The coffee houses were crowded, so Marius strolled along the colonnade, stopping to gaze at the many items displayed in the shop windows. In one, a series of wooden bowls labelled Tonbridge Ware, caught his eye.

Early the next day Marius had risen, dressed carefully, and left the house without taking breakfast. Roger's comments, although bantering, still made Marius uncomfortable.

Leaving by a side door, he slipped across the garden and followed a pathway through the Grove. In due course, he reached the lane leading to the Calverley Estate and Southborough beyond. It was a short step in the other direction to the Walks.

At Smith's, he had idly passed the time watching the company promenade and take their ease at the coffee house. When the midday bell tolled, he realised many of the congregation attending morning service were now seated around him. Mrs Johnson had failed to appear. Disconsolate, and on the point of leaving, it was at that moment Roger Dashwood threaded his way through the crowd and sat on a vacant chair.

"So Miss Roper did not appear. I was sure she'd be most anxious to meet with you again."

Marius pushed away his mug of chocolate, still untouched.

Roger continued to taunt him mildly about his tryst. Finding little response, he was rising from his seat, when Marius said. "It was not Miss Roper. It was Mrs Johnson I was meeting."

Roger dropped back into the chair. Hesitatingly, Marius declared. "I had hoped for a word with her, and I arranged to meet her here this morning."

They sat in silence for some minutes. Finally, Roger interrupted his introspection. "Look Marius, I'm sure she will be in the Walks this afternoon, or tomorrow morning. Let's go back to Ashenhurst House for an early dinner. You can come back this afternoon, and you may well happen upon her then."

Many of the tables around them were emptying as the company began making their way to their lodging houses or nearby inns.

As they strolled along the Upper Walk, Roger remarked. "Did you see the remains of the fire when you walked down Mount Sion? Apparently, one of the houses burnt down during the night."

"No," replied Marius, looking hard at his companion. "I came through the Grove."

Reaching the foot of Mount Sion, the smell of burnt timbers was heavy in the air. A short distance up the slope they came upon a badly gutted, wooden-framed building. In front of the still smouldering shell, stood the local constable, amid a small crowd of on-lookers.

Marius and Roger halted. When fire struck such dwellings, the conflagration was swift and unrelenting. Black smoke continued to spiral skywards. What remained of the structure was still shedding embers. The constable noted them standing close to the picket fence.

"A bad business, gentleman," he said sombrely. "The trouble is these houses are natural fire hazards. The slightest unguarded flame, and they ignite. We were lucky to extinguish it before it caught the others. Though the occupants were not so fortunate, I'm afraid."

"Were they residents?" asked Marius sharply.

"No sir. I'm told a family had taken the house for the season. The gentleman was not at home, but it seems his wife and daughter were. Both perished in the fire."

The strongest premonition gripped Marius. He stared at the constable, then in a voice tightening in his throat. "What was the name of the family?"

"Johnson, sir," came the constable's grave reply.

CHAPTER TWELVE

He found Marius by the paddock watching the horses as they grazed in the shade of the bordering trees. After a few minutes Marius turned to him. "Do you think the constable would allow me to view the bodies?"

"He may have confused the fact that Mrs Johnson's daughter is really her niece," murmured Roger. "You can correct him on that point, but I cannot see why you want to involve yourself."

"I wonder if her husband has been able to identify the bodies? If they were burnt beyond recognition, as a doctor I may be of help."

"I have the strongest suspicion you are about to interfere," Roger commented, concern in his voice. "If I were Mr Johnson, I would not be comforted by a stranger taking such close interest in my affairs."

"He may not be able to bring himself to make the identification. If that's the case, I'm sure the constable would welcome an offer of assistance."

"Marius, it seems whatever I say will not dissuade you. I'm not sure you are doing the right thing. Unless, of course, you feel something is amiss. Do you?"

"No… I just feel sorry I was not there when she needed me," he lamented.

At the burnt-out shell of the house the constable was discussing with the owner when the property might be salvaged. Waiting until the conversation had ended and the constable had started down the hill, Marius caught up with him.

"I presume, Constable, if the house is being made safe, the bodies have been removed?"

The constable was a serious looking man. Of middling height, he carried his spare frame in a stiff, upright manner. His attitude was cool and precise.

"They were transferred to the mortuary on Mount Pleasant this morning, sir. Why do you ask?"

"I was wondering if you would permit me to view them. I do not wish to intrude, you understand. However, as a doctor and knowing the family, I might be of service. Has Mr Johnson identified the bodies?"

"You mean, sir," said the constable, halting and turning towards Marius. "The woman and her niece. I was corrected by Mr Johnson. At the moment, he is too distressed to leave his room at the White Bear Inn."

The constable resumed walking. Marius remained at his side.

"I'm not sure I can allow you to see them before the next of kin," murmured the constable. But it was said with little conviction. "The trouble is, even when he is ready, it will be difficult to identify one of the bodies. The ravages of the fire have not treated the younger woman kindly."

He hesitated. "Perhaps, in your capacity as the family doctor, you could make a preliminary identification. Then, if Mr Johnson agrees, I could accept your confirmation. We could save him further upset, and have the burials arranged without delay."

Marius did not correct him.

"Why don't we go the mortuary now?" Marius suggested. "As you say, the sooner the better."

It was a short distance to the single storey brick-built structure used as a mortuary. The constable banged with his stick on the heavy green door, which was unlocked by one of his deputies. They were ushered into a narrow ante-room, empty but for two rickety chairs and a small table. On the table were the half-eaten remains of a meal.

"I shall wait here whilst you examine the bodies, Doctor," said the constable uncertainly. "I'm sure you don't need me peering over your shoulder."

Closing the door to the inner room, Marius found the two corpses stretched out on wooden planks mounted on tressels. By the weak light coming through a narrow window high on the wall he set about the grim task.

Examining the body nearest the door, Marius noted that much of the clothing was scorched but intact. He recognised the rounded features of Mrs Johnson.

He gazed upon her for several minutes before turning to Miss Roper. She had been found where the heat of the fire had been most intense. It had had a devastating effect. The body was burnt almost beyond recognition. He recollected that the tattered remnants were of the gown she had worn at the ball, and remembered the vivacious creature so much enjoying the evening. Now she lay burnt beyond recognition on a makeshift mortuary table.

He retreated slowly towards the door, still engrossed in his assessment of the bodies. As they lay side-by-side, his eye was taken by their similarity in length. With his hand on the door latch, he recalled that Miss Roper had been noticeably taller than Mrs Johnson. The fashionable shoes she had worn may have added extra inches, but from where he stood they appeared much closer in height.

He returned to Miss Roper's body and looked again at the mutilated, indistinct features. Marius could tell little, and he could bring to mind no distinguishing marks. Moving to the other table, he stared intently at the face. There was little doubt

Mrs Johnson was the other victim. It was several minutes before Marius realised that something was amiss. There was no blackening around the nostrils and mouth, indicating smoke inhalation. Taking a handkerchief from his pocket, he gently parted her lips and swabbed the inside of her mouth. Removing it carefully, Marius saw it was unstained. With the same care he did the same with the lady's niece.

"Were you able to confirm their identities, Doctor?" asked the constable when he returned to the outer room.

"One of the bodies is undoubtedly Mrs Johnson. The other is too badly burnt for me to make a positive identification. The clothing suggests it was Miss Roper, but what disturbs me is that both women appear to be similar in height. I was certain Miss Roper was taller."

Roger Dashwood looked searchingly at Marius.

"What are you saying, Doctor?"

"I'm not sure. I hesitate to say it, but I truly wonder if it is Miss Roper. However, I may have more disturbing news. If I'm right, the two women did not inhale fumes from the fire. If that's the case, they could well have been dead before the fire started."

CHAPTER THIRTEEN

Having persuaded the constable to let him visit the property, Marius arrived at the Johnsons' house early the next morning. Not the most patient of men, curiosity prompted him to walk round the shell of the charred building. At the rear he came upon a door which had sprung from its frame.

Marius pulled it open carefully, and stepped into what had once been the kitchen. The walls were burnt and blackened, debris covered the remains of the wooden floor, and through scorched rafters he could see to a room above. Is this where the fire started? he wondered. Crossing the floor tentatively, testing the floorboards where they existed, he reached the door to the rest of the house.

It opened into a small sitting room. The fire had burnt through the adjoining wall, and though much was intact, the heat had had a most telling effect. A small side table had cracked along its seams, its decorative runner browned and curled. The china lining the dresser was crazed, some of the bigger pieces had shattered, their shards spread about the floor. As Marius surveyed the smoke-blackened room, the front door was pushed roughly several times before surrendering to the presence of the constable.

"Good day, Doctor," he said sharply, clearly put out that Marius was already in the house.

"Good morning, Constable. Just getting the lie of the land. The back door afforded easy access."

The constable sniffed. "And what has your inspection yielded?"

"Nothing that, with your experience, you have not already concluded, sir. No doubt, you also believe the fire started in the kitchen."

The official nodded.

"Interestingly, it would seem the flames did not spread sideways so much as vertically. Probably why this room escaped much of the ravages of the fire, and why the bodies were not consumed, don't you think?"

"I do, Doctor. The quick work of the rescuers saved their destruction, though, unfortunately, not their lives."

Marius was thoughtful.

"Constable, could you point out where the bodies were found?"

"The younger woman was found next to the kitchen wall. That's why she suffered more than Mrs Johnson, who was lying nearer the front door."

Marius noticed that he had not attributed a name to the victim. Had the constable already accepted the body might not be that of the niece.

"Who first noticed the fire?" Marius enquired.

"Those in the adjoining houses were first on the scene. A bucket chain was quickly organised from a well at the rear of the Angel Inn. Others arrived, and the flames were eventually extinguished." The constable pointed to the kitchen. "They concentrated on the back of the house where the fire was fiercest. Several attempts were made to enter the property, but it was too hot, and in any case the door had jammed. I got here at about one of the clock. It was light before it had cooled sufficiently, and we could force an entry."

"So you were here when the bodies were found?"

"Yes. Someone brought a stout length of wood, and we managed to batter open the front door. I lead the others into the house, and found Mrs Johnson lying at the foot of the stairs. Her feet were on one of the steps, her head facing into the room," he declared, broadly indicating her position.

He strode across the room. "As I said, the other body was here, her head close to the remains of the kitchen wall."

They picked their way up the staircase to the floor above. The front bedroom had been damaged by the fire, but the rear bedroom was totally destroyed. Returning to the sitting room, Marius asked the constable what time the neighbours were alerted to the fire.

"Well, as I said, I arrived just before one of the clock. I believe those living close by were roused an hour earlier, by then the fire was well under way."

"May we go into the kitchen where it began," asked Marius, turning to retrace his steps.

Studying the walls and floor intently, he moved to a corner and knelt to examine a heavy deposit on top of two badly-burnt joists. This is where it started, he realised, rubbing a sample of the ash between thumb and forefinger.

The smoke fumes had penetrated the very fabric of the house, and the stench still lingered in his nostrils when he and the constable walked down the hill to the White Bear Inn. Taking mugs of ale, they sat on a bench by a large bay window.

"I suppose I can let the landlord begin salvaging what he can from the property," said the constable.

"It depends on whether you believe the fire was an accident or started deliberately."

"What is your opinion?"

Marius contemplated the question.

"Bizarre accidents happen all too often, and this could be one such occasion."

He raised the mug to his lips.

"However, let us consider the circumstances. Firstly, who would go to the kitchen at such a late hour? Someone may have awoken and desired a hot drink or cordial. A fire was maintained in the hearth, and it would have been the work of a moment to spark it into life. But, in truth, it is most unlikely the fire was caused by an accidental spillage of hot embers. The indications are that it ignited in a corner of the room, and the two walls acted like a flue, carrying the flames upwards.

"There again, at that hour, most people would be in their night attire. The two victims were in their day clothes. And as I mentioned previously, neither of the women showed signs of smoke inhalation, which suggests, Constable, that it could have been a deliberate attempt to burn two people who were already dead."

The constable looked shocked. "I certainly hope such is not the case, Doctor."

"To be sure of the true nature of their deaths, their lungs should be examined. That would prove, one way or the other, if they died as a result of the fire."

"Well, as I said, Mr Johnson has yet to view the bodies. Now you have raised doubt about the identity of the younger woman, it is even more essential."

The law officer rose and picked up his hat. "At the moment he is deeply distressed, so I'm not sure he would agree to his wife's body being probed and inspected. As for the other corpse, if he confirms that it is not Miss Roper, that presents yet another problem."

"Unfortunately, it is one I cannot help you with, Constable," said Marius also rising to his feet. "Though, if you want a medical opinion or advice, you know where I am lodging."

As they passed by the dining room Marius glimpsed Mr Johnson eating a hearty breakfast.

CHAPTER FOURTEEN

"What will the constable do?"

"I'm not sure, Roger. Although if I were he, I would certainly insist upon Johnson attending the mortuary. He was fortunate that he was gambling to such a late hour, and missed the incident. Perhaps, he is saddened by his loss. Though, I have the impression he is not overly upset."

"Do you believe he will agree to your examination?"

"I don't think so, and his wife's death will ever remain conjecture," Marius replied, pursing his lips in thought. "I wonder if the constable checked his whereabouts last night? Determined the time he was last seen in company?"

"Surely, you don't consider him a suspect?"

"Don't be so shocked. It's not the first time a husband has been responsible for his wife's death."

Roger no longer felt hungry, and excused himself from the table.

Moving through the throng, Marius was surprised at the ease he had acquired in holding passing conversations. Roger's influence was more telling than he had thought. They joined a table still discussing the fire. The excited rumour was that at least eight bodies had perished. Marius mentioned nothing of his involvement.

"Someone told me the arsonist locked all the doors after he started the fire, trapping the people inside," declared one. "I wonder where he went afterwards? Perhaps he will strike again."

"Do you think so?" said a woman at the table nervously. "I am lodging in a similar house in Frog Lane."

"Why not?" said another at the table. "Now he has the taste for it, no one is safe."

"I don't believe you should spread that sort of comment, even if it is meant to amuse," Roger Dashwood said in a serious voice. "You could frighten the company and cause panic."

"Actually, there are a lot of people who are already worried about sleeping in their beds for fear of being caught in a fire," stated someone soberly.

The conversation lapsed, then struck up again when the topic turned to the evening's entertainment. Marius felt uneasy. It had only been one incident, and they were not rare occurrences. Yet the fire was stirring people's imagination.

There was movement behind him, and heads turned as a carriage and six turned into the Lower Walk and stopped by the gate. The driver dismounted, and opening the carriage door helped down a well-set gentleman. Casting round, he took up his cane and walked slowly towards the Upper Walk. He was dressed in a bright, brocade frock coat, a matching waistcoat, a full wig and held a white cocked hat under his arm.

"It's Beau Nash," Roger whispered. "I wonder what brings him out at this hour?"

Reaching the company, the gentleman said, "Ah, Mr Dashwood, would you be kind enough to provide me with a chair?"

Roger rose hurriedly to comply. The hubbub of chatter was restored, though many were still regarding Mr Nash with interest, wondering on whom he might be calling. Roger came back carrying a chair with arms, and Nash indicated that he should set it at the table.

"Tell me, Mr Dashwood, is this gentleman Dr Hope?"

The voice was flamboyantly loud. Each syllable given its full value.

"If so, sir, I, Richard Nash, am delighted to make your acquaintance."

He continued. "Mrs Porter gave me full account of your attentions, Doctor. Your ready ministrations to her arm reduced her discomfort, and another physician has confirmed it is not broken, merely sprained. I felt, at the very least, I should express my gratitude."

"It was my duty to attend her, sir," responded Marius. "I was pleased to be of assistance."

Coffee was set upon the table, and Nash fell into easy conversation with Marius, asking him about his arrival, where he was lodging, and his opinion of The Wells.

"Do you gamble, sir?" asked Nash. "If you are of a mind, I can suggest several worthwhile games of Hazard, Pharaoh or Basset. We have some very good tables for our entertainment."

Marius mentioned that he enjoyed gaming, and would be sure to try his hand.

"Well, let me know if I can be of any assistance during your stay in The Wells, Dr Hope."

He edged closer. "Would you, by chance, be looking to set up as a physician in the town? If you were, I could provide you with very worthwhile introductions. Even organise rooms appropriate to your needs."

"You are most kind, sir. However, my intentions are to spend my days here enjoying the town and its attractions. I am not seeking employment until I return to London."

Nash acknowledged his remarks, and making his farewell returned to the waiting carriage. Once more, the driver was attentive to his patron, ensuring he was comfortably installed before driving off.

"Well, well," said Roger, "you have created a stir. I have never known Beau Nash visit upon one of the company. Usually, one seeks audience with him."

The musician was installed in an ensemble occupying the gallery. Two things were in his favour. His competence as a player, and his instrument, the mandolin, was an excellent accompaniment in a Bach fugue or one of Mr Handel's partitas.

The ensemble was commissioned to play in the late morning and in the afternoon, when the company returned to the Walks. The rest of the time he was at liberty to do as he pleased. He had taken lodgings close by, and his frequent passage through the Walks meant he was now an habitué of the area, his presence fading into the background.

Sitting in the gallery he had witnessed Beau Nash's visit, seen him converse with the doctor. After the Master of Ceremonies' departure, The Walks had emptied as the company drifted away for dinner. The other players were packing away their instruments, readying to go their separate ways.

The musician was the last to leave, making his way to a house behind the Lower Walk. Shortly, thereafter, he came from his lodgings, and headed for one of the passageways leading onto the common land of Bishops Down.

They had dined at the Castle Tavern. Neither inclined to walk up Mount Sion past the Johnson house. The inn was crowded, the buzz of conversation masking their exchanges.

"Do you think people are truly anxious about the fire?"

"More than I would have thought," Marius replied. "Still, I suppose if it were deliberate, their concern is understandable."

"The constable should do something to calm everyone's fears."

"What can he do? Someone may have chosen that house, but it might easily have been any other. Perhaps, their fears are justified."

"Do you really believe that to be true?" queried Roger.

"No, I do not," said Marius slowly. "But, you can't go around making accusations without proof. Anyway, what has anyone to gain from the deaths of the two women?"

As they were finishing their meal, Dashwood suggested they accept Mr Nash's suggestion and take a turn at the tables.

"It will lift the gloom of the incident," said Roger encouragingly.

Marius felt that it would require more than an evening's gaming to rid him of his melancholy. He was fast coming to the opinion he must discover more about the tragic event. As they were finishing dinner, Roger announced he had a meeting to attend.

Left to his own devices, Marius decided to stroll in the direction of Bishops Down.

With no particular purpose, he found himself heading on an upward path towards the ridge at Mount Ephraim. He turned along the lane signposted Rusthall, and after a mile or so, the meandering track sought a decision from him.

In the hollow of the hill was a small enclave of dwellings ringing a communal green. Situated at the far end of the village was a church, and to one side stood an imposing manor house, just visible behind a broad standing of trees. Presumably, the village of Rusthall, thought Marius. So, the Lord of The Manor resides next to the church.

To the left, a sign pointed to a bath house. He was torn. Should he continue into Rusthall, or cool himself in the baths' inviting waters. The heat of the summer's day made the decision for him. He turned down the path away from the village. Following another sign, naming the descent through an avenue of trees as the Hundred Steps, he reached the bath house.

Although remote, the spot was enchanting. Surrounding the building were gardens featuring fountains, ornamental ponds and discreet sitting areas. The whole, an arena of tranquility. So much more enjoyable than the baths at Islington Spa, thought Marius. Close to St Bartholomew's, he would go there whenever time permitted. However, set in a pleasure garden, the baths were often crowded.

Inside the bath house, the rooms were decorated in attractive tiling. The only discomfort, which was momentary, was the chill water. Nevertheless, Marius found his brief immersion wholly invigorating. An hour later, emerging into the afternoon sunshine, he retraced his steps to the top of the incline, then down the far side to the village.

In its centre, a number of carriages and sedans lined a bowling green. Strolling towards a knot of spectators, he took a vacant space on a bench to watch the players. However, their antics and distracting cries failed to hold his interest. A movement caught Marius' attention; glancing in the direction of the manor house, he saw a group of people readying to depart. There were three men in an open carriage, and two on horseback. At the gates one of the riders turned in a westerly direction, the others taking the road towards The Wells. As they passed, Marius' eyes narrowed. The horseman following the carriage was Roger Dashwood.

CHAPTER FIFTEEN

At first the soft tap went unnoticed. When it was repeated, Conyers glanced towards the door over his wire-framed glasses.

"Come in!"

A footman sidled into the room.

"Sir, Mr Loveday is asking to see you."

"Tell him I am not available," declared Conyers curtly. Then, recalling the tenor of Pitt's letter. "No. . . wait. Show him into the library, I'll be there directly."

A few minutes later when the Lord of The Manor entered the panelled, book-lined room, the chandler's back stiffened perceptibly.

"Mr Loveday. . . I hope you are well. May I offer some refreshment?"

Taken aback by the cordiality of the welcome, Loveday was suddenly hesitant. "Er. . . Thank you, sir. A mug of cider if you please."

Conyers tugged a bell pull. Then turning, waved the freeholder to a chair.

"Sit down, sir. Let us be comfortable."

They seated themselves either side of a small table.

"Now," opened Conyers. "Do I presume you are here to make another proposal?"

Loveday dropped his gaze to the hat lying across his knees. He clutched nervously at the brim. Raising his head, he looked intently at The Lord of The Manor.

"I must tell you, Mr Conyers, there is no change in the position we freeholders have taken. If anything, because this dispute has lasted these four years, our attitude has hardened."

Conyers' face reflected his growing ill-temper. Containing it with difficulty, he glared angrily at the freeholders' spokesman.

"Then why on earth are we having this conversation?"

Loveday maintained his equanimity. In a calm voice he said. "Because, Mr Conyers, the situation is causing unnecessary upset. Soon, I will not be able to control the other freeholders' actions. A way has to be found, of mutual benefit to all, and it must be found quickly."

As the words rang out, Conyers' resentment subsided. He thought to what Walpole's reaction might be if confronted by dissident mobs during his forthcoming visit. The presence of the Principal Minister in The Wells might be construed as lending support to his entitlement. However, it could just as easily reduce the strength of his claim if there were public dissent.

"I am not persuaded by threats, Mr Loveday. However, our dispute cannot be allowed to harm the growing reputation of The Wells. That would be in neither of our interests."

Conyers looked unseeingly into the empty grate. Stirring, he turned to the chandler.

"Advise your fellows you've talked with me, Mr Loveday. Tell them I am increasingly amenable to some form of compromise. I shall instruct my legal advisers to look again at the last proposal, and tell them to use it as a basis for an agreement which satisfies both parties. Now, I can't be fairer than that."

"I'm not sure that will lessen their disquiet, Mr Conyers. We have heard much the same before."

"Then, convince them, my friend. Tell them a solution will be forthcoming in a matter of weeks."

"I hope, Mr Conyers, for both our sakes, what you say comes about," responded Loveday fervently. "I'll relay your words to my fellow freeholders."

Loveday drained his glass, and they both rose to their feet. The Lord of The Manor advanced towards Loveday, and taking his hand, declared, "Now, be sure to tell them exactly what I have said. Mark my words, our differences will be resolved. I bid you good day, sir."

Ushered from the room, Loveday's hopes were rising. Unsure of his reception when he had called upon The Lord of The Manor, he was leaving with greater certainty that the end of the disagreement could well be in sight.

CHAPTER SIXTEEN

In addition to his usual toilet, Marius washed and dried his hair; and as was his practice in the hospital where wigs were an encumbrance, tied it at the nape of his neck with a ribbon. From the hanging cupboard he chose his second-best pair of breeches trimmed in grey silk, and a full-cut chemise and frock coat suited to a night at the gaming tables.

He looked briefly for Dashwood in the public rooms before setting off for the Walks. Consciously avoiding the remains of the Johnson house, he took one of the lanes meandering down to the town.

As he passed the Presbyterian chapel, a late evening service had just finished. The congregation were dispersing, slowly spilling into the roadway. Forced to shorten his step he spotted Nathaniel Jordan deep in conversation by the chapel door. He was speaking forcefully, emphasising his comments with exaggerated gestures.

What is that is all about? speculated Marius, glancing at the faces of those gathered around the farrier. There were five men listening to his words. Several were clearly not in sympathy with what was being said. One, openly aggressive, was taking the argument to him. A pity I cannot await the outcome, he thought, as he picked his way through the throng of chapelgoers and strolled on down the hill.

The sound of running feet caught his attention. Someone called his name. It was Roger Dashwood.

"Why didn't you wait for me? I looked down Mount Sion, and couldn't see you. So I guessed you'd either taken this route or walked through the Grove."

Marius was non-committal. They continued on to the Assembly Rooms in silence. As they entered, Marius' ears were assailed by the noise and the numbers crowding the tables. Surveying the room, he left Roger to join a group playing Pharaoh.

Spending an enjoyable half an hour, Marius found he had not lost as much as expected. Encouraged, he dallied at another table where a game of Hazard was in progress. A seat became vacant, and he spent the next hour building a small profit. Eventually, rising to take supper, he found Roger Dashwood again by his side.

"Shall we go in together?"

They were ushered to a table already occupied. However, the other diners were close to finishing their meal, and within minutes they were alone. Both were silent until their order was taken. Then Marius commented, "I went to Rusthall this afternoon."

"Did you? You may have seen me. I was visiting someone in the village."

"You were in the company of others leaving a large manor house."

"Perhaps I should explain," Roger murmured, watching Marius closely.

"Roger, there's no need. That's your own affair. It is nothing to do with me."

"I think you should know what I do here during the season."

"Why? We all have our own lives to lead," Marius interrupted, suddenly concerned he might also be expected to account for his presence in The Wells. Dashwood ignored him, unconsciously his hands clenched the edge of the table.

"I was attending a meeting to discuss the growing quantities of contraband coming into the town. Smuggling has long been a popular pastime, but normally it's confined to the towns and villages along the routes to London, its usual destination. Now, a worrying quantity is finding its way into The Wells."

Roger waited while glasses of wine were placed on the table. Looking up, Marius saw his face had lost that carefree look, his eyes dark and introspective.

"Marius, I want to tell you something of my past."

He picked up his glass, and drank deeply. "I mentioned I used to live with my uncles, once Lords of The Manor of Rusthall. The brothers were quite wealthy, until like many others, they took to investing in stocks and securities."

Once more, Roger lifted the glass to his lips.

"They began spending more and more time in London. Hours were passed in the coffee houses in Change Alley."

He looked down at the table, a harshness creeping into his voice.

"All they achieved was the purchase of stocks that were completely worthless. Finally, in 1720, Sir Francis Dashwood, gambled all on trade with the Spanish colonies in South America." He smiled cynically. "When the South Sea Bubble burst, they lost everything."

For a moment, he was lost to his recollections. Then he continued, hurt evident in his voice.

"I had to leave Rusthall. After the deaths of my parents, the only family I'd known simply broke into fragments. I was despatched to an aunt in Bristol. I never saw any of them again. I did not attend the funerals of either of my uncles."

The fork picked at the food on his plate. It was clear he had little taste for what he was eating. Taking another drink, Roger went on.

"But I couldn't stay away. Several years ago I began making a meagre living in the summer months working for the local magistrate. I come down at the beginning of the season, and keep an eye open for people who appear suspicious. Those selling jewellery, or goods of doubtful provenance. I look out for buyers of illegal items. Having lived in the town, you see, I'm known to many of the residents. I soon get to know who are *bona fide* visitors, who are the likely criminals."

Marius said ruefully, "So, it was you keeping watch on the coach the other evening. Presumably, you saw me as a dubious character."

"Not exactly. I was intrigued enough to strike up a conversation with you. It was soon evident you constituted little threat."

Some minutes elapsed before Marius said, "What other subterfuge are you engaged in? Is the magistrate involved in the Johnson affair?"

"No, that's the constable's responsibility. In fact, the magistrate doesn't even know of it."

"Who else was at the meeting in Rusthall?" asked Marius, teasing out the information.

"There was Maurice Conyers, of course, the present Lord of The Manor. Robert Fielding, who represents the Excise Commission in London. Thomas Marshall, a Riding Officer from Newhaven. Mr Phillips, The Wells Magistrate and his assistant. I can't remember his name, and a fellow magistrate from East Grinstead called Flowers."

"As well as yourself," added Marius. "So what came of the meeting?"

"I'm not sure I should even be discussing this with you. After all, you could be the mastermind of the smuggling ring," Roger said wryly.

"Come, Roger. Do I look like a smuggler? I'm just a lowly doctor of physick," Marius exclaimed.

Roger was shaken from his bout of melancholy, but not entirely free of his memories. He said, in the same low voice. "A distressing moment at the manor this morning was to come face-to-face with Bryant, my uncles' footman. He's now the butler. When we saw each other, we were both discomfited. As a child, he was the confidant of many of my concerns."

Roger looked away, his eyes moist. Coughing, he took a handkerchief from his sleeve, turning aside to blow his nose. He played idly with his glass, collecting his thoughts before continuing.

"At the meeting I told them as much as I knew. Identifying a number of stallholders in the Lower Walk whom I suspected of handling smuggled goods."

"No doubt your testimony was the most relevant contribution," commented Marius cynically. "The others probably agreed that it was deplorable state of affairs, and drank tea or port."

"Well," he said, amused at his companion's insight, "we did talk around the problem for two hours without coming to any conclusion. Anyway, enough of that. Now you know why I'm here in The Wells, tell me, what was the urgent need to converse with Mrs Johnson?"

Marius, as so often in the past, re-directed the conversation away from himself. "Do you know a fellow called Nathaniel Jordan?"

"The farrier you mean?"

"Yes. He was on the coach from London with me. For some reason, I feel he could be part of your problem. Everywhere I turn, I see him in hot debate with people who are either freeholders or traders, or possibly both."

"What do you think he is doing?"

"During the coach ride from London, I heard him mention he hoped to set up a farrier's business close to the Walks. Presumably, he is trying to buy some land," said Marius thoughtfully. "Though, his attitude leaves much to be desired."

"Until a few years ago, there were covenants against any new buildings being erected on or near the Walks," Roger said thoughtfully. "Nevertheless, I know a number of freeholders who might willingly sell their shares in the Walks and the titles they hold."

Finishing supper, they decided upon a brief tour of the tables before returning to the lodging house. In the gaming room, Marius threaded his way towards his original seat at the Pharaoh table, but then hesitated.

Playing Hazard at a nearby table was Mr Johnson. Moving in his direction, Marius stood close to his chair. Johnson had been drinking, and his wild calls on the fall of the dice were resulting in heavy losses. After several more throws, Johnson rose unsteadily to his feet and lurched from the table towards the door.

Marius followed as he staggered along the Upper Walk. There was little need for caution, in his drunken state Johnson was unaware of all around him. The moon was full, casting strong shadows across the pantiles and trees lining the edge to the Lower Walk. Nearing the church, Johnson momentarily disappeared into heavy shade. Coming into the moonlight a short distance on, Marius could see he was now walking with purpose.

Instead of going to the White Bear, Johnson turned up the hill to halt before the blackened shell of the house he had so recently occupied. After a short interval, the gentleman retraced his steps to the inn.

Now, why did he adopt that drunken charade? wondered Marius. Was it to elicit sympathy? To give the appearance of drowning his sorrows? Something was most odd about his behaviour.

Returning to the Assembly Rooms, Marius walked under the colonnade which was in deep shadow. There were few people abroad, just a trickle of gamblers returning to their lodgings. Close to the steps to the Lower Walk was a figure he recognised. It was Nathaniel Jordan. Marius paused, and drew back into the gloom.

Standing with Jordan was a tall man, slight of build. There were no distinguishing aspects to his dress, and his features were obscured in the half-light of the lanterns. He had what appeared to be a dark, full beard, apparent even under a flat, broad-brimmed hat. It was clear from the manner of the exchange there was disagreement. Marius could not hear what was said, but it was heated and abrupt. Delivering his final word, the fellow turned on his heel and strode off. Jordan stood there motionless for a moment, before heading in the opposite direction.

In the Rooms, he watched Roger Dashwood successfully call the dice in a game of Hazard, before whispering, "Pick up your winnings, we must leave."

Outside Roger asked, "Why so soon, Marius? I was enjoying some good fortune for a change."

"I have just witnessed two intriguing events. The first was Johnson, giving the appearance of being drunk and sorrowful. It was a sham. More intriguing was the second. Jordan was arguing with someone. I'm not sure, but I believe you've pointed him out to me. I can't recall his name."

"What was the fellow like? Can you describe him?"

"It wasn't easy to tell. But I did notice that he had a beard and wore a distinctive wide- brimmed hat."

"Was he tall?"

Marius pondered on the question. "Yes, taller than Jordan, and thinner."

"It sounds like Adam Loveday. He always gives the impression of being a law-abiding citizen," said Roger, a curious tone to his voice. "Mind you, that could easily be a deception, even though he's the freeholders' spokesman."

"I'm sorry to keep you, Doctor, the parents of a serving girl wanted to speak with me," explained the constable. "They live out at Woodsgate Corner. Apparently, their daughter has not been home recently. Unfortunately, I couldn't help them. No one has reported anyone missing from their employ."

"Forgive the earliness of the hour, Constable. However, I thought a word with you would be in order. It seems a number of people are frightened their houses are about to burst into flame."

"I have been told something of the kind," muttered the constable, looking up at his visitor. "It often happens when there's a fire. It catches the company's imagination, and becomes magnified beyond belief. Who heeds logic when an alarming, yet entertaining, tale is abroad."

Marius took the proffered chair. When shown in by a deputy, he had been surprised that there were so few comforts in the constable's room. All it comprised was a modest, well-worn table and several chairs. The décor, a mid-green wash, was decidedly nondescript.

"However, that was not the sole purpose of my visit. I wanted to ask if Mr Johnson has yet agreed to view the bodies?"

"No, Doctor, he has not. I was wondering how long I should wait before becoming insistent. The powers are there to force his attendance. However, I was inclined to show a little latitude."

"I want to ask a favour, Constable," said Marius, attempting to be casual. "Do you think I could be present, when Mr Johnson visits the mortuary?"

"Hmm … I am not sure. I suppose I could ask him. But, why do you wish to be there?"

"With your permission, I wanted to enquire if his niece wore high-heeled shoes. They were not with the body, and I couldn't see any at the house. I also wanted to ask if he knew the state of her teeth. For a gentlewoman so young, she appeared to have far too many gaps."

Marius did not reveal to the constable that he had other pressing questions to put to Johnson. He was now almost certain one of the bodies was not his niece.

"If Mr Johnson does not come by his own accord," declared the constable, rising from his seat, "I shall request he attends the mortuary no later than Friday."

"When you set the day and the time, perhaps one of your deputies could advise me?" prompted Marius.

It was a perfect summer's morning, the air fresh on a mild breeze. The heat of the day had yet to make its presence felt. With his room on the north side of the house, it would remain cool for some hours to come. He lay on the bed, going over in his mind what he was about to do. The aim was clear. Yet, each stage had to be precise. He knew there was little room for error, everyone must be accounted for. The best time would be when they were all gathered in the house for dinner. The materials would be easy to retrieve. Stored close to the site, the chances of being observed were slight. He rose from his bed, and dressed slowly. He left the room as the church bell chimed ten of the clock.

Marius ate a late breakfast at the Angel Inn. Those taking the waters had now returned, so most of the tables were full. Ordering toast and hot chocolate, he thought over his meeting with the constable, trying to determine what Johnson's reaction might be when informed of the summons to the mortuary.

His mind turned to Nathaniel Jordan. It was clear he was trying to coerce a number of people, but to what end? The fellow wanted to establish a farrier's business close to the Walks. From what Marius gathered the freeholders appeared to be resisting his overtures. Would he take kindly to a rebuff? Marius wondered.

He was convinced Jordan would not let matters rest. Perhaps, I should check his background, he mused. I'll write to my father. He would have the means to find out more about him.

His thoughts turned to Dashwood. He had described those attending the meeting at Rusthall. Could any of them take advantage of their position and be involved in the movement of illicit goods into the town? It was a random thought, but one that began to take shape in his mind. Conyers, the Lord of The Manor, could do well from the controversy. Especially, if it were shown the freeholders themselves were trading in contraband.

As he buttered his toast, Marius considered Fielding's presence in The Wells. According to his wife, he had already spent several weeks in the spa town. Yet from what Roger Dashwood had told him, the only discussion of any consequence Fielding had attended was yesterday at Rusthall Manor. Conceivably, he was employed on other Excise business. Or was he simply ignoring the problem? Taking the waters, and spending his time at the gaming tables? Having met with Conyers and the others, would he now return to London? Surely not when his wife had just arrived? I must have a word with Roger to discover if any further meetings were scheduled, he concluded.

Finishing his meal he made his way to the shops in the colonnade. Leaving his rooms in London in a hurry, he had not brought sufficient clothing for a lengthy stay. He was in much need of linen and other items. In the clothier's shop his eye was taken by a rich brocade fabric that would make up into a waistcoat. Although by nature conservative in his choice of dress, the material appealed to him. Holding the bale, and considering the cut of the garment from a directory, he glanced through the window to see the Fieldings promenading along the Upper Walk.

Hastily completing his purchases, and agreeing to return for them later, he hurried from the shop. The Fieldings were seated at one of Uptons' tables when Marius asked if he might join them.

"Why, Dr Hope," Mrs Fielding gave a wan smile. "I saw you yesterday talking with Mr Nash. Are you enjoying your time in the Wells?"

For some reason Mrs Fielding appeared anxious, looking frequently towards her husband, who gave a curt nod of greeting.

"Are you going to the horse races on Saturday, Dr Hope?" enquired the woman nervously. "I do hear they are a most entertaining diversion."

"Yes, I'm looking forward to it."

"It appears crowds of people attend, and Mr Nash is going to preside over the day's events. I'm sure it will be most jolly." There was a faint flush to her cheeks, and she said it without conviction.

"Are you a gambling man, Mr Fielding?" Marius asked.

"I suppose we shall attend," replied Fielding in an off-hand manner. "I often go to the race meetings on Epsom Downs. Though, to my mind, it has deteriorated with the advent of the touters. They line the route proclaiming what one should enjoy at the course, and jostling to sell their wares whilst you are in your carriage. These days it's more like a roadside bazaar."

"I'm going with Mr Dashwood," said Marius. "If he can tear himself away from his work."

"And what is his work?" Fielding asked in a languid tone.

"Do you know, I really have no idea. He disappears for long periods, and all that is ever said is that he is going about his duty. Still, he seems most assiduous in its undertaking."

"Does he confine himself to the town?"

"No. From what I gather, Dashwood often rides out to meetings, or to perform some act or other. All he states is that he has sharp eyes and ears," responded Marius artlessly. "I'm not sure what he means by such a remark."

"Have you been to any of the balls in the Assembly Rooms, Dr Hope?" questioned Mrs Fielding in a fluttering voice.

"I have been to one, madam. They are most enjoyable. Have you and your husband?"

"Unfortunately, I do not derive much pleasure from dancing. Do I, my dear?" declared Fielding.

She did not reply. His wife seemingly engrossed with her own thoughts.

"Forgive my wife, Doctor. Occasionally she is lost to this world," said Fielding, staring at her.

A serving girl provided coffee.

Fielding suddenly asked, "What business is your family in, Hope?"

"We have a shipping company mainly importing from the Indies. We have a quay and warehouse close to London Bridge."

On a whim, he mischievously expanded on his answer.

"The biggest headache is dealing with the Excise people. When they have queries, shipments can be frequently delayed. There are occasions when it takes up to a week to allay their concerns. Then there is the documentation. As you know, goods are never released by the Excise until the duties are paid, and all the papers signed."

Marius looked questioningly at Fielding, who appeared to take no great interest in his comments.

"Well, time is passing, we must bid you good day, Hope," declared Fielding. Obediently, his wife rose with him, and the couple made their way in the direction of the Well.

Marius sat at the table after they had gone, mulling over the conversation. He was still contemplating Fielding's responses, when Roger took a seat opposite him.

"Had a busy morning?" he grinned.

"Interesting … most interesting," responded Marius, a faraway look in his eyes. "I took coffee with the Fieldings. He has a detached air, but he's acutely aware of all that is going on around him. I was trying to analyse what was said in our conversation. More to the point, what was left unsaid."

Marius stared at him across the table. "At your meeting in Rusthall, did anyone touch upon matters to do with Excise?"

"I recall that Marshall, the Riding Officer, did on several occasions," he said, attempting to recollect the discussion. "Fielding didn't comment. For that matter, he didn't say much during the entire meeting. I thought he showed a marked lack of interest in the proceedings."

They sat in companionable silence, drinking coffee, each occupied with his own thoughts. Music drifted over the Walks. Marius looked up at the gallery where the ensemble was playing a bright, rhythmic piece by Scarlatti.

"Well, I'm hungry," Roger declared. "Shall we return to Ashenhurst House, or eat in one of the taverns?"

"Why don't we dine at the White Bear?"

"A capital idea! In this heat I am not of a mind to traipse up the hill."

Marius did not speak of his motive, but if circumstances allowed, he wanted a word with Mr Johnson about the examination of the bodies. However, there was no sign of him when they seated themselves in a quiet alcove.

The tavern filled as many of the company came to dine. The hubbub of conversation rose. It was a convivial atmosphere, much given to banter and laughter. Slightly apart from the main dining area, Marius and Dashwood enjoyed a platter of cold meats and cider, and sat back contentedly smoking their pipes.

Suddenly, the tavern door burst open.

"There's a fire in Frant Lane!" shouted a man frantically. "One of the houses across the stream is burning! People are trapped inside!"

Utter silence was instantly broken by uproar. The fears that people had been harbouring were released. Many hurried from the tavern, shocked by the news. Marius looked across at Roger. Climbing to their feet, they hastened towards the church. Turning into the lane, they beheld a fearsome sight.

Another wood-built house was in flames, smoke and tongues of fire belching skywards. A chain had formed using water from the nearby stream. Sadly, their efforts were futile. Slowly, the passing of the buckets came to a halt. There could be no survivors. The intensity of the fire, the speed with which it was devouring the timbers, was beyond the efforts of the would-be rescuers. All that could be done was wait until it subsided.

Marius noticed the constable standing with a small group, and walked over to him. His saddened face turned to Marius, misery starkly portrayed in his eyes.

"A thankless task, Doctor," he said, his expression betraying his feelings. "We'll have to wait to see who is lost."

"Whose house was it, Constable?"

"A freeholder by the name of Loveday. I know him well. A man of habit. At this hour he would have been eating with his family. I just pray it was one of those days when habits were broken."

"Constable, I do not want to intrude. However, it seems unlikely you will be able to do anything before tomorrow morning," said Marius sadly. "Could I join you when you search among the embers? I might be able to help in some small way."

The constable was quiet for a moment. "Perhaps, we could meet here at eight of the clock, Dr Hope?"

CHAPTER SEVENTEEN

"This used to be the main room," said the constable in dismay. "I can't make any sense of it."

The fire had done its worst. All that remained were the gaunt outlines of three walls. The rest reduced to crumbling charcoal and shattered masonry. Everything wooden had been consumed. The exceptions were the floorboards in the main living area. Although badly scorched, many were still intact, saved by a thick layer of still-warm ash.

"Constable, if you have doubts about the fire," commented Marius, bending to examine the boards, "it might be worthwhile checking outside for anything that looks suspicious. Something which appears out of place."

I can concentrate better alone, he thought, kneeling in the rubble.

Near the centre of the room he came across the shattered remnants of pottery, once plates and beakers. A meal was either being eaten or being prepared at the time of the fire. A heavy iron pot lay on its side by the stone fireplace, two twisted ladles close by confirmed his thoughts. He dragged his hand carefully through the ash, discovering several knife blades.

Rising slowly to contemplate the ruin, Marius noticed a blackened stick lying by the remains of the back wall. Retrieving it, he chillingly recognised it as a human bone. From its shape it looked like a child's. Putting it to one side, he gingerly felt among the debris. After a few minutes, he had collected a number of shards and splinters. It was difficult to assess how many bodies they represented, but it was evident that among the ashes lay the remains of a number of people.

"Did Loveday have many children?" he asked the constable on his return.

He nodded. "Four. Why? . . . What have you found?"

"By the wall are fragments of bone. It is hard to tell how many bodies were in the room, but from what you tell me, it could well have been the entire family."

"My God! What a tragedy! I know Loveday was a careful man, but do you think the fats and oils he used could have burst into flame?"

"Fats?"

"Loveday was a chandler. He made candles in a room off the scullery."

"Would he have left hot oil unattended whilst having a meal?" queried Marius.

"He might have done. I never knew how he worked. Although he was teaching his elder son, Thomas, to make candles. Perhaps, the boy made a mistake."

"Can you show me where the room was?"

The constable led him to an area where there was a partially collapsed stone bench and the remains of hearth. To one side were a number of large metal cauldrons, used for melting and mixing. Close by were the contorted shapes of a number of tin tubes.

"I wonder if the fire started here?" muttered the constable.

"Wherever it was, it quickly devoured everything in its passage."

They returned to the main living area.

"If those bones are all that's left of the family, why are they all in one area of the room? Unless they clung together in desperation. It just doesn't make sense. At the very least, I would have expected Loveday to try to save his wife and children," said the constable, sadness catching at his voice.

From the burnt-out shell of the room, they made their way towards where the stairs to the upper part of the house had once stood. Marius hesitated, and knelt close to the crumbling, blackened remains of a stone wall.

"What are you doing?"

Straightening, he said uncertainly, "It was just an odour, slightly stronger and different from the smell of burnt timbers, but I've come across it before, I just cannot think where."

They stopped for a glass of brandy at the nearby Gloster Tavern, fortifying themselves against the horrors they had witnessed.

"We seem to share the worst of experiences, Dr Hope. I've been a law officer in The Wells for eight years, never have I come across such a run of misfortune."

"In my view, Constable," said Marius bleakly, "I'm not sure either fire was accidental. We could have two incidents caused by someone with little or no regard for life."

"What possible motive could there be, Doctor? What is there to gain?"

"That, Constable, is what we must find out," said Marius gravely. "I was deeply saddened by the fire in Mount Sion."

He drank from his glass.

"This senseless act provides added reason to discover who was responsible. Whoever it is, if guilty of both incidents, may strike again."

The constable rose from the table. "I must report this to the magistrate. It's my job to apprehend those guilty, but in matters as serious as this, I must give him details of both happenings."

"Before you go, Constable, have you spoken to Loveday's neighbours? I wonder if they heard shouting, even screaming from the house. There may be some merit in talking to them."

"I'll be doing that later, Doctor."

He walked away, his shoulders slumped.

Finishing the brandy, Marius went to the clothier's shop in the colonnade to collect the items purchased the previous day. They were waiting for him, neatly wrapped in a parcel. Tucking it under his arm he strolled along the Upper Walk.

"Good morning, Doctor," said a voice. Turning his head Marius saw Mr Tofts, the musician, coming towards him.

"Are you taking a break from the ensemble, Mr Tofts?"

"Briefly. When we can, we take it in turns," replied the musician.

"By the way, I never did discover what instrument you play."

"The mandolin . . .it has such musical quality."

On a whim Marius asked, "Would you care to join me for coffee? I need to sit for a while. It has been an upsetting morning, even though I am used to unpleasant sights."

They chose a table and Marius caught the attention of a serving girl.

"Has something troubled you?" enquired the musician.

"Yes, the fire yesterday. It not only destroyed a house, it obliterated a family," he said despondently.

"What a fearful thing to happen." The musician looked shocked.

"I am strongly of the opinion, Mr Tofts, there are those in The Wells out to wreak havoc. They have to be stopped," Marius muttered to himself.

"I examined the debris this morning. It was a sickening sight, but I believe whoever did it left a clue."

He recalled the odour near where the staircase had once stood. Some distant memory hovered at the edges of his mind.

"I've just got to work out what it means," he mused aloud. Suddenly, he was distracted by the arrival of Roger Dashwood.

"My dear fellow, I've been looking for you everywhere. I'm sorry not to have been along earlier. Ashenhurst House didn't have a mount available, so I've rented one for you from stables in Mount Pleasant."

Tofts finished his coffee, murmured his thanks and departed.

"Who was that fellow? I'm sure I've seen him before," commented Roger blithely.

"He's called Tofts. Another traveller who came down on the coach with me. He's a member of the musical ensemble," said Marius, nodding towards the gallery.

"Odd sort of dresser, don't you think?"

"Well, it's hard for me to say," smiled Marius. "I could be thought too conservative.

Mind you, I have just asked the tailor to make me a rather dashing waistcoat."

"Is it in the parcel?"

"No. Some linen I have just collected."

"Well, if you are off to Tonbridge, you best be on your way," he remarked. "Though why you can't buy the Ware here in the Walks is beyond me. If you like, I'll take your parcel back to the lodging house."

He retrieved it from an adjacent seat.

"I'll walk to the stables with you. You can tell me of the morning's events."

As they strolled towards Mount Pleasant, he listened intently to Marius' disturbing tale. It drew concern, and by the time they had reached the livery stables, for once Roger was unusually quiet.

A groom gave Marius directions to Tonbridge by way of Southborough. The route, unsuitable for coaches, passed through several hamlets on its way to Bidborough. From there, he was told, he would see the castle and township below, nestling either side of the Medway River.

After bidding Roger good day, he rode leisurely up the hill, passing the Calverley Estate where, briefly, the terrain levelled out. The track rose again to a high point overlooking The Wells. Turning in the saddle, Marius was able to identify the houses on the hillside below, and make out the distant church. However, the Walks were concealed by a broad sweep of trees covering the southern slopes.

On the ridge at Bidborough, he reined in to survey the scene. Tonbridge Castle lay on the north bank of a river bisecting the busy township. In the distance he could see the undulating, green expanse of the Weald stretching towards the distant North Downs.

Urging his mount forward, Marius descended into Tonbridge, making for the main bridge and the Wise Manufactory. The company produced decrative wooden bowls and dishes. Presented to members of the family, they would make very acceptable mementoes.

He spent an hour in the manufactory conversing with the illustrator. An elderly man, bent from his years of painting simple but appealing designs on wooden items. Afterwards he toured the castle, or what remained of it after Thomas Weller had "slighted" the keep and walls during the civil war, to confound its use as a fortification. He took a mug of ale at the Chequers Inn, and afterwards, crossed the marketplace, past the stocks and cornmarket, to the Rose and Crown.

There, he handed in a letter. Being a posting inn on the coastal routes to and from London, coaches from Tonbridge ran frequently to the capital.

CHAPTER EIGHTEEN

"Are you saying that someone else is prepared to pay more, and you're accepting their offer?" exclaimed the farrier angrily.

"He was very persuasive," replied William Bennett, keeping his head low, eyes averted.

"What do you mean? Haven't I explained what this will give you and the other freeholders?"

"I know… I can't explain … But, I'm going to sell my title shares to him."

"I might be able to pay a little more . . . In which case, I would need you to sign over the deeds to me today."

Bennett looked up, greed evident in his eyes.

"Mr Jordan, I have to think of my family, what's best for them."

He looked into the freeholder's face, and leaned forward to emphasise his words.

"Let me put it this way, Mr Bennett," said Jordan menacingly. "If you are so important to your family, I'm sure they would forego a few guineas to ensure your continued health."

Bennett's eyes widened. The farrier seemed very capable of carrying out the implied threat.

"What if I include a barn I have in Waterdowne Forest? It's only a mile or so from the Walks."

Jordan was intrigued.

"I'll pay another twenty five guineas for your title deeds for the Walks and for the barn. That's my final offer, Bennett. It will make you a rich man. If you are thinking about your family, you can't afford to turn it down."

Bennett rung his hands.

"Give me a little time to think about it, Mr Jordan."

"I want to know now, and I will not take no for an answer. As you may well find out," declared Jordan threateningly.

"Let us meet tomorrow. By then I'll have retrieved the deeds."

"Alright, but we won't meet here," relented Jordan. "I'll see you by the bettors' round at the races on the Common. I shall have the money. For your sake, you'd better have the title deeds."

Jordan strode away, leaving Bennett with the feeling he was trapped between two implacable forces. How could he do business with one without incurring the wrath of the other?

CHAPTER NINETEEN

A note was left for him at Ashenhurst House.

> Dr MARIUS HOPE
>
> This is to Advise that Mr Johnson will be Attending the Mortuary at Half past Three of The Clock this Afternoon. You May Wish to be Present in the Outer Office Prior to his Arrival.
>
> Simon Russell – Constable of The Wells

He read it several times before passing it to Roger.

"What the constable is saying, is do I want to ask Johnson if I can be present when he inspects the bodies?" Marius said thoughtfully.

"Why on earth do you want to be there?"

"I want to ask Johnson some questions."

"Surely you could put them to him elsewhere? Why do you have to be at the mortuary?"

"I want to watch his reactions when he identifies the bodies."

Roger said nothing. Leaning on a side chest, he looked out the window to the paddock beyond. At length he observed, "It seems the weather is changing. I do believe it might rain."

"Perhaps it will bring down the temperatures, which would be welcome," replied Marius.

By the time they were ready to walk into the town, it had grown much darker. The clouds heavy and deep. The sky illuminated by continuous flashes of lightning, closely followed by booming claps of thunder. They stood at the main door, neither inclined to venture out. Suddenly, the heavens opened. Heavy raindrops bounced off the gravel pathway. In seconds, rivulets were running across the lawn.

The long spell of sunshine had broken. Disappointed, they retreated to the orangery to lounge in rattan chairs amid the ornamental plants and shrubs. Marius closed his eyes, listening to the rain pounding on the glass roof, while Roger thumbed through a book left on a chair.

"Did you visit the Wise Manufactory when you were in Tonbridge?" he asked languidly.

"Yes. They are producing some bowls illustrated with my own choice of designs."

"When will they be ready?"

"In about ten days time."

Roger moved to a window overlooking the rose garden.

"Shall I come to the mortuary with you?"

"Thank you, Roger, but it's best I go alone. Two of us might appear intimidating."

"Well, we can have dinner together. Then, whilst you are at the mortuary, I'll buy the wine for the races tomorrow," he declared.

They idled away time until the worst of the storm had passed. The sky gradually lightened, and by late morning the rain had eased. Fortunately, Roger had managed to borrow one of the few umbrellas to be found in The Wells, and a little after one of the clock they set off for the Castle Inn.

Because of the poor weather the inn was crowded. When finally seated Marius said, "If you are going to the wine shop, could you do something for me? If Mr Augustus Brown is in the Walks, could you keep a watch on him? It would be useful to know what he is about."

"What do you expect him to do?" asked Roger, his curiosity piqued.

"I'm not sure whether his interest in the Lower Walk is genuine, or a front for something else."

Pushing his plate to one side, Marius began the makings of a pipe. Calling for a lighted spill, he looked around the room and noticed Johnson sitting alone by the fireplace.

"I'll not be a moment," he said, rising and making his way through the tables to the far side of the room.

Johnson was well into his meal when Marius came to his shoulder.

"Mr Johnson, I wonder if I might have a word. My name is Hope . . . Dr Hope. I have been speaking with the constable, and he advises me that you are due to make an identification this afternoon."

Sounding purposeful, Marius added, "In circumstances such as these, where there is evidence of misadventure, it is customary for a doctor to be present. I have the necessary credentials, so I thought it proper to introduce myself. To notify you that I shall be attending."

"I cannot see the need for a doctor," said Johnson, looking up at him. "Still, if it's the law, so be it." He wiped his mouth on a napkin.

"I am dining here, with a friend. Perhaps, when you are ready, we can walk to the mortuary together?"

"When I have finished, Doctor, I'll seek you out."

Displaying unspoken irritation, Johnson returned to his meal.

"What did you say?" Roger asked anxiously when Marius resumed his seat.

"I just mentioned that as a doctor it would be proper to be there at the identification."

"Do you mean to say you invited yourself?"

"Not in so many words. But, yes, that was the result."

"I'm not sure the constable will approve."

"As far as he is concerned, I shall arrive with the fellow. I shall mention that all is in order, and neither will be any the wiser."

"It's a bit risky though, isn't it, Marius?" Roger commented, a hint of concern in his voice. "If the constable discovers Johnson was not given the chance to deny you access, it might become a little fraught."

"It's hardly likely, Roger."

His eyebrows rose questioningly: Dashwood was not convinced.

A little while later, Johnson stopped by their table, and Marius joined him on the short walk to the mortuary.

Knocking on the stout green doors, Marius could not help thinking that all such buildings had a forbidding aspect. The door was opened promptly by the duty officer. In the ante-room the constable was clearly surprised to see the two of them together. Now more attuned to his ways, Marius could perceive the constable was ill-at-ease. His manner hesitant, self-effacing.

"I am here, Constable, although I must emphasise the distress the event has caused will be worsened by this demand of yours to attend upon the bodies so soon," declared Johnson. "Have I not suffered enough without being subjected to further upset?"

"I am sorry, Mr Johnson, but the law requires a formal identification, and we cannot delay much longer before burial," said the constable apologetically.

"I have had a word with Mr Phillips, the magistrate, on the matter," stated Johnson in a disgruntled tone. "In his opinion there seems to be unnecessary haste. Too much concern with the letter of the law. He felt that a longer interval, to overcome the shock of the incident, would have been in order."

So he has spoken with the magistrate, thought Marius. Now I understand why the constable was uneasy. I wonder if he has been told to treat the matter with leniency? If I'd come earlier, he might well have stopped me viewing the bodies.

"Well, we had better get it over and done with. I understand the good doctor has to accompany me," said Johnson, removing his hat and resting his cane against a chair.

Whilst he did so the constable stared at Marius, though made no allusion to Johnson's remark. Instead he said, "I shall remain here, Mr Johnson. There is no need for me to intrude upon your grief. For that matter, I am not sure Dr Hope has to stand beside you."

"If Mr Johnson needs a moment to grieve, I shall withdraw. But what has to be done can be done quickly. Is it not a simple identification?" Marius asked guilelessly

"Come, Doctor," exclaimed Johnson, irritably, and was directed through the inner door by the deputy.

The window, set high in the wall, barely provided sufficient light. The storm clouds adding to the gloom of the chamber.

"I suggest you wait a moment, Mr Johnson, until your eyes accustom to the light."

"No matter, a mere glance will be all that is necessary," he snapped.

Marius pulled back the white cloth that covered the body nearest to the door. In the half-light the waxen features of Mrs Johnson were revealed. In repose she looked calm, almost angelic. A reflection of her nature, Marius thought.

"No doubt about it," declared Johnson, less sorrowful than might be expected. "That is my wife, Mrs Johnson. God bless her."

Marius gently re-covered the body, and they moved to the next table. Once more, the cloth was pulled back, but this time the face, burnt and contorted by the fire, was an alarming sight.

"Can you reveal more of the body?" asked Johnson, with more equanimity than Marius felt he should possess. The cover was turned back further, and fragments of the young woman's dress and her hands became visible.

"It is difficult to recognise Emily from her face, but that is most certainly the dress she was wearing. And the rings on her hands confirm it. This is the body of Miss Emily Roper."

"You are quite sure?"

"I cannot think there could be any doubt," commented Johnson sardonically. "After all, she was my niece."

"I met your wife on the coach travelling down from London. I remember her vividly. I am truly saddened to see her lying here. You have my heartfelt sympathy," Marius said softly. He paused. "I only met your niece on two occasions, Mr Johnson. In the Walks and at the ball in the Assembly Rooms. She impressed me with her bright smile and her elegance."

He looked down at the corpse, taking the right hand he examined the fingers. "You should take the rings with you, sir, and your wife's jewellery."

He turned to the other body, and raised Mrs Johnson's hand above the sheet. Her wedding ring, which was almost embedded in the finger below the knuckle, was the only adornment.

"I do recall your wife was wearing a necklace, bracelets and several rings on the night of the ball, Mr Johnson. Presumably, she must have removed them. Yet Miss Roper still wears her jewellery. Odd, don't you think?"

Staring down at his dead wife, Johnson did not reply. Marius walked back to the other table. He leaned over the corpse and gently prised open the mouth. The upper teeth were intact, but there were a number of gaps in the lower jaw. He could not recall noticing when dancing with her. When she had laughed, her head had invariably been turning sideways to attract the attentions of others.

"Mr Johnson, were you aware of the state of your niece's teeth? Can you recall if she had had any dental treatment recently?"

"I have no idea," Johnson mumbled.

"Do you mind if I ask another question? Was your niece taller than your wife?"

"I would have said she was taller," responded Johnson quietly. "But it may have been an illusion. She wore shoes with raised heels."

"How high were the heels?"

Johnson swivelled round, and glared furiously at Marius.

"Am I correct to assume that as the medical representative you should merely be present, not subjecting me to heavy-handed inquiry?"

"Forgive me, Mr Johnson. It's natural interest," replied Marius, hastily apologetic. "I did not realise I was intruding."

Johnson was not easily mollified. "Tell me, Dr Hope, are you questioning my judgement? Are you suggesting that these are not my wife's and my niece's bodies?"

"It is not my job to comment one way or the other, Mr Johnson."

"Quite so. I was married for seventeen years, and in that time watched my niece grow up. So I should think I knew them both intimately, don't you?"

"I have no reason to doubt that you knew both members of your family well," said Marius.

Johnson turned back to the body of his niece, and slipped the rings from her fingers.

"See that emerald and diamond ring, Hope? I bought that for her on her fifteenth birthday. What more proof do you need?"

He started towards the door.

"May I raise just one more query, Mr Johnson? To satisfy my curiosity, you understand. Your wife is wearing shoes, yet I cannot see those of Miss Roper anywhere."

Opening the door, and in full view of the constable, Johnson spun round angrily. "Listen to me, Doctor. I don't care to satisfy your curiosity. In my opinion you have overreached your position. I shall be speaking to Mr Phillips, the magistrate, about your deplorable conduct."

He walked into the ante-room, and said to the constable, "Why have you allowed this man to question my judgement? I have told him that they are the bodies of my wife and my niece. It is clear from his remarks he questions my veracity. I hold you totally responsible. Phillips will most certainly hear from me on the matter. Good day to you!"

With that he stalked out. The constable turned to Marius.

"Do you realise what you have done?" he exploded. "I now find myself in difficulties, all because you wanted to confront the man. Like a fool, I went along with it. I allowed him to think it was obligatory to have a medical man present. When the magistrate discovers that I was party to the deception, he will rightly take me to task. What have you to say to that?"

"Mr Russell, I am in error," said Marius apologetically. "I admit that my little ploy has gone awry. However, I am still convinced there is more to the incident than meets the eye. If you wish, I shall go to see the magistrate and explain my opinion and your unwitting involvement."

"I suggest, Dr Hope, that you leave these premises. You forget the whole, unhappy incident, and you refrain from meddling in other people's affairs."

CHAPTER TWENTY

As the young man hurried through a passageway by the Assembly Rooms, he was conscious of the fear rising in him. It had been ever-present these past four years. When Daniel Clifford was about to acquire his inheritance, his father's dying words had foretold of dissent: that it would be only a matter of time before there was bloodshed.

The one stall in the Lower Walk he had worked with his father, had grown to three in as many years. Whilst the profits were only to be made when the company was present in the summer months, it had been enough to maintain him and his family. Now he was being pressed to sell other merchandise. He could make much more money, it had been said. Buy things for his children, dress his wife fashionably, enjoy a more prosperous life. However, there was a risk. One, he had told the fellow he was unwilling to take.

Clifford's attitude had not been taken kindly. From being pleasant and persuasive, the man who confronted him had become openly aggressive. There had been no attempt to disguise the threat. Not just himself, but his family was now vulnerable.

He must protect them at all costs, as well as looking out for his own well-being.

A figure stepped out of a doorway. Clifford made to walk past, but suddenly he was gripped by the shoulder, his arm twisted behind his back and he was forced against the wall.

"I am not giving in to your demands," he croaked. "You cannot make me, despite your threats. My stalls are not available, do you hear?"

"My friend, listen carefully. I want you to sell me the titles to your freeholder rights. This is not an idle warning. Loveday thought it was. He no longer has the luxury to change his mind. Live to see your children grow up, your wife by your side. Deny me, and you will follow the Lovedays into oblivion."

The assailant twisted Clifford's arm even further, until he gasped with pain.

"I shall come for you again in a few days time. You will not know when. But, you will have the right answer for me."

With that he dashed Clifford's head hard against the stone wall of the passageway.

CHAPTER TWENTY ONE

There had been little else to say. He had admitted his mistake. However, the constable's anger forswore any attempt at appeasement. Marius cast round for Roger Dashwood, before slumping dejectedly into a seat in Smith's Coffee House. The weather was still sufficiently unsettled to keep most of the patrons inside. He nodded to one or two acquaintances.

Half of the hour later, he was on the point of leaving when Mrs Porter bustled through the door. She toured the coffee house, the weather providing a captive audience. The sound of heavy coin falling into a large bag as the dues were paid would be music to Mister Nash's ears. In due course, she stopped at Marius' table.

"How are you today, Mrs Porter?" he enquired.

"It's kind of you to ask, Dr Hope. Thankfully, the wrist is much better. It still aches, and I frequently need to rest it, but your attentions the other evening were much appreciated."

"Did you know Mr Nash sought me out to thank me?"

"No, I did not. When was that?"

"Tuesday morning. I was sitting outside this very house, when he arrived in his carriage. We had a long conversation."

She smiled at him while opening her large book.

"I have to ask you this, Dr Hope. Have you availed yourself of the gaming rooms, the dancing and any other activities since you arrived? As you know, it's my role to collect the fees for all the pursuits enjoyed by the company," she said in an almost apologetic tone. Clearly put out that she was asking for money, when he had done her a kindness.

"I have, Mrs Porter. Frankly, I have no idea what I should be paying. What does it normally cost?"

She leaned over the table, and said in a low voice, "I will not charge you what I ask of others, Dr Hope. Just give me a nominal sum, and we'll leave it at that."

"That's generous of you, Mrs Porter. Though, I would not want to embarrass either of us by offering too little or too much. Tell me the charges."

"There is an official list of fees, Doctor. Perhaps, if I itemise them we can decide what you might pay."

She opened her accounts book. A large, leather-bound volume, which was patently heavy, and uncomfortable to carry when in pursuit of the company. On the inside page was a schedule of charges, with several scales against many of the items.

"Let me explain how the dues are applied, Doctor. When one first arrives, you are serenaded by musicians. That costs half a crown. The music played in the gallery and at the balls is charged at half a crown to a guinea, according to rank and privilege. It also varies between a crown and a guinea for use of the Assembly Rooms. This allows one to have the company of others, write letters, read journals, enjoy playing at cards and conversation."

Mrs Porter made an amendment to the sheet, then continued. "If one attends any of the balls, the charge is two shillings and sixpence for the gentleman, one shilling for his lady. It is also half a crown to sit in the coffee house if you come regularly, borrow a book from the bookstall, or take the waters from the dipper. It is a shilling for the waiters and the same for the Walks' sweeper. I collect the dues weekly, although I have found it difficult of late with my wrist in a sling."

Mrs Porter surveyed the other tables, and in a low tone, enquired.

"Tell me, Dr Hope, have you used the facilities and diversions since you arrived? If you have, I would ask for one pound and seven shillings. If you've sought the services of a clergyman, it would be a half crown extra. Just give me fifteen shillings. At your pleasure, of course."

"Mrs Porter, as yet, I have not taken the waters or seen a minister. Though, thank you for your indulgence. I'll gladly pay, and now is as good a time as any."

Taking a purse from his waistcoat, Marius dropped the required sum into Mrs Porter's leather bag. She smiled, made an entry in her record book, murmured her thanks and continued her tour of the coffee house.

He waited until the rain had stopped. When a few weak rays of sunshine filtered through the windows, he judged it the moment to leave. He walked under the colonnade as far as the sun dial. The rain, lying on the pantiles in the Upper Walk, was now evaporating. A soft mist rising from the patchwork of puddles. The trees were still shedding raindrops, spraying passers-by with unwelcome showers when gusts of wind swirled around the alleyways.

Marius made it back to his lodging house just before the next downpour. Trotting the last few yards to the house as droplets splashed on the track, already mudded by the day's heavy downpours.

He asked a chambermaid for a jug of hot water, shaved, and was putting on a fresh chemise when there was a knock at the door. Opening it, he found Roger standing there, a broad smile on his face.

"Come in! You look as though you have something to tell."

"I don't know whether it's significant or not, but I found Mr Brown's activities most entertaining."

"Start from the beginning, after we parted at the Castle Inn."

"Well, as you suggested, I strolled to the Walks, but Brown was nowhere to be seen. I bought the wine for Saturday, then rested a while at the Sussex tavern, enjoying a pipe and a bumper. Glancing out the window, I happened see your Mr Brown promenading along the Upper Walk. After a time, he came down the steps to the Lower Walk."

Roger was distracted for a moment, picking up and examining one of Marius' silver-backed brushes.

"Anyway, I moved behind the fish market when he took up a position by the Gloster Tavern. Interestingly, his comings and goings haven't gone unnoticed. The innkeeper told me he is often prowling about there, occasionally going into the tavern for a restorative. When it started to rain he turned on his heel and walked towards the bridge by the lane to Frant."

Roger shrugged off his frock coat, and perching on the bed, continued his story.

"Brown stood by the bridge seemingly waiting for someone. Would you believe, within minutes a small coach halted beside him. He had a brief conversation with the occupant. Then the carriage door opened and this fellow got out. I didn't recognise him, but he was of presentable appearance."

"What happened then?"

"Well, the strange thing was both of them strolled over to the house, or shall I say Loveday's charred ruin. They stood looking at the burnt-out shell for at least a quarter of an hour. Having a fine, old discussion, they were. Unfortunately, I couldn't get close enough to hear what was being said. When their conversation was at an end, they walked back over the bridge and adjourned to the Angel Inn."

"They stayed together?"

"Yes, it was clear that they were still talking about something. At the inn they went into the salon. I was trying not to be too conspicuous. I followed and sat in the taproom watching through the door. When it was at the end, they rose and shook hands. So it must have something to do with business, no one shakes hands socially. I heard the other fellow bid Brown farewell, and leave in the coach which had drawn up outside the main door."

"Did you find out who he was?" Marius asked impatiently.

"Let me finish, Marius. After the meeting, Brown came out the salon clearly pleased with events. He hesitated in the lobby, then decided to go upstairs to his room. That was the end of it," he said, now looking at Marius closely. "However, when I got up to leave, the porter at the front door remarked, "We don't often get a visit from Lord Abergavenny's estate manager"."

Roger looked up at Marius and grinned.

"As the porter walked towards the parlour, I asked if he knew the owner of the Loveday house. He replied, "Lord Abergavenny, of course. He owns most of the land and properties the other side of the stream." So, if I am any judge, your Mr Brown is about to buy the house in which the Loveday family perished."

CHAPTER TWENTY TWO

Marius carried the picnic hamper provided by the housekeeper at the lodging house, and Roger brought the wine and glasses in a carrying box. They strolled across Bishops Down with other racegoers, intent on making their way to the far side of the slope where the marquees and seated areas were located.

After the rain, the sun was now in the ascendancy. A light breeze gently caught at the colourful hats of the ladies, and cooled the gentlemen in their extravagant frock coats. The infectious spirit of the gathering crowds heightening the occasion. Roger was a step or two ahead, looking for a suitable spot by the rails, when a voice hailed him.

"Dashwood! Come, join us! There's plenty of room. Bring your companion."

"It's Mr Conyers," murmured Roger. "Do you mind if we join him?"

Marius shrugged his compliance.

Maurice Conyers, the tenth Lord of The Manor of Rusthall, was a commanding figure. Dressed in white, from hose to cravat, he stood by his marquee welcoming friends and acquaintances. As they drew near, Marius could see a well-rounded man of middle height and years. His plump face smiling beneath a full, extravagant wig. Closer, the cast of his features denoted someone who, although congenial, had firm opinions and would not be inclined to suffer fools. Roger introduced Marius to him, and the pair was ushered to one of several large tables laden with food, wine, cider and cordials.

When seated, Marius looked around at the others in their party, recognising the Fieldings and Augustus Brown.

Mrs Fielding smiled. Mr Fielding nodded, turning his head away in the same motion, giving the clear impression he would prefer to maintain his distance. Brown also inclined his head in acknowledgement, keeping his gaze upon Marius for a moment longer than necessary.

"May I offer you a drink, sir?" enquired the person next to him. "Would you care for some wine?"

Marius murmured his thanks, and a glass was filled. The young woman on his other side remarked on the warmth of the weather, and if it might trouble the runners. With that, Marius was immersed in the flow of conversation around him, though he could contribute little when the merits of individual horses, jockeys, and wagering odds were discussed.

On several occasions he looked around for Roger. Each time he was talking earnestly with the Lord of The Manor. He also saw that their discussion had not gone unnoticed by others at the table. He eventually took his seat, and immediately engaged the attention of the woman next to him. She was soon laughing at his comments, and rocking in her chair. He tells a good tale, acknowledged Marius. Whereas he has a way with the ladies, I find it difficult to hold their interest. Perhaps, he should give me guidance.

"This is a wonderful spread, is it not!" he called over to Marius, who smiled his agreement.

Marius turned to the young woman on his left, and asked if she had decided which horse she favoured in the first race. He added he had not yet had the opportunity to study the runners listed on the many blackboards dotted around the course.

"I am much taken with Runaway Lad. Alas, I have nobody to place a wager for me," she replied, with a slight, sideways smile.

"I would be delighted to place it for you. In fact, I shall choose the same horse, which will make it easier. I have no idea of their abilities. I don't even know which horse is the favourite."

She bent to retrieve her reticule beneath her chair.

"On this occasion, allow me to cover both our wagers," said Marius.

"I'm afraid I cannot. My uncle would not countenance such generosity from one of his guests," she replied. "I have to pay my own way. This is one of his cardinal rules."

"Your uncle being ... Mr Conyers?" enquired Marius.

"Oh, I thought you knew. During the season I frequently stay with Aunt and Uncle in Rusthall. Like father, he is very strict about how I spend my money when I'm here. He is against any notion that others should pay for my pleasures."

"Surely a small wager doesn't constitute paying for your pleasures?"

"He takes his role as *locum parentis* very seriously. He says, whilst I'm in his care, he acts as would my father. Still, perhaps he would not mind on such a day as this. It is the one occasion in the year when he can entertain his many friends."

"Leave it to me," said Marius, amused at her comment. "I'll slip away whilst he is occupied."

Walking through the mass of people he made his way towards the bettors' round, located near the finishing post. This was a new experience for him. He hung back to see how others placed their wagers. Standing in the throng, he noticed Nathaniel Jordan walking purposefully towards a group on the fringe of the milling crowd. I wonder who he is attempting to browbeat this time, thought Marius.

After some minutes, deciding that he now understood how it was done, he walked over to two men offering a range of odds. He declared he wished to place two wagers, for five shillings each, on Runaway Lad. One took his money, the other wrote on the tickets the name of the horse and the amount placed.

"Hang on ter 'em, guv'nor. Could be yer lucky day."

Marius had been so preoccupied with the other guests, and conscious of Roger's lengthy conversation with their host, he had not been fully aware of Conyers' niece. As he made his way back, he saw her turning animatedly to comments around the table. She had a narrow, attractive face, and when amused her eyes sparkled and she emitted a deep, throaty chuckle. She must be in her middle twenties, he thought. Dressed in a white sacque-back gown with a laced front, the blue frills at her collar and around the sleeves matched perfectly the colour of her eyes. What few cosmetics she wore only served to enhance her natural complexion. Marius realised he was sitting next to a decidedly, attractive companion.

Rejoining the table, he discreetly gave her one of the tickets.

"What odds did you get?" she whispered.

"Oh, I forgot to ask," said Marius deflated.

"Never mind, it's fun to hold a ticket and wish. I don't suppose we shall win. I'm never very lucky, and I fear I have probably spoiled your chances as well."

"It really doesn't matter," he smiled. "As you say, it's the enjoyment of cheering on a particular horse, and we can do that together. First, I ought to introduce myself. My name is Marius Hope. I am a friend of Roger Dashwood. "

"I know who you are, Dr Hope. Roger told me whilst you were away from the table."

"Oh, you have the advantage of me. I don't know your name."

"It's Elizabeth Conyers."

"May I, then, Elizabeth, ask you to accompany me to see how our horse fares?"

"That would be delightful, Dr Hope. I'm sure I shall not need a chaperone on such a day as this, although, I should tell my aunt."

Roger was sitting on the other side of the table. As Marius rose, he gave an amused grin.

"I have told my aunt, Dr Hope."

Momentarily distracted, he turned quickly towards her.

"Marius, please."

"Then you shall call me Beth. It is how I am known to my friends," she said lightly, turning to look up into his eyes.

The area near the finishing post was crowded, so Marius suggested they walk a little further up the course. Stopping on a high point, they had sight not only of the finish, but of the left-hand bend leading into the finishing straight, a hundred yards distant.

The course, broadly rectangular, lay at an angle across the slope of the downs. The start and the finish were just below the topmost point. This section was railed on both sides of the course, from the bend to just past the post. The rest, though open land and unfenced, was a clearly defined track, marked by posts. Where Marius and Beth Conyers were standing was a good vantage point, although part of the course was obscured by a grove of trees hiding much of the final bend before the run down to the finish.

"This is an ideal spot," said Beth excitedly.

"What I find fascinating is the number of people close to the bettors' round and the start and finish line," exclaimed Marius. "Is it always so colourful and noisy?"

"Yes, the hubbub of chatter, the shouting and laughter are really quite loud. It adds to the atmosphere, don't you think?" said Beth, smiling up at him.

The eleven runners and their riders were led through the crowd and onto the track. One or two were high-spirited, kicking up the sand as they pranced, waiting to be off. The jockeys held their crops at the ready. A silence fell as they came forward in a ragged line. The starter on the rostrum quickly brought down his flag, signalling a roar from the mass of spectators. Suddenly, the horses were running hard down the slope towards the first bend.

Out of sight briefly, the horses appeared going hard into the second turn at the lowest point of the course. For a moment they were again lost behind a standing of trees. As they emerged along the bottom straight, Marius could see that four horses had opened a gap between themselves and the rest, and the distance was growing.

"I cannot tell which is ours. I also forgot to find out the colours our jockey was wearing," shouted Marius.

"Never mind! When they come round the top bend, we shall be cheering every one of them," Beth called out.

The four horses in the lead were battling it out as they came towards the last corner. Disappearing behind the trees as Beth had predicted, they suddenly exploded into view, thundering down towards the finishing post. A second later the remaining runners passed them, galloping strongly.

"Good Lord! I didn't appreciate their speed," said Marius breathlessly. "Being this close, it's like being in the midst of a cavalry charge."

"I believe our horse was amongst the last, Marius," said Beth dejectedly. "I'm afraid I've lost you your money."

"Perhaps, we shall do better in the next race. Though, I suppose we should now go back to the table."

On their return a small celebration was under way. Roger had backed the winner, and so too had Mr Brown. Bottles of champagne were being opened and passed round the table.

"Did you win anything?" Roger called.

"I never have much luck when I make wagers, Roger."

"Then come, drink to my health. And you, Beth, enjoy the moment with me."

It was fast becoming a light-hearted gathering. Marius noticed even Fielding was shedding his air of indifference. He asked Beth which horse she favoured in the next race. When she mentioned that she was not aware of the runners, he recited the names of six horses. One she chose almost immediately.

"What prompted you to pick Marshal's Field?"

"I have an uncle who was a marshal in the army, and he owns a farm," she said promptly.

"I cannot fault your logic, so I'll follow your lead. I'll put a wager on for both of us. As you have picked the horse, I'll place the money."

"You cannot keep paying for me, Marius. I'll be in trouble if Uncle finds out."

"Surely, not for such a trifling sum. Come on! I'll place the wagers, and we can go where we stood previously. It's a good viewpoint," he said cheerfully.

For a moment she looked distracted. Then with resolve she said, "Wait for me whilst I speak to my aunt again. I should tell her if I am not going to be in her company."

On Beth's return, they made their way to the bettors' round. Marius placed their wagers with the same two men, and returning, passed one of the tickets to her.

"This is the last time I can accept your generosity," she said in a serious voice

"You can pay when you win," he replied, amused at her expression.

The second race commenced with the same tumultuous send-off. The runners disappeared into the distance; but, this time, Marius was more interested in Beth than in the horses.

He could see her teeth gnawing on her lower lip, silently urging on the horse she had selected. When the pack was running along the bottom straight, she was openly mouthing the name of her chosen runner. At the same time, she moved from one foot to the other, as in a slow ritual. Then, as the pack climbed the rise and erupted from the bend, all Beth's actions were concentrated on calling the horse's name. Not that anyone could hear. Everyone was doing the same.

Unfortunately, for all her fierce support, the horse passed the post in fourth place. From elation to dejection in seconds. It had been well placed as it passed them, standing on the knoll. Marius did not say anything for a few minutes. Then she turned to him, slightly pink from her outburst.

"I have done it again, picked another that has lost us money."

"You are surely not downcast at not winning?"

"No, I'm just sorry I have spent your money in vain."

Marius laughed, and picked up Beth's parasol she had dropped in her excitement.

"What if I pick the next horse for us?" he said.

"And I shall pay," she cried.

"I don't think so, not until you win," said Marius laughingly.

So the pattern unfolded. They returned to the table, having first noted the runners and colours for the third race. Shortly, thereafter, having spoken to her aunt and uncle, assuring him of the suitability of Marius as a companion, two wagers were placed on "The Outsider'. A fine chestnut mare, running in blue and gold, and offered at twelve to one.

Beth's excitement, if anything, was even more pronounced. She was cheering their horse whilst it was still on the long top straight, and jumping up and down in anticipation when the horses swept round the final bend. Her efforts were rewarded. She willed home "The Outsider" by two lengths, virtually collapsing into Marius' arms when it finally passed the winning post.

"We've done it!" she cried. "We've done it!"

She smiled up at him in genuine joy. Marius could not help grinning back at her. More at the pleasure of seeing her so animated than in winning the wager. Returning to their table, she held on to their winnings with great glee. On arrival, she loudly proclaimed they had won a huge sum, and this time the celebrations were for their good fortune. Marius stood at her side, openly amused at Beth's obvious delight.

In their absence, the numbers around the tables and standing in front of the marquee had swelled. Glasses were filled, and Beth was toasted roundly for having wagered on the winning horse. Conyers was standing close by the group with several companions. When the glasses were lowered, he beckoned Beth and Marius to his side.

"Beth, my dear, let me present you and Dr Hope to some friends of mine. Sir William Thomas, this is my niece, Elizabeth, and her companion, Marius Hope, a doctor of physick."

Beth curtsied and Marius and Sir William bowed in greeting. The couple were then presented to Lord Alexander and Sir Jeffrey Sutton. The latter recalled that he and Marius had met before. After a few moments conversation, Conyers excused Beth, Marius and himself.

Leading them away, he commented that they should properly make the acquaintance of his other guests who had arrived. There followed a bewildering bout of introductions to many notable names. Marius had the impression that a large slice of the aristocracy had abandoned London and were bent on enjoying Conyers' hospitality.

"I have never encountered such an abundance of the nobility in one spot," he murmured to Beth. "It's like standing in the lobby of the House of Lords."

"If you look round you'll see the Principal Minister, Sir Robert Walpole, heading this way," whispered Beth. "When he arrives, let's slip off and see the fourth race."

"Are you sure we can leave your uncle's party?" asked Marius hesitantly.

"They will all have eyes for Walpole, I doubt they'll miss us."

Marius was not so sure. He did not wish to abuse his host's generosity. But she was already pulling his arm when Walpole stopped to talk with Conyers. A large crowd gathered, and they retreated, slipping away by the side of the marquee.

There was no time to note the runners and their colours in the race. The horses were lining up at the start. It was too late even to place a wager. They reached their viewing point as the starter dropped his flag. Once more, the runners set off down the course to a hearty bellow from the crowd.

Although Beth had not wagered on a horse, her enthusiasm again took hold. She was already stamping her tiny feet in anticipation of the moment they would sweep past her on the way to the winning post.

They rounded the second bend, and hurtled along the bottom straight. In the distance all that could be seen was an ever-changing kaleidoscope of jockeys' colours as the horses jostled for the lead. The runners were in a tight-knit pack as they turned up the hill, but slowly, one of them began to pull away. It was a grey. Its strongly-built haunches giving it strength to cover the rising ground. Riding furiously for home, the jockey, in a bright red and yellow hooped jersey, was now clearly visible as he led the others at full gallop up the half-mile stretch towards the turn.

It seemed to Marius that the gap between the grey and the rest of the field was widening. This is going to be a wonderful sight as the leader and the chasing pack round the bend, he thought, holding his breath at the prospect.

Beth was ecstatic, clapping her hands in readiness of the horses erupting from the final corner. The ground was now reverberating from the hooves of twelve horses as they thundered up the incline and disappeared behind the trees on the apex of the turn.

Marius and Beth, with others around them, were caught up in the drama of the race. Everyone was shouting fierce encouragement. Beth gripped his arm in the excitement. Would the grey still be in the lead? Had the other horses made their run for home, and were they now neck-and-neck with the leader?

The noise was deafening. No one heard the sound of the collision. The grey appeared –but not running – toppling with sickening force towards the side of the track. Spinning and rolling, its legs and neck at increasingly acute angles to its body.

Caught up in its flight were two human shapes. No structure or form to their flailing limbs. As their momentum slowed they fell to the track, only to be lifted, kicked unmercifully, and discarded by the pack which emerged at unstoppable speed. Then they were gone, heading down the course.

The sudden horror silenced those close to the scene. The sickening drama of the incident made all the more terrible by the distant cheering of the unsighted spectators nearer the finishing post. Marius was rooted to the spot. For a fraction of time no one moved. The moment seemed an eternity. Then the small crowd surged forward. Marius looked at Beth, whose face portrayed the shock of the tragedy.

"My God … My God," she repeated.

Too stunned to move, Marius turned her slowly from the sight and held her in his arms. Then he said. " Beth, I must go to them. To see what I can do."

She turned her face up to his, her eyes filling with tears, as the terrible event was replayed in her mind. "Of course," she gasped. "Give me a moment and I'll be with you."

Calling out that he was a doctor, Marius pushed his way through the throng of people standing round the lifeless horse. Thankfully, it had not survived the appalling accident. Two bodies were close by. The jockey was lying awkwardly on one side. He had died on impact. The other body was face downwards, crushed by the following horses. Blood was pooling onto the track. As Marius turned him gently, a voice gasped over his shoulder …

"It's William Bennett!"

News of the incident spread quickly, but failed to dampen people's spirits. However, many close to the appalling accident were deeply saddened by what they had seen. Beth was still sitting on the grass when Marius returned.

"I had better get you back to the marquee."

He spoke softly, helping her to her feet. Beth clung to his arm saying little as they walked slowly towards the party. The short distance gave Marius time to reflect on what had occurred. He had pronounced the two bodies beyond help, and the race officials had acted quickly, removing them and the horse from the track.

Beth's aunt came rushing towards her, her face portraying anxiety. Two other women detached themselves from a group and clustered around Beth, before they all moved into the confines of the marquee. Marcus was momentarily at a loss.

"You look as though you need a stiff drink," declared Conyers, pushing a brandy into his hand. "What exactly happened up there?"

Marius briefly recounted what had occurred, apologising for having exposed Beth to the horrors of the accident.

"Life is full of incidents. You cannot always protect people from pain or suffering, as much as we would wish," murmured Conyers. "Don't blame yourself."

As Marius put his glass on a table, he saw the constable approaching with a determined stride and a fixed set to his face.

"I have a feeling the constable is about to vent his displeasure on me," he murmured to Conyers.

"Mr Conyers … Dr Hope," said the constable heavily.

Marius stood there, fully expecting him to state he should present himself before the magistrate at the earliest moment.

"Dr Hope, could I have a private word with you, sir?"

He excused himself from Conyers, and they drew to one side.

"I was told you attended the bodies. Can you tell me what you believe happened?"

"All I know, Constable, is that I saw the grey leading into the final bend. Then two people and the horse were catapulted into the air. All three died. I was close, but there was nothing I could do for any of them."

"I see. You were not aware what caused the accident?"

"I was not close enough to the corner, Mr Russell. I doubt that anyone saw what actually happened. Miss Conyers and I were some distance from the bend. We had found a high spot that allowed us a good view of the course."

The constable nodded, and thanking him prepared to leave. Then he hesitated, and turned back.

"I must admit I am confused about the details of this affair."

He stared intently at the doctor, then remarked. "We have had our differences, Dr Hope. But, if you are inclined, would you come with me? I would very much welcome your advice."

Marius was surprised. Recognising the offer of the olive branch, he readily agreed to accompany the law officer.

The horses were being called in as they walked back up the course and crossed to the inside of the track. Whilst the roar of the crowd signalled the start of the next race, Marius and the constable entered the trees that fringed the turn. Their pace slowed as the constable bent forward peering at the ground.

"Are we looking for something specific?"

"I'm not sure, Doctor. According to the jockeys, William Bennett pitched out of the trees from this side of the course."

After twenty minutes of checking the area bordering the track, Marius stood up and leaned against a tree. Looking idly around, his eyes rested on the gnarled, exposed roots by his feet. The bark had been abraided in several places, and white root tissue was showing through. Kneeling, he noticed the faint imprints of boot heels in the soft earth. From their position, the wearer had had his back to the racetrack.

"Mr Russell, you should see this," he said, pointing to the outlines of the footprints. "If you look closely, the backs of the heels are deeper than the front, suggesting that if these are Mr Bennett's prints, he toppled backwards. It might possibly account for the accident."

The constable knelt beside Marius, studying the impressions.

"You could well be right. But why would he be standing here in the first place?"

Marius considered the question.

"Tell me, what have you done with the bodies?"

"They have been moved to a tent at the back of the course. After the meeting they will be officially identified, then buried."

"Could you arrange for Mr Bennett to be taken to the mortuary?"

"For what reason, Doctor?"

"I would like to examine the body more carefully."

"Dr Hope, I trust we are not about to repeat a previous, unhappy episode."

He ignored the remark.

"Moreover, I would like you or one of your deputies to be present."

The constable forgot his concerns about Johnson and began to dissemble. "I don't think you will need my presence, Doctor. After all, you know what you're looking for. I certainly do not. I could get in the way."

"Mr Russell, the reason I think someone in authority should be present is to confirm any findings I might come across. It may have been suicide, but if he took his own life, why stand with his back to the oncoming horses? Hardly the best way to judge when to jump.

"There again, if he were merely a spectator, why would a man ignore the race and look the other way? Unless, something was suddenly more important. What would command his undivided attention other than a threat to his life? In my opinion, Mr Russell, an examination could well throw light on the real cause of his death."

Marius returned to the Conyers' party to find that the last race had been run and guests were making their farewells. During a brief moment when Conyers was free, Marius asked after Beth.

"My wife has taken her back to Rusthall, Dr Hope. She professed to be quite well, but I felt it better she recover in her room for the rest of the day."

"Yes, of course," said Marius, disappointed that he had missed the chance to speak with Beth before her departure.

Roger joined him, thanking Conyers for his hospitality. As they walked back across Bishops Down, Marius explained what had transpired when the constable arrived.

"I saw him bearing down on the party, and by the look on his face thought he had come to arrest you."

"So did I," exclaimed Marius. "In truth, he was seeking my help. Anyway, I've requested that he takes Bennett's body to the mortuary."

"For what reason? Surely, you don't suspect more foul play?"

"An examination may show nothing. On the other hand it might confirm that Bennett was deliberately pushed in front of the horse. Apart from the obvious injuries, the body may reveal why he was standing with his back to the course."

Roger took time to digest Marius' remarks. Then he surprised him by saying, "By the way, Conyers has called another meeting at the Manor. It's next Tuesday, and Lord Abergavenny is attending. Why don't you come? It will be an opportunity to enquire after Beth Conyers."

CHAPTER TWENTY THREE

The gentleman was staring out a window overlooking the lawns, his hands clasped behind his back. Without looking round at his visitor, he remarked. "It seems, Mr Jordan, your efforts are paying dividends. How many stallholders are now selling our merchandise?"

Nathaniel Jordan was seated in a deep, comfortable chair.

"Twelve sir, at the moment, and there'll be more soon. I have also managed to acquire a store in Waterdowne Forest, south-east of the town. I believe it was once called the Ivy Lodge. It was pulled down, and the stone used to build a small barn. It could be very useful, more so as few know about it."

"Have you now? Yes, that could be decidedly useful," replied the gentleman thoughtfully.

He returned to his seat.

"However, for the moment, Mr Jordan, I would suggest you temper your approaches to the stallholders. You cannot persist for too long without calling suspicion upon yourself, and possibly me. I would suggest two fires and a freeholder trampled to death are more than sufficient inducements. Mention of these should bring the most obstinate round to our way of thinking. What have you achieved in the other matter, the purchase of the titles."

"That's a lot more difficult, sir. I'll get the stallholders to sell our goods, make no mistake, but despite dire threats to themselves and their families, the freeholders are defiant about parting with their title deeds."

"Yes, I was aware they might not bend easily. There's a profit selling contraband, but many of them could be denying themselves handsome returns when the dispute over ownership of the Walks is finally resolved. I've already passed on the message. I've a feeling they have already taken steps to secure the titles as well.

"So, for the moment, let us concentrate on obtaining the cooperation of the stallholders in the sale of the merchandise. We need as many as we can get."

"I will get them for you, sir, make no mistake."

"Let me make it abundantly clear. It is imperative, Jordan."

The gentleman leaned forward, looking at him searchingly.

"I need to know how you progress. Come back at this hour in three days' time, and tell me all that you have achieved."

CHAPTER TWENTY FOUR

Marius was at breakfast when advised Mr Russell, the constable, wanted to see him.

Meeting him in the hall. Marius led the way through to the orangery. They sat in silence whilst coffee was poured. When the maid closed the ornate glazed door, the constable began.

"Mr Bennett has been removed to the mortuary, as you requested, Dr Hope. Though, I doubt an examination will reveal much. The horses did fearful damage. But, then, I am not a medical man, you may find the answers that elude me."

"I've been giving more thought to what might have happened, Mr Russell. Just prior to being hit, Mr Bennett had his back to the track. A fraction of a second too early, and the horse would have trampled him. Too late, and he would have been knocked back into the trees. The timing had to be precise. I would say, looking over his shoulder to judge the moment would have been much too difficult, don't you think?"

The constable nodded.

Marius chose his words carefully. "So, for the moment, let us conjecture that Bennett was held against his will. Perhaps, by a knife, a sword, even a pistol. His assailant waited for that exact moment. Whether Bennett was thrown back by the strength of the attack, or involuntarily shied away to avoid being killed, I can't say. Hopefully, his corpse will tell me."

"There is another possibility."

Marius looked up sharply.

"I can accept Bennett was standing facing in towards the trees. I took his boots and matched them to the footprints. However, they were the only ones. What I couldn't find were the marks of your assassin. It's a plausible notion, but I could just as easily suggest that Bennett was there a few days ago, and made the marks when it rained. Or, that he climbed a tree to get a better view, and fell into the path of the oncoming horses. All we have Dr Hope, are elaborate theories, not facts."

"Well, with your permission, I shall try to eliminate some of those theories when I examine the remains," said Marius defensively.

109

"There again, there is another possibility. Supposing he had been dead for some time, hidden in the undergrowth, then thrown onto the track during the race?"

"Unfortunately, there's no way of telling how long Bennett has been dead."

"What I am trying to say, Dr Hope, is that you keep an open mind. If you have any preconceived notions about Bennett's death, we might face the situation we had with Mr Johnson. The magistrate knows of the affair, and he will be calling you to attend upon him shortly. Let me speak plainly, Doctor. I do not want a repeat of that episode. I may appear over-cautious, but I cannot allow you to draw the wrong conclusions. I could be seen party to your misguided enthusiasm."

"Sir, having an open mind fetches upon you as well," said Marius indignantly. "Do you really believe that Johnson is the paragon of virtue he claims? How he can state that the body is that of Miss Roper is beyond me. What is more, I am convinced Mrs Johnson, and the other person, were both dead before the fire started."

"That has yet to be proven, sir," declared the constable stiffly.

"No, Mr Russell, it has to be confirmed by a more detailed examination, and permission is being withheld."

"Well, without Johnson's agreement, there is little chance of taking it further, unless I have clear reason to suspect a criminal act, and he has thwarted that by going to the magistrate. He learned you attended the identification without authority, assuming powers you do not possess. This has caused the magistrate to take against you, and accept Johnson's word in the matter."

"Are you saying, Mr Russell, that the fire which accounted for the deaths of two people, is no longer being pursued?"

"No, sir, I am not. I must tell you that after his initial anger at what he termed, your needless intervention, the magistrate and I discussed the fires on Mount Sion and in Frant Lane. Our opinion is that both could easily have been misadventure. On Mount Sion there was an open hearth. A spark, a charred end of wood flares, tumbles to the floor. Those wooden houses quickly ignite."

The constable paused briefly to drink from his cup.

"As you know, Doctor, the Loveday home was used for candle-making. Hot oils and open flames are a highly combustible mixture. It wouldn't be the first time Adam Loveday has had a fire. It has happened in the past. Moreover, if it were deliberate arson in both cases, we could not blame Mr Johnson. On the day the Loveday house burnt down he was elsewhere."

"What do you mean, elsewhere?"

"Witnesses state he was in a tavern in Southborough. One of my deputies rode over to see the landlord. He confirmed Johnson was served dinner on the day in question."

For the moment Marius was nonplussed. He had recognised, unconsciously, that a link might exist between the two incidents. Beyond seeing Johnson as the culprit for the first, he had not seriously considered him responsible for the second.

"Well, if he did not set fire to the house in Mount Sion, I still think he deliberately mis-identified one of the bodies. To me, that is highly suspicious," declared Marius forthrightly.

"It seems that we continue to talk in circles, Doctor. Let me put another thought to you. You know well the effect of heat on the body can lead to contraction of the limbs. The tendons shorten, muscles shrivel. This could easily give the appearance of shortening a body. Don't you think this could account for the difference in height? Mrs Johnson was not near the heart of the fire, she would not have been so affected."

"I took that possibility into account. In this instance the heat was intense, but not sufficiently prolonged to cause physical distortion."

He sat there in silence for a few moments, whilst the constable lighted his pipe. Then he expressed his thoughts aloud.

"I calculate that Mrs Johnson was about five feet in height. When I met her, in the Walks and at the ball, Miss Roper appeared to be at least four or five inches taller. On both occasions she was wearing shoes that gave her an extra two inches or more. So, at the very least, she was three inches taller than her aunt. But, side-by-side in the mortuary, the height difference was negligible. It just does not accord with my memory of the young woman."

"What we have, sir, are incidents where foul play may have been committed. Yet, we have no proof any was intentional. In the matter of the Johnson family, you have suspicions, but no facts. The same applies to the Lovedays. Equally, Bennett's death could also have been an accident. Although, I admit, like yourself, I am inclined to think the worst, to regard it as a murderous act."

Though surprised by the admission, Marius said nothing.

"Frankly, Doctor, I share your view that all three events were intentional. However, as constable of this parish, I have to challenge everything until proof is absolute. I have been the devil's advocate more to get your considered responses. In my opinion we have people abroad responsible for nine deaths."

Marius scrutinised the constable's face.

"So, what is the next step?"

"We have to work with what we have. At the moment that consists of one unclaimed body … Bennett's. Even if we discover that he was attacked before falling in front of the horses, it will not reveal who did the deed, or lead us further in our investigations."

Marius did not immediately respond. He reached into a coat pocket for his pipe. When it was drawing to his satisfaction, he remarked:

"I should tell you of one or two events that may have bearing on the matter, Mr Russell. Firstly, I am sure that Nathaniel Jordan, the farrier, is involved in some way. He has had meetings with men whom I am told are freeholders. From what I gather, they have not been harmonious. Then, suddenly, two of their number are dead."

He continued, "Several days ago, I asked Roger Dashwood to keep a close eye on Augustus Brown, who purports to be a comestibles trader. He appears to be most interested in properties in the Lower Walk. Dashwood told me, at one point, he went to the ruins of the Loveday home, where he met the estate manager for Lord Abergavenny. All of which seems highly questionable."

"Well, Doctor, it seems you have achieved more than I," said the constable. "We should keep a close eye on both these gentlemen."

"I was wondering, is there someone in charge of the mortuary all the time? Although it's Sunday, the quicker I conduct an examination of Mr Bennett, the better."

"I presume the constable was not paying his respects," Roger said. "I saw you were in earnest conversation, and thought it best not to interrupt. What was it about?"

"Not as dire as you might imagine," remarked Marius smiling. "We cleared the air. I would go as far as to say we are on quite good terms."

Roger looked at him quizzically. "I understand that he has reported you to the magistrate."

"He had no choice. Johnson made a complaint against me."

He told him the gist of the conversation with Russell, explaining the constable had to take a dispassionate view. Nevertheless, he had admitted holding similar opinions to Marius. However, before he could exercise his office, firm evidence of wrongdoing was necessary.

"And that's as far as we got," summarised Marius.

Roger nodded, then said quietly, "Are you saying, when you refer to us, you are also involved?"

"Well, on the first occasion I involved myself. This time, in the case of the Lovedays and Mr Bennett, the constable is seeking my help"

"Marius for your sake, exercise a little more caution. The magistrate still has to deal with Johnson's complaint. The consequences could be unpleasant if you cause further upset."

"I've got strict instructions. On no account are you to go near the other bodies," said the deputy, showing Marius into the inner room of the mortuary.

"Do not concern yourself, Deputy, I've no intention of doing so. My sole aim is to examine the remains of Mr Bennett."

"E's a proper mess, and no mistake. I've cleaned "im up best I could. But I warn you, e's not a pretty sight."

The deputy lifted the sheet from the cadaver, and for a moment Marius was transported back to his student days. Shrugging off feelings of disquiet, he gazed upon the broken body. The leading horse had caused the most damage. The subsequent passage of the rest of the field had brutalised it further. There were extensive injuries to the head, left shoulder, chest and abdomen, which must have taken the full impact of the gallop to the finishing line.

"Yer looks a little pale, Doctor. Would yer like a glass of something? Brandy "praps?" enquired the deputy.

Marius readily accepted the brandy. The fieriness of the spirit momentarily catching in his throat.

"You're right, Deputy, he would be unrecognisable even to his own family."

Marius devoted his first attentions to the stomach. However, the damage masked any signs of attack by a sharp blade, and there was no evidence of a pistol shot. He continued his examination moving slowly up the body. The chest and shoulders were not so badly lacerated, but these too yielded no sign of attack.

"Deputy, would you help me turn the body?"

It took the combined efforts of both men to turn the corpse on its face. When it was fully stretched out, Marius said, "I don't believe I shall discover anything, but I cannot ignore any possibility."

He spent half an hour going over the back and haunches of the late Mr Bennett. He found nothing concealed by the widespread abrasions. Once more, he called upon the deputy, and they turned the body back to its original position. The head overhanging the short table.

Leaning over to inspect the shoulders, something made him hesitate. The deputy, who had remained by his side, peered over his shoulder, following every move.

"Found summ'ing?"

"I don't think so. Most of the cuts and bruises here were caused by the sharp edges of the hooves, not the work of an assailant."

He studied the neck, turning the head slowly. As he did so, he saw a thin line of blood hidden beneath the short beard Bennett had favoured. It was several inches back from the chin. In normal circumstances, the wound would have gone unnoticed.

"Deputy, help me pull the body further up, until the head and neck hang fully over the edge."

They eased the corpse along the table. As the neck stretched downwards, so the beard parted to reveal the injury more clearly.

"Could you get me a bowl of water, and some cloth, Mr Jeffries?"

Slowly he cleaned the neck, then peered intently at the wound.

"The knife you have on the table in the ante-room, could you fetch it? And bring a lighted candle."

The deputy went out, to return with candle and knife.

"Yer not gonna" to do anything to the body, are you Doctor?" the deputy asked anxiously.

"Not at all."

He prised open Bennett's mouth, and directed the light into the cavity. He inspected the soft palate and throat, then inserted his fingers. He found where the tissue had been severed. Determining the angle of entry, he proceeded to lay the knife against the side of Bennett's head.

"I believe this is the manner in which he died. It looks very much like he was killed with an upward thrust of a weapon such as this. I can see the entry channel. It was a blade of similar width," said Marius, still turning the head from side to side, assessing the fissure.

"However, it was much longer. I would surmise that it penetrated the victim's brain, killing him instantly. The soft tissue would have yielded easily to the weapon, and the impetus of the blow would have thrown the body backwards."

Marius stood up, returning the knife to the deputy.

"If you give me a pen and paper, I shall formally record the cause of death. I want you to witness the document, Mr Jeffries. To attest to its veracity."

"Right yer are, Doctor. But I won't use this knife when I 'ave my lunch again without thinking of it as a likely murder weapon," said the man gloomily.

CHAPTER TWENTY FIVE

"I'm not sure I should be riding with you, Roger. It might be thought discourteous to arrive uninvited."

The closer they were to Rusthall Manor, the more uneasy Marius became. During a moderately successful time at the gambling tables the previous evening, Marius had agreed to accompany Roger Dashwood. Even at dinner, he had decided that calling on Beth Conyers, to enquire after her health would be an excellent idea. Now, as they neared Rusthall, the wisdom of journeying to see her was in question.

"What if they decline to let me enter? Dismiss me for being too bold for presenting myself on their doorstep?" Marius fretted.

"Calm yourself," Roger grinned at him, amused by his friend's uncertainty. "You are getting into a fine old state. Nothing like that will happen."

Marius was not easily mollified. As they rode up the drive, all his earlier ebullience had disappeared. At the Manor, a footman took the reins of the horses. The main door opened and Conyers himself appeared. Dashwood moved towards him, momentarily leaving Marius standing alone, and all the more uncomfortable. Thankfully, it was shortlived.

"Dr Hope, how nice to see you again," welcomed Conyers. "I presume you have come to enquire after Beth's wellbeing? At the moment she is in the garden. I'll call someone to take you to her."

He turned briefly into the interior of the house.

"Lucy will accompany you, Doctor. Forgive me, but there is a gathering in the library I must attend. Perhaps, we can meet afterwards? I'll mention your arrival to Mrs Conyers. I know she will be pleased that you have called upon us. No doubt, she will wish to join you."

With that he turned on his heel, Roger a pace behind.

"This way, sir," said the maid, leading him from the gravelled forecourt, through an iron gate, and across a wide expanse of grass towards a large canopied cedar. Rounding the tree, Beth was seated on a bench, her head lowered, intent on reading a book.

"There's a Dr Hope to see you, Miss," said Lucy, with a fleeting curtsey. Beth looked up. At the sight of him her pleasure was immediate.

"Marius! What are you doing here?" Beth exclaimed. She stood, walked quickly towards him, taking one of his hands in both of hers. They stared at each other. Suddenly, she realised that the maid was still lingering. "Thank you, Lucy."

Turning back, she asked, "Have you come to my uncle's meeting? Or is this a medical visit to assess my recovery?"

"Professional and social. I wanted to see how you were."

"I'm fine. A little bored, actually. I soon recovered after the initial shock, but my aunt insisted I rest in a darkened room."

She leaned forward conspiratorially. "I'm virtually a prisoner here at the Manor. Have you come to free me? The trouble is she and uncle are concerned for me, so I can't flout their well-meaning hospitality. Anyway, come and sit by me. Before we have company, tell me what happened after I returned to uncle's party."

Marius was taken by her obvious delight in seeing him. The warmth of the greeting was almost unsettling. Not that he didn't enjoy it. Far from it. Expecting the normal feminine reserve, at first he found difficulty in responding in like manner. Beth noted his reticence.

"Don't worry," she chided amusedly. "We shall soon have a chaperone."

"What a pity. I'll have to be more mindful of what I say."

"What would you have said, Dr Hope? If we were alone?"

Before he could reply, Mrs Conyers appeared at the gate in the wall, and came breathlessly across the lawn.

"Doctor, do forgive me. I was with cook when my husband informed me of your visit. I'm sure you need some refreshment. A cordial, coffee, some tea perhaps?"

"Tea would be most welcome, Mrs Conyers," said Marius, rising to his feet.

She gestured to Lucy, who had been lingering at a discreet distance.

"I trust you do not mind my calling to ask after Miss Conyers. I came with Mr Dashwood, who is attending a meeting with your husband."

"It was most considerate of you, Dr Hope. Beth has not felt like leaving the house since the unfortunate incident. I was beginning to think she was a recluse. I've been most worried for her."

Beth, seated the other side of her aunt, pulled a face at the remark, much to Marius' amusement. At that moment, the maid appeared carrying a tray, with Roger Dashwood at her side.

Several paces away, he called, "Listen, my dear fellow, Mr Conyers wants you to join us in the library. It seems there are thirteen of us, which is thought unlucky. He wants you to even up the number."

"What nonsense!" cried Beth, "Surely, he is not that superstitious. Aunt, do something. Dr Hope came to see me."

Roger was taken aback by Beth's outburst. He said hesitantly, "He really is most insistent. Actually, he wants to talk to him about recent events. I was jesting about the numbers," he added lamely.

Beth was not easily calmed. It took her aunt's soothing intervention before Marius was drawn away to the meeting in the library.

"Welcome, Dr Hope," said Conyers cordially, as he was shown to an empty chair towards the middle of the long table. "I should explain the purpose of this gathering. These gentlemen here are much concerned about the amount of contraband that seems to be finding its way into The Wells. We are informed it is hampering legitimate business, and causing unrest among the town's traders."

He looked round the table. "It appears some are selling the goods to the company. Others, who do not want to use their shops or stalls as outlets, for fear of legal reprisal, are suffering unfairly. We need to take action, but it is damnably difficult to find out how it is arriving, who is responsible for bringing it into the town."

"But stop it we must, sir," said a heavily-built man at the far end of the table.

"Quite so, Mr Phillips. We'll come to that in a moment. I was explaining to the doctor, the reason why we are here," said Conyers, with a hint of exasperation. "We have already discussed the effect contraband is having on the community. The problems it is causing, and now, according to Mr Dashwood, perhaps the deaths resulting from it.

"In that regard, I've also been made aware of your involvement," continued Conyers, with a wry smile. "Willing, or otherwise. Thus, it was felt, as you were at the Manor, we should hear your views on the matter."

He surveyed those around the table. "Rather than introduce you all to Dr Hope, when you speak, be kind enough to mention your name."

Conyers turned to Marius.

"Whether the three recent incidents in which you have become involved have a bearing on our smuggling problem, is hard to say. However, as a medical man, your comments may shed light on something we may have missed."

Conyers looked round again at the people assembled in the room.

"As I explained to the gentlemen present, Dr Hope, it is our good fortune that Sir Robert Walpole is also with us today. He has been enquiring about local affairs, so I asked him to join the meeting. I thought it would be useful if he were apprised, first hand, of the issues causing concern. We may well reap the benefits of the Principal Minister's advice. So, gentlemen, let us move on."

Marius had noticed him sitting next to Conyers. As he had the constable sitting beside the individual Conyers had referred to as "Mr Phillips". A discreet glance towards the end of the table was more revealing. He had a florid, full complexion topped by a well-powdered wig. His eyes were small, obscured slightly by a pair of Mr Scarlett's temple spectacles. His air of mild disdain as the constable whispered something to him was apparent to all. However, it was to him that Conyers turned to open the account.

"You may recall that on the last occasion, our Magistrate, Mr Phillips, was prepared to initiate certain steps to identify and apprehend the main culprits. Perhaps, Mr Phillips, you would tell us of your endeavours?"

The magistrate looked around the table. "As you have identified me to the doctor, Mr Conyers, I shall not repeat my name. With regard to the surveillance we have been conducting, I shall ask my assistant, Mr Fines, to report."

The assistant to the magistrate was seated on Phillips' right. As he rose to his feet, Marius sensed he was about to convey failure. It was in the demeanour of the man. He laid his hands on the table, and looked down as he spoke. Of nondescript age, and undernourished, he blinked with each word he uttered.

"I'm afraid," he began uncertainly, "I'm afraid that we have not been able, as yet, to obtain any positive sightings. We have employed a number of people, including Mr Dashwood here, as observers. So far we have been singularly unfortunate in identifying anyone bringing smuggled goods into the town."

The Wells' magistrate interrupted.

"On reflection, perhaps I should have organised the action myself. Clearly, I made a mistake in leaving it all to Fines."

Fines, narrow-faced with watery blue eyes above a receding chin, flushed at the remark. An unwelcome rebuke to make in public, thought Marius.

"I'm sure it's only a matter of time, Mr Conyers," declared Fines, responding to the slight by his employer. "If we keep up our vigil, I'm sure we shall discover who is transporting the goods, and bring an end to the matter."

Conyers nodded to Fines, who sat down in his chair.

"Surely, Mr Phillips," said Conyers thoughtfully, "surely, we can name those selling the contraband?"

"My brief, sir, is not to detain the sellers. It is to catch the miscreants bringing it into The Wells," said the magistrate pompously.

Conyers' voice took on a harder edge. "Tell me, sir, Mr Fines said nothing positive has come of your surveillance of the likely routes into The Wells. Have your people achieved anything during these night-time vigils? Presumably, the goods are coming in at night?" He directed the last remark to the constable.

Mr Russell did not reply. He clearly expected Phillips to answer. When the magistrate lowered his gaze to the papers before him, the constable said, "Dr Hope also knows my name. The men working during the night hours report directly to Mr Phillips, sir. I have nothing to comment on their efforts."

"Are they not members of your constabulary?" enquired Conyers.

"Whilst it was agreed at the last meeting that a night force was needed, Mr Conyers, Mr Phillips later considered that it was beyond my remit. In fact, he took it upon himself to organise the extra men, and finance their employment from his own purse, without burdening the township."

"That's exceedingly generous of you, Mr Phillips," said Conyers grudgingly. His doubts regarding the night-time patrols clearly at odds with the fact that the magistrate was paying for them from his own pocket.

The magistrate accepted the praise, looking sideways at the Principal Minister. "One does what one can, Mr Conyers."

The Principal Minister turned to the Lord of The Manor, and in a loud aside. "Tell me, Conyers, why don't we call upon the militia to lie in wait?"

Mr Fielding, the Southern Controller, was sitting further down the table, facing the long shelves of books arrayed either side of a stone fireplace. He looked up at the remark.

"Robert Fielding, the official representative of Customs House in London. I have to advise, sir, that enforcement of the Excise laws is based principally on catching the smugglers red-handed, at point of entry. We can't afford to have an army loitering in the lanes and undergrowth in the hope of catching the odd parcel of goods. I'm sure I have no need to tell Sir Robert that the Excise Commission does not have the funds to perform all of its tasks. He is well acquainted with the amount allocated by The Treasury. Frankly, whilst I applaud the public-spirited action of the magistrate, I doubt he is spending his money wisely."

"What are you insinuating, sir," declared Phillips, bristling at Fielding's remarks.

"What I mean, sir, are you using the right people? Do they know the district, the terrain, the buildings? Are you paying handsomely for observers who are prepared to take your money without performing their allotted tasks?"

"I find your comment offensive, sir," exclaimed Phillips, his face reddening in anger. "Do me the honour of withdrawing it. Otherwise I shall be unable to sit at this table."

"They are neither intended as a slight, nor as a slur on your good name," said Fielding, unperturbed by Phillips' outburst. "If they have offended you, naturally, I withdraw them. Please accept my apologies."

The Lord of The Manor quickly remarked, "Following a discussion we had the other day, Mr Fielding, you were hoping to seek official approval for a small detachment of Enforcement Officers to be deployed in the town. Have you heard the outcome of that request?"

"Not as yet, Mr Conyers," declared Fielding. "A letter was despatched. I still await a reply. The trouble is, as I explained earlier, Customs House receives many such demands. I am not entirely hopeful they will accede to the request."

"If the problem is as bad as you state, Conyers," said Walpole, "I am sure we can bring some urgency to the matter. I shall be returning to London shortly. Perhaps, a word with the Commissioner of The Board of Excise might produce results."

The Principal Minister's remark was made with the finesse Fielding might have done well to heed.

The discussion dragged on. Marius came to the realisation that they were sitting there in the library not to determine what action should be taken, but, more to parade themselves in front of the Principal Minister. He was musing on the subtle use of Walpole's stay in The Wells by Conyers, when he heard his name spoken.

". . . Dr Hope whether, in his view, they might have a bearing."

Marius looked uncertainly around the table.

"I know that Dr Hope has clear opinions on these recent events," Roger Dashwood quickly interjected. "And, as yet, he accepts that there is little evidence to support some of these notions. Equally, he understands the magistrate's point of view. Nothing can be done without the firmest of proof. Nevertheless, his interpretation of the events in Mount Sion, in Frant Lane and on the racecourse should be heard."

Marius leaned forward and scanned the faces of those sitting round the table.

"Whether or not, gentlemen, they are related to the smuggling is difficult for me to judge. I leave that to the constable. However, let me review the incidents in the order they occurred.

"With regard to the fire on Mount Sion," began Marius, "I recognise that Mr Johnson might have gained the impression a medical presence was required when identifying the bodies of his wife and niece. On reflection, this placed the constable, and the magistrate, in a compromising situation. Suffice it to say, I apologise for the misunderstanding."

"But did it reveal anything?" Roger asked pointedly, giving Marius the opportunity to expand on his concerns.

"Yes, and no. You see. . . " Marius got no further.

"Really! Must we suffer a further catalogue of surmises and make-believe?" commented the magistrate acidly.

"Mr Phillips, the good doctor may have come across something which casts light on our smuggling problem," said Conyers smoothly. "I think I speak for the majority when I say his observations would be welcome." He glanced around, and found no dissenters.

"Pray continue, Doctor."

"As I say, I am not sure I have anything directly to offer concerning the increase in contraband," declared Marius. "I can only comment in my capacity as a doctor of physick, and the effect on the bodies of the unfortunate. In this regard, I cannot accept the two events as the work of a single pyromaniac. The fire at the Johnson's house brought about the deaths of two visitors to The Wells. It could well have been accidental, though there are one or two aspects that concern me.

"The other, at the Loveday house, I am convinced was a deliberate, premeditated act. It was intended to obliterate the family, and it succeeded."

There was a murmur around the table, the loudest, in protest, coming from the magistrate. "Nonsense, there's an arsonist loose in the town."

Marius pressed on. "So, whilst I do not think the first incident was associated with the sales of contraband, the outbreak at the Loveday's house could well have a connection."

"I find your supposition preposterous, Dr Hope," cried Phillips. "What possible bearing could the fire at the Loveday house have on the flow of illicit goods into the town?"

"Mr Phillips," said Conyers patiently, "I would urge you to comment after the doctor has laid out the facts as he sees them. Pray continue."

"Before I do so, Mr Conyers, can we accept that this is, as yet, an unsubstantiated opinion. After a recent episode, it would be unwelcome if what I am going to say went beyond these walls."

Glancing at Phillips, Marius could clearly see the snear directed at him.

"We discuss very close matters amongst those present, Doctor. I can vouch that anything said around this table will be treated in the strictest confidence."

Marius was not easily assured.

"With regard to the second fire, I accept the constable's remarks that no freeholder has lodged a complaint against the farrier, Nathaniel Jordan. But on several occasions, I have been present when he has had heated words with freeholders. It may be he wishes to acquire land for his business. It may be the nature of the fellow to become angry and threatening when in negotiation. However, I should tell you that last week I witnessed Mr Jordan in fierce argument with Adam Loveday. It was much more than a disagreement."

Marius paused to raise a glass of water to his lips.

"When I joined the constable at the house on the day following the fire, we carefully examined all that was left of the building. One thing struck me as odd. At variance with what one would normally expect. The heat of the blaze had been intense, yet there was no indication anyone had tried to escape. I eventually came across the bones of six people in the living room. All along one wall. As though they had been trapped or tied together, unable to free themselves."

"I cannot see a link between this event, this fellow Jordan's involvement, and the contraband, Conyers," said Fielding. "How could seemingly innocent people be killed, if that's what the doctor is implying, to advance the sales of smuggled goods? In my view such a supposition is far too tenuous."

Untroubled by Fielding's comment, Marius continued.

"One should consider the facts. They may be circumstantial, but, there are enough to lead to more than just suspicion. Let us review what is known. Gentlemen, you have stated that contraband is coming into the town in disturbing quantities. Mr Dashwood has observed that it is being sold in the Lower Walk by the stallholders, whom I understand are also the freeholders and own most of the stalls. The leader of the freeholders was Adam Loveday.

"All these factors cannot be mere coincidence. As you have stated yourselves, the sale of contraband is a crime, with considerable sums of money involved. When that occurs, greed and even murder are likely partners. Eliminate Loveday, their spokesman, and you reduce the freeholders' resistance to those bent on using them to sell illicit goods."

Marius noticed the constable nodding. Marius' words created a silence in the library which was broken by a knock at the door. On Conyers' command, two maids entered with refreshments. The moment had passed, there was an upsurge of chatter among those seated around the table.

Taking his cup of tea, Marius rose and walked to a window hoping to catch a glimpse of Beth. He was searching the grounds when there was a voice behind him, "Marius, I was intrigued by your comments about the fires."

He turned to see Sir Robert Walpole standing beside him.

The Principal Minister smiled. "How is your father these days? I haven't seen him since the spring, when you all came to my summer house on the river."

"He is quite well, sir. He still goes to business, though he has promised my mother he will retire later this year."

Walpole looked out at the gardens.

"The King wanted me closer to affairs of state, so he bought the house in Downing Street. Other than the occasional visit to the house on the river and my place in Norfolk, I miss views such as this."

He eased back the curtain and said wistfully, "I had a lovely garden in Chelsea."

Walpole remained motionless, staring across the lawns for some minutes, before turning to Marius. "I liked your concise appraisal of the Loveday incident. It strongly suggests a link between his death and the contraband. Tell me a little more about the first fire."

Marius was surprised he should express interest in incidents that were commonplace in London. He marshalled his thoughts.

"In the case of the Johnsons, I came to know Johnson's wife and his niece quite well. When they were lying in the mortuary I was able to identify Mrs Johnson. It was much more difficult with the niece. The fire had ravaged her features, she was unrecognisable. The body was attired in Miss Roper's clothes, but, I recall she was much taller than her aunt. Whereas the body next to Johnson's wife was broadly the same size.

"Moreover, I am almost certain that the two people were dead before the fire began. There were no signs of smoke inhalation around the mouths, nor, from what I could see, in the passages to the lungs."

"Hmm … do you suspect anyone?"

"Sir Robert, all I can say is that Mr Johnson cannot provide a satisfactory explanation."

"But do you suspect him of firing the Loveday house?"

"No. I'm told he was away from The Wells at the time."

"Do you think the person who killed the Lovedays, could have been responsible for the Johnson's house?" asked Walpole, staring intently into Marius's face. "Could it be, Doctor, that this person, or persons, deliberately killed Mrs Johnson and her niece to enforce some act by Mr Johnson?"

"You make a fair point, Sir Robert. However, thinking about how he has acted subsequently would give lie to that theory," replied Marius. "I have watched Mr Johnson most carefully. He gives a very public display of grief, but, in reality, shows little remorse. Equally, he shows no concern for any form of retribution, or fear that he is a potential victim."

"Interesting, Marius. Can you be absolutely sure the two ladies were dead before the fire supposedly took them?"

"I cannot, sir. What I have given is a fairly accurate deduction based on observation. If I were to examine the lungs, I could tell you with greater surety. Unfortunately, Mr Johnson has withheld that permission."

"It would appear you face a conundrum, Doctor," stated Walpole. "On the one hand, Mr Johnson avows that one of the bodies is his niece, and will not allow it to be examined. On the other, you are convinced that it is not Miss Roper. Surely, if it is not his niece, you do not need to seek his authority to examine the corpse?"

"Then, I would require the permission of someone who is her next of kin."

"Not if you believe her death were not misadventure," said Walpole slowly. "I know what I would do in such circumstances. It's a pity the constable is not an ally."

"Actually, I believe he is, sir."

Walpole smiled. "Why do you believe the circumstances are different in the Loveday affair?"

"Because of how it was done. It was a clear attempt to create maximum damage.

There was no escape. Whoever did it was set on obliterating every last member of the family. It was a calculated act, clinical in its execution. Perhaps a warning of what might be done to others."

The Lord of The Manor announced the meeting was about to resume, and they took their seats around the table.

Conyers picked up the thread of the meeting. "Dr Hope, we have heard your comments about the two fires. Do you have anything to add about the death of the freeholder, William Bennett? I know you were present when it occurred."

"I was there, Mr Conyers and witnessed the accident. At least, I thought it was an accident. However, now in possession of the facts, I have come to a quite contrary opinion. The constable removed the body to the mortuary, and I performed a detailed examination this morning."

"I presume, Hope, you had the permission of a member of his family," declared the magistrate.

"There was no need, sir," responded Marius. "It was an external examination, not an autopsy. However, I should tell you, as you are the official for this district, that the death of yet another freeholder was by the hand of someone who waited for the moment, then plunged a large, wide-bladed knife through the throat into the victim's brain. He was dead before the horses trampled him."

"God's teeth," exclaimed a voice.

"To sum up," said Marius in a measured tone, "my personal belief is that all three happenings were deliberate. With smuggling and the rising sale of contraband commanding everyone's attention, you may well find that this has been central to the deaths of at least seven of the nine people involved in these murderous acts."

CHAPTER TWENTY SIX

For much of the journey they rode in silence. Marius sat in the saddle, deep in thought, barely aware of the route they were following. They reached Bishops Down, and turned onto a track leading to the town.

"What did you think of the meeting?" asked Roger.

"I suppose it was worthwhile."

"Of course, it was worthwhile! Old Phillips certainly got a flea in his ear. He is such an arrogant fellow, so full of his own importance. It's good to see him the butt of someone else's remarks for a change. I thought Fielding was absolutely right, the magistrate's private army has been woefully ineffectual. Phillips will be in a foul mood when I see him tomorrow."

Marius was only half listening. After the meeting, whilst the others were making their farewells, he had gone in search of Beth. Sadly, she was nowhere to be seen. Returning to the house he had encountered Mrs Conyers, who mentioned her niece had retired to her room, and was unlikely to reappear before early evening. At that moment a door off the hall had opened, and Conyers had beckoned him.

Entering the room in which the Lord of The Manor conducted his business, Marius was offered a chair. It was then he noticed the Principal Minister seated by the window.

"I thought I would have a private word with you, Doctor," Conyers had said. "I felt that despite some antagonism at the meeting, which might have dissuaded you from making your point, you carried on. I like that sort of attitude. To put it bluntly, Dr Hope, I would like to enlist your help."

"I'm not certain how I could be of service, Mr Conyers. After all, I've only recently arrived in The Wells."

"Let me explain my problem," Conyers declared, glancing in Walpole's direction. "As Lord of The Manor, I have a duty to the Crown to maintain civil rights. To ensure the people of the town are adequately served by the law. The practice of that law is upheld by the magistrate and his constable."

Conyers took up a spill, and lighted his pipe. When it was to his satisfaction, he continued, "As a consequence, the magistrate, other town officials and I meet regularly as a watch committee. Our aim being to preserve the nature and the dignity of the town. I think it is obvious to all, at the moment, that the problem of the contraband is becoming a sizeable threat."

Marius had maintained his silence, not knowing the direction the conversation might take.

"My position is complicated. For the past few years a number of the townsfolk and I have been at odds over the titles to the land in the Walks."

Conyers paused, looking again at Walpole.

"As a consequence, it is difficult when involved in decisions on behalf of the town, to avoid suggestions of prejudice. I could easily be accused of furthering my own ends. So, I have to tread warily, be sure of my facts, confident of my sources."

He had paused, weighing his words. "You saw what happened today. Invariably, someone has a personal motive, which they bring to these meetings. I am sure they are all honourable men, but, at times their contributions can be flawed. So, how can I confidently propose a fair course of action?"

Conyers puffed on his pipe.

"Let me put it to you. I need someone to tell me what is going on in The Wells. Someone who has no connection with the town, who will relay to me the plain, unvarnished truth. Will you be my eyes and ears, Dr Hope?"

Marius had been taken aback. Of all the possible topics he had thought might be raised when invited into Conyers' sanctum, that had been furthest from his mind. He had stared long at Conyers before responding.

"Mr Conyers, my only intention in coming to The Wells was to deal with a personal dilemma. I believed spending time away from the hospital at which I work might allow me to put my thoughts into perspective. Thank you for your apparent trust, but, at the moment, I would prefer to deal simply with my own problems. In any event, I shall be returning to London very shortly."

The Principal Minister, who had not uttered a word during the exchange, coughed slightly, before remarking. "Marius, I rarely interfere in local politics. Nor do I get involved in regional disputes, unless of course, they are likely to impinge on matters of state."

He sat upright and leaned forward, giving emphasis to his words.

"In this instance, I am considering whether to bring the conflict between the Lord of The Manor and the freeholders before the House. It clearly needs resolution."

Conyers remarked dryly. "One of the reasons for Sir Robert's visit is to discuss an early settlement of the dispute with the freeholders. Now that The Wells is a noted spa, it seems Parliament has become mightily interested in the outcome."

Walpole had continued to gaze at Marius. "In the meantime, the increase in smuggled goods is not being tackled with the urgency it demands. Largely, because of the enmity which exists. You witnessed yourself the magistrate's attitude to applying sanctions to those selling the contraband. Without Phillips' intervention, Conyers is powerless to interrogate the very people with whom he is in conflict. I want action taken against the sale of contraband. Whatever Conyers needs to combat these crimes, I want him to have it. Therefore, I shall ask, on his behalf, will you help him in this endeavour?"

Marius was still thinking of his response to the Principal Minister, when he heard Dashwood comment.

"I suppose you are quiet because Beth disappeared before you came from your tête-à-tête with Conyers. What was that all about?"

The question brought Marius back to the present.

"Did you see Beth, Roger?"

"No, but I have something which I would be prepared to trade. You tell me about your meeting. I'll let you know what Mrs Conyers had to say."

"Mrs Conyers?"

"Yes, she is a mine of information."

Because of the delicacy of Conyers' comments, Marius was obliged to hide the nature of the conversation. Particularly, Walpole's part in the discussion. Instead, he recounted Walpole's earlier comments regarding the Johnson family and the autopsy, allowing Roger to think they were the views expressed by Conyers.

"Do you mean to say he condoned you taking such action without permission?" Roger was speechless: forgetting that Marius had been closeted with Conyers for more than half of an hour. Such remarks would have taken considerably less time to convey.

"He stated, if there were reasonable grounds for suspicion, if what was said did not accord with my observations, I should examine the bodies more carefully."

Roger was silent, lost in thought for the rest of the journey.

Nearing Ashenhurst House, Marius asked, " Now I've told you my news, tell me what Mrs Conyers had to say."

"Not a great deal, actually."

Roger was amused at Marius' crestfallen look.

"However, she did just mention that they would all be attending the ball in the Assembly Rooms on Thursday."

Marius' face took on a thoughtful look. He rode towards the lodging house a more contented man. Then a thought struck him.

"It was interesting to see Sir Robert Walpole at the meeting. Frankly, I can't believe he came all the way from London just to involve himself in local issues. Do you think he came down to take a break from politics whilst Parliament is in recess?"

"Don't you know?"

"Know what?"

"Sir Robert Walpole is in The Wells visiting his mistress, Mrs Skerritt. She is staying at the Old Chancellor House on Mount Ephraim. He goes to see her every day after she has taken the waters."

"I didn't know that," exclaimed Marius. "So that is why he is a frequent visitor to the Manor."

"Was the Principal Minister present when Conyers was prompting you to make an examination of the bodies?" mused Roger.

"Yes. Odd in a way. When I was explaining to Conyers about the problems of conducting an examination, he was listening most attentively. I referred to the need for permission of the next-of-kin, and Johnson's intransigence. Do you know, I had the feeling that he was also keen for me to examine Miss Roper's body. He said if there were grounds to suspect foul play, I should not hesitate."

"What conclusion did you draw?"

"Well, besides thinking of when I could next meet Beth, I have been wondering how I could get into the mortuary. There is no way round it, I'm not going to obtain Johnson's authority."

"What do you mean?"

"If I cannot get his permission, I shall have to attend upon the alleged Miss Roper without it. And the sooner the better!"

CHAPTER TWENTY SEVEN

"'Ullo, sir, what's it this time?"

The deputy stood in the doorway, wiping his hands clean on his breeches. His words distorted by a mouthful of food. Marius was hesitant, but committed.

"This time, Deputy, my job is to examine Miss Roper. The constable and I feel that there is too much mystery surrounding her death to allow the body to be interred. We must first satisfy ourselves she died as a result of the fire."

It was said in direct, no-nonsense terms, the deputy never thought to question him. The inference being that the constable was party to the examination was taken as automatic consent for Marius to enter the backroom and conduct his gruesome task.

"Is Mr Russell joining yer?" asked the deputy.

"Not immediately, though no doubt he will be along in due course," replied Marius, anxious to complete his work and be gone before the constable thought to pay a visit.

"Will yer be wanting any 'elp, sir?"

"I may need you to hold a candle. But, first I'll prepare the corpse. Then I'll give you a call when I am ready, Mr Jeffries."

Marius moved swiftly through the inner door into the room where the two bodies were stretched out on the trestle boards. The air was fetid. The odour of decomposition more pronounced.

"I reckon they'll 'ave ter be gorn soon. "Nother two days and they'll be orf, an' no mistake."

The deputy had followed him, in no way deterred by the thought of the impending autopsy. Marius turned to him. "As you are here, can you help me move her closer to the light?"

They spent several minutes shifting both corpses so that the body of Miss Roper was eventually located beneath the narrow window. Unclothing the body, Marius noticed tiny stress marks and tears in the dress seams, particularly around the arms.

Undressed, it was evident that the dead person had eaten sparingly. Her ribs were proud, covered by only the thinnest layer of flesh.

"That's the trouble wif young girls, these days," observed Jeffries. "They starve 'emselves to keep slim, then wear 'em hooped skirts to make 'em look fatter. I 'spose it's the fashion. Even the shoes must be torture. "Ow they keep their balance when they're inches orf the ground, I don't know."

"She didn't have her shoes when brought here, did she?"

"Now yer mentions it, no she din't, Dr 'ope."

"Never mind, no doubt we shall come upon them in due course."

Marius bent to his task. Taking a set of medical instruments from a small case, he began a procedure he had conducted many times. Making an incision in the thorax, he opened the chest cavity. The lungs were removed and placed in a dish. Marius took them over to a side table. The deputy, quite sanguine, watched with rapt interest.

"What are yer looking fer, Doctor?"

It amused him that Jeffries, the deputy, referred to him as doctor only when involved in medical activities.

"The purpose is to examine the lungs specifically for signs of smoke inhalation. If you would bring a candle to give extra light, we'll set to."

Marius worked slowly and meticulously. Paring away the outer membranes until the inner tissue of each lung was revealed. He called for the flame to be brought closer, looking carefully at the junction where the organs met the bronchii, the tubes bringing air to the lungs.

"What can yer see, Doctor?"

Marius paused. Taking a scalpel, he made another incision. This time freeing a section of the lung. He took it to a well-lit spot beneath the window.

"I have to say, Mr Jeffries, I can see nothing."

"A failure, Doctor?" queried the deputy.

"On the contrary, Mr Jeffries. It proves beyond doubt that Miss Roper, or whoever she might be, did not inhale smoke. In other words, burning down the house in Mount Sion could well have been a deliberate attempt to hide the fact that she, and no doubt Mrs Johnson, were already dead."

Dashwood arrived at the magistrate's house well before the appointed hour. He knew how abrasive Mr Phillips was at the best of times. On this occasion, he was expecting the worst. He had been present when the magistrate was bested in argument. It would not bode well for cordial relations.

Normally he reported to Phillips at the Clarence Tavern, where twice monthly, the magistrate carried out his official duties. However, he had received a specific summons to attend upon him at his residence on Mount Ephraim. Shown into the study, Roger was alone for no more than five minutes when the door was flung open, and Phillips entered.

"My dear Dashwood, thank you for coming to my home," said Phillips civilly. "I trust it did not inconvenience you?"

He was taken aback. Though he managed to keep the astonishment from reaching his face. The magistrate did not wait for a reply, going on to enquire if he would care for a little refreshment.

"Coffee would be welcome, Mr Phillips," he mumbled. This was the first time such courtesies had been shown. Giving the request to a maid, Phillips occupied a comfortable green leather chair, indicating Dashwood to take a seat opposite.

"Now to business. What do you have to tell me? There is no need to refer to any of the items recently discussed. I am sure there are other topics we should be talking about," Phillips said airily.

Dashwood gave a brief review of the new faces in The Wells, their backgrounds and connections. The magistrate listened without interruption. Nor did he make comment when the coffee was brought in. Dashwood took up the conversation once more, giving chapter on the departures. He then moved on to the more detailed assessments of some of the characters making their presence known. Their descriptions were duly relayed to the magistrate, who made a show of writing them down in a laborious hand, dipping his quill frequently in the ink well.

"What about our Mr Jordan. What is he up to at the moment?" asked Phillips casually.

"I have no immediate information on the farrier."

"In my view, he's a bad lot. We need to keep a close eye on him. If it is to be believed he is terrorising the townspeople, we cannot stand idly by. I would suggest, Mr Dashwood, that you make it your main preoccupation. Watch Jordan carefully. I want to know everything he does."

"I believe, Mr Phillips, we know Jordan's purpose. It is to persuade some of the freeholders to sell him land," explained Dashwood. "He says he wants to set up a farrier's business. Can you tell me if any changes of title in his favour have been submitted during the past few weeks?"

"Not to my knowledge," replied the magistrate. "But Fines takes care of such matters. I don't think I have received any documents for my signature that mention his name."

After covering a number of other incidental matters, Dashwood took his leave, making his way, thoughtfully, down a well-trodden path towards the Walks.

Marius was sitting in the Gloster Tavern enjoying an excellent dinner. A full meal and a good bottle of claret deserving of his morning's efforts. He had carefully sewn up the body, and prepared a lengthy document of his findings. Being careful to take measurements and adding those to the description of the corpse.

Then, both he and the deputy had appended their signatures. The report now resided safely in an inner pocket. However, his self-congratulatory feelings were interrupted by the sudden appearance of the constable. He entered the tavern in a determined manner, a grim look on his face. Scanning the sea of diners, he caught sight of the doctor of physick.

As the constable made his way through the crowd, Marius realised that in deciding his reward for the examination, he had forgotten to notify Mr Russell of the results. Judging by the way he was striding across the room, he looked less than pleased.

"Mr Russell, welcome. Come, sit with me," Marius declared expansively.

"This is not a social visit, sir. It may interest you to know I have been in most of the taverns and inns in the town looking for you." declared Russell angrily, as he stood over the table.

"Do you recognise the fact, sir, that you have violated a body without the express permission of the next-of-kin?"

"Have you spoken with your deputy, Constable?" asked Marius, taken aback by Russell's attack. "Before you burst upon me with your allegations."

"I've no need, sir. I asked for your help. I did not tell you to take the law into your own hands."

The constable was conducting his biting reprimand in a high voice. Silencing the diners, and those in the taproom. The constable's face reddened. Marius could see that it would be difficult to abate his fury unless he said something quickly.

"At least I have proved conclusively that she was murdered."

The words hit the constable as he paused for further onslaught. They rang round the hushed crowd now staring at the two combatants.

"What?"

"Sit down, Mr Russell. Let me tell you what I have discovered," said Marius in a quieter tone. Keen to keep his voice from carrying to the enthralled assembly.

"I'll tell you what prompted me to go against your wishes, and what I found as a result."

Marius called for another glass, and poured the constable some claret. He recounted Walpole's suggestion, and what the examination had revealed. He then put his hand to the pocket in his waistcoat, and with a flourish, brought forth the document.

"This is my report, signed and corroborated by your deputy."

The constable was silent for several minutes, reading the document and taking an occasional sip from his glass. Eventually, he looked up. "Does this mean Johnson is responsible?"

"I don't think we can say that. He may well have been gambling when the fire started. However, now we have established that the body, which purports to be Miss Roper, was not a victim of the fire, then a close watch should be kept on him. He may have persuaded the magistrate that I was wrong to make the allegations. Now you and I know differently."

The constable had assumed a reflective mood, looking sightlessly into the distance. He finished the glass of claret, and Marius called for another bottle.

The constable, unaware his glass had been refilled, continued to drink in silence. Finally, he said, "I owe you an apology, Dr Hope. Despite my strong reservations, and the censure of the magistrate, you continued with your suspicions. You had the conviction to pursue them. Perhaps, I was too readily influenced by what Mr Phillips might do. I should have followed my own lines of enquiry."

He deliberated for a moment. "What I should do now, I suppose, is tell Mr Phillips of his misguided support for Johnson. And the sooner the better."

"I have been thinking about that, Mr Russell. Why upset the magistrate further? You and I are aware of the situation. For the moment, that's all that's necessary. Why should Johnson be warned? Which might happen if the magistrate knows of our findings."

Russell stopped short. "You may be right, Doctor. Perhaps, for the time being we should keep this between ourselves."

He rose from the table. "I think we should meet again, soon. Can I expect you at half past ten of the clock tomorrow morning, at my offices on Mount Pleasant?"

"I shall be there, Constable."

Russell put on his cocked hat and walked, a little self-consciously, through the crowded tables.

Marius sat back in the chair holding his glass contentedly in his hand. The confrontation with the constable had not been unexpected. Yet, he had not foreseen it would be so soon, or so public.

He had not relished the thought of explaining his actions. However, this brief dispute had seemingly brought about a partial truce, and dispelled the thought that Mr Russell was the magistrate's pawn.

It was obvious that sitting at the meeting table at Rusthall, being seen to take direction from the magistrate, had also added to Russell's outburst. Phillips' imperious attitude had diminished the constable's status. He had wanted to reclaim it.

Marius filled his pipe and called for a spill. It was evident that Jordan was a central figure in the spate of recent happenings. It appeared his heavy-handed approach was having little effect on freeholders. Although, that could only be determined if Roger discovered whether any titles had been transferred to the farrier.

Then there was the wanton destruction of two homes, and the deaths of so many people. Perhaps, the fires had not been premeditated, merely accidents. Conceivably, a mishap with the candle-making process at the Lovedays. The fact that Johnson's actions appeared highly suspicious did not necessarily mean he was responsible for a deliberate act of arson. Nevertheless, as he had said to the constable, Johnson merited close attention. Marius was sure the man was holding back a number of truths. He was deep in his private world when a raised voice broke through his musings.

"How many times must I repeat myself, sir? I want to know by whose authority have you the right to nose into my affairs?"

Marius looked up to see the towering figure of Johnson standing over him. His wig slightly askew, his walking cane waving aloft. Once again, an attentive silence was cast over the room as diners sat intrigued by yet another outburst. The second time in half of an hour. My reputation in this tavern has reached rock bottom, thought Marius.

"I'm waiting!" Johnson shouted, reddening in the face.

Marius began to rise, but was pushed vigorously back into his seat.

"You're not moving until I have a reply to my question!"

Out the corner of his eye he saw the landlord threading his way through the tables.

"Let me give you the answer you most likely do not want to hear, Mr Johnson," Marius declared, his temper rising. "I have examined the body you state is Miss Roper. I can now confirm, medically, she did not die as a result of the fire. She was dead before it even started. I am in no doubt she was murdered. Her killer left her in the house with the express intention of burning the body to hide his evil deed."

Johnson stared at him first in disbelief. Then in anger as the import of his statement sank in.

"Call yourself a doctor! What do you know? I shall inform the magistrate immediately of your irresponsible actions. Anyway, I wasn't at the house when the fire started."

With that, Johnson turned abruptly on his heel. Pushing past the landlord, he made for the door. Marius sat there, staring at the table. Annoyed that he had been provoked into revealing his hand.

"Are you expecting any more visitors, sir? If you are, would you care to meet them outside? I don't want any trouble in my tavern," said the landlord, clearing his plate and glass from the table.

"Hopefully not. But have no worries, Landlord, I was about to leave," Marius retorted.

He walked slowly along the Lower Walk, and mounted the steps to Uptons' coffee house. Sitting in a shaded corner, he recognised the back of Roger Dashwood. He walked over to join him.

"How did your meeting go with the magistrate?"

Roger lifted his head and smiled. "Better than I could have possibly imagined. Did you complete the examination?"

"Yes, but it created one or two difficulties. I think I need something stronger than coffee," confessed Marius unhappily.

Giving his order, he told Roger what he had discovered in the mortuary. Then he described the two encounters in the Gloster Tavern.

"You won't be welcome there again," he said with an amused grin.

"That's what the landlord inferred. He virtually threw me out," said Marius irritably. "It wasn't even my fault."

"What should be our next move?" Roger enquired.

Drinking the glasses of rum brought to them, Marius outlined precisely what he had in mind.

The nearer to the Assembly Rooms, the more nervous Marius became.

"Are you sure she will be there, Roger?"

"All I can say is that Mrs Conyers said the family would be attending the ball. Anything is possible. They may have changed their minds, Beth may not have come with them, or she has come with her beau."

"Do you mean to say there is someone calling on Miss Conyers?" Marius asked anxiously.

"Marius, I don't know. I was just putting to you all the possibilities. When you think about it, an attractive young lady such as Miss Conyers would have more than her fair share of suitors."

He found Dashwood's remarks depressing. By the time they reached the Rooms, he had lost much of his eagerness. Now he was more subdued, his enthusiasm hidden beneath a closed countenance.

Dancing was in full swing, a minuet was in progress. Marius saw Mr Conyers involved in conversation with others. His wife similarly occupied with a group of ladies. There was no sign of Beth.

However, as the musicians struck up a courtly passage, he saw her on the dance floor partnered by a tall, handsome fellow, elegantly dressed and most attentive. She seems much taken by him, thought Marius. When the minuet came to an end he attempted to move through the throng in her direction. However, the crowded room slowed progress. When he arrived close to Mrs Conyers, Beth had again taken to the dance floor – with the same man.

"Dr Hope, how nice to see you," exclaimed Mrs Conyers. "Beth is much in demand at the moment, Ralph seems to have claimed her attentions."

Her words emphasised the obvious. Beth was seemingly enchanted by her partner.

Her eyes shining, her laughter heard above the music. Marius was downcast. His eager thoughts of an enjoyable evening in Beth's company were dashed. Roger had been right. She already had a suitor, and her eyes were only for him. He mumbled an excuse, and headed for the door.

He sat outside in the gathering dusk. Why is it my feelings are so easily crushed, he asked himself. Yet, another reflection of childhood, when events or people's affections turned in a moment, often leaving him emotionally stranded. This evening was another such occasion.

He had come uncertainly to the ball, pinning his hopes on Beth's instant welcome. Delighting in the prospect of spending time in his company. Why did he always harbour expectations that were rarely achieved? The sound of music was still audible as he sipped the chocolate provided by an attentive serving girl.

Marius let passing thoughts become embroidered by notions of what might have been. Allowing himself a fleeting pang of sadness that Beth was spoken for.

"Dr Hope," said a voice at his side, "do you have a moment?"

It was Mrs Porter. She appeared out of the gloom, this time without her book of account. It seemed to reduce her authority. Now Marius saw her for what she was. A lady in her middle years, worn down by work and dedication.

"Hello, Mrs Porter, may I offer you some refreshment?"

"I won't keep you, sir. But, as you are offering, I'll have a small glass of rum and some coffee," she replied, taking a seat next to him.

They sat in companionable silence whilst the serving maid fetched her order. She returned, placing a small tray in front of Mrs Porter, who sipped from both glass and cup before opening the conversation.

"Dr Hope, I know that certain happenings in the Walks interest you. What you are really about I do not know. You are not like others in the company, seeking pleasure, looking for diversions," she said, giving birdlike glances at some dancers taking the air.

She lowered her voice conspiratorially. "I must tell you there are some strange affairs presently. They haven't said anything to me, but something is worrying the freeholders. Every day in the Walks, I am more and more aware of passing comments, whispered conversations. Feelings are running high."

Mrs Porter drank deeply of her rum. Putting down the empty glass, she wiped her mouth.

"There's no point talking to Mr Nash about it. He's not really involved with the townsfolk, just the company. Always the company," she said, with sudden feeling.

She leaned across the table, and gripped his arm. "I've got to talk to somebody. I don't mix with the company, you see. I live among the people here. I'm concerned for them."

Marius looked at her closely. "Would you like something more to drink, Mrs Porter?"

She was clearly distracted with her own thoughts, failing to hear his offer. Marius caught the eye of the serving maid. Then turning back, he said. "I think you had better tell me what's worrying you."

She began hesitantly. "I know I can trust you, Doctor."

A simple statement, but one which implied conviction on her part. Marius nodded.

"I was speaking with one of the freeholders, yesterday. He wouldn't tell me what the problem was. He was even afraid to talk to me at first. When I told him to take his troubles to the constable, he laughed in my face. He said there was no one in authority who could help him."

Mrs Porter picked up her glass, and as before she drank deeply.

"And he's not the only one. I couldn't get him to say more, but I've got to do something. Then, seeing you sitting here, I thought you were just the person he should speak to." She smiled grimly. Her darkened teeth showing briefly in the half-light.

"I heard about your confrontations in the Gloster Tavern, today. Someone who isn't frightened by overbearing officials or the so-called gentry of the town. In fact, there are several like him who should have a word with you."

"I'm not sure I can be of much help, Mrs Porter," Marius said. "Even if I did hold my own with Mr Russell and Mr Johnson, I have no standing or influence. I am just a doctor of physick."

"Not according to Mr Dashwood."

"What has he to say about me, Mrs Porter?" enquired Marius, a hint of irritation in his voice.

"I met Mr Dashwood the other day, by the bridge in Frant Lane. He was watching two gentlemen. I asked why he was there. His words were that you had asked him to do so. He gave the impression that it was official business."

"I see. Well, it was not exactly official, more personal interest."

"Whatever it was, you seem to me to have your own mind, Doctor. That could mean a lot to some people. Especially, if they had someone they could trust, who would listen to them, give them guidance."

"Well … as I said, I'm not sure I would be of much help. But, I dislike injustice. Particularly, when it affects those not in a position to oppose it. I suppose it would do no harm to hear what the fellow has to say. Perhaps, you could arrange for me to meet him, Mrs Porter?"

"That's kind of you, Doctor," she responded warmly. "I'll speak with the freeholder. I won't tell you his name yet awhile. If he agrees, the next time I ask for your dues, I'll tell you who he is, and where and when to meet him."

137

With that, Mrs Porter drained her cup, and stood to bid him farewell. As she stepped outside the candlelit area surrounding the table, she turned and said. "By the bye, Doctor, someone told me that, these days, Mr Johnson is to be seen regularly in Tonbridge town."

CHAPTER TWENTY EIGHT

"I've learned the title transfer has been lodged. But you misled me, Jordan. There is no deed for the barn."

"It's just a matter of time, sir. The clerk took the note of assignment from the freeholder. He is checking his archives to confirm all is in order before he assigns the property."

"That's just it! Fines has established it was never the freeholder's right to sell. It was rented from the Abergavenny Estate. What was the fellow's name?"

"Bennett."

"Didn't he die at the races on Saturday? Well you won't get your money back. What is more, I'm not going to pay it. And another thing, Brown is going to Eridge Park today. Do you know why? God's teeth! He is going to buy the Loveday house and rent the barn you thought you owned."

Jordan was silent.

"Well, what are you going to do about it?"

"What do you mean?"

"Do I have to spell it out? Brown is going to see Martin Bowes, the estate manager. He intends to acquire both properties. We cannot allow him to complete the transaction. It's as simple as that."

"What do you want me to do?"

"In this instance, nothing violent. Leastways, not as permanent as your other ventures. Just keep him from making the appointment. I'll see to the rest."

CHAPTER TWENTY NINE

"Where did you get to last night?"

Roger slumped down beside Marius at the breakfast table. "We had a splendid time."

"Did you?" Marius murmured disinterestedly.

"There was a jolly party at the end of the evening. We paid the musicians, and danced and drank until one of the clock. What happened to you?"

"I … I felt out of sorts. I stepped outside for some air, and then decided to return to the lodging house."

"Beth wondered where you were. I told her we had come together, but when I searched you were nowhere to be seen. She was quite disappointed. So was her cousin, who wanted to meet you."

"Really," said Marius, responding in the same detached fashion. "What is her name?"

"There is a her. However, I'm talking about a him. His name is Ralph. He is Conyers' nephew. A tall fellow, dresses rather well. They were dancing together when we arrived."

Marius looked up from his plate, relief evident on his face.

"That's why you left!" exclaimed Roger, now grinning broadly. "You thought he was her suitor, didn't you? Well, I'll be damned!"

"I did entertain the notion," replied Marius primly. "Who wouldn't? They were dancing together for a long time, and seemed to delight in each other's company."

"But, he is her cousin."

"I didn't know that last night, did I?"

"Well, a group of us, including Beth, are meeting in the Walks tomorrow morning for coffee. Afterwards, we are taking a carriage to the Gun Inn at Eridge for dinner. Would you care to join us?"

Marius grinned his ready acceptance.

They hired a carriage at the gateway to the Lower Walk. Beth sat between Marius and Ralph Martineau. On the other side, Roger was flanked by Maurice Conyers' daughter, Rowena, and her cousin, Judith.

At first, when they had arrived at the coffee house, Marius had been uneasy. How would he explain his sudden exit from the ball? Fortunately, Roger had taken the lead in conversation, engaging them with a witty description of the people he had recently encountered in The Wells. At one point, he mentioned Augustus Brown, imitating the agitated look on his face whenever they passed in the Walks. It provoked much laughter.

Something caught at Marius's imagination. However, it was fleeting, and he smiled broadly as the pompous image of Augustus Brown came to mind.

So the mood of the group was set. Over coffee, he had mentioned to Beth that feeling unwell at the ball, he had returned to his lodgings. In a way, it was true, for Marius now admitted to himself that he had been decidedly put out seeing her with another man.

Judith, was clearly taken with Ralph. Whenever Marius looked in her direction she was casting glances at Beth's cousin. I wonder if my feelings for Beth are as obvious, he wondered. I'll have to be more guarded. Still, there were no knowing looks when he caught the eyes of others upon him.

The day was warming. A faint breeze wafted over the open carriage as it made its way down Strawberry Hill, and through the Waterdowne Forest. Twenty minutes later they reached the Gun Inn, and in high spirits, made their way into the taproom. Roger lingered, arranging for them to be collected later in the afternoon.

"Right you are, sir," responded the driver. "I'll be back at the inn door in four hours."

"Perhaps that's a little late," said Ralph. "I've got an appointment this evening."

"Don't worry, my dear fellow. You'll have plenty of time."

For some reason Marius took delight that Ralph would not be with them afterwards. Then, almost immediately, scolded himself for taking such an unwarranted attitude towards Conyers' nephew.

They were shown to a table in the orchard at the back of the inn, where Marius, again, found himself seated next to Beth. Ralph took up the conversation.

"Did you see the cannon by the front door, Marius? It's one of the last fashioned on the Abergavenny Estate. For a great many years they were producing iron here, and casting gun barrels and other munitions."

"I didn't know we were in a mining area."

"Why do you think the water tastes so foul, Marius?" Roger said across the table. "Did you know you cannot carry a compass if you drink too much?"

Everyone laughed at his wry humour. Marius sat back contentedly on the bench, enjoying the moment; and Beth's presence by his side. Food came, and as they ate and drank so the mood became steadily light-hearted.

The sun was slowly losing its heat, the shadows lengthening when they eventually rose to take their leave. In the inn, they came across their driver drinking in the taproom. He downed the last of his ale, and wiping his mouth with his coat sleeve, strode to the door and opened it with a flourish.

Marius was the last to board the carriage. The door shut firmly by the driver before he climbed onto his box. With a flick of the reins he turned the vehicle on the forecourt, and they headed back towards The Wells. Breasting the rise before descending the gentle slope through the forest, they were conversing about the visit upon Marius by Beau Nash. Suddenly, the driver lunged forward, and whipped up the horses. He half-turned his head and shouted, "A coach has been raided. I'm not stopping in case the brigands are waiting to surprise us!"

Ahead of them, in the dip before it rose up the hill beyond, they saw a small coach. Both doors open, a figure lay in the track.

"My God, it's Brown!" exclaimed Marius, as the carriage thundered past. "He always feared he would be attacked. Stop the carriage, I've got to get out!"

The anxious faces around Marius made him add, "Just slow down! I'll jump! Then go as fast as you can!"

It took some minutes before Brown regained consciousness, and Marius could help him into the coach.

"From what I can see you've suffered a number of contusions, and you'll be badly bruised," Marius told him. "But, at least you're alive. Now, I'd best drive you back to the Angel."

Brown had said nothing all the time he was being attended to by the young doctor. When he was eased gently onto the coach bench, Marius went looking for signs of the driver. He was nowhere to be seen.

Sitting on the driver's box, Marius' thoughts were much about the day spent with his companions. He had made his hurried farewells to those in the carriage. He had smiled down at Beth as he stood to leap from the slowing vehicle.

"Come and visit me on Tuesday morning, Marius!" she called when he jumped.

At the hotel, porters carried Brown to his rooms, whilst Marius asked the innkeeper for brandy, bowls of cold water and flannels.

"Mr Brown has been attacked on the Eridge Road," he explained. "I don't think he is badly hurt, but he will need rest. In the meantime, I shall apply cold compresses to his arms and back."

Brown was lying on the bed, dressed in his outer clothes. Despite his groans and a reluctance to cooperate, Marius managed to remove his frock coat, waistcoat, shirt and undergarments. It was evident he had been subjected to a rain of blows to his body and arms. When asked to lay on his side, Brown did so slowly, complaining all the while of the pain he was suffering. Marius observed the wounds closely. None had broken the skin, but the bruising was darkening rapidly in a criss-cross pattern across his back and shoulders.

"This is going to be cool to the skin, Mr Brown," said Marius, as he put the flannels in the water, rung them out, and covered the injuries.

"Ye gods, man!" he shouted. "It's freezing cold! Do you want my heart to stop?"

"You want to be able to move relatively freely, don't you?" Marius said in exasperation. "If I don't do this, you will stiffen up and be confined to bed for a week."

Despite frequent shouts and exclamations that the doctor was doing his best to bring about maximum discomfort, the hapless victim grudgingly allowed him to continue. Later, when Brown had dressed and regained some degree of composure, Marius said, "You can now drink the brandy, it will help you sleep."

He took the proffered glass and downed it quickly. Marius poured him another small measure, and a glass for himself, and took it to a chair by the window.

"I am grateful for your attentions, Doctor, though I feel your methods are a little extreme," said Brown, in a passing show of gratitude. He lay on his side on the bed, levering himself up occasionally to sip the brandy.

"Have you any idea who they were, Mr Brown?"

"None at all. We were rolling along when I heard a cry, and the coach came to a sudden halt. The doors were wrenched open, and ne'er-do-wells pulled me from my seat. Two of them brandished wooden clubs, another demanded I surrender my purse."

Brown paused, reliving the unpleasantness of the moment.

"It seemed to take forever to remove it from my waistcoat pocket. A brigand with a club hit me about the arms, which made me stumble and fall. Then two of them poured blows on me from every angle."

He was silent for several minutes.

"The ringleader shouted to them to stop. Lying on the ground I managed to free the purse. Whereupon, one of them snatched it from me. Another began hitting me again. I rolled over and put up my arms to ward off the blows. I suppose I must have passed out. When I came to, you were standing over me."

"Did you recognise anything about the men who attacked you?"

"No," said Brown quietly. "I kept my head down. I didn't want to look at them. All I could see were their shoes."

"Anything significant about those?"

Trying to force some recollection of the incident. Brown lay back, and closed his eyes.

"Now I think of it," he murmured. "Now I think of it … one of them was wearing shoes with decorative leatherwork. There was tooled piercing around the heel. I thought it odd that a ruffian, a highwayman, would wear footwear of such taste."

Marius' memory was pricked. He thought back to the coach journey from London.

"Mr Brown, could one of your assailants have been Nathaniel Jordan?"

Brown thought around the question and nodded in affirmation. Marius rose from the seat and walked over to the bed.

"The point is, when we came to The Wells on the coach, such shoes as you describe were worn by the farrier. He was most likely one of your assailants. What about the other voices? Had you heard any of those before?"

"Not that I can recall."

"Do you think there was a reason you were attacked, other than robbery?" Marius enquired.

"What do you mean?" said Brown sharply.

"Did they hit you first then demand your money, or vice-versa?"

"It wasn't as clearcut as that. As I said a moment ago, why don't you listen? One of them hit me at the same time as another of the brigands shouted at me to surrender my purse."

"Forgive my inquisitiveness, Mr Brown, but may I ask you where you were going?"

Hiding his reluctance to answer, Brown rounded on Marius. "Why do you want to know? I'm a law-abiding citizen, minding my own business. You have no jurisdiction over my actions. After all, it was just a robbery."

"Mr Brown," said Marius in a deliberate voice. "I don't think you appreciate the danger you were in. If it had been a simple case of robbery, it would have been just one or two footpads. A gang will rarely stop a small coach carrying one man. It's not worth it. So, the probability was they were intent on doing you harm. Perhaps, some sort of warning."

"What do you mean?"

"If they took your money," declared Marius, "it could be purely to hide the real purpose of the attack. Most likely, they were intent on stopping you reaching your destination. I asked you where you were going. This, surely, must be the key."

"Dr Hope," Brown said imperiously, "I believe where I was going, what I was doing, is my own affair. I see no reason why I should tell you. Now, sir, I shall bid you good day. Please let me rest after my ordeal."

With considerable effort Brown turned over, pulling up the covers and closing his eyes. Standing by the bedside, Marius suddenly felt dismissed. He hesitated, then turned on his heel and went out the door, shutting it gently behind him.

The coach was still standing outside the inn door attended by the porter.

"Tell me, were you on duty earlier today?" Marius enquired. "When Mr Brown ordered the coach?"

"Yes, sir. I'd just taken up my position in the lobby when he asked how he could rent one for the afternoon. I told him it could be easily arranged. He then turned to go into the dining room, his parting words being that he would see me after dinner."

"Did he ask you to do so later?"

"Now I come to think of it, he came into the lobby at about half past the hour of two. A man … I didn't notice him until that moment … met Mr Brown and escorted him through the door. I thought no more of it."

"Did you tell anyone of Mr Brown's request?"

"I didn't need to, sir," came the response. "With his loud voice, he broadcast his intentions throughout the inn."

"I wonder who it was who procured the coach?"

"All I can tell you, sir, is that it came from Mr Simon's yard near the Calverley Estate. The name of the stable is painted in small letters on the side."

Marius took directions from the porter. Climbing onto the box he drove the coach to the livery stables. Pulling into the yard, Marius tied the reins to a convenient rail. A rotund fellow, roughly dressed in breeches and a short waistcoat, sporting a battered cocked hat above bucolic features, was shouting orders to two young grooms, sending them scurrying to various parts of the yard. When they were working to his satisfaction, he came over to Marius.

"You've got ter keep 'em on their toes, otherwise they takes advantage," he said, wiping his hands on a handful of straw. "Now, sir, what can I do for you? Have you finished with the coach?"

He peered at Marius intently. "Though, I can't say as I recall 'iring it ter you."

Marius explained that he was returning the coach on Brown's behalf.

"Can I ask you how the hire was arranged?" he enquired.

"His name was Brown, sir. He paid the price, a sovereign for the day, and drove out the yard immediately it was ready."

"Tell me, Master, can you describe this man called Brown?"

The yard master scratched his side whiskers, removing his hat as he did so, letting his hand run through a ring of grey hair. There was a red welt across his forehead where the hatband had impressed its mark. Jamming it firmly back on his head, he replied, "As I recall 'e was of modest height, light in body. He wore an 'at, low over his eyes. I didn't really get a good look at his face. But, he paid his due, so I saw no 'arm in letting him 'ire it."

Thanking him, Marius walked away deep in thought. Nearing the entrance to the yard, he glimpsed a smithy set to one side of the stables.

The blacksmith was hard at his labours, working a length of metal which he beat and plunged repeatedly into the white-hot coals. His young assistant was in a sweat as he worked the bellows. The sudden flarings brought back the memory of the smell in the burnt-out shell of Loveday's house. That was it! Horse hair mixed with tallow. Farriers use this combination to start their fires, and to quicken the burning of dead animal carcasses. Marius recalled the compound was also used in the confines of hospitals to dispose of waste matter and body parts.

CHAPTER THIRTY

"Most satisfactory, my dear fellow, Now we can trade on a much broader scale."

The other was silent, not immediately replying. When he did so, his voice was thoughtful.

"Bowes was eager to accept our offer. I must admit, getting hold of the building in the woods was a stroke of good fortune."

He rose and moved to a side table, where he moved an ornament with a small sweep of his fingers. Adjusting it thoughtfully, then casting his head to one side to study its new location.

The gentleman who had congratulated him, added.

"However, we must be careful not to invite Walpole's interest. The sooner he goes back to London the better. We don't want him fired up by Conyers, and for a troop of Enforcement Officers to descend upon us."

"I've already told Jordan to be more circumspect."

"One can't sit back either," said the other forcefully. "Everything must be in readiness. Use all the stallholders in the Walks. We need the sales to reach their peak as soon as possible. Don't confine the distribution. Use the stews in the lanes, coachmen, bathhouses. We've got to create sales throughout the town."

"What about securing the title deeds?"

"You just concentrate on moving the contraband. Don't concern yourself with other matters."

"And this inquisitive doctor, what about him?"

"As I said, leave that small matter to me."

CHAPTER THIRTY ONE

He had gone directly to the constable's office on Mount Pleasant.

"I could send two of my deputies to apprehend Jordan," Russell said thoughtfully. "Unfortunately, you still haven't given me one solid reason for taking him into custody."

"Look, Constable, it is a well-known fact he has been using threatening tactics against the freeholders to secure building land. He is a farrier, and I am certain Loveday's house was fired using farrier's tinder."

"You don't see my problem, Dr Hope, do you? Again it's all circumstantial," explained the constable wearily. "Give me indisputable proof, and I'll have him immediately under lock and key. But I can't do anything about his supposed actions. Surely, you must see that?"

Marius had stared at him, then turning on his heel marched out. Walking back to the lodgings at Ashenhurst House, he cast his mind over the facts as he saw them.

There was little doubt Jordan was an insufferable bully. His manner was overbearing and cynical. There was every reason to believe he had orchestrated the attack on Brown. Even the partial description cast him as the principal suspect. However, Marius came to the realisation that his dislike for the man could well be colouring his judgement.

The constable was probably right in paying little heed to my demands, he accepted. In the heat of the argument, he had forgotten to mention that someone, presumably the man posing as the driver, had hired a light coach whilst purporting to be Augustus Brown.

The letter had been left that same afternoon.

Dear Dr Hope,

I Should be Delighted if You Could Join Us for Supper on Wednesday Evening. An Impromptu Gathering at Seven of The Clock .

Despite the Short Notice, I Very Much hope You will be Able to Attend.

Your Obedient Servant –

Doctor John Brett, The Grove

He re-read the note. I wonder why I should merit such an invitation, he mused. Pondering on its brief contents, Marius decided to go. If anything, to learn what mattered to the residents of The Wells, and compare them with the opinions he was receiving from the company. He penned a brief reply, giving it to the porter to arrange delivery.

"I wasn't aware you knew Dr Brett. Indeed, you must be an acquaintance of long-standing to merit an invitation," remarked Roger dryly. They were seated on a bench in front of the Gloster Tavern. The landlord keeping a wary eye on Marius.

"I have heard of him, of course. I know that he owns a large amount of property in the town. But, I have never met him," replied Marius, amused by the air of pique in his companion's voice.

"Odd then that he should invite you, don't you think? I've spoken to him on numerous occasions, socially, you understand. Never been to his home. In fact, to my knowledge, few have, and certainly never for a meal."

"Well, there must be a reason for singling me out. Perhaps, he thinks I'm going to set up in The Wells, and will use the evening to dissuade me."

"John Brett doesn't practise physick, anymore. He gave that up long ago when he inherited everything from his uncle. Mind you, a lot of good that's done him. He has been in and out of the courts fighting his aunt and Pickering. The man she later married."

"Why is that?"

"It seems that Brett's uncle owned a hundred acres of land in the heart of The Wells," Roger explained, enjoying a measure of ale. "But when he died, there was no money to pay all the many bequests he had made. Nevertheless, the Pickerings still pocketed all the rents and proceeds. So, the good Dr Brett took them to court. The dispute has been going on for years. You would do well not to refer to the subject when enjoying his hospitality."

Marius reflected on his comments. "Do you think Brett invited me because he heard about Nash calling on us in the Walks?"

"Most likely, my dear fellow. Or, that you have the ear of the Principal Minister." Marius refrained from comment.

They sat in idle contentment watching the company going about their day. The boulevardiers strolling the Upper Walk. Many seated at tables, others chatting in small, companionable groups. People in the Lower Walk were buying food for the day at the gaily-bedecked stalls, and choosing their needs at the open shop fronts. Shoppers were clustered around the fish market, peering intently at the day's catch.

As Marius raised the mug to his lips, a heavily-built figure in an apron emerged from a butcher's shop, a cleaver in his hand. He walked across to one of the stalls. An argument flared, and the cleaver became the focal point of the gathering crowd's attention. It whirled in emphasis to the indignant harangue. Suddenly, people scattered as voices were raised. A punch was thrown. The cleaver came down on a bare arm.

Stallholders rushed to restrain the butcher, who was pushed and kicked to the ground.

Seeing one of their kind under attack, a group of shop owners came to his aid, armed with a variety of weapons and clubs. An open brawl between the two factions erupted. Casualties were quickly exacted among the stallholders, and several stalls were pulled over, their wares trampled under foot. The scuffle was brief, but bloody. As rapidly as they had appeared, the shop owners melted from the scene.

Marius' professional concerns took hold. Calling Roger to follow, he ran across the square to where the fracas had taken place.

All that remained were weeping women tending those lying on the ground. Marius shouted for water and cloths to bind the wounds. The call was answered by the womenfolk from the shops, who responded, albeit grudgingly, to his demands. Fortunately, no one was critically hurt. Marius was able to clean and bind many of the cuts and abrasions, and restore the men to their feet. The only serious wound was to the stallholder involved in the initial skirmish. His arm, above the elbow, was deeply gashed.

"You will need this to be stitched," Marius said panting heavily. "And it should be done now, before you lose too much blood."

An anxious look came into the fellow's eyes. Uncertain whether he should allow it to be sewn, or risk the consequences.

"Well, what's it to be?" questioned Marius. "Let me say, if you don't, you could bleed to death. Even if you survive with such an open wound, infection could quickly set in. Then you would lose the arm completely."

The man's face was now white with shock, and loss of blood. He nodded, slowly.

"Don't worry, I know what I am doing," said Marius, more gently. "I am a qualified doctor of physick."

The relief was fleeting on the man's features, the fear of pain taking a firmer hold of his imagination.

"Roger get some spirit from the tavern. Quickly, please. Enough for him to drink four good measures, and for me to cleanse the wound."

At his request, one of the women went to the haberdasher, and returned quickly with strong thread and needles. Several stallholders moved the injured man into the shade of one of the stalls. Marius removed his frock coat, rolled back the sleeves of his chemise. Dashwood reappeared with a jug and glass; and whilst the arm was prepared, gave the patient ample measures of rum in quick succession.

"I'm afraid we shall not have time for it to take effect," murmured Marius. "Hold him down, Roger, when I start."

With that the needle was threaded, soaked in rum, and the suturing commenced. A half-stifled scream rang out, which stopped many of the distant company in their tracks. Thereafter, the cries were muted when a cloth was stuffed into the man's mouth. It took no more than a few minutes. The patient's eyes shone with relief when the gag was removed, and he was released from the tight grip. Helped to a standing position, his friends led him slowly away. At that moment, the constable arrived with several of his deputies.

"I see you are involved as usual, Doctor," commented the constable dryly.

"In truth, sir," Roger spoke out spiritedly in Marius' defence, "he has just saved the life of one of the unfortunates who were attacked."

Russell stared at him, intrigued by his intercession.

"Well, Constable, I would not go that far. There was an injured man, a stallholder, who sustained a severe wound. It might easily have done for him," observed Marius.

The constable muttered. "I meant no offence, Dr Hope. It just seems remarkable, that of late any incident that occurs in The Wells and you're at the heart of it."

"As long as I can provide some help, and am not the victim, it does not trouble me," he replied, clearing up after the minor operation.

The constable told the deputies to collect statements from those who had witnessed the incident.

"Can I buy you a drink, Doctor? You too, Mr Dashwood," invited Russell.

They resumed their seats outside the tavern.

"Have you any idea what caused the brawl, Doctor?"

Marius shook his head.

"Well, I think I know," declared the constable. "And I'm sure my deputies would verify my concerns. It's to do with the sales of contraband. There are a few shops in the Walks selling a little, here and there. More worrying is the amount being sold by the stallholders."

The constable leaned on the rough wooden table.

"So much so, it is now affecting the shop owners' trade. Today, tempers boiled over, and they retaliated. Frankly, there could be further bloodshed, and next time there could be serious loss of life."

"Surely, Mr Russell," said Roger firmly, "now is the moment to deal with the stallholders selling illicit goods?"

"You are right, Mr Dashwood. But, in truth, they are of little real consequence. If I put them in prison, there will be others ready to sell a few ankers of rum, tea, or a yard or two of lace. They each deal in modest amounts. It's the number of them trading that's the problem. There are even dealers selling from premises around the town. No, I want the real culprits. Those bringing in the consignments."

"If you apprehended a stallholder, couldn't you get him to reveal his source?" questioned Roger.

"Until now, I have had an understanding with the traders. I turn the occasional blind eye, and they keep me informed if something criminal is in the offing. Though, these past weeks it's as if a barrier has gone up," said the constable dejectedly. "They turn away when I stroll through the Walks. They are frightened to talk to me. Seemingly, they fear the consequences."

"I felt Mr Phillips, the magistrate, was a little too glib at the meeting in Rusthall," said Marius thoughtfully. "However, now you explain the reluctance to stop the sellers, it makes sense. What must be a worry is the control the suppliers seem to have."

The constable drained his mug, and was rising from his seat, when Marius said,

"Incidentally, Mr Russell, I have heard that our Mr Johnson has been seen in Tonbridge. I wonder why he is spending time there?" Raising his eyebrows quizzically, he stared intently into the constable's face.

"He will certainly be in The Wells next Monday, Doctor. The funerals of his wife and niece are taking place. If you are of a mind to attend, may I suggest you keep a discreet distance."

Roger went off to obtain more ale. Marius sat back, spying Mr Tofts in the musicians' gallery. He was busily playing his mandolin in accompaniment to a lively tune led by two violins.

"Whenever the constable stops by, I always feel I have done something wrong," said Roger on his return. "Still, he has a difficult job, and no mistake."

Marius sipped his ale and mumbled agreement. Over the rim of the mug, he saw Mrs Porter gradually making her way along the Walks.

"I would say Roger, you probably have another five minutes."

"Five minutes? What do you mean?"

"Mrs Porter is heading this way. In no time at all we shall be her target."

He looked round, witnessing the hastily vacated tables. A clear sign that an early sighting of her was encouraging many to make a prompt exit.

"Look, old chap, I've got one or two things to attend to," he murmured. "Why don't we meet at the Well in half of the hour? We can go back for dinner together."

Marius nodded his acceptance. Roger, with another quick glance towards the collector of dues, strode off in the opposite direction. Shortly thereafter, she stopped by the table where he sat enjoying the sunshine.

"Dr Hope, are you well?"

He smiled up at her. "Why don't you take your ease, Mrs Porter?"

She sat on the chair so recently occupied by Dashwood. The question of his charges was dealt with quickly. Again her demands were not onerous. Although Marius declared all that he had enjoyed in the past few days, he was asked an arbitrary sum, which was noted in the book of account.

"I wanted to speak with you, Doctor," she said in a low voice. "It's about the matter I brought up the other evening."

She looked around, anxious to avoid being overheard. But her role as gatherer of levies ensured she was given a wide berth.

"Do you recall what it was?" Her tone had the edge of uncertainty.

"Of course, Mrs Porter. How could I forget. Though, you will remember, I queried if I were the right person for your friend to talk to."

She ignored the comment. With another hawk-like glance over her shoulder, she whispered. "He wants to meet you tonight."

CHAPTER THIRTY TWO

Daniel Clifford crept from his house in Frog Lane. He had left his jerkin and breeches downstairs before retiring, and left unfastened the latch to the bedroom door. His wife lay in gentle slumber, the children snug in another room. He had carefully descended the stairs, avoiding the steps which creaked. Dressing in the darkness, he had gone out by the back door and taken the path down to the Frant Lane.

Now, was not the time to have second thoughts. But it was hard to press ahead with the meeting. Telling someone of his problems might well be the cause of vengeance visited upon his family. The doctor had agreed to meet him a half of an hour before midnight. He would be waiting among the trees by the cold baths close to the Sussex Tavern. Thank goodness the moon was out, and Clifford could more easily follow the track.

He was sweating freely as he entered the copse, the foliage filtering the pale light. He was fearful of blundering through the undergrowth. Making noise could attract attention. Slowing his step, he moved forward cautiously until he reached the tree line bordering the southern end of the Walks. Clifford paused. Catching his breath, he eased his way into the shadows, noting the dark shape of the baths to his left.

It was some moments before he summoned up the courage to cross to the meeting place. Suppose it was an ambush. Hope was not there, but his persecutor was. What then? Shapes and shadows moved with the changing light – real or imaginary? He scuttled across like a rabbit, stopping in the middle of the lane, as last minute fears welled up. The remaining few yards took an eternity.

"Is that you, Clifford?"

Relief flooded through him. He recognised the doctor of physick.

"Calm yourself. I wish you no harm, sir," murmured Marius. "Come deeper into the shadows, away from prying eyes."

Marius led him to a small clearing. Another man rose to greet them, and Clifford, seized with dread, turned to run.

"Don't be afraid! He's a friend, I assure you. Let me introduce Mr Roger Dashwood. You can have every confidence that whatever you say to both of us will not be repeated to a soul. On that you have my word," declared Marius gravely. "Come, sir. Sit by us, tell us what concerns you."

The doctor and his companion sat on a knarled tree trunk. Clifford moved to join them. His unease palpable. Marius looked intently at the man. Short, narrow of build, a plain shaven face, eyes wide with fear.

"What I have to say, Dr Hope," whispered Clifford, "is not something I reveal lightly. I have been warned if I so much as let drop a single word, reprisal will be swift. They have even threatened my family."

There was a catch in his voice as he made the last comment. He cleared his throat.

"They want me to trade in illegal goods. I have three stalls in the Lower Walk. So far, I have rejected their demands. But now they want the title deeds to my share in the Walks as well."

Clifford, wiped his brow, and blew his nose on a spotted handkerchief.

"I don't know how much longer I can hold out."

"Do you know who they are?" questioned Marius.

"There are two of them. One is that farrier, Jordan. I don't know the other one. I have never seen his face. It has always been dark. He is no taller than myself, but seems much more dangerous. Both have made it clear they would not accept refusal. They have assured me if I continue to stand out against them my whole family will suffer."

"I thought Jordan was behind it all," muttered Roger. "An unpleasant a fellow as you're ever likely to meet. I don't know of his henchman."

"Have you been offered money to sell contraband?" enquired Marius.

"No. He said my reward would come from profit on the sales."

"The trouble is," said Marius, stroking his chin, "you tell us it is Jordan, and we are convinced that it is. But we have to catch him, or this other man, red-handed. You need someone with you when they are demanding your involvement, then we can take the matter to the constable."

"I can't go to the constable!" cried Clifford in agitation. "No one can trust him. Look what happened to Loveday."

"What do you mean?"

"Loveday went to see Mr Russell. The next day his house burnt down. His family with it!"

Marius was shaken by the remark. The constable had told him none of this. Was he more caught up in the smuggling affair than Marius had considered? He was only half listening when Clifford said, "Only a week ago, one of them caught me in a passageway in the Walks, and told me this was their final warning. Hand over my title deeds, or my family will suffer just like the Lovedays!"

CHAPTER THIRTY THREE

Roger led their mounts across the gravel forecourt.

"It won't rain, I'm certain of it," he said glancing skywards. "In fact, I do believe the day will improve. It's brightening already."

Marius smiled. He was looking forward to the visit to Rusthall Manor, to see Beth once more.

"Don't you think we're somewhat early. After all, we are not expected before four of the clock when the family take tea," Roger commented. "I know you can be a little anxious at times, but it shouldn't take us two hours."

"I thought we might visit the baths at Rusthall before going on to the Manor," said Marius cheerfully. "It would do us both good."

"Hmm … I'm not sure about that. I've had my share of the waters, inside and out, this summer. Anyway, I'm told the temperature in the baths is too low to be enjoyable, and the towels are rough to the skin."

Marius tutted sympathetically. "Do you know, Roger, sometimes, you really are lacking in fortitude."

"Well, I feel the cold. People like me can take the heat of the day, but dislike it intensely when it is cool. Personally, I see no joy in sitting in an ocean of cold water in the mistaken belief it is doing me good. As a doctor, you can't tell me that shivering is good for your health."

"No," responded Marius, now grinning hugely. "It's good for the soul. Consider it as a penance for all your wrongdoing."

"Are you saying, sir, that I have committed an offence?"

"Even if you haven't physically," declared Marius, enjoying himself at Dashwood's expense, "I am convinced that you have had impious thoughts. And, if you haven't, then regard the dip in the baths as a credit against what is likely to come."

They rode down Mount Sion, and along a bridle path on the upward route to Rusthall.

They were silent for much of the journey. Marius reflecting on the last moments of the conversation with Daniel Clifford. It had taken much for him to reveal his predicament. Particularly, as he felt his family was in danger. They had spoken for more than an hour on what might be done. But, inevitably, with the constable's ever-constant plea that unimpeachable evidence must be furnished, until one or other of Clifford's aggressors could be caught in the act, little could be achieved.

"Give me the name of someone who can corroborate your story," Marius had said, 'and I'll take it straight to Mr Conyers. He is a man pledged to uphold the law in this parish." In the end they had parted with Clifford seemingly more bewildered. He had thought by unburdening his concerns, the matter might be resolved. Now, he felt vulnerable at the expectations upon him. He had promised to give Marius' request earnest consideration; but the doctor of physick was inclined to believe he would provide no further help.

As they reached the lane to Rusthall, Marius reined in his horse. Roger, caught unawares, travelled a short distance further before wheeling and pulling his mount alongside.

"Why are we stopping?"

"I was thinking … could the Lord of The Manor be involved? I know it sounds preposterous, but consider the facts."

"What are you saying, Marius?"

"Conyers could benefit by being in league with the smugglers. Don't you see? If willingly or unwillingly, most of the freeholders were trading in contraband, and thus committing a criminal act, it would put them at a tremendous disadvantage. When they were exposed, who do you think the authorities would favour when deciding the settlement of the Walks?"

"Well, I can assure you that Conyers is very much on the side of the law," exclaimed Roger. He added, "You certainly have some quaint notions at times."

They rode on until their horses breasted the rise above Rusthall. Marius nodded in the direction of the village. "I wonder if anyone else is party to your discussions? Someone who listens in."

"Why are you so obsessed with the Rusthall household? For goodness sake let it be, Marius."

Tying the reins of their horses to a hitching post in the shade of an oak tree, they descended the long flight of steps to the building in the valley. Behind a tall desk, in the gloom of the entrance hall, sat a forbidding figure. Marius had not seen him on his first visit.

Occasionally, when the clouds broke, shafts of light shone through a nearby window. They fell upon the desk, highlighting motes of dust that swirled each time the pages of a large ledger were turned. The light glinted on a pile of silver coins, throwing a passing reflection into the man's face, bringing a gleam to eyes set deep in a heavily-lined face.

"Gentlemen, can I be of service?"

The voice matched the appearance. Marius answered for both of them, giving Roger little chance to change his mind.

"Thank you, we shall bathe, and afterwards enjoy a massage."

A note was made in the ledger, money exchanged, a bell was rung. As the peal subsided, an attendant in a full-length robe appeared. He led them along the tiled passage to a spacious changing room.

"Here we are, gentlemen," declared their escort. "When you have undressed, attire yourselves in these bathing robes. Then make your way to the bath just along the corridor."

He pointed to a door set in the opposite wall. Marius arranged his clothes carefully on a bench, and slipped on the voluminous white, cotton wrap, using a tie of the same material to fasten the garment.

First through the door, Roger slowly descended the steps, grimacing all the while as he eased himself into the water. Marius grinned at his companion's obvious discomfort. Taking a breath, Marius stepped boldly into the bath.

It seemed colder than when he had last visited. However, as he lay back until the water lapped his chin, gradually, he began to relax as his body adjusted to the temperature.

His thoughts turned to the afternoon, and how he might engineer a few moments alone with Beth. Did he have any feelings for her, or was it an attraction that would diminish as summer moved into autumn? For the first time he considered her presence in his life. The notion seemed very agreeable. But that might be a distant future, of more immediate concern was whether or not he should return to the hospital.

Oddly enough, since arriving in The Wells, he had not given much thought to his predicament. Soon he would have to make a decision. Whether, despite recent setbacks, the hospital still held attraction for him. Or should he practise elsewhere?

Closing his eyes, Marius floated in the bath, with just his nose proud of the water. He let his mind wander over the events that had engulfed him. In the few weeks since his arrival, he had become a medical authority on dubious deaths. He had been asked by the Lord of The Manor to act as his personal observer; and he had fallen for his niece's charms. The last thought came so easily, that it surprised Marius. He found himself admitting his affection for her both pleased and dismayed him. How could I entertain such feelings when I have spent so little time in her company?

Nevertheless, he lay there in happy contemplation. Shifting unhurriedly, moving an arm sporadically, producing gentle waves that rippled away from his body. Around him the noise of the other bathers receded.

It seemed only the briefest time had elapsed before Roger, wallowing nearby, decided he had had enough. A massage was infinitely preferable. He climbed from the bath, water tumbling in all directions.

"Marius, my teeth are chattering. You can turn blue if you wish, I'm off for a warm rub-down."

It also seemed that the temperature was not to the liking of others. Shortly thereafter, Marius found himself alone in the bath. A solitary figure, floating, remote from immediate cares. His thoughts turned again to Conyers' request. Had he been beguiled into acting as his unwitting accomplice? Relaying information that, if he were part of the smuggling ring, might actually help The Lord of The Manor avoid exposure. The soft eddies, relics of the departed bathers, took Marius this way and that. Time was forgotten.

A deeper turbulence lapped across his face. A rush of water interrupted a breath. He spluttered, attempted to stand. But, as his shoulders cleared the now churning waters, hands were applied to his heaving chest. Unbalanced, he toppled backwards. As he floundered, Marius' eyes opened. The watery distortions revealed the shadowy outlines of two figures. Suddenly, recognising his assailants was less important than freeing himself from their clutches.

This was impossible. No one could drown him at will. It would be the work of a moment to free himself. Try as he might, hampered by the bathing robe, he felt himself sinking. The need to breathe was inexorable. He sobbed, catching at the hands, his strength fading. The instinct to survive took over, logic no longer a consideration. He grabbed at the arms pinning him down. In desperation, through the gathering mist came the realisation, if he could not use his hands he must resort to his feet

With a despairing effort, fuelled by panic, Marius kicked out making abrupt contact with someone above him. As if demented Marius launched a rain of blows with his legs. Suddenly, he was free to move. Surging upwards, he gasped for breath. Through paroxysms of coughing he turned to see his two assailants, both fully dressed, clambering up the steps. A door slammed, there was a shout, Roger appeared, and was knocked into the water beside him.

Marius was far from caring. Bent double over the side of the bath, retching threatened to overwhelm him. After what seemed an eternity, he gradually regained his composure. His heart was pounding. An ache enveloped his entire being. Roger waded towards him, putting an arm under his shoulder he was helped from the bath.

"What the deuce happened, Marius?

Marius could not speak. Dumbly he shook his head.

Eventually, he managed. "Just let me sit on the side for a minute."

An attendant was fetched, and they stood over him anxiously. Finally, he was raised to a standing position, then half carried to the changing room.

"Now, can you tell me what happened?"

"When you left," said Marius painfully, "I was alone in the bath, oblivious to all around me. I lost track of time, until suddenly, I was forced under the water by two men."

He stopped to regain his breath.

"I thought I was going to die, Roger. Fear made me kick out. By good fortune, a foot connected with one of the attackers. It must have knocked him into the other. I managed to get to my feet. They gave up, and were escaping when you came to find me."

Roger smiled ruefully, "I was wondering what was going on. I got pushed in when they ran for the door."

He sat on the bench next to his clothes. Unconcerned that they were fast becoming sodden. He reached for a towel, and sluggishly dried his face and hair. Standing up, he slowly towelled the rest of his body. After resting once more, he began to dress into wet clothes. His breeches and shirt had suffered most. Both were saturated and crumpled. He shrugged on his coat without tying his cravat, and sat down, exhausted from this simplest of exertions.

"Marius, will you be all right if I leave you for a moment?"

He raised a weary hand.

He was still there, slumped on the bench, when Roger returned with an anxious Lord of The Manor.

He had ridden to the Manor. Conyers had immediately called for his carriage and two footmen. Hurrying to the cold baths, between them they managed to get Marius up the steep steps to the ridge. At the Manor, he was carried by the footmen to one of the bedrooms, where Roger helped him undress and ease himself into the bed. A short time afterwards Conyers came in, bearing a large glass of brandy.

"Do you feel able to tell us what happened? Dashwood has given only a garbled account," said Conyers, showing concern.

"Can you give me a little time to rest, sir? I cannot think straight for the moment. I have the most appalling headache. If you don't mind, I'll tell you all a little later."

He drank the brandy and closed his eyes in an attempt to relax and ease his discomfort.

When he awoke he was disorientated. Neither recalling where he was, nor how he came to be there. Slowly, his memory returned, and with it the unsettling thoughts of the incident in the baths. He was attempting to rise from the bed, when there was a light knock on the door. The handle turned, and Beth came into the room.

"You're awake?" Her eyes expressive in their disquiet. "Aunt and I visited your room several times. You have been sound asleep."

She walked towards the bed, staring at him intently. "Are you feeling any better?"

"I think so, Beth," Marius answered slowly. "But I still have a most unpleasant headache."

She had reached the bedside. "I must be quick, in case my aunt discovers me in a man's bedroom." Looking at him gravely, she asked. "What happened to you in the baths, Marius?"

"On our way to Rusthall I persuaded Roger to take a bath and massage with me." He found it was also difficult to speak.

"Roger soon gave up, saying the water was too cold. I lay in the bath alone. Suddenly, two men attacked me. I managed to fight them off, however, by then I had inhaled so much water, was so desperately short of breath, that I was weak, and faint. It seemed to take forever to get out the bath, and dress. Roger and your uncle brought me here."

Beth's eyes slowly filled as Marius told of his experience. She bit at her lip when he had finished and said nothing. She walked to the window, staring out across the lawns. Then, in a small voice, "I was worried when uncle told me you were unwell. I had not realised you had been the victim of an attack."

Beth returned to the bedside and took his hand. Tearfully, she murmured, "Oh, Marius, what would I have done if they had succeeded?"

Marius placed his other hand gently over hers.

"Dearest Beth, it would take a great deal more for the world to be rid of me."

"Well, you are not to tempt fate again. I insist you don't put yourself in such dangers," she sniffed.

Marius smiled. At that moment, Roger came through the door.

"My dear fellow, how are you feeling?"

Beth hastily disentangled herself from his clasp.

"He's a little better, Mr Dashwood," she said acerbically. "No thanks to you."

With that, she walked quickly past a puzzled Dashwood. The bedroom door slammed, a signal of her displeasure.

The knock on the door was peremptory. It opened immediately to admit a maid with a jug of warm water and clean towels. Marius awoke as the heavy curtains were opened with a flourish. The rings rattling and clicking on the poles. The sun brightened the room, and he half-closed his eyes until they grew accustomed to the light.

"Good morning, sir, how are you today?"

"Infinitely better, thank you."

Roger appeared in the doorway. "I've been up ages," he declared. "Do you feel able to join us on the terrace for a light breakfast?"

"Give me a while to ready myself."

Fortunately, his wet and crumpled clothes had been freshly laundered, and, as the maid left, he noticed them laid on the back of a chair. His breeches, waistcoat and frock coat had also been dried and smoothed.

A short time later, Marius made his way downstairs and through to the terrace beyond. Roger was sitting with Conyers, talking in hushed tones. The conversation halted when Marius walked towards them.

"Marius. Come, sit down. Are you well enough?" asked Conyers solicitously.

"I'm feeling something of a fraud, sir. All that happened yesterday is far behind me. Apart from a few aches, I am really quite well."

"Glad to hear it."

"Let me get you something," said Roger standing up, and ushering Marius to a chair. "What do you wish to eat? Some fish?... A few kidneys?... Some eggs perhaps?"

"Shortly, Roger. For now I'll content myself with tea and lemon."

Conyers was occupied with his meal and said nothing further. Marius drank his tea slowly, looking down at the table in contemplation. Roger resumed eating, but kept glancing at Marius, waiting for him to speak.

Conyers put down his knife and fork and cleared his throat. "Marius, are you able to tell us any more of what occurred?" He beckoned to one of the maids, requesting hot chocolate and toast.

"Mr Conyers, I find it hard to believe it myself. But, I now realise … yesterday someone tried to kill me."

"Good grief, are you sure?" cried Roger. "I mean, I was with you at the cold baths. Supposing they had come after me as well?"

"It was only two people, Roger, not a mob."

"Marius, do you know why you were assaulted?" asked Conyers, ignoring Roger's concerns.

"The only conclusion I can draw, Mr Conyers, is that someone believes I am close to finding out more than is good for me."

"Have you discovered something that might lead to our smugglers?" he enquired.

"In truth, I don't know."

"Well, I can't think we have," said Roger imperiously. "I would certainly know if we were on their heels."

The maid returned with Conyers' hot chocolate. Marius found himself casting envious glances at the toast brought to the table.

"Help yourself, Marius," smiled Conyers. There was a companionable silence around the table while they ate, although, Roger found it hard to contain himself. At length, Conyers stood up, commenting that he had to attend to certain matters.

Now alone, Roger was anxious. "What are we going to do, Marius?"

"I'm not certain there is anything we can do. The fellows who almost drowned me were no doubt working for someone. Who, I have no idea."

"We can't just wait for them to come at us. They may be more successful next time."

"Well, we shall have to see," Marius answered, in an introspective manner.

"Humph. I don't think we should simply wait to be attacked. We've got to do something about it."

"Roger, I'm feeling more weary than I thought," said Marius. "I think I'll rest for a short while. Perhaps, we can resume this conversation when we ride back to The Wells."

At the foot of the stairs he met Mrs Conyers.

"Mrs Conyers, I must thank you most kindly for your hospitality."

"Dr Hope, we would do nothing less," she responded warmly.

"If it's convenient, madam, I'd like to rest just for an hour. Then Roger Dashwood and I will be on our way."

"As I said, Doctor, use the house as you please."

With the merest of curtsies, she excused herself and made for the drawing room.

"Mrs Conyers, a moment if you please. Have you seen Beth this morning?"

"She went for an early ride with her cousin. She should be back within the hour."

Irrationally, he felt a tug of jealousy. As he turned to climb the stairs Marius wondered which of the cousins it was. Then, dismissing the thought from his mind, he went into the bedroom.

The knock on the door awoke him.

"May I come in, Marius?" Beth asked, looking quickly over her shoulder.

"Of course. I must have fallen asleep."

"I understand you are returning to The Wells, this morning," Beth said, walking to the bedside. "I cannot stay but a moment. It's not seemly."

"Dear Beth," said Marius, putting out his hand. "When can I see you?"

Beth smiled, and looked into his eyes. "Tomorrow afternoon, cousin Rowena and I will go for a ride in the carriage. When we are out, I shall decide, on a whim you understand, to visit your lodgings. To enquire after your well-being. I could see you then, if you wish?"

Marius squeezed her hand in anticipation.

Beth laughed, passing a gentle finger across his cheek, she retreated from the room.

CHAPTER THIRTY FOUR

"God's Blood! How could you have wasted such an opportunity?"

"He was fortunate. He started kicking out, and I lost my footing. I fell against Luther, and Hope managed to struggle free. We only just had time to get out the baths."

"Well, you've warned him. He'll be ready for you next time, make no mistake."

"Do you want us to finish what we started?"

"Yes … But not right away. Wait until his guard is down."

"Can you wait much longer?

"That's not your concern. Now I must weigh up the best course of action. Thanks to your bungling, you've made my work doubly difficult. Now get out! I'll tell you when next to go against this meddlesome doctor."

The gentleman sat back in the chair and reviewed the situation.

What should have been the simple despatch of an interfering busybody had now been made much harder. It was a race against time to complete the task and bring closure to the enterprise, without this fellow Hope, nosing into their affairs. He must not be allowed to discover the real purpose of all that was going on. A close eye would have to be kept on him to make sure he did not stumble upon the real purpose of his plan for The Wells.

CHAPTER THIRTY FIVE

After a late meal, Marius retired to his room to prepare for his evening with the Bretts. Sitting on the bed, he thought again about the incident at the baths. More intently on his moments with Beth. If the look in her eyes were anything to go by, he felt sure his feelings were returned.

He recalled the conversation with Ralph Martineau. Prior to their departure, Marius had come across him in the library playing a form of patience. It was evident he was not concentrating, for the play of the cards was repetitious.

"How are you feeling, Marius?" Ralph had asked without turning his eyes from the table and the cards spread before him.

"I have recovered, thank you, Ralph," said Marius, standing at his shoulder. "How was the ride this morning?"

He smiled wanly. "I didn't feel up to it. I rather wanted to keep my own company."

He played for several minutes.

"Did you know it's Emily Roper's funeral on Monday?"

"Yes … I did," he replied, surprised Ralph was also aware of the event.

"I knew her rather well, you know."

"Really? I had no idea."

"Well, it has only been a few weeks. At first, I had the strong impression she returned my feelings. Then, for no apparent reason, she seemed to distance herself from me," said Martineau quietly. "I can't think I did anything to offend her. Emily seemed to enjoy my company. Then, almost overnight, she went to great lengths to avoid me."

"Ralph, I didn't know you were well acquainted," responded Marius, at a loss for something to say.

"I shall go to the funeral, of course."

He stared at the cards in his hand, but made no effort to play. After a few minutes, he looked over his shoulder.

"Are you sure you are up to riding back to The Wells? God, what a frightful thing to happen."

"I think they must have followed us from the town. What I cannot understand, now I think about it, is why we didn't see them."

An opportunity to lay a run of cards presented itself. Ralph was immediately distracted. After a moment, still absorbed in his game, he murmured, "Perhaps, they were hiding at the top of the common?"

"Perhaps," said Marius.

After a few minutes, having watched Ralph fail to capitalise on an obvious opening, he drifted from the room. Something about the conversation prompted a half-thought: which at that moment eluded him.

At half past six of the clock, dressed in new breeches, a fresh chemise and cravat, and sporting an elegant frock coat, Marius set out for the Grove. He had his silver topped cane, not for any continuing frailty, more as a weapon against possible attack. Roger had offered to walk with him.

"Thank you, but I cannot live an existence where I have to be accompanied everywhere," he declared firmly. "Whomever has taken against me I shall have to deal with on my own terms."

Nevertheless, he was apprehensive as he strode along the tree-lined path. It would be all too easy to lie in wait amongst the foliage. He quickened his step. Fortunately, it was no great distance, and suddenly the house loomed before him.

The main door was opened to the distant ringing of a bell by a sombre-faced footman. Grey-haired, with a shuffling gait, he led Marius into the depths of the house. Opening the double doors of a large sitting room, he announced him to a group of people in amiable conversation.

During the slight pause, a distinguished looking gentleman of middle years, dressed in an elegant blue frock coat, came forward. Close up, his florid features showed a kindly disposition. A brief smile tugged at his mouth.

"My dear sir, I'm so pleased you could join us. My name is John Brett."

He took Marius by the arm, and led him to several of his guests standing by full-length windows overlooking the gardens.

"Let me present Dr Hope. He has recently come down from London. This is the Earl of Buckingham, and his wife, Marianne. I believe you are already acquainted with Mr Augustus Brown."

The Earl, a man advancing in years, was clearly discontent with his lot. He was above average height, though this was diminished somewhat by a slight stoop of the shoulders. His countenance was dominated by a well-veined nose, and a tight, disapproving mouth.

He wore a periwig which had seen better days. He nodded to Marius, turning at the same time to gather a glass of wine from a tray carried by a serving maid.

His younger wife was a small, timid-looking woman. Her over-whitened features cracking slightly in the rictus of a wan smile. She said nothing, maintaining a long-suffering, apologetic air.

Turning to the comestibles trader, Marius enquired, "Are you feeling better, Mr Brown? You look heartier than when we last met."

The Earl, now holding a full glass, sniffed loudly. "So, you know about him being savagely attacked on the way to Abergavenny's place, do you?"

"Hope attended me in his capacity as a doctor of physick," muttered Brown

"I did not have to do much, for there was little damage," commented Marius, noticing Brown's sharp look in his direction. "Most of Mr Brown's injuries were superficial. It was more the nature of the attack. It appeared to be something of a gesture by his attackers, not like the acts of violence we hear so much about on the roads these days."

"It laid me low, Dr Hope!" declared Brown, clearly put out. "I am still feeling the effects of it several days afterwards."

"Forgive me, Mr Brown. I was not attempting to minimise the ferocity of the attack, or the result. I know only too well what such an assault can do."

Brown was not easily mollified.

"Well, Brown, you're here to tell the tale," said Buckingham, amused by Marius unknowingly pricking Brown's bubble of self-pity. "It could have been worse. You might not have been with us at all. And if you aren't now buying the Loveday house, I'm sure there are many other properties suited to your needs."

Brett joined them, and the conversation turned to Marius and his recent *contretemps* with the constable, followed by Mr Johnson, in the Gloster Tavern.

"I happened to be dining two tables away, Dr Hope," acknowledged Brett, with a knowing smile.

Marius said ruefully, "Did you know the landlord no longer believes I'm a desirable patron?"

At that moment, the footman opened the doors to announce Mr Phillips, the magistrate. Brett went forward to greet him, and to introduce him to his other guests.

"I believe you know most of those here this evening, Brotherton."

Marius nodded in acknowledgement, glancing at Brown as he did so. He was startled to see a glare of irritation fleetingly cross his face.

"Have you met Mr Augustus Brown?" queried Brett. "He has recently arrived, and has visions of opening a business here."

"Good evening, sir," proclaimed Phillips, looking at Brown with interest. "What type of business do you have in mind?"

Brown adopted the attitude Marius had noticed in the coach, when he had declared his intention of opening a number of grocery outlets. However, on this occasion the pomposity was moderated, and his air of self-importance carried little conviction.

At the dining table, Marius found himself between Mrs Brett and the Countess of Buckingham. Contrasting opposites. One garrulous, the other reluctant to utter the slightest word.

"Doctor, what is your opinion of The Wells now you have been here for a few weeks?" demanded the hostess. She continued without awaiting his reply. "Personally, I do not welcome this invasion each summer, present company excepted, of course. The shops and stalls are crowded, traffic clogs the roads, the mode of dress is far too liberal, and there's frequent brawling."

Marius glanced at the Countess, who gazed steadily down at the plate before her. He turned to Mrs Brett, about to respond, when she resumed her diatribe.

"When the company disperses in early October, when everyone goes their separate ways, what happens? They leave behind a whole army of unemployed servants, unpaid bills and broken furniture. The town is badly used, and the carriageways in a far worse state. Every year the town repairs the thoroughfares and the fences, only to do it all again ten months later."

Mrs Brett looked around the table awaiting words of support. Her husband drank deeply of his wine. Buckingham confined his attentions to the meal before him.

Marius commented mildly. "You have a point, Mrs Brett. Tell me, have there been no improvements since The Wells became a popular resort? The shops may be overrun, but have you not noticed they stock a wider range of items? Nowadays, you can buy things in The Wells that were once only available in London. It seems to me, there are more facilities available in a country town than one would normally expect."

Mrs Brett looked sharply at her husband, silently summoning him to take up her argument. When he failed to comment, she went on.

"Dr Hope, I cannot think why you would believe we want all these things at our disposal. My husband and I, and most other residents, desire our town to be unsullied. If it means going without the pitifully few amenities you identify, then that is a price we would gladly pay."

The Earl of Buckingham smiled, "Come, come my dear, you can't mean that. If I remember rightly, it was the town's expansion and demand for property that provided your husband with his good fortune. You can't have it both ways."

"John, I want you to tell the earl that his remarks are out of place," snapped Mrs Brett.

"Madame, forgive me," said Buckingham, his amusement under the thinnest of disguises. "I meant no slight. I was just recalling a little local history."

"Mr Brown," said Brett hurriedly. "Did you recognise any of your attackers?"

"At first, I thought I might know one of the assailants. On reflection, I now know I was mistaken," mumbled Brown, not looking at Marius. Yet aware of the curious glance in his direction.

He added. "I realise I might have been quick to condemn the wrong man."

Marius could not contain himself.

"I find this change of heart somewhat baffling, Mr Brown. When I attended upon you, you were convinced of the identity of one particular assailant. Far be it for me to state his name, but surely you cannot now say you were in error?"

"You, of all people," stated Brown in irritation, "must appreciate how a blow to the head can affect one's judgement. You forced me into making an instant identification. When I recovered, having had the chance to reconsider, I came to the conclusion it was not Mr Jordan."

"Are you referring to this farrier who's in the Wells?" enquired Brotherton Phillips.

"I regard it as inappropriate to refer to him by name, Mr Phillips. Particularly, if Mr Brown no longer believes him to be the culprit," said Marius with feeling.

"What I find, Dr Hope," said Phillips imperiously, "is that you condemn, all too quickly, the unintentional shortcomings in others. Yet find a ready excuse for yourself when flounting both convention and the law."

"More wine, Brotherton?" pressed Brett, anxious to diffuse the likelihood of confrontation. It was not to be.

"I am intrigued by your remarks concerning our young doctor, Mr Phillips. What are you referring to exactly?" asked Buckingham, titillated by the thrust and counter-thrust of the exchanges.

Marius was smarting at the magistrate's comment. Though, for once, he resisted voicing any protest at the unfairness of the remark. He applied himself to the dish before him.

"I think our magistrate is giving the good doctor a wigging," interrupted Mrs Brett. Now retaliating after Buckingham's earlier barbs.

Marius looked up, noting the apprehension in Brett's eyes. Again, he refrained from responding.

"You are a little officious at times, my dear fellow. You always seem to take your function as the magistrate so seriously," reflected Buckingham. "Don't you think so, my dear?"

He turned to his wife for confirmation, staring at her intently.

"I won't get a peep out of her tonight, I can't think why I asked."

Phillips was engaged in chewing something from his plate, and his reply was delayed. The earl lost little time in striking whilst he had the advantage.

"What I cannot understand, Brotherton, is why you allow this damnable dealing in contraband to go on. I suppose you know about the altercation in the Walks yesterday? If you want to appear magisterial, you ought to put a stop to it?"

Red in the face, Phillips was hastily trying to finish his mouthful.

"Mind you," said Buckingham, now quite enjoying himself at the magistrate's expense. "I can't say no to the odd bottle of brandy, or tobacco, at such reasonable prices. What about you, Brett?"

The host was sensible enough to ignore the remark. However, Buckingham was loath to let it go.

"Tell me, Brown, when you have set up your emporium, are you going to make a few discreet purchases from the stallholders to fill your shelves?"

"Certainly not! I'll have you know, sir, I am a law-abiding citizen. I'm not about to compromise my dealings when I open here."

The evening continued in much the same vein. Courtesies were thinly veiled. It seemed to Marius, everyone around the table was, at some time, the butt of pointed remarks. Some were amusing, some ironic, others laying bare personal feelings. Marius was the first to take his leave. When the main door closed on him, his relief was palpable.

CHAPTER THIRTY SIX

Taking his ease in the orangery, Marius thought about the previous evening. It had gone awry when he had displayed exasperation with Augustus Brown. If the trader were unsure, it had been wrong to argue the point. Although, he had the strongest feeling Brown had deliberately altered his opinion. Not through uncertainty: perhaps, it now suited his purpose. Had he been paid? Were there those who could smooth his business path if he kept quiet? Or, had he been threatened?

He dismissed the idea of payment. Brown gave all the appearances of being financially comfortable. Had the attack been both a warning and a deterrent? Supposing he had been warned before journeying to Eridge, and ignored the threat?

It was all too likely that he had been roughly-handled, then firmly advised not take the matter further. But, by whom? The distributors of the contraband? Did they want the site of the Loveday's house for themselves? Marius's reverie was abruptly interrupted by Roger Dashwood.

"I thought I would find you here, Marius," he exclaimed, looking pleased with himself. "Now you can tell me how it went."

"Oh, there's not much to tell. I argued with Augustus Brown, also a guest at Brett's table. That set the tone for the evening. Thereafter, it was a meal beset by carping criticism, ill-manners and sheer rudeness. I departed as soon as it was seemly to do so."

"Who was there? I presume there were others besides Brown."

"Yes, I met the Earl of Buckingham and his wife. A quiet soul, who gave the impression of being downtrodden. Your employer, Mr Phillips, was also there. I didn't know his name was Brotherton."

Roger grinned. "So you've met the local nobility. If I know the earl, it was probably he who was the cause of any mischief. He is renowned for spreading disquiet."

"Now you mention it, he did prompt Mrs Brett to retaliate on a point. I can't remember what it was, but her reaction was quite waspish."

"I don't know why Brett associates with him. For that matter, I can't understand how Buckingham can find it in his heart to mix with Brett. After all, it was Brett's uncle who wrested much of his property from the so-called earl."

"What do you mean so-called?"

"It's another aspect of the Brett family fortunes that has never been publicly aired," recounted Roger knowledgeably. "His uncle was an apothecary. He was also working as an agent for Buckingham, through a fellow called Marsh. It appears he lent the earl vast sums of money. Then as cool as you like, uncle Brett took a number of properties in lieu of debts. A bit underhanded in my opinion."

"That could well account for his manner at the table," said Marius thoughtfully. "From what I'm told, he is like it all the time," murmured Roger. "Have you heard of Lady Muskerry? He is her son by her second husband, Viscount Purbeck. He poses as the Earl of Buckingham. Frankly, the claim is highly suspect. Particularly, as the real Duke of Buckingham petitioned for its rejection some years ago."

"Did I tell you Mr Phillips also tilted at me," said Marius. "He took delight in reminding me that I was intolerant of the shortcomings of others. Self-righteous in my own eyes, even when in the wrong."

Roger grinned at him.

"What's so amusing?"

His grin broadened. "Well, he's right. You get that indignant look on your face, and you adopt a holier-than-thou manner."

"Nonsense!"

"And you don't realise you're doing it."

"Balderdash!"

"You are also pigheaded when you think you're right. Even when it's clear to everyone else you're not."

"I'm not like that at all. I listen to others, seek their advice."

"Really?"

"Of course, I do."

"The paragon of sweet reason. Honestly, Marius, you should stop and look at yourself once in a while."

It was said in an amusing, unassertive way that Marius could not take umbrage. He stared at his companion. Almost searching for an image of himself in Roger's eyes. Then his face creased into a smile.

They returned to the orangery after dinner. The weather was still cool, though, the early morning showers had now abated. They lounged in the rattan chairs, exchanging the occasional word, content with the silences. Suddenly, they heard voices, and the clatter of footsteps on tiled floors, growing louder as they came along the corridor. A maid opened the half-glazed door, followed immediately by Beth, and Conyers' daughter, Rowena.

"Beth, what a pleasant surprise!" exclaimed Marius, jumping to his feet.

"We were enjoying a brief outing, and being close to Mount Sion, it came to us that we should call upon you," declared Beth, as though she had prepared what she might say, and was rushing, breathlessly, through the words.

"We wanted to be sure you were improving after your ordeal, didn't we, Rowena?"

"I'm extremely well, having rested much of the day," said Marius, engaging her glance, unable to look away. In that moment, he forgot those around him.

"Forgive my friend. I do believe the little incident at Rusthall has waterlogged his brain," Roger said. "He has forgotten every courtesy. Won't you be seated. Would you care for some tea?"

"Sorry, Beth, what am I thinking of?" stuttered Marius.

"Pay no regard to Roger, Marius. I do believe it's his little joke," responded Beth, sitting on the sofa. He quickly sat by her side.

"Are you being truthful? Are you really much improved?"

"Truly, Beth, I am completely recovered."

Marius looked into her eyes, taken aback to find compassion, concern, and something else in the manner she returned his gaze.

"Miss Conyers, it is quite pleasant now in the garden. Would you care to join me for a stroll around the herbaceous borders?"

Roger was directing his attention to Beth's cousin.

"A splendid idea, Mr Dashwood."

With no further word, he opened the double doors, and descending the steps they began a gentle stroll among the flower beds.

"Marius, we cannot stay long. But, I was anxious to see you." She blushed. "I mean, to ask after your health."

"Beth, I have been thinking about you every minute since you came into my room yesterday."

Two pink spots blossomed on her cheeks. "Marius, I hope I did not appear too brazen. Coming unannounced into the bedroom, and blatantly making an assignation for today." Her face a little downcast at the thought of what she had done.

"My dearest Beth," said Marius, taking one of her hands, cool and delicate in his grasp. "How could you suppose, for one moment, that your comments might be deemed bold. I delight in the fact you can say to me exactly what you think. I would never believe you less than perfect."

"Now you are mocking me," said Beth, a little uncertainly.

"Far from it," exclaimed Marius, still with her hand in his. "I know we cannot be long together, for appearances sake. Just tell me when we might meet again."

Out the corner of his eye, he could see Roger and Rowena turning towards the orangery.

"My aunt and several of her friends are going to a recital at Eridge Park on Tuesday afternoon. Why don't you attend? We can meet there without fear of comment."

"I shall be there," declared Marius. The couple in the garden were but a few short steps from the door.

"Beth, there is something I must tell you. I wouldn't want you to hear this from anyone else. Your uncle has asked me to work for him. He feels that as a stranger I might more easily be able to discover something of the distribution of the contraband. He may mention it to you. I wanted to be the first, so that you did not get a wrong impression."

Her eyes widened. Marius could not tell whether from surprise, anger or disappointment. Beth stood as the pair came into the orangery.

"We must go, immediately, Rowena," said Beth, tight-lipped, making her way towards the door.

"Good afternoon, to you," she nodded in Marius' direction. "Goodbye, Roger. Do not bother to see us to our carriage."

The last comment was so emphatic, both men stood stock still. Rowena looked at them half-apologetically, before following her cousin. The click of their shoes came loud on the tile flooring, then the main door closed with a thump.

"Why do I get the feeling you have just said something out of place, Marius' commented Roger dryly.

CHAPTER THIRTY SEVEN

It was Monday morning. A chilly, north wind catching the mourners unprepared as they clustered around the two open graves. Marius was standing well back in the shade of a broad yew tree. Although less exposed to the weather, he still felt the occasional gust as it blew across the graveyard. The scudding clouds had darkened, rain was threatening.

The minister conducting the ceremony noticed he was in imminent danger from the elements, and picked up the tempo of the service. It was with obvious relief to the cleric, and those paying their respects, when the last words were intoned.

Marius had made his own farewell and a snatch of prayers for Mrs Johnson a little earlier. Now he was more attentive to the bowed heads among the gravestones. Why, he wondered, were the bodies not taken back to London and buried in a local cemetery? Again, Marius opined that Mr Johnson wanted to bury the evidence with all speed. But, who is likely to believe me, he thought. Anyway, even if a crime has been committed, the time had come to inter the bodies. Though, that did not mean their deaths were to be forgotten.

Marius was convinced that the two people now coffined, and being lowered into the ground were victims of a murderous act. He silently vowed that he would not stand passively by and allow whomever had committed the deed to go unpunished.

The service was done. The minister picked up the skirts of his cassock, and hastily departed. By contrast, the small group around the grave was slow to disperse. Among them, Mr Nash and Ralph Martineau.

Marius witnessed Johnson stride away, ignoring the convention of thanking those who had attended. Another figure moved away from the knot of mourners. He recognised the constable putting on his hat and pulling his coat tight to ward off the chilling breeze.

As he descended the path, Marius stepped from his vantage point.

"Does the constable of this parish attend every funeral?"

"Doctor," Russell acknowledged him. "I won't ask what brings you here, although you don't look as cold as I feel. It's supposed to be midsummer. It's more like late autumn."

"Let me buy you something to warm your bones, Mr Russell," invited Marius, smiling at the constable's exaggerated discomfort.

The mass of people inside the Grove Tavern gave the low-ceilinged bar room a warmth not lost on the constable, whose temperament rose with his temperature. Marius found a convenient table, away from the throng, and a serving maid provided a jug of mulled wine.

"I noticed Johnson depart the burial directly the service was over," remarked Marius.

"Uncommon quick, in my view," commented the constable. "He showed no gratitude to those attending. In fact, he seemed annoyed at my presence. Probably just as well he didn't notice you among the trees."

"Tell me, Mr Russell, are the deaths of the two women still being investigated?"

A hint of irritation crossed his features.

"Of course. I've mentioned it before. Do you think we would conclude the case just because the bodies have been buried?"

"Well, I'm not sure of official procedures," replied Marius. "As much of your time is absorbed with the smuggling problem, the matter might not have seemed so pressing."

"Dr Hope, the reason for the fire may be unsolved, as is that of the Lovedays," responded the constable grimly. "Believe me, I am not ignoring the need to discover the cause of both and apprehend the culprits."

Marius said nothing. He judged from the remark that the constable now thought the fires were the work of different people.

"Can I fill your glass, Mr Russell?"

"No. I must be about my business. As you say, there is much to do."

Marius could see the constable had been pricked by the enquiry. But, he did not want him to leave before raising another issue. Searching for something to delay him, Marius leaned forward, and said in a low tone.

"I had an interesting meeting late on Thursday night. One of the stallholders revealed that he and his family are being threatened. If he does not become part of the selling ring in the Lower Walk, they will exact a dire penalty."

The constable subsided slowly back into the chair.

"He also mentioned," said Marius covertly, "that he is being pressed to sell his title deeds. It's clearly Jordan. But, as you have already stated, proof is essential."

Russell stared at him intently. Marius felt a stab of guilt that he had revealed the nature of the meeting. Particularly, as Clifford had been so scathing of Russell's efforts. More worryingly, Loveday had sought out the constable only for his house to be razed a day later.

However, Marius had noted the grief Russell had suffered when searching through the ruins. Not even the finest of actors could have portrayed such intensity of feeling. He was convinced the man was not playing a double game. Well, almost.

"Will he get the proof, Dr Hope? Will he be able to produce witnesses to the threats? What is his name?"

Marius felt concern. He tried to deflect the questions by declaring that he never saw the freeholder. It was dark. In any event, he doubted if he would have recognised the face.

"How did he communicate with you in the first place?"

The conversation was becoming increasingly difficult. He had to change the subject before the constable got too close and he let slip Clifford's name.

"He used an intermediary. A note was left at my lodgings."

Russell continued to gaze at him.

"By the way, I wanted to ask you something, Mr Russell," Marius said in an attempt to deflect the interrogation, "have you come across a Mr Augustus Brown, a trader in comestibles? Leastways, that's how he describes himself. He is seeking to open a shop in The Wells selling foodstuffs."

"Is he is that large, over-dressed gentleman, who carries such an obvious air of self-importance?"

Marius nodded, then asked the question.

"If he were to buy what remains of the Loveday house, would he be able to build on the site?"

"I believe there are covenants prohibiting any commercial premises being erected. The land and buildings on the south side of the stream belong to Lord Abergavenny. Still, I suppose he could allow some dispensation. Though, to my knowledge he hasn't done so far."

"He seemed so sure of his ability to build his own premises. But, if he hasn't bought it, that's the end of the matter."

Russell shrugged, and sat back in his chair. Now was the time to steer the conversation in another direction.

"If Lord Abergavenny owns much of what lies to the south of the Walks," Marius casually enquired, "what are Conyers' interests? From what I've heard, the present Lord of The Manor has title to most of the land between the Well and Rusthall."

"It's more complicated than that," commented Russell. "The Walks are jointly owned by Conyers and a number of freeholders."

"As Lord of The Manor, does his role include looking after the civic welfare of the town?" enquired Marius guilelessly.

"Bearing in mind that the centre of The Wells is the Walks, then, yes, he does. In fact, he has taken on that responsibility more so than any of his predecessors. Of course, he doesn't do it alone. He, and a number of prominent citizens, have formed a self-appointed watch committee."

"Including the magistrate?"

"Yes," murmured the constable. "And his presence means that I have to attend as well."

"So, when contraband began appearing in The Wells, this committee addressed the problem. How long has Conyers been Lord of The Manor?"

Russell was now looking at Marius quizzically. "Nigh on sixteen years."

"Do you know where he came from?"

"I understand his family have farms and land near Guildford. Look, Doctor, I know why you are asking these questions."

Marius was taken aback. He knew when he started digging into Conyers' background, Russell might guess his motive. Certainly not this quickly, and how could he possibly know the reason.

"Really, Mr Russell, I was just interested in the public spirit Conyers inspires amongst the town worthies."

"You don't fool me, Dr Hope. Wanting to know all about Conyers is just a roundabout way of finding out more about his niece," said Russell, smiling broadly.

Marius was startled. He looked down at his drinking glass to hide his feelings, searching for something to say. At that moment, Beth had been furthest from his thoughts. Colour tinged his cheeks. Russell, however, took his reaction as embarrassment that he had been found out in his quest to discover more about the Conyers' family.

Marius, assuming a slightly sheepish demeanour, remarked, "You attend the meetings at Rusthall, Mr Russell. I just wondered if there were anything about the man I should guard against. I was hoping to learn if there were any pitfalls to avoid. Subjects not to touch upon. If I can encourage him to like me, he might accept my calling on his niece whilst she is at the Manor."

"I would strongly suggest, Doctor," said the constable, an amused smile playing at his lips, "you don't refer to the present conflict with the freeholders. That's a very sore point."

CHAPTER THIRTY EIGHT

He sat through an hour of Monteverdi. To Marius, the operatic recitative was like someone talking over the music. It was ineffably dreary, and seemed to prolong the moment when he could search for Beth.

At last, the interlude. The audience rose, already talking in ringing tones about what was to follow. A string quartet playing some pieces by Bach, a German composer whose name was on everyone's lips.

Marius moved with the crowd into the hall at Eridge Park. He stood near one of the large, full length windows overlooking the well-tended grounds.

"I didn't think you would come," said a voice softly behind him.

Turning he saw Beth, an uncertain look on her face.

"I thought we had agreed I would."

"Not after my abrupt departure on Thursday. I was angry with you. How could you let yourself be involved in uncle's affairs, Marius? You don't live here anymore than I do."

"Your uncle is very persuasive. There seemed little alternative."

"Why must you put yourself at risk?"

Her annoyance showed in her slightly raised voice. A number of heads turned in their direction.

"Whoever it is has already tried to rid the world of you," she whispered fiercely. "Why embark on another venture which could place you in danger?"

"Actually, your uncle asked me to become involved that day when I was called into his meeting," murmured Marius.

"So, the episode in the bath house was the smugglers' way of warning you off." Two pink spots on her cheeks were again in evidence.

"I didn't know I was a target. In the future, I'll take greater care."

"I saw what they did to you, Marius, and, I do not care to see you attacked again. What if next time they are more successful?" she sniffed.

"Beth, I cannot withdraw my services. You must see that."

"Of course, you can. It's not your responsibility."

Then, she seemed to relent.

"Oh, for goodness sake, Marius. You had better not do anything, or go anywhere without Roger. I shall tell him myself, he must be your constant guardian."

Marius smiled. "All the time?"

"No . . . just some of the time." She returned his smile.

"Beth, my dear, we should be taking our seats," interrupted Mrs Conyers, making her way towards the couple. "Dr Hope, will you excuse us?"

"Perhaps, we can speak again during the next interval, Marius?" said Beth, looking over her shoulder, and inclining her head demurely as she was led into the music room.

The gloom was swept away. A surge of contentment washed over him. He was uncertain if he could endure the next part of the programme in anticipation of her company.

As the hall emptied, on a whim he chose to occupy himself in the garden for the coming half of the hour. Ignoring the main entrance, he wandered through the ground floor of the house. There were numerous doors, but, none seemed to offer an exit.

However, at the end of a dark passage, Marius glimpsed an orangery, which suggested a most likely route.

As he neared the glazed door he heard voices. The conversation was in low tones, and Marius could not clearly discern what was being said, until one word caught his immediate attention. His name. Someone had said, "Hope is now in the Lord of The Manor's employ".

Keen to learn the owners of the voices, Marius peered cautiously into the orangery from the shelter of its darkened entrance. It was difficult to overhear the exchanges, and all he could make out were the shapes of two men distorted by the designs in the glass panels.

Suddenly, the shapes began to move. Marius darted back along the corridor, and slipped into the first room he came to. Just as he closed the door, leaving the merest gap, two men hurried past. He did not see one, but the other was Robert Fielding, the Excise Official. It was he who had mentioned his name.

Marius remained behind the door for several minutes, dwelling on what he had heard. Why was he the subject of a discreet conversation? Playing back the phrase in his head, Fielding had clearly said he was working for Conyers. What business was that of his? More importantly, how did he learn of the arrangement?

Marius went cold. The only person he had told was Beth. A brief moment ago Marius had felt elated, now he was pitched into deep despair. He could no longer trust her. A wounding hurt brought to the surface all the old emotions he had tried to subdue. He wanted to leave, hide his feelings, forget all that he had believed was enchanting and appealing about her.

He marched through the house, out the main door and headed for the stables. A groom came forward with his horse. Climbing swiftly into the saddle, Marius urged his mount into a canter. A Bach sonata for violin and piano emanating softly through the windows went unheard.

"Why, Marius, I have been looking everywhere for you. I thought you had left," said Beth as he entered the hall.

Marius studied her for a moment, seeing the change come over her face as she realised something was amiss.

"Dr Hope, what did you think of the recital? Wasn't it perfectly splendid?" exclaimed Mrs Conyers. She came bustling towards him, accompanied by Rowena and two companions.

"I do find this composer quite captivating, don't you? And the quartet was outstanding. Lord Abergavenny brought them down from London, you know," continued Mrs Conyers blithely, ignorant of Beth standing by Marius, looking at him in puzzlement and dismay.

He nodded, not taking in her remarks. His mind fixed on Beth. A short while ago, Marius had flung himself onto his horse, intent on escape. He had galloped through the lodge gates, jerking the reins in the direction of The Wells. Distance was all. Disillusioned, as in the past, the immediate resort was to rush from the cause of his upset.

But, as his mount slowed to a trot, it came to him this was not the solution. It would not insulate him from his affection. He had to find out why Beth had told Fielding, and he had to hear the reason from her own lips.

He slowly retraced his steps. I shall confront her, he decided. Demand to know the answer, whatever the circumstances. Now caught up with Mrs Conyers and her friends, his nerve was failing him.

"Marius, I really, must show you the fountain in the rose garden," declared Beth, cutting across her aunt's exotic prose. "Aunt, forgive Rowena and I whilst we take Marius to see the fountain before the interlude is over. Come Rowena."

With that she grabbed Marius' arm. Accompanied by her cousin, too perplexed to say anything, the trio made for the garden.

Outside, away from the throng, Beth said, "Rowena, wait here. I shan't be a moment." With that she ushered Marius a short distance, turned, and without preamble said. "Now what is troubling you? Have I done something to make you angry with me?" No one had ever been so forthright. Taken aback, Marius hesitated.

"Marius, I am not prepared to suffer my aunt's wrath without an explanation."

Marius looked at her. He could see clearly the concern in her eyes, and the inward curl of her bottom lip. She was anxious, but determined.

"Beth," he said uncertainly. "When you were annoyed with me after I told you I was working for your uncle, did you mention it to anyone?"

"Is this what it's all about?"

Her mouth set in a firm line.

"No, of course I didn't. Why should I? When I returned to the Manor, I asked uncle about it during the evening meal. Truly, I have said nothing to anyone outside the family."

"Are you sure? It's important."

"If you think I would let something like that slip out, you don't know me at all well," said Beth sharply. "Frankly, I am upset you consider me likely to do such a thing."

Beth was angry. The two spots of colour on her cheeks a distinct warning .

She started to walk off, when he said.

"Well Fielding, the Excise man knows. A half of the hour ago I heard him telling someone in the orangery."

Beth turned slowly. The intensity of her emotions plain to see.

"Do you seriously believe I would reveal what you told me to a soul?" she uttered indignantly. "Marius, I am furious with you for even contemplating such a notion."

"Beth, I'm truly sorry," he said in abject apology. "I reacted without thinking. It's always been a failing of mine. I was devastated when I overheard what was said. You were an easy target to blame. Please, forgive me."

The last few words were said with such remorse, that Beth walked back to him and rested her hand on his arm.

"I shouldn't be so sensitive. When you first told me about uncle's request, as I said, I was put out. I did confront him at the dinner table. But, believe me, I didn't make it public. Now I must go back. Rowena is waiting for me. No doubt, Aunt Isabelle will be furious at my behaviour," she murmured.

"I'll return with you. Hopefully, I can pacify her."

Close together, they walked back to where a bewildered Rowena was standing. They went into the hall, joining the others as they made their way into the music room. Beth's aunt led the group, head high, a stiffened back. Her displeasure obvious to all.

CHAPTER THIRTY NINE

He dismounted in the Manor stable yard as the village church bell sonorously tolled midday. The deacon should inspire more enthusiasm, thought Marius, as the pauses between the peals lengthened, suggesting the sanctity of the moment had surrendered to boredom on the part of the bellringer. As the last reverberation echoed away, a groom came forward and took charge of his mount.

"Marius! Good to see you, my dear fellow!"

Conyers came through a gate, followed by Martineau, his nephew.

As Martineau disappeared towards to the house, Conyers asked eagerly, "Anything to tell me?"

They walked across the lawns and sat on the circular bench under the tree.

"Several things, sir. Though of no great importance, I'm afraid. Leastways, of no bearing on the smuggling problem."

"Oh!" Conyers was crestfallen. "Well, I suppose it's too early to expect any significant revelations."

"I'm not sure that, even with time, I shall uncover much that will be of value, Mr Conyers."

"Well, you might as well tell me what you have discovered so far."

"I was invited by Dr Brett to spend the evening with him. He had a strange assortment of guests. The Earl of Buckingham and his wife, Mr Phillips, the magistrate, and Mr Augustus Brown, a comestibles trader. Do you recall I mentioned how his coach was attacked on the way to Eridge Park. What amazed me was that Brown vehemently denied Jordan was his attacker."

"Why would he have cause to do that?" queried Conyers. "You told me he was convinced it was the man by his shoes."

"I couldn't understand it," Marius said wryly. "He was quite subdued. As though he had been pressed into reversing the accusation. I was angered by his change of heart, I must admit, and said as much. My outburst had a curious effect. It prompted argument and ill-temper for the rest of the evening. I was pleased to leave."

Conyers stared across the surrounding fields, shading his eyes from the sun.

"I have met the Buckinghams. In my opinion, he would most likely have seized the opportunity to bait some unfortunate. He has that turn of mind. Was he confrontational with the others?"

Marius nodded.

"I'm not surprised," added Conyers. "Did anything else come of the evening?"

"No. However, I went to the Johnsons' funeral on Monday. Afterwards, I had a lengthy discussion with Mr Russell."

"I know all about that," Conyers said sharply, dismissing the event. "Ralph attended the service, though I can't think why."

Marius was needled by the interruption. Although, anxious for any tidbit that might help combat the smuggling epidemic, there was no need for Conyers to ride roughshod over his telling of the episode.

He retaliated. "Did Beth tell you I overheard my name linked with yours at the concert at Eridge? It seems common knowledge I am now your lackey."

Conyers had the grace to look shamefaced. "Yes, she did. I cannot think how that might have happened. I have not mentioned it to a soul."

"Could it have been an inadvertent remark in front of the servants?"

"No"… there was hesitation in his voice. "I'm sure whenever I have made comment, they have not been present."

"So the topic has never been raised publicly?"

Conyers looked uncertain. "Well, I might have referred to it at the dinner table, in front of the Principal Minister. But, not outside the house." He was silent for a moment. "If one of the servants did overhear, it could only have been an unintentional remark in a tavern. It's easily done. Still, no harm. I'm sure it is of little consequence, my dear fellow."

Marius was not so sure.

"The other item of news I have is about a meeting with one of the freeholders."

Conyers was suddenly attentive.

"I received a message that someone wanted to have a quiet word with me. We met by the cold baths close to the Sussex Tavern."

"Why didn't you mention it when you were last here?"

"If you recall, sir," said Marius, "I was not entirely myself."

"Quite. I'd forgotten the circumstances," mumbled Conyers.

"It appears he is being threatened on two counts. As well as being pressed to sell contraband from his stalls in the Lower Walk, someone else is demanding he sell his title deeds."

"Has he any idea who is pressing him to do such a thing?"

"I said I could do little to help without knowing who was issuing the threats and substantiated by the strongest evidence."

Conyers sat on the bench deep in thought.

"This is an interesting development," he murmured. Then turned to Marius. "Why, may I ask, did he seek to speak with you?"

"It seems he has little time for the authorities in the town. He has no respect for the magistrate, and feels the constable is ineffectual," replied Marius. "In fact, he believes that if he speaks to either, his life could be in jeopardy. In his view, that's what happened to Loveday."

"God's teeth!" exclaimed Conyers.

A footmen came hurrying across the grass.

"Mrs Conyers has asked me to inform you the Principal Minister has arrived, sir."

CHAPTER FORTY

They were just as he had envisaged. The illustrations and the delicacy of the painted lines running their circumference were ideal.

It had been an easy ride to Tonbridge. Setting out soon after breakfast, he had arrived at the Wise Manufactory by late morning. His purchases had been carefully wrapped, and stowed in the saddle bags. After another tour of the showroom, he departed in good spirits, content that the wooden bowls would be well received.

Crossing the town bridge, Marius hesitated. Rather than face the uncertainty of eating on the road to The Wells, a good dinner might be best taken in the town. He turned and rode the short distance to the Rose and Crown opposite the corn market.

After a hearty platter of cold pork, washed down with cider, Marius was about to prepare a pipe, when the notion took him to stroll through the yard.

He halted by the table his fellow travellers had occupied on the journey from London. He rested his hand on the chair taken by Mrs Johnson, feeling the sudden loss, a sadness hard to explain. The memory of her sitting there, the smile lighting her face was vividly recalled. Almost immediately, Marius' melancholy was replaced by anger that she should have been so cruelly taken. He slowly retraced his steps. In his reverie, he almost walked into the innkeeper who was crossing under the archway to another part of the inn.

"I beg your pardon, sir," he exclaimed, as their shoulders brushed. "I didn't see you for the moment."

"My error, sir," said Marius. "I was lost in thought."

On a whim, he added, "Tell me, innkeeper, do you know someone by the name of Johnson? I'm told, he is a regular visitor to the inn."

The man's long green apron over his shirt and breeches was topped by a tousled head and a moustache of great expanse, covering much of his lower face. The eyes were bright and knowing. Marius realised that here was a fellow who would know a deal about people, but would likely keep his counsel.

"We do have a lot of travellers here, sir. I can't be knowing every one of them. Can you describe him? I might be a bit clearer in my mind if I could conjure a face."

Marius gave him a description, which he recognised was less than adequate. He suggested his height, his figure, and the manner in which Johnson dressed. However, he found it difficult to put into words the man's demeanour or character.

"No … I can't rightly say I've seen the gentleman," said the innkeeper, shaking his head. "Perhaps, if you had a likeness, I could have given a better opinion."

Marius thanked him, and continued his walk towards the bridge. A creaking, wooden structure that had clearly served the townsfolk well over the years. Now, it was showing signs of wear from the fall of hooves and the countless passing of wheels.

The water beneath was flowing sluggishly. Marius stopped to watch the boats rowed by those intent on enjoying an afternoon on the river. Some exhibited an ability to hold a straight course. The majority, though, steered erratically, frequently bumping into others, splashing all in the process.

He sauntered to the shade of an old chestnut tree, its branches reaching out over the water. Children with their parents strolled past. It was a joyous summer's day. The warm weather encouraging a lightening of spirit, a general air of well-being. As Marius watched the revellers, being on the water was suddenly appealing. With the cool breezes on the river, he would not get too hot, and the exercise would do him good.

He crossed back over the bridge, and found the boatman.

Moments later he was seated in a small boat, dipping the oars with only the faintest of splashes as he manoeuvred his way through the untidy flotilla. Marius rowed strongly, sending the craft forward at an even pace. It felt good to bend his back into a rhythm which demanded physical effort. After ten minutes of hard pulling, he found himself clear of other craft which tended to linger within sight of the castle and the bridge. The noise of the townsfolk faded.

Shipping the oars, he took his pipe from a pocket in the frock coat which lay on the wooden board opposite. The sound of the river lapping the banks, gurgling in the hollows, and gently slapping the sides of the boat was soothing. A moment of tranquillity to be savoured.

The pipe lit, Marius drew on it contentedly. The boat drifted lazily. Among the overhanging trees, birds were whistling, calling their rights of territory. A peaceful, memorable afternoon, when the simplest pleasures provide feelings of serenity.

He stretched back, putting his feet on the board seat. In a reclining position, he looked up at the blue sky, the sun warm on his face. The flow of the river gently carrying the boat along.

He wondered, idly, if one could sail on the river where it was less crowded. Where it was wider. Where did the river go? If it flows to the sea, could one sail down to the estuary? There were no boats of any size here, Marius noticed. But where it was wider and deeper, presumably there were bigger craft. What might they be used for? Carrying coal and wood perhaps? Taking cargoes or passengers down to ports at the river mouth? A silent, yet efficient means of transport. Marius sat up. A more serious use of the river had come to mind. Could they smuggle goods by river? He had heard from the constable that sales of illicit goods were also increasing in Tonbridge.

Returning the boat, he retraced his steps to the Rose and Crown. The innkeeper was again in the yard, and nodded to him as he made his way to the stables. Still deep in thought, the two men passed each other, before Marius turned, and said. "A moment, sir. May I again ask something of you?"

The innkeeper's eyes were guarded. Unconsciously, he wiped his hands on the apron.

"Do many craft come to Tonbridge? I mean large carriers of goods coming up river?"

"Yes sir, especially in the summer. They bring up coal, iron ingots for the smithies, and the like. They go back laden with grain, meat and wood," replied the innkeeper, still uncertain where the conversation was leading.

"Just between ourselves, you understand," said Marius leaning closer. "Can one buy anything from such boats?"

"Meaning what, sir?"

"You know. Is there, by chance, a little extra spirit for sale? Or perhaps some tobacco or tea?"

Marius was trying his utmost to appear a ready buyer of smuggled goods. Whether or not the deception was fooling the innkeeper, it was hard to tell.

"I have money that I could use freely for such purchases. Being new to the area, I'm at a loss to whom I should speak," he said, in a conspiratorial manner. Looking over his shoulder to check they were alone, Marius realised that the man could well be buying wines and spirits cheaply for his own premises.

"I would not be revealing the source of my information, you understand."

The innkeeper nodded, but his countenance was closed, his attitude non-committal, confirming Marius' dawning suspicions. He tried another tack.

"Let me put it this way," said Marius softly. "If I could set up a regular supply, buying what I require, I could be very generous to those who made such introductions for me."

The innkeeper nodded slowly several times. "I don't rightly know, sir. I'm not saying there is, I'm not saying there isn't. I could check, I suppose."

It was obvious that he was looking for a little silver to help negotiations.

Marius reached into an inner pocket, and discreetly passed over a handful of coins. They disappeared quickly beneath the apron.

"How do I know, sir," said the innkeeper, a little more affably, but with an edge to his voice, "you are not encouraging me to reveal something, then inform the constable?"

"It would be my loss, sir," commented Marius, with a knowing smile. "I would be giving you money which, doubtless, the constable would not repay, and I wouldn't get the goods."

"You best leave it with me, sir. As I say, I'll make enquiries. Come and see me again in a week's time. By the way, you'd better tell me your name."

"Marius Hope, innkeeper. Tell me one thing, if you would." Marius tapped his nose, as if a partner in intrigue. "If smuggled goods were coming into the town, wouldn't they best come by river?"

"You could be right, sir," said the innkeeper. "Particularly, as the constable's men are abroad at night, keeping a watch on the roads."

"So what do you think?"

"Well, if they were bringing in contraband by river, how do they get it to The Wells?" asked Roger.

"I have not considered that aspect. I'll deal with that later," responded Marius, still enthused by his deduction. "What I need is a map showing the River Medway. I must find out about the towns and villages along its course, and the best place for contraband to be unloaded and brought here."

He rose, left the orangery, heading for the library. Twenty minutes later he was back.

"I think I have the answer!" he said smugly. "Take a look at this chart. The ships come to the mouth of the estuary, and are met by smaller craft."

He tried to spread the map, but the heavy roll of linen resisted his efforts. Eventually, he secured an end with several ornaments and gradually unravelled the sheet.

"Then they ferry the goods to Tonbridge, and land the items for The Wells about here," declared Marius with a flourish, pointing to a broad area with his finger.

"I don't want to undermine your enthusiasm, Marius," Roger said calmly. "Do you realise that the mouth of the Medway is in the estuary of the River Thames?"

"So?"

"You're a Londoner. You must know how paranoid the good burghers are about the possibility of a Dutch fleet sailing up to the city walls again. That is why men-o-war are on permanent station in the roads. Do you think a ship full of contraband is going to run that gauntlet, then anchor in full view whilst its cargo is unloaded?"

"I hadn't thought of that," said Marius crestfallen. He sat back in the chair, and closed his eyes in thought.

Lighting a pipe, Roger added, "Nor should you forget the locks that run the length of the Medway. I can't see how your smugglers would negotiate them without waking the lockkeepers. If you look at the map, you'll see there are any number between Tonbridge and the sea."

Marius stared moodily through the windows of the orangery. For once he was completely deflated by his companion's logic. After some minutes, he turned to him.

"Roger, I want to tell you something I should have mentioned earlier," he said, clearing his throat. "I was told to be discreet, and to keep it to myself. However, I dislike keeping secrets from you, and I fear, others already know it."

Roger took the pipe from his mouth, and placed it carefully on the table. He leaned forward in his chair.

"When we were at Rusthall, the day I was brought into the meeting, you may recall Conyers and Sir Robert Walpole took me aside. The gist of it was I was asked to be Conyers' man. To report on anything untoward happening in the town."

Roger stifled a remark.

"The problem is, at the concert at Eridge last Tuesday, I overheard my name mentioned by that Excise man, Fielding. He was telling someone I was spying for The Lord of The Manor."

"Who was he talking to?"

"I don't know. When I told her I had agreed to work for her uncle, Beth was none too pleased with me. When I jumped to the conclusion that she might have, unwittingly, told someone, she was furious I should even consider it likely. However, someone at the Manor must have let it be known."

"Beth had reason to be upset if it led to the attack in the Cold Baths," said Roger, picking up his pipe. "If you didn't see the other person Fielding was talking to, did you get any impression of his clothes, height, demeanour?"

"No . . . I could only make out Fielding," reflected Marius.

"Have you mentioned it to Conyers?"

"Yes, when I was there a few days ago. He dismissed it as a servant overhearing comment in the house, and unthinkingly passing it on in a tavern."

"That is not your understanding of how it might have come about?"

"No. I'm positive there's more to it than that. I just wish I knew the answer."

CHAPTER FORTY ONE

"I can't think Walpole is likely to press for a military presence, so apply whatever measures you think fit. We need all the stallholders to trade in our goods. Do you understand what I'm saying, Mr Jordan?"

It was a hurried conversation. A moment snatched between engagements. The gentleman stood back in the shadows, lest he be seen in the farrier's company

"We must be sure to keep up the supply. Are you ready to receive tonight's shipment?'

"Quite prepared, sir. The packhorses will be here at two of the clock. They'll be unloaded, and safely on their way back before anyone stirs."

"I repeat, I want nothing to jeopardise our efforts, and we need to maintain ready quantities of tea, rum, brandy, wines, and silk. Can we do that?"

Perhaps, I didn't make myself clear, sir," said Jordan. "We can provide extra quantities of everything. All we need do is increase the number of horses in the convoy."

The gentleman was silent for a moment. Logic dictated he gave way to the man in charge of the operation.

"Well, make sure you keep up supplies to the stallholders, and get them all involved," he muttered.

CHAPTER FORTY TWO

"You seem to be acquainted with most everyone in the town, Roger, do you know a competent artist who could produce a likeness?"

"Why do you want such a thing? Is it for a certain lady?"

"No! I want a portrait of Johnson."

"Whatever for?"

"When I was in Tonbridge the other day, an innkeeper was reluctant to reveal if he knew Johnson, or he had visited the inn. He suggested he could better tell if he were presented with a likeness. "

"Well, I do believe you're in luck. I know the very person. A master at capturing likenesses."

As good as his word, he had commissioned a portrait artist. Roger then lingered in the vicinity of the White Bear Inn, waiting for Johnson to appear. On the second day, late in the afternoon, when close to giving up, Johnson came down the lane from Southborough and rode into the stable yard.

Following him into the inn, Roger was pleased to see the fellow brush the dust from his coat and call for some ale. Slipping out, he raced off to find the artist.

They had both enjoyed several glasses of Madeira at a table close to where Johnson was taking his ease. After half of the hour, when he retired to his room, Roger asked,

"Did you get a good look at him?"

"I would say I have seen enough, Master Dashwood," said the fellow in an equable tone. "Come and see me tomorrow afternoon. Then you'll discover if I have captured him."

At the top of Mount Pleasant they turned into a lane leading to a chapel. There were several wooden houses set back from the verge bordering the track. Roger led the way to one which was clearly in need of repair. The flimsy porch was in imminent danger of collapse, and a number of window panes were cracked. The limewash on the outside of the building was discoloured and peeling, many of the exposed timbers needed replacing.

199

Roger banged loudly on the door.

After some minutes, they heard shuffling in the passageway, and the door was opened to Roger's energetic knocking. An elderly woman, bowed by years, and despite the warmth of the day, wearing a heavy shawl, peered up at him. Her narrow face was lined, however her dark eyes were bright, undimmed by age.

"I see you have forgotten who is standing on your step, Martha," he declared. "Are you not going to invite me in?"

"It's not you I'm looking at, Master Roger," she replied, still staring myopically in their direction. "It's him! Your companion. He looks shifty. How do I know I can trust him?"

"Who is it Martha?" came a call.

"Quick, before Thomas gets angry with you," said Roger, in his mellowest tone. He smiled at Marius. "Martha used to work for my uncles at the Manor."

"Whoever it is, tell them to come in." The voice, again from deep within.

Martha was not convinced, nevertheless she slowly edged aside to let Roger pass. Marius made to follow, but she blocked his way. The man in the house shouted once more, "For pity sake, woman, let them pass."

Marius hurried along the passage, to emerge into a large, high-ceilinged studio at the rear of the building. Peering round Roger's shoulder, there propped at an easel was the artist.

"Ah, Master Roger, I was wondering when we might have the pleasure of your company."

Putting down his brushes and palette, the man swung himself sideways into a seat. It was then apparent that below a normal-sized head was the stunted body of a dwarf.

"Let me offer you, and your young friend, some refreshment. Martha, pour some cider for our gentlemen visitors."

"Thomas, I want you to meet Marius Hope. Marius, this is my old friend, Thomas Loggan."

Thomas Loggan settled contentedly back into the well-cushioned chair.

"So, old friend, is it ready?" asked Roger softly.

"Actually, it was easier than I thought. It was done by the time we had dinner," replied Loggan.

He pulled himself out the chair, and hobbled to the far side of the studio. As he passed, Marius saw a face lined with experience and suffering. Eyes bright, alert to everything around him. His dark hair full over a massive brow. He wore the simple, brown woven clothes of an artisan. Tucking several rolls of parchment under his arm, he limped to a table, and began unrolling the sheets as his housekeeper returned with the cider. They took the proffered mugs.

The drawings were spread across the table. There, before them was the face of Mr Johnson. His piercing eyes, heavily-veined nose and aggressive mouth all clearly defined in both sketches.

"Remarkable, sir," exclaimed Marius.

Roger smiled, nodding to Thomas.

"Didn't I tell you, Marius, this is a man of considerable talent. You should see his paintings, they are quite outstanding."

While he drank his cider, the artist showed Marius a number of his works.

"Before I go back to London, Mr Loggan, could you undertake a portrait for me. I shall be quite prepared to pay your price."

"When you are ready, Mr Hope," he replied. "You now know where I live. I also have a hut at the end of the Walks. If you wish, you can visit me there."

When the two drawings were rolled and safely wrapped, and Marius had paid for the two works, Loggan said to him.

"We've known Master Roger since he was a child. When he asked me to prepare a likeness, I did not ask him the reason. However, Mr Hope, I am a righteous man, please assure me these are not for any unlawful purpose."

Marius returned his gaze. "You need have no such concerns, Mr Loggan."

He hesitated, then, glancing at Roger, continued, "I believe this man killed his wife, sir. I have no way of proving it. Yet, he is acting suspiciously, and I need to find out where and what he is doing, then, maybe I can secure his arrest."

"Marius thinks that with a likeness, people will be able to identify the person. To prove he has been up to no good." added Roger.

Loggan nodded, and leaning heavily on a stick, escorted them to the door.

CHAPTER FORTY THREE

They were dining in the Sussex Tavern when the constable stopped by their table. He accepted the invitation to join them, and when their pipes were safely lighted, the conversation turned, as ever, to the overriding topic. The constable waved an arm to clear the smoke.

"By the way, Doctor, have you heard anything more from the freeholder who wanted a private word with you?"

Roger looked sharply at Marius, who coloured slightly under his gaze.

"No, Mr Russell, I'm still waiting for him to contact me."

"Well sir, if you hear anything, let me know."

After Russell had drained his glass and departed, Roger said in a low voice, "I didn't know you had mentioned our meeting with Clifford to the constable. I understood he did not want him involved."

"He did," replied Marius. "I considered what he said with great care. Eventually, I decided that he has nothing to fear, and it would be better to have Mr Russell on our side. I didn't reveal Clifford's name."

"Surely, that was not your decision? It seems to me you've been a bit high-handed, Marius, telling a man Clifford doesn't trust."

"I thought it was for the best," replied Marius, nettled by Roger's outburst.

"Well, I hope your faith is well-founded. You don't have cause to regret your openness."

"Don't you believe him to be trustworthy?"

"I do not need to give him the benefit of the doubt. Frankly, neither do you. I just cannot see why you were so anxious to mention the meeting to him. What compelled you to do such a thing?"

Marius was irritated by Roger's comments. At the same time, he realised he had overstepped the boundaries of confidentiality Clifford had urged upon him. Moreover, he had also told Conyers of the incident. Had he unthinkingly put the freeholder at risk?

"Perhaps, I have been a little hasty."

There was an awkward silence, during which both men withdrew into their own thoughts. Finally, Marius said, "I have to tell you, Roger, I also told Conyers of the meeting. I even gave him Clifford's name."

Roger did not reply, but looked deeply into his glass.

"I did what I believed was for the best," said Marius, annoyed with himself for giving in to foolish impulse. "I still feel that to be the case, if it helps curb the smuggling and reveals those behind it."

"Everyone knows who's behind it. There are any number of smuggling gangs looking for opportunities to expand their networks," Roger snapped. "Selling to the company in The Wells is a perfect way for them to do business."

"I'm not sure I agree with you," murmured Marius. "The constable mentioned that smugglers supply goods, they rarely have to coerce people into selling them. They leave that to others."

"Well, they're in a hurry. The season ends at the end of September."

"Perhaps, though I still feel that there is more to it."

"What do you mean?"

"I'm not sure," Marius spoke slowly, weighing every word. "I have the impression someone is behind it all, providing the necessary funding, intent on creating disharmony."

"And making a lot of money," Roger declared. "Whoever it is must be investing heavily, but the returns would be substantial."

Marius effected not to hear him.

"Frankly, I have my doubts that anyone is masterminding such a scheme," Roger continued. "It's likely no more than over-ambitious fishermen on the coast taking advantage of The Wells' transient population. You mark my words."

Marius looked across at his companion.

"In which case Clifford has little to fear. Telling Conyers and Russell should not lead to any repercussions."

But he was aware of a slight note of concern in his voice.

The sudden evacuation of tables around them gave notice of Mrs Porter's impending arrival. With as much haste as was consistent with good manners, a number of the company departed the tavern. Others, with beverages untouched, plates still laden, sat in silent expectation of her demands. Affecting as much nonchalance as they could muster.

However, Mrs Porter was in no mood to linger. At that moment she was not concerned with demanding dues, marking payments in her book. She came directly to their table.

"I've been hoping to find you these past few days, Doctor," she murmured breathlessly. She cast a glance around her. No one was close. Leaning forward, she said in a hushed voice. "Daniel Clifford wants to see you."

"When?"

"It has to be tonight. He said he could meet you at the same place as before, at eleven of the clock. Can you be there?" Mrs Porter asked anxiously.

"That's not a problem," murmured Marius. "Just tell him to make sure no one knows of the meeting, or follows him."

A pang of conscience prompted the comment. Marius realised that the broken confidence was now troubling him.

"He told me to say he will have all the evidence you need," whispered Mrs Porter. "He will also have someone with him who will confirm what is going on."

"Will he now?" Then tell him Roger Dashwood will accompany me. He knows he need have no fear of him."

She nodded, "I'll let him know to expect two gentlemen at the baths."

Then, in a louder voice, "Thank you, Dr Hope. That settles the matter, nicely."

Mrs Porter rose, turned her head slowly to espy others whose fees were unpaid. Then intent on pursuing the company who had resumed their seats near the Well, she strode purposefully in that direction.

"I shall leave too, Marius," said Roger. "I'll see you later at Ashenhurst House."

He drank from the glass of wine, untouched on the table since the difference of opinion with Roger. His mind turned to the forthcoming assignation with Clifford, wondering what the strength of the information might be. Hopefully, it would help identify those responsible for distributing the contraband. He now felt sure it was being organised for a purpose. Would the illicit imports continue to grow, swamping the trade of the genuine shopowners? Was it being done to upset the business of The Wells? If so … Marius' thoughts were interrupted.

"Why, Dr Hope, how are you? I was just saying to the earl, what a splendid evening we had at Dr Brett's. He is such an excellent host, don't you think?"

"Then this dreadful woman came to my table. At the meal at Bretts, she said nothing. I thought she was the subdued wife of an overbearing husband. How wrong I was. She was talkative beyond measure. She and that pompous, would-be courtesan occupied me for a full hour, talking inanities about the social life of the town."

Marius was still fuming about the chance meeting at the tavern with the Earl of Buckingham and his Lady.

"She is well-known for her gushing, small-minded chatter, Marius. There are many like her in The Wells." Roger was amused at Marius' irritation.

"As a resident, I should imagine she is at her wit's end during the winter, when she has few on whom she can impose her sparkling conversation. Anyway, let's ignore her. I want to discuss the meeting with Clifford."

"Mrs Porter said he will be accompanied. Unfortunately, she didn't give us a clue to his companion's identity."

"She is merely the messenger, Roger. I'm sure she knows little of what Clifford wants of me, or even his predicament."

"Mm . . . what you do want me to do?"

"We'll split up. I think on this occasion we have to be more careful. I shall go to the bathhouse just before eleven of the clock, and stand under the trees to the right of the entrance, as I did previously. If anything is untoward, I can slip into the wooded area to the side of the baths. I would like you to be across the track. When I meet with Clifford and his unknown companion, await my signal."

"If you don't shout out in the first minute, I join you, is that it?"

Marius nodded.

"To be honest, Marius, I don't think it much of a plan. We have to consider the possibility that Clifford won't be there, and the ruffians who attacked you in the cold baths might, and they could easily overpower you before I had the chance to intervene. If you believe him trustworthy, why don't we ask the constable and his men to accompany us?"

"No," said Marius decisively. "I gave Clifford my word such meetings would be just between us. No one else present. I can't change that agreement. He wouldn't trust me."

"Marius, the rules have already been altered. You've told the constable, and given his name to Conyers."

Marius stared at Dashwood. Hesitatingly, he said, "I believe I made an error in breaking Clifford's confidence. I was full of myself, too ready to show I was succeeding where others were making little progress. Maybe I wanted Conyers to think well of me."

"Surely, Marius, you can see the merits in safeguarding your person. After all, you've been attacked once. It's a simple precaution. Clifford need not even know of it."

"Let us hear no more about the constable, Roger. My mind is made up. I'll meet you in front of the lodging house at half past ten of the clock. That will give us more than enough time to take up our positions."

"As you wish, Marius," said Roger coldly. "This time, however, you can rest assured I shall be armed."

CHAPTER FORTY FOUR

He shivered. Not cold, more in anticipation, even concern. He had been squatting among the trees with a view across the track to where Marius was supposedly hiding. It was a moonlit night, with hard shadows casting deep pits of darkness. Marius was there, somewhere, but he could discern no movement. There was no sign of his presence. Why doesn't he wave a hand, some slight indication? He was becoming anxious.

They had reached the bathhouse in good time, and taken up their agreed positions. That seemed ages ago. A coach had passed earlier, followed shortly by two figures on horseback. No one on foot. I'll allow another ten minutes, he decided, then cross the track.

Time passed slowly. His legs ached with the strain of bending low. Easing himself up, he moved forward slowly, to the edge of the shadows. Then, in a crouching run, he crossed the track and gained the standing of trees opposite.

"Marius?" he queried in a loud whisper.

"You make enough noise to wake the dead, sir," said a voice in his ear.

Roger was startled. "I couldn't see anything of you. And it's long past the time when Clifford should have arrived."

"I was thinking the same. I suppose we shall have to abandon our vigil, and see him another day," Marius said disconsolately. "I doubt he will be coming now."

"This was the agreed spot, was it not?"

"If you remember, last time we met in front of the bathhouse. But, at a later hour. At eleven of the clock, there are still people abroad. Clearly, we couldn't loiter in front of the building. I presumed Clifford would take the same precautions as ourselves."

"Shall we return to our lodgings?"

"I suppose we must. There's no point in waiting any longer."

"I wonder if he could be on the other side of the baths? He could have done the same as us. Stand among the bushes on the slope."

"Surely, he would have shown himself by now?" After all, he must have been aware of you scuttling across the track. He couldn't miss you in the moonlight."

"Well, before we go back, shall we check if he's there?"

"Right, I'll slip past the front of the bathhouse."

He eased himself forward, and took stock of the lane, alert to the possible sounds of travellers.

"Follow me," urged Marius. "If you hear a vehicle or riders, hide yourself."

They moved carefully to the edge of the building, and then walked rapidly across its wide frontage. Nearing the entrance, the sound of wheels approaching at speed caught their ears.

Suddenly, a coach, its passengers clearly in a hurry, was closing on them rapidly.

"Hide in the shadow of the doorway. I'll take the alcove by the buttress," Marius hissed, moving swiftly forward and darting into the angle of the jutting support.

The coach rolled by, the driver's whip cracking, the jarring sounds of revellers inside the rocking vehicle. Then it was gone. Silence.

"Are you all right, Roger?" said Marius after a moment. There was no reply.

"Roger!" he called.

Standing upright, he peered round the buttress into the shadows of the doorway. Dashwood was not there. One side of the double doors was ajar. In two strides Marius was in the porchway, and pushed open the door. Roger was bending over a figure on the floor. Shafts of moonlight illuminated the prostrate, bloodied form of Daniel Clifford.

CHAPTER FORTY FIVE

His face was grave.

"I tended him as best I could, but he was in a sorry state. Eventually, when I could do no more, Dashwood and I made to pick him up. But he was in considerable pain."

"What did you do then?" enquired Russell.

"I left Dashwood with him, and went to Dr Brett's house. It was the only place I could think of. I fear he was not best pleased to be wakened," said Marius, grimly recalling the moment. "However, having explained to one of his servants that his services were desperately needed, he came from his bed and ushered me into the library.

"I had little time to explain. But Brett has a quick mind, and rapidly grasped the essentials. Taking up his medical bag, we went first to a shed by the side of the house, and took a stout board. I carried it down to the bathhouse. Brett applied tinctures and salves to Clifford's obvious wounds. After which the three of us got him onto the board, and Dashwood and I carried him to the doctor's house."

"Did anyone see you?"

"Fortunately, no. The servants were abed. We managed to transport him up to a room at the back of the house. I'm sure he has internal injuries. It's hard to tell just how serious they are."

"You say he had a companion," said Russell, relighting his pipe, which had gone out whilst his attention was elsewhere. "Where was he when all this was happening?"

"It may have been this unknown fellow who assaulted Clifford. There was certainly no one else near the baths. Leastways, not that we could see."

"Can Clifford identify his attacker?" enquired the constable.

"He hasn't regained consciousness," replied Marius, wringing his hands. Now dreading that he had given out Clifford's name. "Frankly, I'm worried he may never do so."

"Is that Brett's opinion as well?"

"It is an unspoken understanding between us. If he can last through the next few days, he may have a chance. But, neither of us could gauge the extent of his injuries.

He may well have suffered damage to various organs when his ribs were broken. We simply cannot say."

"Will you tell his wife?"

"I think, in the circumstances, it best come from you. The trouble is, I don't want to reveal Clifford's whereabouts. If his assailants think he is still alive, they may try again."

"But, you can't keep the poor woman away from him. Supposing he were to die before she had the chance to see him," declared Russell, standing up impatiently. "I am afraid, Doctor, she will have to see him."

"In which case I'll accompany you when you visit her," said Marius, accepting the gravity of the constable's remark. "After that, I shall ride over to Mr Conyers, and tell him of the incident."

"I suppose you can trust him, Dr Hope?"

Marius stared intently at the constable. Hesitatingly, he replied, "I'm not entirely certain, Mr Russell."

"You have some slight concerns?"

"At the moment, they are more uncertainties."

"Do you feel able to confide in him?"

Again Marius hesitated. "I'm not sure I should, for the moment."

"That's your choice, sir," said the constable. There was a depth of meaning in his words.

They halted outside the house in Frog Lane. When the door opened, Mrs Clifford gasped and clutched her hands together.

"What have you come to tell me?" Her face was drawn, her eyes quick and staring.

"May we come in, Mrs Clifford?" asked the constable.

She stepped back, allowing them access. In the small, cluttered living room her children were standing close together, silent and fearful.

"Mrs Clifford, I have grave news, I'm afraid," Russell said in a quiet voice. She stood stock still, her eyes now closed, summoning up an inner strength to ready herself for the constable's next words.

"Your husband has been the victim of a savage assault. He has been severely injured."

"But, he … he is still alive?" Tears ran down her cheeks as she waited for the answer.

"Yes, though …"

She exhaled slowly, then cried. "Thank God! … Thank God!"

"Mrs Clifford, your husband is dangerously ill," added Marius. He glanced towards the constable. "You must come to him immediately."

She turned to Marius.

"He's at death's door, isn't he?"

"Yes, Mrs Clifford, he is. I have done what I can for him. The rest is in the hands of the Lord."

She nodded, then wiping her eyes, went to her children and comforted them.

A short time later, Marius and Mrs Clifford walked to Dr Brett's house. It had been difficult to deter the constable from accompanying them. Marius had declared that the fewer who knew his whereabouts the safer he would be.

Mr Russell had not taken kindly to being excluded, until Mrs Clifford had declared she would thank him not to be present. Without further comment he had bowed his head in her direction, and strode out the house.

It had been a painful moment for Marius to witness her distress at the sight of her husband's body. In the daylight, the wounds were even more pronounced. He lay on the narrow cot, deep in a coma, barely breathing. His face sickly pale, twitching frequently as pain coursed through his limbs.

Mrs Clifford knelt by his side, stroked his forehead, and murmured in his ear. She stayed by him for some minutes. Then rose, and said. "Thank you, Doctor, for attending him. Now, he needs me as well. I'm sure he heard me. I must come back after I have seen to the children."

Marius was alarmed. "Mrs Clifford, rest assured I will do all within my power to bring him back to us. Please recognise he is in much danger. Not just from his injuries, but from those who inflicted them upon him. If they discover he still lives, they likely will try again. Next time, perhaps, with more success."

Mrs Clifford bit at her lip. "He needs me here, Doctor. I have to see him."

"Well, if you think it wise, do so before it is light of a morning, and after dusk. Whatever you do, make no mention he is alive, or tell his whereabouts to a soul."

They made a quiet exit through a side door.

After parting, Marius went to the constable's office.

"I'm sorry, Mr Russell, for the secrecy. I meant no slight, My overriding concern is for Clifford's safety. I'm sure you appreciate that."

"Do you honestly think I would reveal to anyone where he is, Dr Hope? If you do, you have a low opinion of this constabulary."

It was evident Russell was still smarting from his dismissal. Employing his age-old tactic of changing the subject, Marius remarked, "By the way, Mr Russell, I have a notion to explore the Medway River. It could well be a possible route for the contraband. I have to go in that direction tomorrow, so Dashwood and I thought we might check if the smugglers use the waterway to transport their goods."

"I suggest you take the greatest care, Doctor. If you come across anything, don't be foolhardy and tackle it on your own. I don't want to learn of yet another incident."

Leaving the office, he turned towards Bishops Down, climbing the path to the

Queen's Grove. The wind was blustery, and the weak sun unlikely to tempt any but the most hardy to endure the waters at this early hour.

Marius sat on a bench, staring down at the Walks. A barrage of questions arose. When Marius had seen the broken body of Clifford on the unyielding flagstones, his first thoughts had been, who had known of the meeting? Whom had he told?

The images had been sharp. Dashwood, Russell and Conyers. No one else. Had one of the three been responsible for this savage attack? Had one of them feared what the freeholder might reveal? His mind refused to disengage from the endless merry-go-round of unanswered questions. In the lukewarm light of day, he accepted that Roger could readily be excluded.

That left Russell and Conyers.

Marius reviewed the occasions when Russell had faced adversity. He had witnessed the personal horrors the constable experienced when confronted by the two fires, and the tragic deaths on the racecourse. He had seen the depths of sorrow and hurt portrayed in the man's eyes, and the determination to avenge such wrongs. Marius came to accept that the constable would never countenance such violence.

Which left Conyers.

Once more, the spectre of The Lord of The Manor loomed. The thought that he could well be working for his own gain, oblivious to the shattered lives of others, could not be easily dispelled.

CHAPTER FORTY SIX

"I do not wish to be acquainted with every little act, sir. I have stated what I want. Just bring it about without connection to my name and with all speed. Is that understood?"

"I am well aware of your demands, sir. But, there are times, and this is one, when you should be aware of what has happened."

"Frankly, when you resort to violence, I most certainly do not want to hear of it. Just don't kill any more freeholders."

"What I am trying to say, sir, is that he might well be dead."

"What!" the gentleman was incandescent with rage. "You fool! I've told you repeatedly, injure, possibly maim them, but do not kill. Loveday was the example. That was enough. Otherwise, it could undermine all my work, and be an expensive lesson for us all! For your sake, you'd better hope Clifford lives. Do you hear?"

CHAPTER FORTY SEVEN

"My husband prompted me to ask if you were free to join us for dinner next Saturday, Dr Hope?" said Mrs Conyers brightly. "Before Beth returns to her family."

He was startled. Beth's colour deepened. "I was going to tell you, Marius, but Aunt Isobelle has mentioned it before I had the chance."

Mrs Conyers had come into the hall as Beth and he were making their farewells. Interrupting the couple, she had blithely proffered the invitation. Suddenly, Marius was saddened to think this might be the end of their brief acquaintance. In that moment he knew his feelings for her were growing deeper. Marius had been discreetly holding her hand. Involuntarily, his grip tightened.

Beth gasped, and glancing up, caught the look of hurt on his face.

"I am only going home for a short while," she said quickly. "Father has written. He wants me home to celebrate mother's birthday. I shall be away no more than a week."

"Oh," was all Marius could utter. Both were silent.

"Er … Thank you , Mrs Conyers. I should be delighted."

"Until Saturday, Dr Hope!" she called, as he rode down the sweeping drive.

Roger was having more luck than Marius in the Gaming Room. He had enjoyed a number of winning hands at Pharaoh, and held his own at Hazard. Marius had lost steadily. Leaving the tables, they went in search of supper. At the table Roger enquired. "What do you care to drink, Marius? Something that will help you concentrate, I should think. I don't believe you even saw the cards you were dealt."

"I'm a little out of sorts, Roger. It will pass."

"I hope so. When you are gambling, you should have all your wits about you."

Over their meal, Marius studied his companion.

"I've been thinking, Roger," he said slowly. "You and I should return to the hunt, to discover where Mr Johnson goes. Perhaps, striking north of Tonbridge towards Sevenoaks, to check if he is known in any of the villages. He may drink in Tonbridge, but he doesn't lodge in any of the inns. Yet, he is frequently away from the White Bear several days at a time."

"Is that what has been occupying your thoughts?"

"No." He hesitated, reluctant to reveal the true reason. Someone was prying. He started to withdraw to his old self, putting up protective shutters. Roger watched him closely.

"You don't have to tell me, old friend."

The wine was at Marius' elbow. He poured for both of them.

"I have the strongest notion Conyers could be at the heart of this smuggling affair. I know I've voiced it before, but it seems the meetings he arranges could simply be to provide him with the news of others.

"As you've said yourself, nothing ever comes of the discussions at the Manor. Just think, the magistrate tells him where his surveillance people are stationed. They see neither hide nor hair of the smugglers' caravans. The constable reports the displacement of his deputies. Incidents happen when they are elsewhere. The Excise officers outline their strategy. They never uncover sign of the smugglers' whereabouts or sources. Frankly, Roger, the more I think about it, the more convincing is the case against him."

"What are you going to do?" Dashwood asked in a neutral voice.

"Nothing! I have no proof. What I do know is that I cannot continue to enjoy his hospitality for much longer."

"What about Beth?"

Marius twirled the glass in his hand.

"Roger, today Beth told me she was going back to her family. I was devastated. I have been unable to think of anything since."

"My dear fellow, you must do something about it. If your heart dictates, follow her. Don't just allow her to leave."

Marius smiled. "It's not as bad as that. She is coming back. What surprised me, when her aunt told me, was the sudden realisation of how much I feel for her."

"Love does strange things, Marius. No wonder you couldn't play cards," said Roger, recharging their glasses.

"I'm going there for dinner next Saturday. Mrs Conyers has invited me to bid Beth goodbye. After that, I won't be going there again, until I have either proved Conyers is central to this whole business, or he has no connection whatsoever with those involved in the smuggling . . . or the purchase of the titles."

Roger kept his counsel.

"I'm also very worried about Clifford. You were right, Roger. I should not have exposed him to danger by revealing his name. If Conyers were the architect of his beating, I will never forgive myself. What is more, if he survives, can we protect him?"

They lapsed into silence. After several minutes Marius again took up the conversation.

"I know you will not agree, but I spoke with the constable earlier today. We both went to see Mrs Clifford, and I took her to visit her husband at Brett's house. It was all I could do to persuade her not to tell a soul that he was alive, or his whereabouts. She finally acknowledged that if word were abroad, whoever they are might attempt to finish the deed."

Roger nodded.

"I have something to tell you, Marius. Whilst you were at Rusthall today, I rode out to the village of Groombridge. Actually, I should say I followed someone to Groombridge ... Nathaniel Jordan. Guess who he met?"

"Roger, you really are the most exasperating fellow. Who was it?"

"John Bowra."

"I've heard the name. Who is he exactly?"

"He is a surveyor of some standing. He has designed and had built a good many properties around The Wells. Though, perhaps, his greatest work so far is the construction of a mansion in Groombridge. Like yourself, young Bowra's father was a medical man in Sevenoaks."

"I wonder why Jordan wanted to speak with him? From what you say, Bowra seems a reputable fellow. Why would he wish to associate with the likes of the farrier?"

"Actually, there are strong rumours Bowra has two sides to his life. On one hand, he is a successful draughtsman. On the other, he is suspected of controlling a smuggling ring that supplies establishments in London."

Before Marius could react, Mrs Porter bustled into the salon. Surveying the crowd, she made directly for their table.

"Sit down, Mrs Porter," invited Marius, then in a whisper. "Have you spoken with Mrs Clifford?"

She nodded mutely.

"Before we came to the Rooms," said Marius compassionately, "I visited Clifford. There is little change. He has suffered a massive beating. At the moment he is stable, in that his heart is regular and there are no sign of a fever. But he is still in a coma."

"Thank you for telling me, Doctor. I know his wife is out of her mind with worry. But she wouldn't tell me why."

Mrs Porter, sat there for several minutes with her head bowed. Finally, she sighed and made to rise.

"Sit if you would a moment longer, Mrs Porter," said Marius.

It was almost unheard of for the dues collector to take her ease at a table among the company. There was a lull in the surrounding conversations as she became the object of diners' interest. Slowly, the chatter rose to its previous level.

Roger sat opposite the collector, wondering when her thoughts would turn to her major preoccupation. Looking at him, she gave a half-smile. "No worry, Mr Dashwood. You're safe for the moment."

Once more, she rose to leave. Yet hesitated.

"There is something I wanted to mention, Dr Hope," she murmured.

Roger and he looked up enquiringly, Mrs Porter again subsided into the chair. Looking about her, she whispered.

"Mr Nash has been threatened. There are people who want him to remain in the Wells, not return to Bath."

"I thought he was staying longer than normal," Roger observed. "He is usually quite insistent that once everything is organised, he is off to Bath. Yet, here he is, still in residence some months into the season."

"What was the nature of the threat, Mrs Porter?" asked Marius.

Suddenly, she seemed reluctant to answer, colouring slightly. She dropped her head.

"It was something he let slip when in his cups the other evening. I'm not sure I should comment on the reason, Dr Hope," Mrs Porter mumbled. "It's a private matter."

"Come, Mrs Porter, at a time like this, we can have few secrets between us," Marius replied in a low voice.

She was unsure. It would not be thought kindly to reveal anything of the darker side of her employer's life.

"I can't say, sir," she blustered. "It wouldn't be seemly."

"Mrs Porter, if I judge the situation correctly, a slightly bruised ego does not compare with the attempted murder of Mr Clifford," said Marius grimly.

It came out with a rush.

"Mr Nash, through no fault of his own, owes a lot of money, Gambling debts, which he cannot meet. Someone has purchased his promissory notes. Whoever it is, is threatening to reveal that he is without means if he leaves for Bath. It would be a scandal for a gentleman in his position."

"What does he intend to do, Mrs Porter?"

"As far as I know, Dr Hope, he is too terrified to do anything, for fear the news might become public."

When she had left, Marius said, "What's your opinion, Roger?"

"It could well be true, Marius," he leaned across the table and whispered.

"Just between ourselves, I have heard rumours that our Master of Ceremonies has been involved in, shall we say, manipulating the cards. There are several people I know who believe Beau Nash has gotten himself caught up in a scheme to fix the tables," Roger said uneasily. "If it became public that he was also penniless, his reputation would be at an end. Occasionally he wins, but, it appears he more frequently loses. Lord Chesterfield said he wondered not that Nash could lose, but where he gets the money to lose."

CHAPTER FORTY EIGHT

"It must be a powerful reason for Johnson to journey this way so often. Do you think he is someone's guest whilst recovering from the deaths of his wife and niece?"

Halting on the ridge at Bidborough, Marius had put his thoughts into words.

"Most probably," Roger agreed. "I have the impression he would soon conjure an invitation from someone of note."

"It's like searching for a needle in a veritable haystack," exclaimed Marius. "I cannot think we shall have much success in running him to ground."

"By the bye, I made no mention of Johnson at my recent meeting with Mr Phillips," said Roger, looking sideways at his companion. "And, of course, not a word about Clifford. However, I did tell him I had seen Jordan with John Bowra."

Marius frowned at the thought that it had been raised at Roger's weekly review with the magistrate.

"You mean their meeting at Groombridge?" he qualified.

Roger looked at him quizzically. "Why not? I happen to work for Phillips. It was quite trivial."

"It's just that I feel uncertain about Phillips knowing as much as ourselves," remarked Marius. "I suppose you have told him of all the incidents that have occurred during recent weeks?"

"Most things."

He was becoming sensitive to Marius' unstated concerns. His tone was a little sharper.

"Phillips says I am his eyes and ears. In truth, all I do is pass on information which, for the most part, is common currency."

"Perhaps I am naturally suspicious," said Marius, yawning. Since the night of Cliford's attack he had enjoyed little sleep, frequently spending long hours at his bedside. It was Dr Brett who had suggested he would take over Marius' duties and that Marius take a few days rest.

They descended the hill alongside the quarry towards the town.

In the Chequers Inn there was desultory chatter among the few early drinkers. A tap boy appeared, several glasses of ale clutched in his hands. Seeing the two men, he called over his shoulder for the landlord.

Another door swung open to emit his bulky presence. A tall fellow, with a ruddy complexion, above a thickening girth. He was wearing the traditional innkeeper's apron. Momentarily halting, a guarded look fleetingly crossed his face.

"And what can I do for you two fine gentlemen?"

"We would like beds, sir, for this night, if you please," requested Marius.

The innkeeper made a show of checking a dog-eared book. Eventually, he nodded.

"Do you need help with your baggage, gentlemen?"

"We have it in our hands, thank you, landlord," Marius replied, lifting his saddle bag. "If someone could show us to our room, that will be sufficient."

The tap boy led them up the narrow stairs to a small, plain room overlooking the stables. In it were two narrow cots with rough, woollen coverings. Depositing their saddlebags on a chair they returned to the taproom below.

"Not a very cheery reception, Marius. I'm sure there are better rooms to be had."

"Perhaps we should have stayed at the Rose and Crown across the street. Still, it doesn't matter too much, we are only here one night," Marius replied. "More importantly, if we are to make enquiries about Mr Johnson, whom do we ask?"

"If Johnson stopped here, he would have tied his horse to the hitching rail by the stables. I don't think we are likely to get much from the innkeeper, let's show Johnson's likeness to the groom. He could well have seen him. He may even have noted the route he took."

Whilst Roger returned briefly to their room, Marius stood at the front door looking towards the corn market in the centre of the town. Burly labourers were unloading sacks of grain. Merchants inspected their contents, searching for signs of wild rye, while farmers looked on anxiously. A stiff breeze occasionally wafted the wheat ears from the buyers' hands, sending them swirling across the paved market floor.

Marius caught a slight movement. Turning he glimpsed the landlord in a doorway taking stock of him. He quickly turned on his heel and slammed the door.

When Roger joined him, he said in a low voice. "I believe someone has been searching my bag, Marius."

"Anything missing?"

"No ... leastways, not that I could detect. I have the feeling some of my things had been disarranged, and I'm sure the oilskin covering Johnson's likeness has been unwrapped."

"Whilst you were upstairs, the landlord was surveying me very intently. I wonder what that suggests?"

"Perhaps, we should find other lodgings?" Roger said uneasily.

"Well, I am sure we are safe for one night. We'll be back at Ashenhurst House tomorrow."

In the yard, they waited for the groom to seat a large gentleman on his horse. Heaving him up the mounting steps was demanding. It was a monumental effort, on both parts, to get him into the saddle. Patting the horse's hind quarters as it moved off, and deftly palming the coins he had been given, the groom turned towards them.

"Gen'lemen, shall I get your mounts?"

"Before you do so," said Marius, "can you spare a moment?"

Roger unfurled the rolled parchment.

"Have you, by chance, seen this man whenever he has visited to the inn?"

The groom stared at the likeness, stroking his chin. "I may 'ave. What's it to you?"

Roger was disarming. "This man is thought by the magistrate in The Wells to be a possible witness. Nothing more. As we were in Tonbridge, Mr Phillips asked us to make enquiries on his behalf."

The man was clearly not at ease, although less defensive. He continued to gaze at the likeness.

"Well, I 'ave seen him 'ere in the yard. Tended "is 'orse a few times. Though, I've never passed the time of day with "im."

"When was the last time you saw him?" Roger enquired.

"I would think about four, maybe five days, ago. My mate might 'ave seen "im since. 'E was working in the stables in the afternoons last week."

"When is your mate next here?"

"'E's 'ere already. 'E's mucking out the stables."

Just then a figure, trundling a barrow of well-used straw, came through large, double doors into the yard.

"Ned, come over 'ere! These two gen'lemen wan'' a word!"

The man hesitated. Turning his head to check a route for possible flight.

"Don't take on! They jus' wants a word."

Slowly the man and his barrow approached them.

Marius edged away as the stench reached his nostrils.

"Ned, I understand you know of this man?" Roger said forcefully. Not allowing the groom to deny knowledge of Johnson. Ned looked at his fellow-worker, undecided if he were about to be blamed for some misdeed.

"It's alright, Ned," said Roger. "As your friend is aware, it's no more than a minor enquiry. We were requested to seek this fellow's presence, for he is needed as a possible witness."

"To what?" responded the groom nervously.

"A small matter … scarcely of importance. His comments might help to clarify matters for Mr Phillips, The Wells' magistrate. As to the nature of the request, I believe it concerns a certain personage's will."

The suggestion that it was nothing criminal, or possibly related to the man's own deeds, made him more responsive. In a high-pitched tone, almost a whine, he said,

"Yer, he comes here of'en. Though, I ain't seen him for two, maybe three days. He'll be by shortly, you mark my words." Ned wiped his hands on his breeches. "Not a very good tipper, though. A bit surly, if yer asks me. Full of his own importance. Come to think of it, 'e don't come in on a Saturday an' Sunday. So, you might have to wait "till Monday. But, as I says, e'll be here."

Marius nodded. "Does he ever stop for any length of time?"

"No more than an 'our or two," replied the first groom, ready to add to the conversation. "Ain't that right, Ned?"

Ned agreed. "No more 'an an hour or two. Then on his way."

The first groom went for their horses.

"Tell me Ned," said Marius, "Which road does he take when he leaves the inn?"

"Well, sometimes, 'e takes The Wells road. I've seen "im 'ead orf in that direction. Sometimes 'e turns north."

The horses were led into the yard. Roger went to mount, when Ned added

"Several times, when I was in the corn market, I sees "im take the fork towards Maidstone."

A morsel, but, decidedly useful. The route they would take had been so determined.

At the next inn they enjoyed an early dinner. The innkeeper, his customers and stable hands had not recognised Johnson from the likeness. Nevertheless, Roger was still keen to follow the road eastwards.

"After all," he surmised, "if he were staying at a house only a short distance from Tonbridge, he would hardly break his journey in the town if it's not much further on."

Yet another occasion when Roger's simple logic surprised Marius.

They continued towards Maidstone, stopping in Hadlow, and at inns in the hamlets of West Peckham and Mereworth. The response was the same. No one had seen the gentleman.

In the late afternoon they retraced their steps to Tonbridge. Marius was disappointed that no further sign of Johnson had been found, and was beginning to doubt the choice of route. However, Roger was convinced that, with a little extra time, they could uncover his whereabouts. His indomitable spirit kept Marius from being too despondent.

"I'm not sure I want to spend any time here," said Roger, as they climbed the stairs to their room. "What do you say to an evening at the Rose and Crown?"

"I'm inclined to agree. Though, first, I need to rest. I'm not used to lengthy periods in the saddle. My back feels stiff," said Marius, with feeling. "I'll join you a little later."

In fact, it was much later. Lying on the bed to ease his aching body, he had fallen into a sound sleep, awaking with a start shortly after eight of the clock.

In the taproom of The Rose and Crown, it was crowded, noisy, and smoke thick in the air. At first, Roger was not to be seen. Then a gap opened in the throng, and in the centre of the room, Marius saw he was seated at table with two other people.

Making his way through the milling drinkers, Marius caught the arm of a serving girl and ordered fresh ale for himself and those at the table.

"Marius," exclaimed Roger. "What kept you? I've been telling my friends here about this crazy doctor friend of mine from London. They probably thought you didn't exist."

His voice was loud, his face flushed. "Sit down, sit down, old friend. Meet my companions. They're sailors, would you believe. I said they were a damn'd long way from the sea, but it appears they sail the Medway River."

The mugs of ale arrived. Roger continued in his talkative fashion. Marius sensed the two sailors were now keeping their counsel.

"Your health, gentlemen," toasted Marius. Silently, the two raised their mugs.

"I've been telling them, Marius, about your adventures. Nothing like that happens to me. Yet my new-found friend, in just a few weeks, is an ally of the constable, the emissary for the Lord of the Manor, and the confidant of Walpole, the Principal Minister."

Roger stared into his mug, momentarily lost in his own muddled thoughts.

"My companion has a lively imagination, gentlemen. I must admit circumstances have taken charge of me since arriving in The Wells," said Marius blandly. "But, nothing as exotic as he is suggesting. I am merely a doctor of physick."

"What sort of doctor chases after rogues, may I ask?" said the shorter of the two sailors.

"Has Roger told you that? Well, it is partly true. I get incensed when someone kills his wife and appears to get away with it," added Marius soberly.

Roger looked at him owlishly.

"Will he get away with it?" asked the other sailor, taking an interest in the turn of the conversation.

"Not if we can help it!" exclaimed Roger, coming out of his reverie.

"What can you do about it?" questioned the first, leaning forward to catch the reply.

"Let me tell you the story, you can judge for yourselves."

They remained for another hour, and more mugs of ale, listening to Marius, asking questions, and giving freely of their advice. As the evening passed, the sailors' reservations slowly evaporated. Fuelled by the alcohol an easy camaraderie developed.

At a late stage, he could not recall when, Jacob, the sailor who had first treated Marius with suspicion, said, "You being a doctor of physick, perhaps you'd come and look at our captain's arm. On the way upriver, he caught a blow from a swinging mainsail. That's why he he's not with us tonight."

A little unsteadily, they made their way to the wharf by the great bridge where the barge was moored.

"Aye, aye, captain, we've got visitors," called Owen, the sailor who had invited them. Roger was giggling and leaning unsteadily against Marius, who was suddenly unsure they could safely negotiate the single, narrow plank stretching between the quay and the barge.

After a moment, a head appeared above the locker doors. "Come aboard, gentlemen," came a gravelly voice, coarsened by tobacco.

Nimbly, the two sailors crossed the gap, beckoning Marius to join them. He took a deep breath to steady himself, then held on tightly to Roger as he pushed him towards the strip of timber. Arms came forward and grabbed the helpless Dashwood, dragging him onto the deck.

Marius shuffled sideways several steps, then also felt his arms taken and pulled aboard. He landed in a heap, and rising shakily to his feet, he heard one of the sailors explain, "I've brought a doctor of physick aboard, cap'n. Me and Owen thought he could take a look at your injury."

Ushered below decks to the crew's quarters, it took a moment for Marius to adjust to the lantern light. It was then he perceived a short, wiry man in his fifties with his right arm tied across his chest.

"May I inspect that, Captain?" enquired Marius, moving towards him.

"My men should not have disturbed you, Doctor. It is badly bruised, nothing more. It was a result of my own carelessness. It will heal."

"Well, as I am here, I might as well examine it."

Marius removed the arm gently from the makeshift sling, and began a careful assessment of the damage from the fingers upwards. The man winced on several occasions, and Marius was immediately apologetic.

"Well, you're right. Although, the arm is badly bruised, I can find no evidence of a break or fracture. Let me retie the sling for you, sir. All I can suggest is that you treat it gently for the next week or so."

"Thank you, Doctor," responded the captain, whilst his arm was re-bound. "Now let me offer you a little hospitality for your trouble."

Seated round the small wardroom table, glasses of rum materialised, and soon they were enjoying lively conversation.

"Do you travel the length of the river, Captain," asked Marius, whilst Roger and the two sailors were briefly caught up in a humorous exchange.

"As far as Rochester, Doctor. We do the trip, there and back, twice a week."

"So the river is navigable?"

"It would be if you could avoid the twenty three locks," interjected Owen. "Some are more difficult than others. Yalding Locks are hard to manoeuvre in. The undercut at East Farleigh can be dangerous, and at Allington, this side of Maidstone, you can still feel the effects of the tide. You've got to know what you're about."

"Why do you ask, Doctor?" prompted the captain.

Roger, who had been sitting quietly, with his head resting against the bulkhead, replied, "Marius has a theory that contraband is coming into Tonbridge and The Wells by river."

He was totally oblivious to the sudden chill in the air. No one responded. The captain put down his glass, and asked quietly. "Are you with the Excise?"

"Heaven forfend! No, of course not! I should explain," said Marius, hastily, glancing at Roger. "When I was visiting a household in Rusthall recently, I met an Excise official. A Mr Robert Fielding. After the ladies had withdrawn, the conversation turned to the spate of smuggling affecting The Wells." Marius raised and emptied his glass. It was not refilled.

"Anyway, we were putting forward our ideas, over the port, on how the smugglers brought it in. I was boating on the Medway the other day, and the thought came that this could be a possible route. Nothing more, I assure you."

A wary silence prevailed. It occurred to Marius that the barge crew were probably not adverse to a little illegal trading. Sailing from Rochester, they could easily bring goods upstream.

"Obviously, it arrives by night. If, as you say, there are numerous locks to navigate, that dispels the notion it comes in from the estuary," concluded Marius.

The atmosphere lightened, but was still unsettled. However, the subject had been raised, and Marius was keen to pursue a further thought.

"Tell me, Captain, purely personal interest, would there be other ways smugglers could use the river to supply contraband to the town?"

The man eyed him carefully in the flickering light. Tapping his pipe on the side of the table, he filled then relit it before replying.

"Doctor, the only way smugglers might bring it in would be to load their boats between the town bridge and the lock gates at Branbridge's Mill, near East Peckham."

Dashwood's head jerked forward. He had fallen asleep. The crew were now exchanging uneasy glances. It was plain they had reached the end of their welcome.

"Well, gentlemen, we must bid you both goodnight," said the captain. He turned to Jacob. "Bosun, see these two gentlemen ashore."

Marius hefted Roger to his feet, and he and the two crew members manhandled him up the short stairway to the deck. Staggering to the gangplank with Roger in his arms, suddenly, the task of making the crossing seemed more daunting than ever.

"Jacob, I would be obliged of your help," said Marius, holding onto Roger's semi-comatose form.

"If you put him down, Doctor, we can each take an end and carry him across," said the sailor, his smile showing briefly in the light of a swinging lantern.

Marius let him slip to the deck, and dragged him to the edge of the plank.

"I'll take his shoulders, Doctor, if you take his feet," suggested the sailor. "I'll walk backwards. All you have to do is follow."

He turned to Owen. "Bring some more light over."

Marius was grateful he would not be the first to venture across the gap. Owen held the lantern high over the tableau, as Jacob eased past Marius, edging between the prone body and the deck housing.

His foot momentarily caught the unconscious Dashwood, and he was unprepared for the result. Rearing up at the slight blow, Roger cannoned abruptly into the sailor's legs. Off balance, Jacob lurched sideways with a cry. Tumbling, the bosun fell against Marius. Both were pitching backwards when the shot rang out, and the dead weight of the sailor pinned him to the deck.

CHAPTER FORTY NINE

Marius was uncertain if he had been shot.

He tried to extricate himself, pushing at the body lying on top of him. His hands slippery with blood, found little purchase. The lifeless limbs of the sailor impeded his every effort.

He knew that suffering was not immediate. Would he soon be overwhelmed by the intense pain from the gunshot? Marius breathed deeply, then slowly he wriggled sideways until, at last, he was free of the dead weight upon him. Cautiously sitting up, he waited, every fibre of his being alert. Moving his legs and arms, the next hurdle would be standing.

When Marius staggered to his feet he heard the sound of people running, drawn by the sound of the gunshot.

A crowd quickly gathered on the quayside, silenced by what they were witnessing on the barge. Pushing his way through the throng, a darkly-dressed, thickset man took charge.

"Captain, explain the incident , if you please."

The commander of the vessel turned from the rail, his face grey and drawn. "I was in the cabin when I heard a scuffle topside, then a shot," he said falteringly. "I rushed on deck, and there was one of my men dying, before my very eyes."

"Did you see who fired the shot?"

"All I saw was Jacob, my bosun, bleeding like a stuck pig," he responded in bewilderment.

"You, sir," ordered the man on the quay, looking at Marius. "What is your involvement in this affair? Why are you on board? Did you or your companion cause this incident?"

He stared at both of them suspiciously.

"They didn't have any weapons on them," the captain responded. "And the sound of the shot didn't come from the deck, but from the quayside. I don't think either of them did it."

Marius was grateful for the captain's intercession. He realised how easily Roger and he might have been taken for the assassins.

He had been questioned further by the officer. Though searching in his inquiry, Marius remained constant to his story. Roger, much the worse for wear, was being helped by the sailor and himself. A shot rang out, and the sailor had been mortally wounded. No, he could not think of an explanation for the extraordinary occurrence.

All the while, Roger was oblivious to what was taking place. He was leaning into the rigging, content with his own thoughts.

Marius had to repeat his story of the incident a number of times, the constable listening for any flaw in the telling.

"So what happened when you left the quarters below?" his inquisitor demanded curtly.

"When we got him up the steps, the fresh air must have bemused him further. One moment my companion was lying on the deck, the next he sat up, catching the legs of the now dead sailor. He toppled into me, and as we both fell the sound of a gunshot rang."

"Who was the ball intended for?"

The same question had crossed Marius' mind.

"I have no idea," he replied, turning towards the captain. "Did Jacob have any enemies?"

"None who would wish this harm upon him."

The official eventually turned to his assistants.

"See these two gentlemen to their lodgings. Advise the landlord not to let them leave before I speak to them in the morning."

They made their unsteady way ashore, and with the escorts aiding Roger, they made the slow journey along the embankment and across the square to the Chequers Inn.

In the morning, the same two men accompanied them to a building on the south side of the bridge. It was then Marius discovered they had been interrogated by the constable of Tonbridge, Mr Bridger.

"You are both free to go," said the constable reluctantly. "But, I shall notify the constable in The Wells to exercise the strictest vigilance. I feel you both know far more than you are saying about the murder of the sailor. Frankly, I find it hard to credit that you, Doctor, have nothing else to suggest other than it must have been a random firing from the quayside."

CHAPTER FIFTY

"I suppose there was a misunderstanding, and you had nothing to do with it?" asked Russell, part serious, part amused.

"I must tell you Mr Russell, it was a shock to be so near to a gunshot," replied Marius. "For a moment I was completely deafened."

"Not just a little concerned the ball was meant for you?"

"Why on earth should it be?"

"Dr Hope, are you being deliberately naïve? I'm sure you have considered the possibility."

Halting at the door of the hosier's shop, Marius dwelt on the constable's inference. He had thought to prepare himself for the visit to Rusthall by buying new stockings. En route, he had encountered the constable walking in his direction, and the officer had chosen to accompany him to the Walks.

"I suppose the possibility had crossed my mind," said Marius reflectively. "But how did they know I was on the barge?"

The constable smiled ruefully. "How can you be sure you weren't followed to Tonbridge? That you have not been under observation since you arrived in The Wells? The message from the constable of Tonbridge was that the shooting was highly suspicious. You could just as easily have been the murderer, or the intended victim. It seems Mr Bridger has yet to make up his mind. That's why you and Mr Dashwood are now under my surveillance."

"It might have been that the sailor was involved in something, and someone took revenge," commented Marius uncertainly.

"Perhaps, I should carry out Mr Bridger's wishes and lock both of you up. It might save your lives."

Russell waited while he made his purchases. As they strolled along the Upper Walk, Marius gave account of the conversation that had taken place on the barge.

"I quizzed the captain about contraband being brought in by river. I suggested that it might be off-loaded from ships onto sailing barges in the Medway estuary. He

231

readily dismissed the idea." Marius tapped his pockets, checking that he had his pipe.

"It would appear there are too many locks between Tonbridge and the river mouth. Impossible to negotiate them all in the dark. Plus the fact that it would have taken more than one night to sail the distance."

The constable nodded. "Still, I suppose it was worth investigating. Did you mention it to anyone in Tonbridge?"

"You mean to your fellow officer? No, not that I had the opportunity. When in his company, he seemed to occupy much of the conversation, bombarding me with questions."

"He is naturally suspicious of anyone who does not provide satisfactory answers. Clearly, you failed to do so."

As they moved through the throng surrounding the Well, Marius was amused to note the anguished faces of those new to the pleasures of the waters.

"So, can we forget about the river as a means of transporting contraband?" enquired the constable.

"Not necessarily," replied Marius. "Although it's not practical to ship it from the estuary, the captain did mention the possibility of goods coming overland to a store that served both Tonbridge and The Wells. If such a store were near the river, they could easily sail into the town when dark, and no one would be the wiser."

"Where would the boats be loaded?"

"He reckoned any point up to four or five miles down river. Before you get to the village of Yalding."

"What about the contraband destined for The Wells?"

"He suggested it would be easy to bring it here by the back trails."

"But they would have to pass the magistrate's men patrolling the pathways and lanes around The Wells."

"If they use packhorses," replied Marius. "There must be any number of tracks and byways into the town. And, in all probability, Mr Phillips has stationed his force on the south side, expecting the goods to come up from the coast."

"Do you think the river banks should be checked?"

"Well, Dashwood wants to look for Mr Johnson's whereabouts nearer Maidstone. He could also scout along the river."

"Is Johnson important to you?" The constable looked at Marius questioningly

"You know my feelings on the matter, Constable. Something is not as it should be with that man. But, whether or not we can find where he lodges, and in what circumstances, remains to be seen," said Marius bleakly.

"Don't you think, Doctor, that you are trying to make a case out of straw? I don't much like the fellow, but you could be thought to be mounting a vendetta against him?"

Marius halted, causing the constable to move on a few paces. He stared after the official. His words rushing to spill out. "God's wounds! No! Why should I do such a thing?"

However, as a denial it held all the elements of a question of himself. The constable waited for Marius to reach him. Three short steps, but sufficient for Marius to query his own motives.

"I suppose it's a possibilty," he said in a low voice. "Perhaps, I could be pursuing an unworthy cause … I'm no longer sure."

They continued their passage across the bridge and past the church in silence. It was broken by the constable.

"I must advise you, Doctor," said Russell, in an authoritative voice that surprised him. "I believe you should let the matter rest, and, furthermore, cease your interest in the smuggling problem. I shall inform Bridger that you are under close observation. I shall also request him to check possible landing places along the river."

Thinking back to his concerns about trust, and keeping the spread of information to as few people as possible, Marius exclaimed, "Is that wise? Forgive me, but surely it would be better if you looked for any likely sites where the smugglers might store goods, or load their boats."

"Meaning what exactly? Are you saying that he is not trustworthy?"

"Not at all. But there is always the chance he could, inadvertently, let slip he is searching the river bank, thus revealing his intention to the smugglers."

"A fine point, Doctor. I suppose I could send two of my deputies to investigate your theory. No one else need know or be involved."

This last comment was said in an uncompromising tone. It was clearly meant to exclude Marius. When they reached the foot of Mount Sion, the constable seemed to hesitate before making up his mind. "Do you have a moment, Doctor? Would you permit me to buy you a mug of ale?"

They entered the Angel, taking seats by a window overlooking Bishops Down. Served by one of the maids, Russell drank half the contents of his mug, before saying, "I want you to tell me, to assure me, Doctor, that Daniel Clifford is safe? Is he mending? Importantly, when will he be coming home?"

"Mr Russell, fortunately there are signs he is on the mend," said Marius, surprised, and a little apprehensive. "Though, it's difficult to say with any certainty if he will fully recover."

"In what way do you mean?"

"Such a beating, clearly intended to kill, will inevitably affect his mind as well as his body," explained Marius.

"Is he able to walk yet?"

"I have not encouraged him to try."

"His wife has been to see him, I presume?"

"A number of times. She is anxious, but manages to hide her concerns. I am surprised at her fortitude. She is obviously fearful for Clifford's health, as well as his safety."

"Where is he being kept?"

"I am still reluctant to answer that Mr Russell," said Marius quietly.

The constable stared at him for a moment, then standing, said, "Let me refill your mug, sir."

With fresh ale before them, the constable gave a faint smile.

"I respect your feelings, Doctor. You may believe it's for the best that no one knows where he is. However, I can offer Clifford greater protection. My men could take it in turn to guard him."

"You may be right, sir. Nevertheless, they could also draw attention to Clifford's whereabouts … with far worse consequences."

As they were leaving the inn, the landlord approached Marius. "Doctor Hope? This letter arrived for you on yesterday's coach."

Glancing at it, he recognised his father's hand. Paying the innkeeper a penny for the postage, and an additional sixpence for its safe deliverance, he tucked the envelope in an inside pocket.

Outside the inn, about to part, the constable said, "One final thing. I am afraid we must discount Jordan being Clifford's attacker. On Friday evening he was seen drinking in the White Bear."

"I was so sure he was the one," murmured Marius thoughtfully.

With Clifford much on his mind, he felt the need to visit the patient and check his progress. Now concerned that he might be followed, he took a circuitous route through the wooded grove before approaching Dr Brett's house from another quarter. Knocking at a side door, it was opened at once by the butler.

"I saw you coming down the path, Doctor," said the man conspiratorially.

CHAPTER FIFTY ONE

Marius readied himself for dinner with the Conyers. His new stockings were comfortable, and although the chemise had seen better days, it was set off by an extravagant purple cravat, complemented by a figured cream silk waistcoat. Marius took a frock coat from the hanging cupboard. Easing it over his shoulders, he gazed in the cheval mirror. It cast just the right tone. Dark plum with delicate gold tracery on the broad lapels and facings on the wide pockets. Turning slowly, he checked his dress from several angles before declaring himself ready for the occasion. Shortly thereafter, a knock came at the door and a voice declared his driver was waiting. On this occasion, Marius had decided to hire a hackney coach.

As it made its way up the incline to Mount Ephraim, Marius thought over the morning's events. He had been certain Jordan was Clifford's assailant. However, when he put it to the injured man in the cramped, dark room under the eaves, Clifford's recollection of his attacker bore little resemblance to the farrier.

"I remember thinking, as he came out the trees, that he didn't look like you, Doctor," said Clifford, screwing up his eyes as if better to recall the scene. "The shape was all wrong, you see. He came out in a rush, and seemed all hunched up. Even so, I reckon he was no taller than myself."

Clifford faltered at the bitter memory.

"Then he hit me. I don't remember much else."

The coach slowed as it reached the top of the rise.

Marius accepted that the constable must be right. Jordan was far taller than Clifford. He also had an imposing physique, suggesting he would have neither the agility nor the soft tread of a smaller man. However, what was uppermost in his thoughts was the content of the letter from his father. Returning to Ashenhurst House, Marius had removed his clothes. Pouring a bowl of water from the jug, he had washed away the grime of his journey from Tonbridge. As he was putting his coat in the cupboard he remembered the letter hurriedly stuffed in a pocket at the Angel Inn.

LONDON
21th August 1736
My Dear Marius,

We hope you are Enjoying your Sojourn at The Wells, and that the Curative Powers of the Waters are to your Expectation!

Your Request for Details concerning Mr Nathaniel Jordan Took Longer than I had Anticipated. It was Harry who Eventually Had The Good Fortune to Meet with a Carter from Chelsea Reaches. He Stated your Man has a Yard and Smithy in Fulham. It would Appear that Whilst Mr Jordan is not Particularly Well-liked, he is a Competent Farrier and Enjoys a Thriving Business.

He is Absent at the Present Time, which Might Confirm that He, too, is Passing his Days at the Spa.

The Only other Comment I would Offer also Came from the Carter. It Seems Jordan is a Short-tempered Fellow, Quick to take Offence, and Often likely to Exercise his Fists and Feet if he Feels Slighted in any Way.

Your other Enquiry about Mr Robert Fielding was Easily Despatched.

Your Brothers and I Have Come across Him at Customs House on the Quay. He Enjoys a Notable Role in the Excise, being Southern Area Controller, Responsible for Much of the Kent and Sussex Coastline. He is also Away Touring his Domain, so He could Easily be in the Vicinity of The Wells.

I have Little to Report about Mr Augustus Brown. No One could Tell Me Much about the Man when I Visited one of his Grocery Shops. The only Tidbit I Gleaned Was that he Dotes on his Wife, and one Wag Implied that He Conducts his Trade Primarily to Satisfy her Whims and Fancies!

You Enquired about Mr Maurice Conyers. In His Early Days He was a Builder. There are Rumours that in this Capacity, He was Thought Headstrong, even a Little Unscrupulous!

Be cautious.
Your Affectionate Father.

Marius had mulled over the contents of the brief letter. Now, as they approached Rusthall, he wondered whether it would be wise to convey any of the events, or his concerns, to the Lord of The Manor.

When Marius descended from the coach, Beth came from the house to greet him. Hurrying across the gravel, she said, "Quickly, let us spend a moment together! I'm off home tomorrow, and we won't see each other for a week."

They made their way towards a side gate. One of the footmen at the main door to the Manor hesitated when he saw them, then withdrew into the interior. They crossed the lawns towards the large cedar tree. Releasing his arm, Beth plumped down on the seat.

"So, did you discover Mr Johnson's whereabouts?" she enquired breathlessly.

"No," replied Marius, vesting a glance over his shoulder to see if anyone were approaching. "We showed the likeness to a number of people. A groom at the Chequers Inn in Tonbridge confirmed he was a regular visitor. No one else seems to have spotted him. Although, a farm labourer at an inn on the road to Wateringbury, thought perhaps he recognised the likeness. But, I'm sure he said that so we would buy him some ale. At dusk, we returned to Tonbridge."

"Oh! what a pity."

"Dashwood is still sure we shall find where he goes, and that it is somewhere near Maidstone. Frankly, I'm not so sure. I just cannot believe Johnson would go in that direction."

"So, it was a wasted journey?"

"Not completely. In fact, it was quite rewarding, except for one incident."

"What do you mean?"

"Well, you know I've harboured this notion that the contraband might be brought by boat up the Medway River. We spent the evening with some sailors from a barge that sails between Rochester, Chatham, and Tonbridge."

Marius again glanced towards the house.

"Later, Dashwood and I went aboard their vessel and spoke with the captain. He said it would be impossible to sail through all the locks in one night. What is more, the lock keepers would note the smugglers' craft."

Marius sat down next to Beth.

"He also added something very interesting. If they couldn't use the whole length of the river, perhaps they have a store not far from Tonbridge. From there they could load their boats and sail the few miles into the centre of the town. They might well use such a store to send goods by packhorses to The Wells."

"Is that really a possibility?" queried Beth.

"Mr Russell thinks it might be. He is going to send his deputies to check the river banks."

"It's a wonder he hasn't warned you off this investigation, as well," said Beth with a wry smile.

"He has, after the incident in Tonbridge."

"What incident?"

"As Dashwood and I were leaving the barge last night, one of the sailors was shot."

"Gracious! Why would anyone do such a thing?" exclaimed Beth, shocked at his words.

"I'm not sure he was the intended victim," replied Marius. "We were helping Roger off the barge, when the fellow stumbled, and fell in front of me. That's when the shot rang out. The ball took him in the chest."

"What are you saying, Marius? They were trying to shoot you?" Beth's face flushed with sudden anger. "Why do you get involved in these happenings? This is the second time you've been attacked. Really, Marius, have you no thought for others?"

With that, she ran towards the house, as her aunt was approaching from the opposite direction.

Dinner was frustrating. Beth averted her eyes throughout the meal, and said little. He tried to engage her in conversation, but she was withdrawn and distant. He was surprised to see that the Fieldings had also been invited. When the ladies withdrew, it left Conyers, Martineau, Fielding, and himself at the table.

"This inability to halt the illegal trade is very vexing," declared Conyers. "What about the presence of that fellow, Jordan? Has anyone got anything to say about him?"

Marius was anxious not to be too forthcoming. In fact, he attempted to be disarming.

"I received a note from London just today. Nothing of any great moment. It appears that Jordan is what he purports to be. A farrier looking to develop his business in The Wells. A rough and ready fellow, but keen to set up premises to take advantage of the summer trade."

"What prompted you to enquire after Mr Jordan, Doctor?" questioned Fielding.

It was Conyers who responded. "He has been seen in the vicinity of several incidents, that's why. And he gives every appearance of trying to browbeat the freeholders."

"Really? For what reason?"

Marius silently wished Conyers would not be drawn. But, the Lord of The Manor, content after a good meal and mellow with good wine, was in an expansive mood.

"Dr Hope discovered he is trying to obtain land for his business by approaching the freeholders, and offering to buy their titles. When they decline, he resorts to heavy-handed threats," said Conyers, refilling his glass. He added, "He probaby doesn't realise that no one wants to sell to him, or anybody else at the moment."

"Why is that, sir?" asked Fielding, drawing The Lord of The Manor further.

Marius turned to the Customs official. "Have your Riding Officers detected many more landings on the coast since the increase in contraband, Mr Fielding?"

"What? Oh, some, Dr Hope," said Fielding. The interruption had broken the thread of the conversation.

"May I offer anyone more port?" enquired Conyers.

Thereafter, the conversation turned to fishing. A pastime The Lord of The Manor had recently adopted under the tutelage of his nephew. He became quite animated, and was still discoursing on the subject when they retired to the terrace to join the ladies.

As the gentlemen made their way towards where they were sitting in the shade of a rose-covered pergola, Marius realised, unhappily, that Beth was not among them .

CHAPTER FIFTY TWO

"Tell me again, slowly this time."

"Hope appeared on deck supporting Dashwood, who had obviously drunk too much. Then, a sailor stumbled in front of the doctor at the very moment I pulled the trigger."

"What happened then?"

"I didn't stop to find out. The shot took the crewman in the chest. He would have died instantly."

The voice was menacing. "You realise, don't you, that this is another bungled attempt. I was prepared to give you the benefit of the doubt over the incident in the bathhouse. This time there is no excuse."

All bombast left the would-be assassin. Suddenly, he was nervous of the dark figure before him. His reply took on a pleading tone.

"I couldn't know that the sailor would lurch forward. One minute there he was, a clear target, but his guardian angel put someone in his place. You can't allow for that!"

"You should have waited until Hope was on the boarding plank. Then, there would have been no mistake."

"Give me another chance," he said anxiously. "Look, I won't let you down, I promise."

"It could be too late for Hope's *coup de grâce,* and your opportunity to carry out my orders."

Fear crept into his voice. He knew the cold-blooded regard the gentleman had for life or property. "I mean it, sir. I'll get him next time, just you see. I won't let you down."

For several long moments the gentleman stared at his agent, before hissing, "I shall expect nothing less."

CHAPTER FIFTY THREE

"And that's about the size of it, Roger."

He had said little whilst Marius recounted the events at the dinner table.

"Clearly, you couldn't comment on Fielding, being that he was present," Roger said thoughtfully.

"I don't know what it is, Roger, but I still feel uneasy about Fielding. Something doesn't ring true."

"All Excise people give me that feeling."

"What do you mean?"

"Well, you can't tell if they are prepared to uphold the law, or ready to take bribes and look the other way."

"Why do you say that?"

"It happens all the time. Recently the Mayor of Winchelsea acquitted the well-known smuggler, Thomas Darby. Last week Thomas Moore, one of Rye's notorious free traders, was bailed by the local magistrate himself. Everyone, from Riding Officers to magistrates and officials are bribed or coerced."

"I'm sure they are not all so easily persuaded," said Marius, with a righteous look on his face. "On the quays, my family find the Excise people firm but fair. There's no question of bribery."

"Let me explain something, Marius." Roger leaned towards him. "Inspecting cargoes and manifests is an altogether different affair to catching smugglers. The Excise employ Riding Officers to patrol the shores, keep watch on possible landings. Yet, every one of these officers has ten to twenty miles of coastline to guard. If they discover where and when the smugglers are landing, what can one man do against fifty to several hundred? It's often safer to turn a blind eye. After all, they have to provide their own horse and they only get paid twenty five pounds a year."

"Surely some smugglers are caught?"

"Naturally. However, a hogshead of wine or some tobacco will often ensure their freedom, and they're soon up to their old tricks."

"I didn't realise that people were so easily bought," said Marius lamely.

"They're not only bought, they're threatened as well. A number of Riding Officers live in the very communities which depend on smuggling for a living. In Kent, a lot of farmers and their workers do. Particularly in the wintertime when there is little work to be had." Roger tapped his pipe on the tiled floor of the orangery. "They're called "ten shilling men". One night's work for the smuggling gangs will earn them more than three weeks' wages on the land. So if their livelihood is endangered, they will visit that same threat upon their local Customs Official."

It dawned on Marius why the current problem in The Wells was not easily extinguished. The shopkeepers may oppose the influx of contraband, they were losing custom to street traders and stallholders. But, with so many involved in the smuggling network – villagers, farmers, fishermen, even churchmen who made their crypts available for storage – the Excise would find it difficult to suppress the amount flowing into the town.

"I wonder if Fielding is in collusion with Conyers?" Marius went on, without waiting for Roger's reply. "That might be the answer. They are working hand-in-hand. Why didn't I see it before."

"For goodness sake, Marius, where do you get such notions? What proof have you got? There's not a shred of evidence to support it."

"Perhaps, there isn't. However, it's a strong possibility. Fielding seems to be his friend. He is often at the Manor, and whenever I see them together they are in a huddle talking in low voices."

"Hmm … You'll be saying Phillips is involved next. Even the constable and Beau Nash."

Marius was quiet for a moment. Then he jumped to his feet.

"I must attend upon Daniel Clifford. I want another word with him about his attackers."

Roger continued sitting comfortably in his chair, as Marius made his way through the potted plants, slamming the door behind him .

"I find it difficult to recall exactly what happened, Doctor," said Clifford, easing himself into a more comfortable position on the cot. "One minute I was standing in the shadows. The next, I was down on my knees, my head ringing from the blow."

"It will take a while for you to recollect the details," comforted Marius, who had heard the same explanation every time Clifford had the energy to speak.

"Tell me, Daniel, do you remember why you wanted to see me? Do you have more of the names of those threatening you? Can you identify any of them?"

Clifford's eyes turned away. He was hesitant and uncomfortable. In a tremulous voice he said, "Since lying here, Doctor, I've had time to think the situation through.

I don't want my family hurt. If I recover, I want to live in peace with my wife and children. If they want, they can have my title deeds, and I'll sell their contraband."

"What does the sale of your titles have to do with selling goods in the lower Walk?"

"I don't know, sir. But if they want the rights to the land on which the Walks have been built, I'm not going to oppose them. My family, and others, have long owned the land between the stream and the track to Eridge. This is what is in dispute with the Lord of The Manor. If it will save us, they can have the titles."

Marius stood up from the low chair by the bedside.

"You said earlier it was Jordan who was trying to persuade you to take his goods." Clifford moved restlessly. "Yes … The second was shorter and thinner."

"Have other freeholders been approached for their titles?"

"I'm sure of it. They haven't declared it openly, but, I believe they've all been threatened with violence, just like me."

"The point is, Roger, Clifford was saying most of the other freeholders have been pressed to sell their titles."

He was still sitting in the orangery. Content to take his ease while Marius paced the floor.

"I cannot understand why anybody should want them. The rents can't be that much."

"They're not. The freeholders get ten shillings a year. Or did until four years ago when the agreement lapsed. Don't you remember me telling you how Thomas Neale, the Lord of The Manor, got them all to sign a fifty year lease?"

"So what is happening? They can't take back their land for grazing can they? Do they want the buildings pulled down?"

"They would like to have more of the monies the Well attracts. But, even a marked increase in their rents would not warrant anyone buying up the titles."

Marius was silent. Then it was evident he had come to a decision.

"Well, whatever the reason, I mean to find out."

"How can you do that?"

"By going to London! Asking some serious questions."

CHAPTER FIFTY FOUR

Marius waited impatiently for the Tuesday coach to London. Roger stood beside him at the bowling green at the top of Mount Sion. The first of the travellers had struggled up the hill. The weather was miserable, and Marius did not relish the journey. Gusts of wind whipping up a light drizzle, dampening the passengers as they huddled beneath the standing of oaks.

"When do you return, Marius?"

"I'm sure my enquiries will not take more than a few days. I'll probably stay the rest of the week with my family." He added, "With Beth at her home, it seems a convenient time to be away from The Wells."

"How is your romance progressing?"

"I don't think it is," said Marius ruefully. "When I went to dinner on Saturday, I told her about the shooting in Tonbridge. She didn't speak to me for the rest of the day."

Roger grinned. "An excellent sign."

"What do you mean?"

"Marius, there are times when your na vety really does surprise me. She likes you, so she cares for your safety."

Twice now the term had been applied to him, in as many days. Perhaps, I am naïve on occasion, thought Marius, when I cannot see the obvious.

"Beth was furious. She declared that this was the second time someone had tried to do away with me, and on the next occasion they might succeed."

"She is even more concerned for you than I thought."

At that moment, the empty coach appeared over the brow of the hill. The commotion which followed whilst people jostled for their seats and stowed their hand luggage, left him little opportunity to pursue Roger's comments.

On the first stage to Tonbridge, Marius, was seated between a full-figured lady and an equally rotund gentleman. At the coaching inn outside Sevenoakes, the gentlewoman alighted. Her place taken by a man of narrower build. Though at first talkative, he soon lapsed into sleep.

Marius began to think about whom he should seek out, and the sorts of questions he would ask. All the while a thought nagged at him. If Clifford had not survived the attack, would it have strengthened Conyers' hand. With yet another freeholder's death, the rest might have capitulated and released their titles. Conyers had sufficient ready wealth to snap them up. But the question arose, what did he have to gain from owning all the titles to the Walks? Perhaps, if he owned the land, he could more easily force the shop owners and the stallholders to sell contraband. They would have little choice. Sell the goods or lose your tenure and the right to own stalls in the Lower Walk. Conyers would then be in the ideal position to organise their flow into The Wells.

The fire at the Lovedays could have been at his instigation. Even the callous murder of Bennett on the racecourse. Marius recalled he had been quite sanguine when told of Bennett's death.

Prior to coming to Rusthall, when he had been a builder, Conyers would have encountered many lawless elements. People he might now employ for his own ends. Marius also realised it would have taken little to arrange the incident at the cold baths, and the shooting on the barge. For a man such as Conyers, rendering harmless anyone who would oppose him would be the work of a moment.

He had the wealth and the means to enforce his will. Sickened by the thought that Beth's uncle could well be the mastermind behind both villainous schemes, Marius journeyed the rest of the way his mind in turmoil.

It took all his persuasive powers to get the hackney coach to take him to Chelsea. Cursing under his breath, the driver had grudgingly agreed to drive him out to Wilderness Row, near the Hospital for The Maimed. Though he demanded double the fare for the journey.

Knocking at the front door an hour later, he had been welcomed by Frederick, the footman, who immediately hurried into the withdrawing room to announce his arrival. His mother, closely followed by his father, came quickly into the hall and embraced him. He was drawn into the room, where one of his sisters greeted him just as warmly.

"What a delightful surprise, Marius. Have you eaten? Are you staying the night?"

His mother bombarded him with questions as she reached for the bell pull to summon the housekeeper.

"Mrs Edwards, my son will need his old room prepared, and a hot meal, if you please."

Marius's father went to a cabinet and poured him a brandy.

"Now, my boy, what brings you here at this hour?"

A hasty meal was set for Marius in the dining room, and whilst he ate, he apprised his father of all that had happened during recent weeks. How, seemingly, there were two schemes afoot. The first to deluge The Wells and the surrounding towns with smuggled goods. The second, to force the freeholders to dispose of their title deeds.

"An interesting situation, Marius. Tell me, how can I help?"

"Father, what I need to find out is who currently holds the titles, and the present share holding of the Walks. Importantly, to discover the changes that have taken place. If I can find out who has the major interest, it could well lead me to the people behind it all."

"I suppose the best person to speak to is John Castaing," said his father, his forehead creased in thought. "He's a noted jobber. You'll find him in the city, at Jonathan's Coffee House in Change Alley. He was the first to produce a list of securities and prices, and he keeps an up-to-date record of all such transactions. If anyone can tell you who has bought what, and when, it's John Castaing."

"I might also want to make some enquiries at Customs House," added Marius. "Could you give me the name of a reliable contact?"

"Leonard White has been our regular Excise Officer for years. Our company knows him well. He's often to be found in the warehouse, or on one of our vessels checking cargoes against manifests."

"Tell me, Father, are there occasions when he is the recipient of your generosity?"

His father laughed uneasily. "What do you mean by that remark?"

"Do you ever attempt to bribe him?"

"Well, I suppose there are moments when your brothers and I, nothing specific mind you, encourage him to complete his checks quickly. If a ship has been delayed, a little inducement to clear the cargo so that we can move the goods quickly, does no harm. Why do you ask?"

"No reason," said Marius, laying down his napkin, finishing his glass of wine. "I was just interested to learn how you oil the wheels of commerce."

He was silent for a moment.

"You sent me some details of Maurice Conyers, the Lord of The Manor of Rusthall. Some years ago, he bought the title from the Dashwoods. Do you know how I can find more out about his family and friends?"

"I can make more enquiries, Marius. It should be quite easy to come by such information."

The next morning Marius rode in his father's carriage to the company offices. Greeted warmly by his brothers, they gathered in his father's room to discuss the information he was seeking. At eleven of the clock, Marius set out for Cornhill.

On the corner of Change Alley, the smell of roasted coffee beans was overwhelming. The emblem of a Turkish coffee pot hung, unnecessarily, over the door. Pushing it open, Marius' ears were assailed by the noise. An unceasing din accompanied the manic rush of men scurrying from table to table. Chairs constantly being scraped across the floor, business being conducted with a shouting passion. All the while, waiters urbanely manoeuvred their full trays through the milling crowd, seemingly oblivious to the cacophony.

It took several minutes for Marius to gain a waiter's attention. Eventually, he was guided to the rear of the coffee house where it was quieter, though still an assault to the ears. In a corner sat an elderly man dealing with a never-ending stream of visitors to his table. An opportunity presented itself, and Marius slipped into a chair.

"Do I know you, young man?" queried the gentleman.

"Mr John Castaing?"

"That is my name, sir."

"Mr Lawrence Hope said you might be able to help me."

"Did he now? And who might you be?" asked the gentleman, taking a sip of his coffee. Marius could see it had long since gone cold.

"I'm his son, Marius."

"Ah … The doctor of physick. The difficult one," commented Castaing, waving an arm to summon a fresh cup.

"Difficult?"

"Well, unfathomable, shall we say."

Marius suppressed his surprise that his father had thought him to be the more perplexing of his children.

"Anyway, how may I help you, Doctor?"

"Mr Castaing, I am anxious to discover the current owners of shares in the Walks in The Wells."

"You mean, of course, the spa town," declared Castaing, screwing up his eyes as he brought the facts to mind. "Even in London it has reached our ears that since the lease expired there has been no resolution of the true rights of ownership."

"Yet, if I understand correctly, some of the titles, and therefore, some of the shares have been traded," said Marius, leaning forward to catch Castaing's words in the interminable din around him.

"There is no doubt in that respect," replied Castaing. "I traded the shares for Sir Francis Dashwood after the South Sea Bubble burst fifteen years ago."

"Really! But surely the Dashwood brothers sold the rights to The Lordship of the Manor to Maurice Conyers?" exclaimed Marius.

"That maybe so. Nevertheless, some Rusthall stock was included in a parcel of shares I sold for them. Like many at that time they badly needed the money."

"So you would know the current status of the holdings?" asked Marius eagerly.

"Not without checking trading records, and speaking to fellow jobbers. It would not merit comment in my journal, the *Course of Exchange.*"

"Would that take long, sir?"

"I cannot stop to do so now. As you can see, I am busy," responded Castaing, looking round the crowded, smoky room. "Allow me a day to familiarise myself, to summarise the stock ownership. See me tomorrow at this hour."

Several men were now standing behind him, anxious to do business. Marius rose to his feet, thanked Castaing, and made his way through the throng to the main door. Slipping out into Change Alley, he was returned to a more measured world. One which had a welcome serenity after the frenzied interior of Jonathan's Coffee House.

He waited outside when Marius disappeared through the door. He had no wish to draw attention to himself. He had followed the doctor of physick since his departure from The Wells. His remit, to observe and report on his actions. No one had mentioned the tedium of waiting endlessly when Hope was occupied. An hour later his quarry had emerged. Once more he took up pursuit, striding out in his wake down Cornhill.

On his way back to the family business, Marius turned into Customs House, a short step along the quays. He entered the building, uncertain of what he wanted to achieve, and whether he should ask for Mr White. Just then, someone touched his elbow, and turning he was confronted by a porter.

"Can I help you, sir?"

"Er … I am looking for Mr Robert Fielding. I would have a word with him, if you please." Marius had been unprepared for the appearance of someone who queried his presence. For a moment, he was at a loss to think of a reason for visiting the building.

"Mr Fielding is not here, sir."

Marius was suddenly unsure how to continue. He could think of no way to gain information about the Excise official.

"Did I hear you mention Mr Fielding?"

Another porter came from a cubicle beneath the stairs. "He is away visiting Riding Officers and Harbour Surveyors in his region at the moment, sir. He won't be back in London for a couple more weeks. Though, if it's urgent, I believe we have means of contacting him."

The porter went back into his cubby-hole and returned carrying several sheets of paper. Standing beside him, the porter held out the pages, squinting to read them. Over his shoulder, Marius could make out the script. It was in an ornate sloping hand, liberally sprinkled with curlicues. The signature at the foot achieved with a large, ostentatious flourish.

"He left these notes, sir. In case we needed him. You can reach him in The Wells, or send a message to the Excise Office in Hastings. He'll be either with Mr Collier, the Surveyor-General for Kent, or Major Battine, who's in charge of Sussex."

Walking back along the quays, Marius was convinced Fielding had spent little time on official matters. Since his arrival, Fielding had not been away from The Wells. Presumably the Customs official was taking a holiday with his wife before resuming his duties. Yet, with smuggling so rampant, surely the demands of office would be foremost. Perhaps Conyers had made use of his expertise to discuss the growth of the contraband. Although, on the occasion Marius had been in attendance, Fielding had made no significant contribution. All he appeared to do was doodle with his pen, and at Conyers' table, drink copious amounts of port.

As he contemplated the Excise Officer, something fleetingly crossed his mind. Tantalisingly close, though too elusive to dredge from the recesses.

"Master Hope!"

A shout from a warehouse doorway was closely followed by the appearance of a short, bow-legged man. Well into his middle years, his face seamed with the lines of age and honest toil, he came bustling towards Marius, a wide smile of greeting on his face.

"Well, well … I haven't clapped my eyes upon you for many a year."

"Dr Simons! How good to see you!"

"Visiting your father?"

"Briefly. Then I am returning to The Wells."

The little man stared up into his face. "I thought you were practising at St Bartholomew's. Have you moved to The Wells?"

"No," Marius smiled. "I have taken a break from the hospital to spend a little time at the spa. That's all. No doubt I'll be back in London shortly."

"For a moment I thought you'd abandoned the profession. You're still a doctor of physick, are you not?"

"The same as yourself, Dr Simons."

Marius did not tell him that as a child he had frequently watched him practise his calling along the quays. Mending broken bones, of which there were many; attending to minor ills and abrasions, and occasionally, tragic death among the wharfmen. The risks were legion. Men working on the river were constantly in danger from shifting cargoes, slippery gangplanks, and untidily stacked loads. The skills and compassion Simons brought to the never-ending demands of these men had contributed to Marius' choice of profession.

"I've been examining the remains of another poor soul dragged from the river," said Simons, explaining his presence near the family business.

"A wharfman?"

"No, someone of note. Or was once, I think. Unfortunately, there is little now to tell of his being. In fact, but for the fine clothes he was wearing you would be hard pressed to tell the gender. He has been in the water too long. Perhaps you could give me your opinion, Marius?"

Marius briefly experienced the uneasy feelings of his student days. He was about to demur, when his professional instincts took hold. Simons led him into a warehouse to a corner at the rear of the building. Removing the soaking cloth, he uncovered the corpse, which lay on a makeshift examination table. Little remained intact of the face and hands exposed to the water. Eaten by fish and other creatures, in places the white of the cranium and finger bones showed through.

"The body has been buffeted by ships as they have manoeuvred alongside," declared Simons. "Virtually every bone in his body is broken. As I mentioned, the only indication that it was a man of some substance is his clothing."

He lifted the edge of a frock coat. "You are more accustomed to this finery. Would you say it was expensive? Could it have been tailored for the poor fellow?"

The garment was waterlogged, and badly torn. Nevertheless, Marius could see that the frock coat had been bespoken, made for the ample frame that lay before him. Where a pocket had been tugged away he could see the stitching was of the highest quality. The cut and styling had been undertaken by a craftsman. Most noteworthy were the buttons.

"This was a costly item, Dr Simons. Made specifically for the man wearing it. What intrigues me are the buttons."

Marius turned one to the light beaming in from a window high in the roof.

"Look at the intricacy of the design in the shape of a lion, and using gold and silver together in this way. I don't think they can be English. More likely of French or Italian origin."

"You mean the fellow was a foreigner?"

"No … I don't think so. The cut of the coat is English," commented Marius, twisting the button to catch another facet of the light. "Could I take this as a sample? One of my brothers might know its source. It could help in establishing his identity."

"By all means. Though I can't think it's too important now. No one, to my knowledge has reported anyone of quality missing."

"You don't know," said Marius. "The body could have drifted up or down river. It might have entered the water some distance from here. Caught by the current, and delivered to the quays."

"According to the men who found him, he was jammed in the wood piles just below us. What is more, he was caught in the top of the cross members, which suggests he went into the river at this very spot."

CHAPTER FIFTY FIVE

Marius pushed open the coffee house door. Although prepared for the hubbub, it was still bewildering that business could take place in such a chaotic atmosphere. Mr Castaing occupied the same corner.

"My dear fellow, come sit beside me!" he shouted, waving an arm invitingly. "I've had a splendid morning, and the rest of the day looks equally favourable."

Castaing took a noisy sip from a large cup.

"Now, to the task you put me. A very interesting situation, if I may say," commented the jobber. "First of all, there is no record of any stock being offered during these past weeks. But that might suggest they have been sold by private treaty, not offered on the open market."

Castaing paused.

"I have also checked the registry. I have to advise you that no sale of shares has been officially recorded."

Marius sensed Castaing was holding something back. There was a light in his eye that hinted he had something yet to reveal.

"Go on."

Castaing grinned impishly. "However, I did find the reference to that sale of shares some fifteen years ago by Sir Francis Dashwood, one of the Manor Lords."

Marius remembered Roger's words concerning his uncles' losses when the South Sea Bubble burst. The family's subsequent misfortunes, and the enforced sale of the Rusthall Manor.

"Would that have been the shares you sold on their behalf, or when the title was sold to Maurice Conyers?"

"This relates to the earlier transaction," replied Castaing emphatically. "As I mentioned, the Dashwoods sold a large number of shares to assuage their losses. These included a parcel relating to the Walks and Rusthall Manor. Not that they were worth much, at that time they were desperate to turn anything into money. Now, let me see."

He rummaged among papers lying on an adjacent chair.

"Here we are," he exclaimed, pulling a single sheet from the pile. "As I thought. Among the various stocks for sale they also put two hundred and twenty-five shares in the Walks on the market."

He continued to peruse the document. "They should have sold their stock and rights to the Walks and the Lordship of the Manor there and then. But, I recall they wanted to hold the minimum to warrant the title. Pity, they had to sell them in the end for far less money."

Castaing looked over the glasses perched precariously on the end of his nose. "That's as much as I have discovered, Dr Hope."

He studied Castaing's countenance for a few moments.

"Tell me Mr Castaing, do you know how many shares in the Walks they retained? "

"According to my notes, it would appear they kept back three hundred and eighty four. The minimum holding for The Lordship would have been three hundred and seventy five."

"Mr Castaing, would you know who bought them?"

"I have notes of virtually all the transactions that take place here and in Garraways, my boy. Let me refer to my records."

Castaing delved deeper into the mound of papers. He searched among a number of folios before withdrawing several documents with a small cry of satisfaction.

"I thought you would ask me that question."

He pored over the papers. Finally, Castaing lifted his head. "It appears that they were sold, with a number of other lots, to a company called Jansons. How very interesting."

Marius sat there uncomprehendingly. "Why so, Mr Castaing?"

"My dear Doctor, Jansons was the company that constructed the buildings in the Walks some fifty years ago."

He was welcomed into the confines of Number Ten, Downing Street, and shown into a side room. A few minutes later Walpole burst through the door.

"Marius, good to see you. I must tell you straightaway I haven't much time. I'm leaving for Norfolk, shortly. The carriage is being made ready as we speak."

"I trust I won't keep you long, sir," replied Marius. A little put out by the man's attitude. The meeting had been arranged several days earlier.

"That must have sounded a trifle abrupt. Forgive me. I've just had a tedious hour with Talbot, the Lord Chancellor. Come, sit by the window, tell me your news. What has prompted your return to London?"

Mindful of the need for brevity, Marius updated him on recent happenings, and the even greater concerns about the rise in contraband.

"There is now open hostility among the townspeople, especially by those fearing for their livelihoods. Only the other day there was a fracas between the freeholders and the shop owners. Tempers frayed. Blood was spilt. Who knows when there will be open warfare."

Walpole was looking at him seriously as he recounted how the events had taken a far worse turn.

"No one, it seems, can stem the flow of goods, which are now offered quite freely. If action is not taken soon the town's economy will be ruined. To say nothing of The Wells as a popular spa. I am convinced, Sir Robert, that the military has to be used to be bring down the smugglers," Marius said earnestly.

The Principal Minister sat in silence, before commenting.

"I accept there is some justification, Marius, but, you will also appreciate this would be a major step. If I sanction the use of dragoons, their role must be as a counter-offensive against clearly identified insurgents. The soldiers' orders must be precise, their tasks clearcut."

"I can assure you, Sir Robert, that the freeholders in The Wells fear for their lives. No one should be allowed to serve such threats upon them, or be so blatant in their commission. When local efforts come to nothing, surely a higher authority must be employed?"

"Hmm … I do not lightly countenance the use of troops," stated the Principal Minister. "I should tell you I was speaking with the Commissioner of Customs recently. He informed me that he has asked The Southern Area Controller to advise the need, or otherwise, of Enforcement Officers in The Wells. He is still awaiting that report."

Walpole looked intently at the young doctor of physick. "What you are asking me to do is discount any action on his part, and opt directly for the deployment of military force."

"Sir Robert," said Marius boldly, "we cannot close our eyes to the fact that in The Wells things are worsening by the day. It must be halted. Stallholders, shopkeepers, and residents should be safe from threats and violence. Of course, it could be a test. How far can they go before the authorities react. Just think, if ignored, illicit goods could be distributed even more widely, then you would have an even greater problem."

"Perhaps Marius. But a detachment of Enforcement Officers might well do the job without the call for an armed contingent of dragoons."

"I am sorry, Sir Robert, I disagree. The only effective way to rid the town and surrounding villages of this illegal trade is the application of military force. The Enforcement people would be ineffectual." Marius stood up impatiently. "What you are not aware of, sir, is the parallel plot. One directed specifically against the freeholders. Compelling them to sell their titles to the Walks may be a ploy to divert attention away from the flood of contraband. Most probably, its aim is to reinforce their sale."

"What are you saying, Marius?"

"I have discovered that certain people are anxious to obtain the title deeds to the Walks. Once they have them, they could force contraband sales up still further. What we are facing is a double conspiracy. Make the tenants bend to your demands, and you could sell as much and whatever you wish. I implore you, Sir Robert, sanction the use of the dragoons, or the town will face an insurmountable problem."

He resumed his chair.

"I am strongly of the opinion, sir, that there is much at stake, involving large sums of money," Marius declared, taking a bold step into what was merely conjecture.

"Do you have absolute proof of such trickery?" demanded the Principal Minister.

Marius was suddenly confronted with the question to which he had no complete answer. How should he reply? Should he declare that Conyers was behind the scheme? Should he admit he knew little, that any response was better than nothing. How would Walpole react to the use of soldiers merely to dissuade the smugglers, when commonsense suggested that once the dragoons departed, it would quickly resume?"

Walpole interrupted his thoughts.

"As yet, you do not know who is behind either conspiracy, do you?"

"Sir Robert, I am sure I will be able to discover the identities of the conspirators and furnish the necessary proof," submitted Marius, struggling to carry his conviction.

Walpole stared at him. Then the decision was taken.

"You shall have your dragoons! However, I shall not advise the Generals or The Secretary At War. Although, out of courtesy I shall have to send a note to the Commissioner at the Board of Excise.

"I've got an idea how we can provide your force another way," declared the Principal Minister. "However, the stipulation is, Marius, before they are deployed, any action taken, Conyers must have evidence of who the conspirators are and from where they operate."

"We shall do all in our power to have the identities of those involved by the time the dragoons arrive, sir."

Walpole looked at Marius intently. A smile tugged at the corners of his mouth. He reached for the bell-pull to summon his secretary.

"I'm relying on you, Doctor. Now, I am fast running out of time. Let us attend to it with all speed. I'm going to write three letters. The first is to Lionel Sackville, the Duke of Dorset, who is in my cabinet. He and I were chatting after a meeting only yesterday, before he left for his country estate.

"We were discussing our defences, and he mentioned that currently there is a detachment of dragoons at the military garrison in Dover. Sackville is Lord Warden of The Cinque Ports, and that role still retains the power to "muster". So, I shall request him to free the detachment of its immediate responsibilities, and for the dragoons to make their way in one week to The Wells. Their orders will be to root out the smugglers, distributors and sellers of contraband endangering the local economies. The officer in charge to report to Mr Robert Fielding, the Southern Area Controller of Customs and Excise."

"Sir Robert, may I request an amendment?" asked Marius hesitantly.

"What's that, Doctor?"

"May I suggest the officer reports to Mr Conyers? He has the facility to bring together the various bodies. The magistrate's office, the constabulary, the clergy and the town fathers. If the officer seeks him out, they will be able to mobilise all the parties concerned into a more united force."

"Hmm … A fair point. I'll make the change,"

Walpole instructed his secretary accordingly. He then dictated the next letter to the Commissioner of The Board of Excise, and the third to Maurice Conyers, The Lord of The Manor of Rusthall.

"Return with the finished documents for my signature and seal as soon as you can," he instructed.

When the door closed, Walpole leaned back in his chair.

"I would suggest, Marius, that you deliver the note to Sackville personally, in case he needs more information. It won't delay your return, for he will be at Knole Park, near Sevenoakes. The coach goes past his estate. Now, before we go our separate ways, tell me, whom do you suspect?"

Marius contemplated the point.

"It's more a question of whom I can eliminate. In all truth, even Mr Conyers could be a candidate. I would dearly welcome proving he is not a party to this devilish plot. In fact, sir, my reason for suggesting you appoint him as organiser was a means of either incriminating him, or hopefully, confirming his preparedness to uphold the law."

Marius continued, uncertainty in his voice. "Whilst sitting here, I've been thinking of a simple way to prove it, one way or the other," he said gravely. "It means one alteration to the letter destined for Mr Conyers."

"Well," said the Principal Minister, "I've been delayed thus far, I might as well spend a little more time confirming that Conyers is either friend or foe. Tell me what you have in mind."

Marius spent the weekend at his parents' home in Chelsea. His two brothers came to dinner, and his younger sister was joined by her husband.

"If only Margaret could have been with us, it would have seemed just like old times," said his mother wistfully.

In the evening whilst his siblings were around the piano singing the latest ballads, Marius sat beside his father on a well-padded sofa. Both enjoying their brandies, and listening to the light-hearted banter.

"By the way, Father, I noticed some building activity across the Row," commented Marius, basking in the kinship of his family. "Is it part of the hospital? Are they creating more accommodation for the soldiers?"

His sister called brightly, "It's not the Hospital for The Maimed, Marius. They are building a new pleasure garden. It's about time they had more pleasing diversions in Chelsea."

Her husband took up the conversation. "Apparently, it's going to be quite splendid. There's going to be a large rotunda where they'll play music throughout the day. There'll be walks, even a boating pond."

"I should imagine Walpole is pleased he moved to Downing Street after all," commented his father dryly. "Yet another free household. When he was paymaster to the hospital, decidedly better than that awful Lord Ranelagh, he also had use of that rather fine house across from the Row. Totally without charge, of course."

Benjamin, his elder brother, remarked, "I can't imagine why James Lacey, the fellow who owns The Drury Lane Theatre, is involved. I can only presume the builder is using his talents to add showmanship to the project."

"Who is the builder, Father?" asked Michael, his other brother.

"I met the fellow the other day. He called to check we were not being inconvenienced by the works. His name is Solomon Rietti."

"Rietti! I know that name. He does the actual construction work for a lot of builders," said Benjamin.

"Including Jansons?" asked Marius blithely.

"Yes, I believe so. Why?"

Startled, Marius looked up. Another conflicting thought.

"Nothing of consequence, Benjamin, just idle thoughts."

The chatter around him turned to other topics, and, for a moment, Marius was lost in contemplation. Much had happened since travelling to the spa town. Most of it he had recounted to his family. However, one subject, about which he had been reticent had been his growing affection for Beth. Was it time to mention it?

He turned to his father. Then, changed his mind. "By the way, I met Dr Simons yesterday," said Marius, placing his glass on a side table.

"He works too hard," muttered his father, gently swirling his brandy, watching it gather in the bowl of the goblet. "Yet, you can't stop him. He never seems to leave the riverside these days."

"Incidentally, Marius," he continued, "I have some more news about the Conyers' family. Originally from Ireland, they settled in London and made their fortune in property. Interestingly, Maurice Conyers' sister married his erstwhile business partner, Robert Martineau."

The elder man took a moment to light a cigar.

"When Conyers moved to the country, some fourteen years ago, he relinquished his interests in the company. Martineau took over, and has expanded it considerably. Nowadays, he is much more involved in building development. Some say he has over-extended himself. Still, that could easily be rumour, put about by his rivals. From what I can gather, he is doing rather well for himself."

"Your efforts are much appreciated, Father."

"Tell me, was Castaing able to shed any light on the owners of the title deeds, Marius?"

"Not in any great detail. Though he did uncover the fact that Jansons, the company that erected the buildings in the Upper Walk, now own a parcel of the shares."

"Really? I wasn't aware they were up for sale."

"They were sold by the previous Lords of The Manor, Roger Dashwood's uncles, after the South Sea Company crashed," commented Marius. "They were included in a raft of stocks and shares they disposed of to ease their financial straits. Though, it didn't help much. They had to sell everything shortly afterwards."

"So what is the present stock holding?" asked his father. "Who owns what at the moment?"

"I've been trying to work this out for the past few days. I haven't got far. From what information I have, it seems that out of an original issue of one thousand shares, the Lord of The Manor, Maurice Conyers, now has three hundred and eighty four. The freeholders have two hundred and ninety one, though I have it on good authority they have been selling theirs. Lord Abergavenny has a hundred, and Jansons, two hundred and twenty five."

His father nodded, absorbing the details as he again swirled the brandy in his glass. Suddenly, he glanced across at Marius.

"If I've calculated it correctly, Marius," his eyes narrowed as he mentally re-checked his figures, "Conyers and Abergavenny together own less than half the stock. Whoever is buying the freeholders' title deeds, which represent two hundred and ninety one shares, if they also acquired Janson's share holding, would have the controlling interest.

"But, why would they want it?" mused his father. He laughed. "Unless, they want to develop the area and build another Ranelagh Gardens."

"That could well be the key to the whole sorry business," said Marius thoughtfully.

CHAPTER FIFTY SIX

Although he journeyed in reasonable comfort, the swaying coach encouraging him to doze, his thoughts would not let him rest. Marius had learned a great deal during his brief visit to London. But how much was relevant?

According to Walpole, Customs House had urgently demanded Fielding advise the best use of Enforcement Officers. They were still awaiting his response. Could it be he had much to lose if Enforcement Officers were called to deal with the matter? If the Excise men working along the coast were open to bribery, who is to say their superiors were above suspicion?

At Sevenoaks he walked wearily up the hill in the wheel ruts of the coach and on through the town to the gates of Knole Park. The Duke of Dorset received him, and breaking the seal, read the letter from the Principal Minister.

"What's the fellow up to this time, I wonder?" said the duke, bemused by its contents.

"However, you can leave it with me, Dr Hope. I shall refrain from asking more about the request, and do as he proposes. I shall send a courier to Dover at first light."

That evening Marius took a room at the Royal Oak Hotel, almost opposite the gates of Knole Park. Retiring early, the constant assessment and re-assessment of events precluded any notion of slumber.

He reviewed the encounters with Fielding. In retrospect, instead of giving him a studied air, Fielding's quiet demeanour could easily have been deliberate, calculated not to draw attention to himself. When first invited to sit in on the meeting at Rusthall, Marius clearly recalled Fielding's lacklustre interest, even when questioned directly by Walpole. He had appeared withdrawn, sitting at the table, occasionally making notes, more often scratching neat little designs on the paper before him.

Again, something caught at the edges of his mind. A fragment, momentarily out of reach, yet seemingly noteworthy. Exasperated, he turned his thoughts to the Manor Lord. He was deeply troubled by Maurice Conyers. Appearance suggested he had little need for additional wealth, but who was to say he had no wish to increase his personal fortune. Beneath the welcoming exterior could easily be an iron resolve to strengthen the power of his position. Would he deliberately set up a smuggling ring, then use the freeholders as a distribution network? If he procured all the shares in the Walks, added to those obtained from Jansons, he would be in an inviolable position. All the more able to coerce the freeholders into selling contraband. Moreover, the enduring dispute over ownership would disappear.

But was he instrumental in compelling the freeholders to surrender their rights? With a quarter of the stock sold before he bought the Lordship, would Conyers go beyond the law to seize the shares from the hapless freeholders? What made it worse was Marius' growing fondness for his niece. If Conyers were masterminding blatant thuggery, even stooping to murder, bringing him to task would undoubtedly jeopardise his relationship with Beth.

The following day he caught the coach to the Wells. When it halted at Ashenhurst House, Marius was apprehensive of what lay ahead.

CHAPTER FIFTY SEVEN

When Hope had failed to join the coach at the pump in Sevenoakes, the fellow continued on to The Wells, uncertain why the doctor had cut short his journey. Outside the Angel Hotel he had taken up his case and crossed to a post-chaise standing amongst the trees. The curtains were tight drawn. The horses standing patiently, other than the occasional stamp of hooves on the dry earth, and the chink of the snaffle chains.

Once seated, it had moved off, taking the upward track to Mount Ephraim. Ten minutes later it came to a halt beside a high brick wall surrounding one of the larger houses on the ridge. The leather springs creaked as the man descended.

He entered through a small side gate, and crossed the lawn towards the beckoning candlelight. Passing through open French windows, ajar in the cool of the evening, he halted before the small group waiting expectantly for his arrival.

"Gentlemen," he exclaimed, dropping his case on the ornate carpet, and draping his cloak on a chair. "Interesting news."

Handed a glass of wine, he took a long draught, before setting it on a side table.

"Our friend Hope has been busy, and very inquisitive. He met with Castaing at Jonathan's Coffee House on two occasions. It could mean he was making investments," he looked for a moment into each of the faces staring intently at him. "More likely, he was inquiring into certain share dealings, and in particular, the present owners of the stock in the Walks."

"What does Castaing know?" asked one of the four standing around the new arrival. "There haven't been any official details released."

"Hope is no fool," responded another, raising an unsteady glass to his lips. "If Castaing has given him the background, he could easily interpret the situation."

He wiped his brow with a large, red handkerchief.

Another well-dressed gentlemen in the room commented, "I take a different view. There is little Hope could learn from his visits to Jonathan's. So, he may have heard that Jansons picked up a portfolio of various shares some years ago. But, there the trail ends. Whatever he might conclude is, at best, conjecture. In all probability, he has reached a dead end, and is hopelessly confused."

"That may be the case," added the new arrival thoughtfully. "He certainly looked bewildered when he left the Coffee House."

"It's all right for you to take such a casual attitude, sir," declared the nervous gentleman, his face now quite red. "You have less to lose."

"My friends, please," interjected the one who had, thus far, kept his counsel. "We achieve little by losing our tempers."

Turning to the messenger, he said. "Tell me, what else transpired?"

"Dr Hope also went to see the Principal Minister. In fact, he spent over an hour with him. It must have been significant. In an inn off Whitehall, I discovered from one of the household footmen, that Walpole was off to his estate at Houghton to attend a shoot. To get there in one day would mean setting out soon after breakfast. Yet, because of Hope's visit, he delayed his departure."

"It may be happening sooner than we think," murmured another of the group.

"Perhaps it is, perhaps it isn't," remarked the newcomer. "But you should prepare accordingly. More so because, before his meeting with Walpole, Hope paid a visit to Customs House. It's near his family's business on the quays."

"What does that mean?" asked the red-faced gentleman anxiously.

All eyes were fixed on the messenger.

"I followed him into the building, there were any number of people passing through the doors, so it was not obvious I was dogging his footsteps. I stood to one side and overheard him ask one of the porters how he might contact Mr Fielding. The reply was that presently Fielding was away from London, conducting one of his regular tours of the south-east region."

"Well that's true," remarked the quieter gentleman. "What then kept him so long with Walpole, I wonder?"

"My belief is that they spoke about the smuggling problem, and the heights it has now reached," smiled the new arrival retrieving his wine glass from the side table. He slowly raised it to his lips, but held it in front of his face in contemplation.

"Why do you think that?" asked one.

"Both Hope and Walpole came out the building in Downing Street together. They were also accompanied by an official messenger, who took to his horse as the Principal Minister's carriage departed and Hope strode off up Whitehall."

Once more he returned his glass to the table without drinking.

"Fortunately I was mounted and chose to follow the messenger, who went with all speed along the embankment. And where do you think he went?"

"Don't play games with us, sir!" exclaimed the florid-faced gentleman. "Damned well tell us!"

"To Customs House. He dismounted in front of the building, and rushed through the doors. I was just in time to hear him state he had an urgent letter from the Principal Minister for the Commissioner. I am in no doubt it was a call to rally the Enforcement Officers. Which means, you probably have less time than you imagine to complete the project."

CHAPTER FIFTY EIGHT

"So, now you know as much as I do."

They were eating in the White Bear Inn.

"The trouble is, I don't think I'm any further forward. Though it's clear the smuggling, the threats to the freeholders, the sale of the title deeds, are all related in some way."

Roger said nothing. He sat opposite, staring into the mug of ale before him. Marius picked at his food. It had cooled during the telling of his exploits, and finally he pushed the plate away.

"I didn't realise my uncles were in such desperate straits," he muttered. "When the South Sea Company went down it must have been an horrendous time. They tried hard to retain the lordship, but, in the end, were forced to sell out."

He looked up. "They lost everything, and all I cared about was my own well-being."

"You were very young, Roger," sympathised Marius. "How could you possibly understand at the time."

"I was angry with them for spoiling my life. I never forgave them, you know. I never spoke to them again. Now I realise what they were up against, I feel quite penitent."

Marius called for another pitcher, hoping it might help blot out Dashwood's melancholy. But as he turned back to his companion, Roger was grasping for his arm to draw him back into conversation.

"Still, I haven't told you my news, have I?" he said excitedly. Marius could never attune himself to Roger's mercurial changes of temperament.

"Er … No. Did something happen in my absence?"

"Two things actually. When we went part-way along the Maidstone road, you will recall I was keen to investigate further," Roger said, a self-satisfied look coming over his face. "So, whilst you were away, I decided to retrace our steps, to continue along that road. I also saw no harm in checking for possible landing sites on the Medway between Tonbridge and the village of East Peckham."

"I thought the constable was going to inspect the river banks, Roger."

He raised the mug to his lips, drank deeply, and looked across at Marius with a triumphant gleam in his eye.

"It seemed perfectly sensible to me that if I were searching for Johnson, I should combine the two activities. After all, they were in the same direction."

Roger leaned across the table, lowering his voice so that Marius had to move towards him.

"I rode to Tonbridge, and took the path along the north side of the river. It peters out in several places, and I was forced back onto the roadway. However, I discovered that, just after a hamlet called Snoll Hatch, I could get down to the riverside. I had taken a flagon of cider and some cheese, and thought to sit on the bank for an impromptu meal."

Roger stopped to light up a pipe. He took his time tamping down the tobacco in the bowl, and some minutes with his tinder, before puffing in satisfaction. Marius knew it was a ploy to heighten interest.

"Where was I? Yes, at the river's edge on a sunny day. Having eaten and set my pipe, I contemplated the view. I must have fallen asleep. When I awoke it was late afternoon. The sun had moved round, the change in the light creating deep shadows in the reeds and tall grasses on the far bank. It was then I made out the faint outline of a pathway from the river to distant buildings. I could not see too much because of the haze. But, it could confirm what the barge captain was saying, could it not? What do you make of that?"

"I'm impressed, Roger," declared Marius, smiling across at his companion. "It might suggest a landing point for the smugglers, though it might be a way to the river for nearby villagers."

"I thought of that. They can reach the river where it runs close to the village without walking a mile or so upstream. Anyway, that's not the end of the story, my dear fellow," said Roger excitedly. "I was stirred to investigate. The nearest crossing is at Bambridge's Mill, up near East Peckham. So I made my way back to the lane."

He took another swig from the mug. Then, grinning, he asked, "Who do you think I saw?"

"I've no idea." Marius was becoming exasperated as the tale was prolonged.

"Johnson! I almost rode into him! Fortunately, I was hidden from view by trees along the wayside. I managed to rein in my horse as he passed. Then I followed him."

Marius was suddenly attentive.

"He stopped briefly in Yalding to make some purchases. Then, he rode on towards Teston, and crossed the bridge at West Farleigh. I must say I was jolly good at keeping him in sight without him seeing me."

Marius thought that Johnson must have been much preoccupied with his own thoughts not to have spotted him. But he refrained from making comment.

"In the next village, I think it's called East Farleigh, where there are lock gates and a weir, he turned up a short path and rode into a stable yard behind a cottage. I made my way towards it on foot.

"Do you know, Johnson almost saw me. I was crouching behind a rough flint wall when he suddenly appeared and was walking towards me. I was frozen to the spot. Fortunately, he turned off, opened a small gate and went in at the back door."

Roger paused again. Staring into the middle distance, as if recalling the scene.

"What then?"

"Well, after recovering my wits, I made my way cautiously towards the front of the cottage to see if I could see anything. I tell you, I was shaking for fear someone might see me," Roger said with feeling. "I crawled under a window, then slowly raised my eyes to peer in. Guess what I saw?"

"For goodness sake, Roger, just tell me!"

"There he was, in the embrace of a woman! I couldn't see her face, her back was towards me. There was no doubt. It was your friend, Mr Johnson!"

"Well, I'll be damned! So there is trickery. We shall have to discover who this paramour is. It could well be the key to what happened in The Wells. What did you do then?"

"By the time I had remounted it was dark. I made my way back to Tonbridge and stayed in the Rose and Crown for the night. The following day I was in two minds whether to ride the south bank of the river, or tell the authorities in Tonbridge."

"What did you decide?" enquired Marius anxiously. Aware of Mr Russell's remarks.

"I decided to return to The Wells and put the matter before the constable."

"I'm pleased you did, Roger," said Marius thankfully. "Let him deal with it from now on."

"He told me of the warning he had given you," Roger said with a chuckle. "Anyway, he is going to send two deputies to examine the river bank and the buildings I saw. What do you think of that, Marius?"

"I am truly impressed, Roger."

"I thought you might be. Though, perhaps, I was a little fortunate."

"Nonsense. You had the wit to seize the opportunity," praised Marius.

Dashwood grinned, a trifle smugly.

CHAPTER FIFTY NINE

"Dr Hope," interrupted a maid. "You have a visitor, sir. Shall I bring him through to the orangery?"

"If you would be so kind."

"For goodness, sake, Marius," Roger exclaimed, "you should ask who it is. It could be someone you might not care to see."

"If that is the case, my dear fellow, I shall be greatly disappointed. However, if it is whom I believe it to be, I shall be greatly relieved."

There were footsteps. The door opened.

"Mr Conyers, sir," declared the maid.

The Lord of The Manor swept in and slumped into a chair. He looked both preoccupied and deeply concerned in the same moment.

"Marius, I must speak with you."

"First let me get you some refreshment," Marius said, then added, "I can't tell you how good it is to see you, sir."

"Perhaps not when you hear what I've got to say."

"On the contrary, I'm sure to be delighted," said Marius. His voice tight with anticipation.

"Dashwood, will you excuse us?"

"There's no need for him to leave Mr Conyers. Roger may not know every detail, but he will soon be aware of much which concerns us," said Marius firmly.

"Well, if you think that's wise, so be it," replied Conyers, clearly agitated.

Glancing briefly at Dashwood, Conyers returned his attention to Marius.

"Yesterday, a messenger arrived from London with a letter from the Principal Minister. I won't repeat all its contents, but suffice it to say, a troop of dragoons will be arriving in The Wells in two weeks time."

Marius nodded and smiled. "Anything else?"

A frown passed over Conyers' brow.

"The letter also mentioned that I should dissuade you from becoming too involved in matters concerning smuggling, and the disposal of certain title deeds," muttered Conyers, looking round at Roger. "Sir, I really believe we should discuss this between ourselves."

"I have to correct you on several aspects, Mr Conyers. Firstly, the militia will be here, in The Wells, in one week's time. The other is that Sir Robert Walpole suggests that I am "a hothead, needing to be controlled for my own safety"."

"How the deuce could you possibly know what the Principal Minister has written? Anyway, he categorically states the troops will be arriving in two weeks time."

"Forgive the artifice, Mr Conyers. You see, I suggested the contents of the letter when I called upon Sir Robert. I also owe you an apology," said Marius, now feeling some small embarrassment.

"What do you mean, sir?" said Conyers, looking at him sharply.

"Let me explain. You also read that smuggling is the key to the whole affair. The sale of the title deeds, or shares, in the Walks, is a ploy to divert attention. Now, if that were the case," said Marius, hesitantly, uncertain how next to proceed without provoking anger, "you could be in an invidious position. Until we discover who is masterminding these two schemes, you, sir, might well have been accused of encouraging the freeholders to sell their titles and trade in illicit goods."

Marius halted, searching for words of diplomacy. However, in that moment, he opted to state his thoughts openly.

"You could have appeared to be the unlawful beneficiary of the sale of those title deeds. You have admitted to me people are suspicious of your involvement in the town's affairs. Forgive me, but it was essential to clear away any lingering doubts. This letter from the Principal Minister was also intended to establish your *bona fides.*"

"I don't understand you."

"Well, sir, if you had not acquainted me of the gist of Walpole's letter within hours of its receipt, the only logical interpretation was that you wanted me to be unaware of the Principal Minister's actions, and were, indeed, party to the plot."

"Good Lord, how devious," exclaimed Conyers.

Marius examined Conyers' face for possible upset. Waiting for the truth to dawn that he had considered him a key suspect.

"If you were involved," continued Marius, 'advising you that the dragoons would arrive in two weeks may have induced a false sense of security. Moreover, keeping me in the dark would have given you time to stifle my attempts to expose the guilty parties."

Conyers got to his feet, and stared hard at Marius.

"I am not happy that you could ever doubt my standing in this affair, sir. Not happy at all."

He wandered towards one of the large windows, and looked out at the garden for some minutes. Marius and Roger said nothing. Conyers turned and with a sigh, said, "But it's logical I suppose, to be suspicious of everyone connected with these happenings. Come, we shall talk no more of it."

He walked back to where Marius was sitting.

"But, how do I afford you protection, as it says in the letter?" he enquired, then came to a decision. "Let us discuss it further at supper tomorrow. I shall be busy all day making the arrangements Walpole has requested. Shall we say six of the clock? I shall expect you both. Good-day, gentlemen."

"Mr Conyers, a moment sir, before you go. You are not involved with passing any information to others, that we know. I'll tell you plain, I feel sure someone in your household is. We cannot ignore the possibility that if details of conversations are being bandied around, then whoever it is, knows about what you, your committee, and those who attend upon you, discuss in private."

"Damnation, Marius, you go too far!" exploded Conyers, his face reddening. "How dare you accuse anyone in my employ of treachery!"

"I'm sorry if it upsets you, Mr Conyers. But, you cannot deny the obvious," said Marius calmly. "Unless, of course, you can suggest other ways information is leaving the Manor."

"I thought for a moment he was going to take against you, Marius," said Roger. "You were taking a fearful risk in the way you handled it. Especially, the accusation that a member of his household is giving away secrets."

"Perhaps you're right, Roger. I find, at times, I speak without considering the consequences. As for finding out whether or not Conyers was party to a possible conspiracy, I had little time to devise a way to establish his complicity, or otherwise. Walpole's letter was the only thing I could think of."

"Anyway, my dear fellow, it worked. Tell me, what did the letter say?"

Marius reached into a pocket and withdrew an envelope.

"This is a copy. If necessary, it was to be given to Conyers if he disputed my knowing about the dragoons."

Marius passed over the letter.

AUTHENTICATED VERSION –
dated Friday 31st August 1736
My Dear Conyers,

The Availablity of Contraband in the Wealden Townships must be Eliminated. To this End, I have, today, Notified the Commissioner of Excise I am Despatching a Troop of Dragoons to The Wells, and for the Officer in

Charge to Liaise with Yourself on the Deployment of his Force.

Ordinarily, he would Report to the Southern Area Controller. However, as You are already Acting as Convenor of the Officials responsible for Local Law and Order, it seems Appropriate that the Chain of Command Resides in Your Hands.

The Troop will arrive at Rusthall in One Week's Time from the Date of This Letter. Please make all the Necessary Arrangements for them to be Billeted, Horses Stabled, and Both Provided Rations whilst under Your Command.

Dr Hope has kept Me properly Informed of Developments in The Wells and Nearby Tonbridge. Judging by Recent Happenings, I am Concerned for his Safety. He is, by Nature quick to React, not always Wisely. He may well Jeopardise his Own Wellbeing as well as any Plans You Deem Appropriate to Overcome the Problems.

Are you Aware, he now Believes that the Rise in Contraband in the Area is Related in some Measure to the Unwarranted Pressure being applied to the Freeholders to Surrender their Title Deeds in the Walks. He Now Believes He Knows the Miscreants behind this Dreadful Plot, and is Determined, Shortly, to Reveal their Names.

I Look to You to Advise him Strongly of the Risks he is Taking, and to Afford all Necessary Protection.

Yours Sincerely

Sir Robert Walpole
Downing Street
London

Dashwood folded the letter.

"H'mm … If The Lord of The Manor had been the villain of the plot, I can well understand why he would have kept quiet. No doubt, he would also have been far more assiduous in your removal if he thought you were about to reveal the culprits. A dangerous game, Marius."

"As I said, it was the only course I could think of at the time."

"Do you really believe the smuggling and the sale of the deeds are linked in some way?"

"Frankly, I'm not sure. It may be just unrelated suspicions on my part," commented Marius. He grinned. "My father even suggested the aim of the whole affair was to erect more buildings in The Wells. But, that's hardly likely. Conyers' hands are clean. What I cannot reconcile is why the intimidation of those holding titles to the Walks coincides so exactly with the arrival of the contraband."

Marius took a clay pipe, filled it, and lit the tobacco.

"Who would carry out either?" Roger queried. "And for what purpose?"

"That, my dear Roger, is the vital question."

"How do you intend to answer it?"

"I'm not sure. What I am sure of is that Conyers is not involved. Though, someone at Rusthall is. And we shall flush them out at supper tomorrow night."

"After your comments, I'm surprised Conyers didn't cancel the invitation," Roger murmured.

"I suppose reason prevailed. After all, he cannot refute logic."

"Logic doesn't enter into it when you touch upon family loyalty. Once in a while, Marius, consider others' feelings before you make bold statements. Anyway, what convinces you that someone is revealing secrets?"

"Little things," replied Marius grimly. "Firstly, I overheard Fielding and that other fellow discussing my involvement at the recital at Eridge Park. Then, I told Conyers that you and I were going to Tonbridge, and someone took at shot at us. I even told him I was going to London, and I had the strongest feeling I was being followed. If we have proved that Conyers is not the culprit, someone in his household most certainly is."

CHAPTER SIXTY

He slowly moved his weight onto his left leg, trying to ease the discomfort. Hidden among bushes that flanked the drive, he had an angled view of the Manor House, bathed in the soft glow of moonlight. Now and then, when clouds dimmed the scene, he was extra vigilant.

He was also weary from having taken up the position four hours earlier. The feeling now dawning that it had been a waste of time, and a vindication of Conyers' viewpoint. No one was letting secrets be known to outsiders. Marius was close to admitting the Lord of The Manor was right.

He thought about Roger, posted near the stables. He would also blame him for his unwarranted assumptions. Putting him to unnecessary inconvenience because of misplaced suspicions. I'll wait here another ten minutes then return to Ashenhurst House, Marius decided. I cannot imagine anyone leaving the house at this late hour.

It had seemed such a good plan. Grudgingly, Conyers had played his part at dinner. Letting it be known to those at the table, and to the serving staff, that he had received a letter from Sir Robert Walpole, which was of the utmost importance. To Marius' dismay, Beth, now returned from her family, had been the first to enquire of its content.

"Come, Uncle," she had pleaded, "don't keep us in suspense. What does he have to say?"

"My dear, how can I tell you of a private matter?"

"Surely, if Sir Robert sends a note to your home we are all involved," commented Beth, her head tilted to one side questioningly. As if to emphasise that everyone should be told. Reluctantly, Conyers had explained.

"My dear, our Principal Minister has at last acceded to my request. In two weeks time he is sending a troop of dragoons to apprehend those smuggling contraband into the town. Now we shall be able to restore The Wells to some sense of normality."

"I'm sure our flamboyant Master of Ceremonies will be pleased, if he is even aware of what is going on," replied Beth.

"Beth!" said her aunt, "be sensible of your remarks! Mr Nash is not to be spoken of in such terms."

"Well, Aunt," added Ralph, "I'm sure he is well suited to his position. But there are times he is somewhat vague, is he not?"

"Ralph, I forbid you to say such things about Mr Nash. Tell them to desist, Maurice."

"My dear," said Conyers, a smile playing at his lips. "I'm sure no hurt was intended."

"Does Sir Robert want you to do anything else, Uncle?" asked Ralph.

"He has requested I organise the dragoons' efforts, and take responsibility for their deployment."

"Surely, that would be the role of the Southern Controller of Excise, would it not, Mr Conyers?" Marius had asked, knowing full well the answer.

"It would appear that as I am coordinating the local efforts against the smugglers, I am best placed to marshal the troops," Conyers had replied.

The conversation at the meal progressed to other topics. Later, when they were entertaining each other in the music room, Marius had spoken briefly with Beth about her visit home, but had had no opportunity to converse in private. Eventually, Roger and he had retrieved their horses from the stables and departed for their lodgings at eight of the clock. Now, it was close to midnight, and still no sign of anyone stirring in the house. Marius transferred his weight to his right leg.

"Marius," came a softly-spoken voice. "Quick! Where are you?"

In the stillness, alone with his thoughts and concerns, Marius was unprepared to hear someone so close. His heart lurched.

"There you are," whispered Roger urgently. "Come on! Something is happening!"

It took a moment for his heart to stop racing. Fortunately, Roger could not see the startled look in his eyes.

"We must hurry. Where have you left the horses?"

"They're behind us, among the trees."

"Come on then. There's not a moment to lose. Someone has saddled a mount in the stable block, muffled its hooves, and is leading it towards the gates."

They made their way through the undergrowth to where the horses were tethered.

"Come on. He will get away before we can follow him," Roger said anxiously. The retreating figure was just visible. Marius wished, fervently, that it was a man.

"Marius, what are you doing here at this hour of the morning?"

"I've come to see your uncle, Beth," he replied, now uncertain about the meeting. Fierce indignation had been replaced by concern. The realisation that Conyers would find what he had to say unpalatable. Nevertheless, he had a duty to perform.

"I believe he is in the morning room," said Beth. Her eyes alight with curiosity.

"Shall I lead you to him?"

Marius now wished Roger had accompanied him. However, when suggested, he had declared it would be best done alone.

"You look very serious, Marius. Is anything wrong?"

"I have something to tell your uncle, Beth, which will not please him."

"Oh! Do you want me to stay when you speak to him?"

"I think not. I'm not certain how he will react."

Beth stopped and looked up into Marius' face. "Well, I'll be close by if you want me." Beth knocked on the door, and opened it for him to enter.

"Marius, my dear fellow, come in, come in," welcomed Maurice Conyers, placing his newspaper on a side table, and coming forward to greet him. However, as Marius approached he could see signs of unease in his eyes.

"I didn't sleep well for fear that you might call upon me this morning," he said, as Beth closed the door. "Did someone leave the Manor last night?" he enquired anxiously.

"I'm afraid so Mr Conyers, and we followed the person concerned."

"Damnation! Which of the servants was it? I should have known better. I thought I had their trust and respect. How could any of them do this to me?" ranted Conyers, outraged at the idea someone in his staff could so readily disclose confidences.

"I'm afraid, sir, it was not one of your servants," said Marius quietly.

"What do you mean? Surely, it could not have been anyone else?"

Marius' expression betrayed his feelings.

"I am sorry to tell you, sir, we followed your nephew, Ralph Martineau to Mount Ephraim. He spent more than a half of an hour at the house of Mr Phillips, the magistrate, before returning to the Manor."

"What arrant nonsense!" shouted Conyers. "You are maligning my own nephew, sir! I won't hear of it! Get out! Leave my house at once!"

The door burst open. Beth appeared white-faced, quickly followed by her aunt, who went to Conyers' side.

"Maurice, what on earth is going on?" she cried. "Heavens! We can hear you throughout the house."

"This impudent fellow has had the effrontery to accuse Ralph, my own sister's boy, of going behind our backs and revealing private conversations to others! Kindly leave, Dr Hope! Now!"

Beth stared at Marius. "How could you say such a thing, Marius? "I thought you were an honourable person! One I could trust."

She fled the room without giving him another glance.

CHAPTER SIXTY ONE

Marius hesitated at the site once the residence of the Johnsons. With his hands on the picket fence, he stared into the dark recesses of the burnt-out shell. A great deal had happened during his time in The Wells. Sufficient to distract him from the uncomfortable reality of life at the hospital. Though, in truth, he had swapped one set of unpleasant experiences for another.

Beth had rejected him, and seemingly, there was no way of regaining her favour. Marius had impugned her family, accusing her cousin of being a common telltale. Relaying every morsel of news of what transpired at Rusthall Manor to the local magistrate. Perhaps, Phillips had been of the same mind as Marius. There was every reason to believe the Lord of The Manor might be central to a plot with far-reaching consequences.

Obtaining the majority of the titles to the Walks would quash any thoughts of an impartial settlement between himself and the freeholders. The fact that Conyers was blameless of involvement was known only to Marius.

Ralph Martineau could well have been an innocent dupe. Persuaded by Phillips to note loose comment at the Manor simply to ensure the titular Lord was acting without personal prejudice.

When told of his dismissal, Roger had immediately suggested they spend a night at the gaming tables. It would lift his spirits. Marius had been reluctant. After the upsetting episode at Rusthall, he had not been in the mood. However, despite his protests, Marius had been persuaded to join him in the Assembly Rooms. But, as the evening progressed, he had become more and more out of sorts. His lack of interest in the fall of the cards ensured he lost heavily. After an hour of play, Marius had made his way back to Ashenhurst House.

His grip tightened on the rough wood of the picket fence. He thought back to his arrival, and the kindly attentions of Mrs Johnson. She had touched him deeply. It may have been because his mind was in turmoil. He had been at a loss to reconcile the problems he faced at St Bartholomew's, and had run from the situation.

Yet another example of his reluctance to face the realities of life. He had met Mrs Johnson at a low moment, and unconsciously seen in her a caring person. Even their brief conversations had been liberating. Now, those moments were gone. As Marius stood where Mrs Johnson had perished, he vowed to seek out the truth of her death.

His mind fixed on the Johnsons, he strode up the hill. Soon he could see the black outline of Ashenhurst House against the night sky. A breeze swaying the branches of trees, leaves rustling as wayward gusts caught at them.

Was that a footfall? Suddenly, his wits sharpened. In the half-light he could see little. He turned his head slowly, to catch unfamiliar sounds. After a moment he continued, but with more urgency in his step.

Nearing the bowling green, he turned down the path leading to the lodging house. Bushes fringed the track, casting shadows in which imagined enemies could so easily lie in wait. Marius was urged to run for the shelter of the building. With his frock coat thrown open, arms pumping, he sprinted the short distance to the sanctuary of the large double doors, open and welcoming by the light of lanterns bracketed either side the entrance.

He leaned against the doorpost, catching his breath, chiding himself for his irrational fears. Pulling away, about to enter the building, a hand touched his sleeve. Marius stood stock still, incapable of movement. Waiting for the inevitable blow and oblivion.

"Dr Hope, sir?" A hesitant voice behind him.

Every emotion coursed through his body. But, the overwhelming sensation was relief. He was safe. Exhaling deeply, he turned slowly to face the person clutching at his arm. It was someone he had seen before, but could not immediately place.

Marius stared at the slightly stooped figure, tidily dressed in well-worn breeches and a coat that had seen many years of wear. The eyes were, at once, compelling and sad. He was a man of middle-age, and without a wig, his sparse hair was lank and untrimmed.

He withdrew his hand.

"Doctor, I'm sorry if I startled you. My name is Fines. I'm a friend of Daniel Clifford."

Marius recalled the man. He was the magistrate's assistant. He had been sitting at the table at the meeting in Rusthall Manor.

"I remember. You work for Mr Phillips, do you not?"

"Yes sir, I do." The clerk looked nervously over his shoulder. "Can I speak with you in private, Dr Hope? It's important, sir."

It was clear Fines was anxious not to be seen. "You'd better come in."

He led the way to a vacant sitting room. Lighting candles, Marius enquired if he wanted something to drink.

"A mug of ale would be welcome, sir. If you don't mind?"

He went to the kitchen and found a serving girl. Rather than let her have sight of the clerk, he carried two full mugs back to the room. Settling in a chair, Marius looked at the man before him. "Well, Mr Fines, how can I help you?"

He was clearly agitated. The candelabra on the adjacent sideboard casting the clerk's face into nervous, mobile planes of light and dark, emphasising his distress.

"As I said a moment ago, Dr Hope, I'm a friend of Mr Clifford." He dropped his head. The long pause which followed made Marius enquire, "Is that it, Mr Fines?"

"No, sir, it is not. I was with Daniel the night of your meeting at the bathhouse. When we were attacked, I ran off."

Fines was feeling the uncomfortable burden of guilt, for he quickly blurted out, "There was only one person with a cudgel. But he came at us with such ferocity, Daniel went down under the first blow. I was hit across the back, and sent sprawling," recounted Fines, looking into the distance as each word brought back the reality of the skirmish.

"Then, as he belaboured Daniel, I managed to get up and run for it." Fines stopped again. "I should have helped him, Dr Hope," he anguished. "The fellow was just too strong for me."

"Calm yourself, Mr Fines. I'm sure there was little you could do."

As Marius uttered the words, he acknowledged that fetching help would have been the least the clerk could have done. It was the merest chance, and Clifford's good fortune, that he had been found so promptly.

"Did you hear me, Dr Hope?"

Distracted, he had not heard the question when it was first posed.

"Sorry, what did you say, Mr Fines?"

"The trouble is, sir, Daniel seems to have disappeared. I don't know whether he is dead or alive. His wife won't tell me anything."

Marius leaned forward. "He is not dead, Fines. He is extremely ill from his wounds, but he will live."

The clerk's relief was palpable.

"Thank The Lord! Where is he, Dr Hope?"

Caution prevailed.

"I cannot tell you. You must understand that for his own safety, the location has to be kept secret. Even from his wife," Marius added. He did not want the fact broadcast for fear of reprisal against her.

"No, of course not," muttered Fines. "However, when you next visit him please convey my concerns. It has weighed heavily on me these past days."

"I'm sure he will understand," said Marius, finishing his ale, and standing to encourage Fines' departure. As they moved towards the entrance, for want of something to say, Marius enquired after the magistrate's health. He received a non-committal reply.

"Thank you for putting my mind at rest, Doctor," said Fines at the door. "Please let me know how Daniel progresses."

He raised his hat, and started along the pathway. Marius was tired after a harrowing day and anxious to be abed. Snuffing out the candles in the hall, he took his first upward step on the stairway, then halted. Marius cursed his sluggishness of mind. Dashing across the hallway, flinging open the main door, he sped down the path.

"Mr Fines! A word with you, please!" shouted Marius.

Fines, who had gone but forty yards, spun round.

"Sir?"

"Tell me Mr Fines, if you know why Daniel Clifford wanted to see me, and you were with him that night, could you be the one corroborating his story?"

Fines looked furtive and unsure. "I don't want anything to do with it, Doctor. I shouldn't have gone with Daniel. It's lucky for me the attacker didn't see my face."

"But, surely, you want Clifford to be able to resume a normal life when he recovers?" enquired Marius bleakly. "He won't if he has to remain in hiding. The sooner this matter is brought into the open, the safer it will be for everyone."

"You don't understand, Doctor. I fear for my life. I know too much."

"For God's sake, Fines, Clifford is your friend! Would he act like this if you were in similar difficulties?"

"Probably. If he wanted to protect his family. Look at what happened to the Lovedays."

"What did happen to the Lovedays?" asked Marius. Then he realised what Fines was suggesting. "They were killed, weren't they, as a lesson to others."

"Go back to London, Doctor. Forget it ever happened," snarled Fines, turning to walk away.

"Listen, Fines," said Marius, snatching at his coat, spinning him round. "I've been shot at, half drowned, and now I've lost the love of my life because of this affair. I'm not leaving until, whoever it is, is brought to justice. If you value your miserable life above helping not only one friend and his family, but others in peril, then you are not the man I took you for."

He let go the coat suddenly, and Fines dropped to his knees.

Marius turned back towards the lodging house.

"Dr Hope, sir," called a tremulous voice, 'a moment. Perhaps we might continue our conversation?"

They sat in the same small sitting room. The hour was late.

"I'm not sure I know where to begin," muttered Fines abjectly. "I've been working for Mr Phillips for the past six years. I look after the court records, note and apply fees and penalties, and keep the calendar of official events," he related, as if by rote. "I also liaise with Mr Nash to make sure the chronicle is accurate."

Fines hesitated, before proceeding more slowly, choosing his words.

"I also keep the register of property owners in the town. This entails recording all changes to deeds and titles." He paused. "Do you think, sir, I might have something to drink?"

"What would you like?"

"A glass of brandy would be welcome, sir."

Marius went through to the dining room. Everyone had long since retired. He removed a decanter and two glasses from the sideboard. Returning to the sitting room, he gave Fines a generous measure, pouring only a modest amount for himself. He would need all his wits about him.

"Please continue, Mr Fines."

"Some weeks ago, sir ... I can recall it clearly. It was the last Wednesday in July. I always do my list of unpaid fines on that day every month. Well sir, Adam Squires, one of the freeholders, came into the office with a Mr Jordan to register the sale of his title in the Walks."

Fines put the glass of brandy to his lips, savouring the dark liquid. "Squires was content with the price paid, and happy to sign away his entitlement and shares in the Walks."

He looked across intently at Marius. "Mr Phillips was there at the time, and when Squires left, he took Mr Jordan into the inner room. I could not hear much of the conversation. Anyway, shortly after Mr Jordan left, another gentleman arrived. A Mr Augustus Brown. I showed him into the magistrate's room. A little while later Mr Phillips came through with signed documents, and told me to put them away, there and then, in the archives."

Fines again halted briefly to drink from his glass.

"After an hour or so, they both went off to dinner. I slipped into the room where the records are kept, took down the file on the sale, and discovered that the new owner was listed as Mr Augustus Brown. I thought nothing more of it, until I found out that the gentleman had arrived only a few days earlier from London. Odd, don't you think?"

Marius nodded, saying nothing. Fines sat hunched in his chair, staring into the empty grate. After a moment, he went on.

"During the past weeks, there's been a steady trickle of freeholders coming into the office, confirming the sales of their titles - all to Mr Brown. I was at a loss to understand why they were selling, and for such modest sums. Then six days ago Daniel Clifford told me. The freeholders were being threatened into selling their title deeds and consequently their shares in the Walks. Sell or suffer the consequences. He laughed harshly. "And we now know what that means."

"Mr Fines, do you believe Mr Phillips is party to the sales of the title deeds?"

"I'm not exactly sure, sir. He was only in the office the first time a sale was registered. And that seemed an amicable agreement. I thought the price was fair to both Squires and Mr Jordan."

"From what you have told me, the fact that Clifford was threatened, then beaten when he did not sell, is surely proof of a conspiracy, is it not?" declared Marius. He stood up abruptly. "One minute, Fines, before you go. I want to retrieve something from my room." He walked swiftly to the door, and ran up the stairs. He was returning with the document a few moments later, when Roger came through the main door.

"My dear fellow, I thought you would be abed."

"Roger, I can't explain now, but join me if you would."

Marius came into the sitting room, followed by a bemused Dashwood. Fines leapt to his feet.

"Don't be concerned, Fines. Mr Dashwood is an associate of mine, and the soul of discretion," said Marius quickly.

"I don't want any trouble, sir," said Fines apprehensively. "Like me, this gentleman works for the magistrate."

"You have my word, Fines. What we discuss will not implicate you in any way. Isn't that right, Mr Dashwood?" said Marius, turning to look at him directly.

He nodded slowly in affirmation. "Mr Fines, you also have my word."

Fortunately, thereafter, Roger remained silent.

"Now, Fines, I want you to tell me exactly how many titles have been registered from the time Squires came into the magistrate's offices unto the present moment."

"I have kept a careful record, sir. I had them written down when Clifford and I set out to meet you."

He took a much-folded scrap of paper from the inner recesses of his coat. He searched other pockets before happening upon a well-used pair of spectacles. Hooking the distorted wire frames over his ears, he unfolded the sheet. He stared intently at the neat writing for a brief moment, then looked up.

"To my knowledge, Doctor, sales of title deeds, equivalent to two hundred and forty three shares have now been registered. That includes the Loveday titles sold by his brother, who was next of kin."

Marius leaned forward. "Mr Castaing, a jobbing broker in London, gave me details of the original share issue. Of the one thousand shares, the freeholders had three hundred and ninety one. We can reduce this figure to two hundred and ninety one, because Lord Abergavenny has a hundred of them."

Marius stopped, and looked deliberately into the faces of the two other men. "So, of that two hundred and ninety one," he said thoughtfully, 'according to your figures, Fines, only forty eight shares are now held by freeholders."

"Apart from Lord Abergavenny, I didn't know how many shares they held, Dr Hope. But if what you say is correct, the forty eight shares are in the hands of three freeholders," said Fines, looking down his crumpled sheet 'and Daniel Clifford has twenty nine of them."

"Do you have the names of the others who haven't sold?"

"Yes, if you want them."

"I say, Marius, what's this all about?" Roger enquired.

"The figures Fines has provided confirm my suspicions. Someone is hell bent on acquiring the majority holding in the Walks," declared Marius. "And it would appear it is Mr Augustus Brown, unless someone is manipulating him."

"Well, it can't be Phillips," stated Roger. "He doesn't have the money."

"Perhaps not," said Marius, looking again at the paper in his hand. "However, he could be aiding someone to lay their hands on the titles. Frankly, I cannot believe it is Brown. He wouldn't have the stomach or the cold-blooded temperament for such ruthless acts. But more to the point, whoever it is, is not far from achieving his aims."

"How so, Marius?"

"According to Mr Castaing, Jansons, the London building company, acquired two hundred and twenty-five shares from your uncles before they sold the title and remaining shares to Conyers. Conyers and Abergavenny, together, hold four hundred and eighty four shares, and they're unlikely bed fellows."

Marius stopped for a moment, once more totalling the various holdings.

"Our friend, Mr Augustus Brown, is the owner of two hundred and forty three shares. Just supposing the holding Brown has acquired was added to those shares owned by Jansons. These two amounts would come to," Marius hesitated, scribbling figures on a corner of the piece of paper in his hand. "They would total, four hundred and sixty eight shares. Do you see what this means?"

Roger Dashwood and Fines stared at him.

"Frankly, Marius . . . No," Roger declared, looking confused.

"It means, Roger, that if Jansons and Brown are in collusion. If they managed to snap up those remaining forty eight shares from the three remaining freeholders, they would have governing control of the Walks."

Silence hung heavily in the small sitting room. Marius rose to his feet, and began pacing the floor.

"I wonder if I'm mistaken?" he said, looking intently into two bewildered faces. "Instead of obtaining the shares to create a ready means of selling contraband . . . what if I've got it the wrong way round?"

"What on earth are you talking about, Marius?" asked Roger, bemused by his friend's ramblings.

"I mean, Roger, what if, all along, the smuggling has been just a device to mask the real motive? What if its purpose was to distract everyone, whilst the conspirators' intention was to take control of The Walks?"

CHAPTER SIXTY TWO

Leaving his chair, he began pacing the length of the ornate carpet.

"So what did he have to say?"

"The militia will be coming to The Wells two weeks from now."

"I've been expecting this. So we must be sure to complete our work in time. We shall have to stall their arrival. That should not be too much of a problem."

"I fear it could be."

"What do you mean, sir?"

"I am given to understand the dragoons will not be commanded by The Southern Controller of Excise. That duty will fall to the Lord of The Manor."

"Who has dared to suggest this form of command? The Commissioner of Excise? I'll dispatch a message this very day demanding he revoke such a ridiculous proposition!"

"It would appear, the order has come from The First Lord of The Treasury, from Sir Robert Walpole himself."

CHAPTER SIXTY THREE

They were at breakfast when the porter came to their table.

"Begging your pardon, Dr Hope, a deputy has a message for you from the constable."

He said it in a low voice, but it was audible to others in the dining room. All eyes were upon him as he made his way to the hall.

"Good morning, sir," said the deputy, rising from a chair. "The constable asked me to convey his compliments, and say could you call on him as soon as was convenient this morning?"

"Do you know why?"

The deputy coughed, and looked away. "I'm not at liberty to say, sir."

"Very well, Deputy, tell Mr Russell I shall be with him in the hour."

"Take a seat, gentlemen. May I offer some refreshment?"

"No thank you, Mr Russell," uttered Marius sharply. "We have much to do. Can we get to the substance of your call?"

Roger glanced quickly at Marius. However, it appeared the constable had not taken offence. Instead, he merely smiled.

"Of course, Doctor. I won't detain you long. I just thought you might like to hear of our recent investigations along the banks of the Medway."

"So things have happened, Mr Russell?" Roger said excitedly. "Good news, or bad?"

"I would say interesting, Mr Dashwood. Come, sit down. Let me bring in my two deputies. I'll let them tell their story."

The constable went to the door. There was a murmured conversation, and he led in the two men.

"Gentlemen, repeat all that you told me earlier. You start Jeffries," said the constable.

Jeffries, a small, wiry fellow with a mournful expression, took off his cap, and held it to his chest.

"Well, sirs, me an' Clapton 'ere, rode to East Peckham and picked up the river on its outskirts. We didn't want no one to see us, so we was very careful, like." Jeffries paused.

"Where exactly is East Peckham?" asked Marius.

"It's a village, Doctor, not far from Yalding," explained Russell.

Jeffries glanced at the other deputy, then carried on. "We rode over to Snoll 'atch, like Mr Dashwood told us. "Id our 'orses in a copse, din't we Clapton, and then makes our way down to the river."

He sniffed, clutched at his cap, and continued. "It would 'ave been about six of the clock. So me an' Clapton, wandered, discreet like, along the bank. There was nobody about. I "spect we must 'ave walked three or four "undred yards up an' down from where we left the 'orses. Sudden like, I sees a small gap in the other bank. The long grass, weeds an' reeds sort of "id it from view. It must'a bin what Mr Dashwood, 'ere, saw. Anyways, I calls Clapton, an' 'e comes over."

Dashwood leaned forward, deeply interested in the unfolding tale.

"I says to my mate, this could be a likely spot where they ties up and loads. O" course, we was on the other side, wasn't we, an' couldn't see all that much. Anyhow, there was bushes an' trees about, so's we could "ide."

The door to Russell's room opened. Another deputy brought in a tray of mugs.

"Have a drink, man, and you Clapton, before you carry on," said the constable. Each gratefully took up a mug of ale.

"Mr Dashwood? Doctor?" offered the constable.

"Continue, Jeffries."

"Like I said, gen'lemen, we takes up positions that gives us a good view of the river, across open fields to some buildings in the distance. An" we waits."

"And?" prompted Roger, eager to hear what occurred.

"Nothing, sir. Me an' Clapton waited all night. Nothing. So's about seven in the mornin', it was getting" a bit warmer then, we takes orf our jackets an' caps and rides into East Peckham for something to eat."

"Is that it?" cried Roger. "I thought you were going to tell me you'd seen the smugglers."

"We did, sir, but not "till the next night," muttered Clapton. Taller and younger than Jeffries, he had a mass of unruly red hair that burst from beneath his cap. He took a step forward, to stand alongside Jeffries.

"We bought some cheese an' ale, an' spent the rest of the day in "iding. About nine that night, Jeffries an' me made our way back to the river, an' "id in the same bushes. Din't we," he looked at his fellow deputy.

Jeffries picked up the tale.

"After midnight, we sees lights in the buildings "cross the river. There weren't much moonlight, but after 'alf of an 'our, we hears the sounds of 'orses, and the creaking of carts. We also 'ears the sounds of oars. Then, blow me, someone lights lanterns, an' there's a scene you wouldn't believe."

He took a gulp of ale. Marius glanced at Roger, who was transfixed.

"There, right in front of us, was a river barge with the sail down, nosed into the bank. There must 'a been some boarding 'id among the reeds, for it was well tied up, an' planks across to the bank. In no time at all, about thirty men was loadin'' the barge with all manner of sacks an' barrels." Jeffries paused again. Complete silence in the room.

He coughed, importantly, and went on.

"About twenny minutes later, they'd finished. The lanterns went out, an' we 'eard the oars pulling the barge to the centre of the river, then the crack of the sail. The 'orse an' carts disappeared as well."

"Well I'm damned! What about that, Marius, eh?" Roger was clearly delighted.

"Well done, Mr Dashwood," commented the constable smiling. "Your hunch was correct. However, we haven't finished. Tell them the rest, Jeffries."

Jeffries grinned. "Well, sirs, me an' Clapton thought we ought to find out more. So's we rode into East Peckham, crossed the river at Bambridge's Mill, and walks along the bank. After a short distance, we sees some buildings. We ties up the 'orses, and creeps towards the nearest of two barns where there's lights. We was "iding, not knowin" exacly what to do, when the large doors opened. About thirty pack 'orses comes out, attended by as many men, I should reckon," he turned to Clapton for confirmation.

"At least that many, Mr Jeffries," affirmed Clapton.

"What did you do, then?" asked Roger.

"Well, sir, we couldn't see 'em proper, but we could 'ear the sounds. An'' we follers 'em."

"Where did they go?"

"Roger, let them tell the story in their own time," murmured Marius.

"Thank you, sir," said Jeffries, nodding to him. "The 'ooves was covered in sackin', cos, they barely made a noise. An'' they takes to the back ways. Still, Clapton an' me manages to stay with 'em, though well behind, all the way to The Wells."

"Good Lord!" muttered Roger.

"Anyways, on an 'ill, close to The Wells, the caravan splits in two. About half the 'orses goes down into the town, an' the rest turns towards Waterdowne Forest. We follers the lot heading into the town, where they disperse quiet like."

He took another quaff of his ale.

"Congratulations, gentlemen," said the constable. He turned to Marius and Roger.

"Well done, indeed Mr Jeffries and Mr Clapton," Marius added, as they trooped out the office.

Roger could hardly contain himself. "Well now, what do you think of that, Marius?"

"Absolutely splendid! You were right to persevere."

He was suddenly self-effacing. "Well, you thought of the possibility first."

"Gentlemen, you both contributed. The magistrate will be delighted. Particularly, if this turns out to be the store from which supplies are being distributed. He can stand down his people guarding the byways, and save himself money," remarked the constable, a wry smile on his face.

"Mr Russell, I'm not sure we are quite ready to tell the magistrate," said Marius, disquiet in his voice.

"Why ever not, sir?"

Marius looked down, uncertain how to proceed.

At that moment, there was a knock. The door opened, and Jeffries stepped into the office.

"Beggin' yer pardon, sir. The Lord of The Manor is 'ere. "'E wants to speak with Dr 'ope, urgent."

CHAPTER SIXTY FOUR

"Have you found out where Clifford is being kept?"

"I still can't discover his whereabouts. But I'll keep trying."

"His wife must know where he is. She's not grieving, so he must be alive."

"I'll find him, sir, don't worry. Then, once we get his signature the others will crumble."

"I worry about you. You need to control yourself. If you had killed him, we would have lost everything. Now, get out there and find him ... Before it's too late!"

CHAPTER SIXTY FIVE

"My sincere apologies, Marius."

They had been left alone in the constable's room. Conyers was beside himself, mopping his brow, twisting the handkerchief in his hands.

"You must understand he is my sister's only son. He has, to my certain knowledge, never before acted so disloyally. Still, whether or not he knew to what extent he was revealing confidences, or was just passing on gossip, he betrayed me."

Beth had been deeply upset by Ralph's condemnation, and gone immediately to her room. Later, Conyers' wife had gone to her, and Beth, between her tears, had declared she was perplexed. She could not believe Marius was one to make accusations lightly. At supper, Isobelle Conyers had told her husband of the conversation. By then he had calmed down sufficiently to consider his niece's comment. Although, he had still dismissed the notion his nephew would seriously report his affairs to others.

"Then, this morning, I learned that Beth had taken an early breakfast, said goodbye to her aunt, and Robertson had driven her to the family home in Guilford," reported Conyers dejectedly. Marius felt his heart lurch. He hurriedly looked away.

"When that occurred, Mrs Conyers said there was nothing for it but to put it directly to my nephew," declared Conyers. "I honestly thought he would refute it as mere fabrication."

"I stated firmly that he had been accused of revealing to others private conversations taking place in my household."

Conyers paused, his features portraying his dismay.

"He denied the accusation. As I expected, of course. But, when I told him that, just before midnight on Wednesday, he had been followed to the home of the magistrate, he revealed his treachery."

Conyers looked the picture of misery.

"How could he? How could he?" he kept murmuring.

Marius stood up, walked over to place a hand on the shoulder of the distraught figure.

"Perhaps, sir, he did not realise what he was doing."

"He said that, Marius," muttered Conyers. "He said Phillips was concerned I might be taking advantage of the situation. It would help everyone if he were made aware of all that could affect the future of the Walks."

"What was your reply?"

"I said it was still betrayal. Nothing could forgive that."

Marius did not comment that this pointed strongly to the magistrate's involvement.

"Where is Ralph, now, Mr Conyers?"

"Gone back to his family in London, with his tail between his legs."

"Perhaps it is just as well," said Marius, thinking on what was now likely to happen as events unfolded.

"Now, sir, if you don't mind, I would like the constable and Roger Dashwood to join us. They have something to report that might bring some cheer."

"The trip I made to London, and the recent discoveries were most revealing," declared Marius. "As a result, I think we should discuss what we now know, and what's to be done to overcome both sets of problems."

"Marius," interrupted Conyers. "Before we continue, I feel it my duty to tell the constable what has befallen my family."

"As you wish, sir."

Conyers, with some difficulty, recounted the events of the past hours at Rusthall.

"I'm sorry to hear that, sir, I truly am," said the constable. "However, what am I to think about the magistrate? Is he involved in some measure in this?"

"I heartily believe that to be the case, Mr Russell. Let me tell you why," said Marius. He related his conversations with Clifford. Referring to the deaths of Bennett, and the Lovedays as examples to the freeholders; and how they had been subjected to relentless pressures, physical abuse, and threats upon their families if they did not agree to sell smuggled goods and part with their title deeds.

"Mr Castaing gave me details of the holdings. What was interesting, Jansons, the original builder of The Walks, holds two hundred and twenty five shares."

"So that's where they went," Conyers muttered.

"Lord Abergavenny has one hundred shares. Until recently, the freeholders had two hundred and ninety one. Now, let me tell you of a meeting I have had with Mr Fines, the magistrate's clerk."

For the next half of an hour Marius gave the details told to him by Fines. Starting with the sale by Squires in the magistrate's offices, and the parade of freeholders as they surrendered their birthrights.

"Fines could no longer sit there registering the transactions without doing something about it," Marius stated, vividly recalling the inner conflict faced by the clerk. "He was uncertain whom he could trust, especially if the magistrate were involved. Finally, he came to me."

"Can we prove the title deeds, representing the shares, were sold under duress, Dr Hope?" asked the constable.

"Hopefully, we can. Although, our first task must be to prevent the last three freeholders losing their titles in the same manner. If they did, the balance of power in the Walks could shift irrevocably."

"What do you mean?" questioned Conyers.

"Well, sir, I don't know if Jansons is involved. Though, at the very least, the company could sell its shares for a goodly sum. Then, whoever is behind the scheme, would have controlling interest."

"I could approach Jansons, and offer to buy them," declared Conyers.

"I am of the opinion, sir, that whoever is masterminding this venture, already has the option to purchase them. You wouldn't create such an elaborate plot in the hope that afterwards someone holding a block of shares would sell to you."

"My God," exclaimed Conyers aghast. "What do we do?"

"We ask Mr Augustus Brown why his name is shown as the buyer of the freeholders' deeds' stated Marius. "According to Fines, his name is on every transaction."

"It was my understanding he was looking to buy a property to sell groceries," said the constable.

"He was also badly beaten when on his way to Lord Abergavenny's Estate. It would appear he was going there to buy the Loveday property," said Marius. "Although I know little of the man, I have a strong impression he is merely a pawn in a highly complex plan. I think you'll find he knows next to nothing about the affair, Mr Russell."

"I'll get my deputies to go to the Angel Inn, and bring him in for questioning."

"Do you not think that might give the game away?" asked Marius, stroking his chin. "If he is being watched, they'll know we are on to him. Why don't I wander into the Angel and engage Brown in conversation. I attended upon him when he was injured. It could be seen as a visit to check on his health."

"That might be a better solution, Doctor."

"What about the matter of protecting the three freeholders. Presumably Mr Clifford is one of them?" queried the Lord of The Manor.

"He is, sir," replied Marius. "In fact he owns twenty nine of the remaining shares. Fortunately, he is tucked away out of harm's reach."

"I must tell you, Mr Conyers, you have not heard all of it," stated the constable. "Again, thanks to these two gentlemen," he nodded towards Marius and Roger, "we have found the warehouse from which the contraband is distributed to Tonbridge and The Wells."

Conyers turned to Marius. "How on earth did you manage that?"

"Well, I only had the notion the goods might come into the area by river. Dashwood found the likely spot, and Mr Russell's two Deputies witnessed the shipment into Tonbridge, and the caravan of packhorses bringing goods to The Wells."

"What you haven't said," added Roger. "is that there could be another store in Waterdowne Forest, which they are also using to supply the town."

"I must say gentlemen, you have been busy," declared Conyers, surveying them with interest. "Now, perhaps we can bring this whole sorry episode to an end."

CHAPTER SIXTY SIX

Beneath the bombast, Brown was a worried man.

"Let me be more precise, Mr Brown. You may choose to believe the purchases of the title deeds were legal, but do you realise you could be party to conspiracy, even to murder?"

"How dare you accuse me of such an unspeakable act! Do you know who you are talking to? I'm a respected businessman!"

Not finding Augustus Brown at the Angel Inn, Marius had strolled towards the Walks, coming upon the gentleman as he crossed Frant Lane. Attempting to portray a light-hearted manner for fear of being watched, he had smiled all the while he related the wrong-doing of the trader's actions.

"If you want to preserve your reputation, sir, I suggest you tell me what has been taking place."

"Listen to me, Hope, you have no authority to question me in this manner."

"You are right, sir. It should be the constable. However, he would have to observe the demands of the law, and do you know what that means? You would be immediately imprisoned to await trial."

Brown was silent.

"Let me acquaint you with the facts. At least seven people connected with the purchase of the deeds have been murdered. Another, to my certain knowledge, had been beaten within an inch of his life. And for what? So that you can put your signature to the transfers of title."

Brown's composure was crumbling.

"It wasn't my idea," he croaked, a voice thickening with despair. "I was told my wife would be seriously harmed if I did not come to The Wells and do their bidding."

"Which was?"

"To be the nominee titleholder of deeds sold by the freeholders," said Brown falteringly. "I didn't ask them to sell them to me. I was just told when to go to the magistrate's office."

"Who issued the threat? Who told you to come to The Wells?" asked Marius, his voice hardening.

"No one. I was informed by letter. They backed up their threat by severely beating the manager of one of my shops."

"Walk with me to the Gloster Tavern, Mr Brown. I feel you need a restorative," said Marius, suddenly conscious of the wretched man's predicament.

"That's his story, Mr Russell. As I thought, Augustus Brown is another victim in the plot."

"Did he know why he was attacked when journeying to Abergavenny's Estate?"

"It would seem Brown is ever the businessman. If he had to come to The Wells, and given the reason as opening a store in the town, then why not pursue the idea," explained Marius. "When Loveday's house burnt down, Brown saw an opportunity. It's owned by Lord Abergavenny, and he was going to see the estate manager, Martin Bowes, to finalise its purchase. It appears his principals were not of the same opinion. They applied a harsh deterrent."

"Is he prepared to admit to his actions?"

"Yes. Provided he and his wife can be protected."

"Tell me, Dr Hope, what is his relationship with the magistrate?" asked Russell.

"I tried to draw him out. He was not sure if Phillips was involved. Although, he did say that the magistrate never once queried his role as signatory, or asked the purchase price of the titles."

"Thank you for agreeing to see me so promptly, Lord Abergavenny"

The sixteenth baron rose from his chair to greet him.

"Not at all, Dr Hope. I've heard something of you, so I was intrigued when I received the message. Come, sit down. How can I be of service?"

"I think, my Lord, that I should start at the beginning. It's a lengthy tale."

For the next hour Marius recounted the details of the plot to swamp The Wells, and the surrounding district, with contraband. Abergavenny listened intently, only once interrupting to ask if he wanted refreshment. Eventually, the narrative focussed on the parallel conspiracy to acquire the title deeds, and thus the majority shares in The Walks. It included Marius' strong opinion that the former was now a device to divert attention from the latter. At the conclusion, Abergavenny sat back in his chair.

"My word, Hope, this is a pretty kettle of fish. So, you believe we can do something about it? I certainly hope we can, I've no wish to see the freeholders taken down by such villains."

"We still don't know who they are, sir," admitted Marius grimly. "But, I am certain we are close to finding out."

"You say 'us', Doctor. There are others attempting to foil this little scheme?"

"Yes, my Lord. Mr Russell, the constable, of course, and Mr Conyers. For reasons I have made apparent, we have not spoken to the magistrate."

"What are their roles in all this?"

"The constable is at this very moment surveying the barn in your forest at Waterdowne, and noting the arrivals and distribution of goods. His deputies will try to identify the men working there."

"Humph! I'd forgotten about that building. We haven't used it for years. Since it was rebuilt on the ruins of the old Ivy House."

"Mr Conyers is making all the necessary arrangements for the dragoons. They arrive on Wednesday."

"Quite. Well, you know there is no love lost between Conyers and myself," said Abergavenny. "Still, if you are satisfied he's not implicated, and prepared to help restore order, then you can count on my support. Tell me what you want me to do."

Marius put to him the course of action he had suggested to the others.

"I want you to buy the title deeds and the shares of the three freeholders who have yet to part with them, my Lord."

"Why on earth should they sell them to me?"

"Simply to safeguard their lives," said Marius. "Let me explain. I got the idea from Augustus Brown. If you buy them as the nominee, with a written undertaking to restore them to their rightful owners, it's a sure way to foil the people behind this conspiracy."

"Well, I don't see any reason why not. If they are agreeable, then so am I," declared Abergavenny.

"There is another aspect I should mention, my Lord," murmured Marius.

"What's that?"

"I want to broadcast the fact that you are going to purchase the title deeds. Moreover, the transfer will take place at a specific time on a particular day at the magistrate's offices. I was thinking of eleven of the clock next Thursday morning."

"If you wish, I can be in attendance. I see no harm in that," commented Abergavenny.

"Perhaps there isn't. However, I must warn you, sir, those behind the scheme have gone to great lengths, including murder to acquire the deeds. My belief is that they will attempt to sabotage the purchase."

"Hmm … I see what you mean," said His Lordship, frowning at the thought.

"I think we can thwart them, and bring them to justice. However, let me know if you still wish to participate after I have told you how we can accomplish it."

Marius left Eridge Park several hours later. During that time he had also paid a visit to the stables, and spoken at length with Lord Abergavenny's coachman. Discussing the choice of vehicle, the route into The Wells, and the absolute need for secrecy and caution.

"Hello, Doctor, good to see you. I'm feeling so much better. If I'm careful, I reckon I could go home," said Clifford, leaning on one elbow.

"Do you now, Daniel? I'll be the judge of that."

He examined Clifford carefully. He was still far from making a full recovery. Under the bruises, there had been internal bleeding, evidenced by several haematomas. These swellings would have to subside a great deal further before Marius was satisfied Clifford was finally on the mend.

"I'm afraid you have still some way to go, Daniel."

"My wife needs me at home, sir. She's finding it hard to cope without me. What's more, she's frightened for the children's safety."

"Just what could you do if you were at home?"

"Well, at least I could look after the kids whilst she works the stalls."

"Listen, Daniel, I'll make sure your family is well-guarded. But, you'll have to stay here a couple of days more," said Marius firmly. Then he added. "I also want you to receive some visitors."

Clifford looked at him with a mixture of fear and suspicion.

"I thought you said no one must know where I am, except my wife."

"That's true. Though, there are some things you should know," said Marius. "With the exception of yourself and two others, all the freeholders have been forced to sell their titles."

Marius sat on the end of the cot.

"If those behind the plot relieve you and the two others of their just rights, all will be lost. Even if you could mount a legal challenge, it would take years for the case to be heard in chancery. Then, there would never be any certainty the freeholders would win. To preserve your ownership, to get back the title deeds, we must fight, and first that means you seeing some visitors."

Clifford's features took on a hunted look. "Others might find out where I am. How can I defend myself?"

"I'll arrange with the constable to protect you and your family. You'll be quite safe, I assure you."

There was no doubt Clifford felt vulnerable. Yet, Marius could see from the set of his face that he felt a responsibilty towards his fellow-freeholders.

"What's the purpose of them coming to see me?"

"I want you to persuade them to sell their shares to Lord Abergavenny."

Clifford snorted. "I thought you wanted us to keep them."

"This way you will. If Abergavenny buys them, those who have been forcing the freeholders to sell to them won't get control. Then, when everything is straightened out, his Lordship will sell them back to you."

"I like Lord Abergavenny. He has always been a fair man," said Clifford, his eyes tightening in thought. "But, what guarantee do we have he'll do so when the time comes," he asked searchingly.

"He will sign a declaration to that effect."

"Hmm … I'm not sure. These things can be ignored. We wouldn't be able to take Lord Abergavenny to the courts."

"Look! Do you trust me?" said Marius, interrupting Clifford's half-formed protests.

"Of course I do, Doctor. You saved my life."

"Then put your confidence in me. I will vouch that everything will come out in your favour."

"That's a big commitment, Dr Hope. Even though I trust you, I doubt you could make good any of our losses." said Clifford. Then, with sudden resolve, he said. "But your word is good enough. Tell them to come and see me. I'll get them to sell, you mark my words."

Dashwood had been busy.

A rare event for him. He had actually sought out Mrs Porter.

"A word, Mrs Porter," said Dashwood, lifting his cocked hat.

"Well, Mr Dashwood, I don't often catch up with you," she said with a wry smile. "Have you been left a small legacy? Enough to pay your dues?"

Discreetly looking around, he whispered. "Dr Hope needs to see Mr Fines tonight at his lodgings?"

"Mr Fines? Can't you go to the magistrate's office and ask him yourself?"

"I'm afraid this is too important, and too dangerous for me to be seen with him, Mrs Porter."

"The doctor you say. I've got a lot of time for Dr Hope. More than some others I could mention," she said with a sniff. "As it happens, I could see him. Fines takes his dinner at the Grove Tavern. I'll make a surprise visit and collect dues whilst I'm there. What time tonight and where?"

They met in the constable's offices at seven of the clock. Conyers reported he had sent word to Dover for the detachment of dragoons to come to Rusthall by a circuitous route, to avoid any possibility of being seen.

"I've sent a map which takes them around the town and delivers them to the Manor at Rusthall."

"Well done, Mr Conyers," said Russell. "What news of your efforts, Dr Hope?"

He told them of Abergavenny's compliance. That his Lordship would be at the magistrate's offices at eleven of the clock on Thursday morning. He also confirmed that Clifford would attempt to persuade the other two freeholders to assign their shares to Abergavenny.

"Does his Lordship understand the possible dangers?" enquired the constable, concern in his voice.

"Yes. I mentioned he would be accompanied by a military escort, which set his mind at rest."

"Excellent," said Conyers. "I don't have much time for the fellow, but his participation is welcome."

"It's vital, Mr Conyers," muttered Russell. "By the way, Jeffries has seen the two freeholders. I might have antagonised them if I'd gone. They all agreed to visit Clifford, and will meet my deputy at the bowling green atop Mount Sion tomorrow afternoon."

"Dr Hope will join them there and take them to Clifford. Wherever that is," commented the constable, looking keenly at Marius.

"What news of the comings and goings in Waterdowne Forest, Mr Russell?" enquired Conyers.

"I've had a watch kept on the barn, sir. Thus far, my men have not recognised any of the visitors. Nevertheless, they will maintain their vigil."

They turned to Dashwood. "Mrs Porter said she will ensure Fines comes to Ashenhurst House at eleven of the clock tonight, Marius."

He added. "By the way, I've got a meeting with Mr Phillips tomorrow morning at the Clarence Tavern. I'll mention I've learned that a detachment of dragoons is coming to The Wells by the weekend. That will shake him. If he is caught up in the plot, and Fines then informs him of the forthcoming sale of the remaining shares to Abergavenny, he is likely to suffer a seizure."

"So," declared the constable. "When we meet tomorrow, Dr Hope will have had a chance to brief Fines, and Mr Dashwood can tell us about the magistrate, and his reaction to the early arrival of the dragoons."

He entered the orangery by a side door, which, since dusk, had stood slightly ajar. The dim light from a shrouded lantern allowed him to thread his way through the palms and shrubs, until he stood before the figure in a rattan chair.

"I got your message, Dr Hope."

"Thank you for coming, Mr Fines," he said, in a low voice. "Come, sit by me. We have much to discuss."

Marius went over what was required of the clerk. Fines raised no objections to his role, rather, he relished the idea of playing an active part. He raised several queries, as well as commenting on points they had not considered. When everything was clear, Fines departed silently in the manner of his arrival.

After the side door had closed softly behind his visitor, Marius contemplated the strategy devised by such an ill-assorted group. He could find little fault with the plan. Though, he was all too aware one small error could upset the most carefully-laid schemes.

CHAPTER SIXTY SEVEN

"I hope this is important. It's a risk for me to be seen too often in your company. Servants talk. At this time of day, someone could see my coach."

"I assure you it is. I've had news that could confound the whole project."

"What! It's too late for that! I cannot ... will not allow anyone or anything to wreck my efforts."

The gentleman of the house wrung his hands.

"It's very difficult. It seems that the militia could be here sooner than we thought."

"Bah ... Then we'll finish this week. You play your part in completing the paperwork. Those remaining title deeds must be in my possession within the next forty eight hours. Make sure of it!"

"You don't know the whole story."

"I don't need to! The final turn of the screw is about to be applied. We've found out where Clifford is. My man has been following his wife, and eventually she led him straight to the hiding place. Would you believe, it's Dr Brett's house."

"What will he do?"

"What he does best. Persuade him to comply. Now I must go. You know what has to be done. Don't contact me again until it's over."

The gentleman sat down heavily, mopping his brow with a handkerchief. The delicate gilt chair creaked alarmingly under the weight.

"There's something else you should know. Abergavenny is buying the remaining title deeds. It's all agreed, apparently. The sales between him and the freeholders will be finalised when they gather in my offices at eleven of the clock on Thursday morning."

The visitor strode back, towering over the individual now cowering back on the chair.

"How dare you let this happen! I won't allow it, do you hear!"

"I can't do anything to stop it."

"Yes you can! You have no option! I want those last few titles!"

He stopped and thought for a moment.

"What if Abergavenny doesn't arrive to register the sale? We'll be there instead to persuade everyone of them to sell to us. In fact, I've no need to reach Clifford. No doubt, he'll be with the other freeholders when they come to the office."

He looked down with contempt at the man. His mind racing as to how he could overturn Abergavenny's intentions.

"I can make sure Brown is present as well," he mused, tapping his cane on the floor. "Then he can then transfer all the titles to me."

He made to leave, then hesitated.

"Where is the thirty thousand pounds I gave you for the shipment, Phillips? Have you passed it on yet?"

"Well, yes, most of it. I held back the balance of ten thousand pounds, which is due to be paid on Friday, when the consignments arrive."

"Give me the money! I need it!"

"You don't understand! It's due the Hawkhurst Gang. I daren't not pay."

"What little I care! Get it!"

Crushed, the magistrate left the room, to return with a parcel wrapped in oilcloth.

"By the way, Phillips, get word to Jordan! I want to see him immediately!"

CHAPTER SIXTY EIGHT

"You should have seen his face when I reported I'd heard dragoons were likely to be in town this weekend," Roger said. "Phillips' face went purple. I thought he would suffer apoplexy. "Where did you hear that?" he cried." "I told him it was common knowledge. Several stable yards were preparing to receive them."

"Do you know if Fines did as he was asked, Dr Hope?" enquired the constable.

"Yes, I met him briefly when he was eating his dinner. Apparently when the magistrate arrived at his offices, Fines put it to him exactly as we discussed. He went into Phillips' room and explained he had been contacted by three freeholders. As a man, they were going to sell their shares to Lord Abergavenny. According to Fines, the magistrate's jaw just dropped open."

Marius looked at the faces fixed intently upon him.

"Fines told me he shouted, "They can't do that!" Fines told him that it was all arranged. He had prepared all the documents exactly as requested. The funds and documents exchange would take place at the offices on Thursday at eleven of the clock. At that time Lord Abergavenny and the freeholders would present themselves to complete the formalities."

"What did he do?" asked Conyers.

"According to Fines, he leapt from behind his desk, and rushed off. He did not reappear during the rest of the day."

"Gentlemen, I have just one item which troubles me," said the constable, concern in his voice. "I was stopped by the landlord at the Angel Inn this morning. As you know, I asked him to report Mr Brown's movements to me. He informed me the gentleman did not occupy his room last night."

"We need him to transfer the titles to the freeholders," exclaimed Marius. "Damnation! Why didn't I think how he might react. I wonder if he has returned to London with the intention of removing himself and his wife to a place of safety?"

Then another unwelcome thought came to him. "Unless, of course, he has been secreted away."

"We can't account for how people will respond to situations, Marius," Roger murmured. "I'm sure he'll turn up. If not we'll just have to go through with the plan without him."

Suddenly, the elation of bringing all the threads of the counter-plot together was dampened by the news.

CHAPTER SIXTY NINE

"Jordan, you are now working directly for me. Forget about the contraband. You've got people who can organise things in your absence, haven't you?"

"Yes, sir. That shouldn't be a problem. Except, we are expecting a large delivery in the small hours of Friday morning. I should be there with Mr Phillips when he makes the outstanding payment."

"Don't worry about that. We've far more pressing matters to attend to."

"What is it you want me to do?"

"We need to act to avoid a disaster. I want you to muster enough men prepared to take against Lord Abergavenny and his people. I don't want him killed, you understand, just out the way for two or three hours on Thursday morning."

"Abergavenny? I reckon as though we would have the law hounding us forever if harm came to his Lordship. I don't think we could get many people to take against him, sir."

"Not if I offered to pay each man fifty pounds?"

"Fifty pounds! I reckon they'd kidnap their own mothers for that. How many do we want?"

"As close to thirty men as possible. You'll probably have to provide them with weapons, and ensure they all have mounts. Take this three thousand pounds, and make sure the job is done."

He unwrapped the oilskin, and counted out the sum. Jordan's eyes were transfixed on the parcel.

"Listen, Jordan, there's also a handsome bonus in this for you. But cross me, and you won't live to tell the tale."

It was said with such menace, Jordan recognised it would not pay to defy the man.

"Right, when I've got them together where should we meet?"

"At the barn at eight of the clock on Thursday morning. Not a minute later. Is that perfectly clear?"

Jordan nodded.

"Before then, come here tomorrow night and tell me of the squad you've put together. Then I'll go over the details how we marshal our forces, where we spring our surprise."

Shortly after Jordan had departed, there was a light tap on a window. The gentleman was expecting the caller. Having dismissed the servants for the evening, he opened the door himself.

"Come in, my friend."

An hour later the man left. Fully aware of what was required of him, in his pocket was one hundred guineas for his services.

CHAPTER SEVENTY

"But, you could miss it!"

He was wavering. Each of his arguments had been countered, but still he showed reluctance.

Roger Dashwood leaned forward.

"This is just as important, I assure you. It could clear up the matter for once and for all."

The constable searched his desk. Finding the piece of paper he wanted, ran his finger slowly down the page.

"Very well! Just make sure you're here by seven of the clock on the day. I'll arrange the horses and provide a few light weapons, just in case."

CHAPTER SEVENTY ONE

"Now, let us go over it once more. Four of Jordan's men will accompany Brown to your offices an hour before they are due. Make sure they are hidden from sight. Their job will be to persuade the freeholders to complete the sale to Brown. This will be done as soon as you tell them Abergavenny is not coming. Do you understand?"

Phillips' nodded his assent. The gentleman looked intently at the magistrate.

"I'll also make sure my man is close by. When the registrations are completed, I want you to bring Brown to my rooms. We can then conclude the final stage of the takeover, when Brown assigns everything to me."

"But if I'm seen doing that, it could jeopardise my position."

"Don't worry. After his signature is on the document, Brown won't be telling anything to anybody."

Phillips blanched.

"I don't like it. It's too risky for me even to be seen with Brown."

The gentleman responded quietly. "My friend, you will be present to confirm the exchange with the authority of your office. That's the way it will be."

"What am I going to do if I'm suspected?"

"I suggest you leave The Wells. After all, you've made a great deal of money from this little venture."

"You don't understand. I have connections, my home is here."

"Listen to me, Phillips, for a high price, you've been a willing accomplice. You should have considered the consequences before you got involved. Now, you will do exactly as I tell you."

CHAPTER SEVENTY TWO

Marius overslept. Dragging himself from slumber, he washed and dressed slowly. Breakfast had long finished, so he chose to stroll down to the Walks to take coffee at Uptons.

Although thwarting the plot against the freeholders had occupied much of his time, his thoughts constantly turned to Beth. Particularly at night, in the solitude of his room.

Conyers had apologised for the accusation against his nephew. Although deep down, Marius knew The Lord of The Manor felt aggrieved at the revelation. It impugned his family's name. Unhappily, he came to the conclusion that whatever his feelings for Beth were, they would never be reciprocated.

It was now a closed chapter. In that moment he realised that without her company he no longer wanted to stay in The Wells. The memories were too deeply etched. The sooner everything was resolved, the sooner he could return to London. To a way of life that would not expose him to hurt and unhappiness. Going back to the hospital, accepting the routines and ill-reasoned strictures was now fixed in his mind. It seemed the only course. He had mentioned to Roger he would be leaving. He would pack over the weekend, and early next week take the first available coach for London.

"Dr Hope!"

He looked up. It was Mrs Porter.

"You were far away, Doctor. Forgive me for disturbing you."

"I'm sorry, Mrs Porter. You are right. I was thinking what I have to do. Anyway, I'm glad you're here, I need to settle my dues."

"Why so, Doctor? Not leaving us, I hope?" she said almost pleadingly.

In a low voice, Marius said, "Have no fear, Mrs Porter, everything will be resolved before I do so."

"Oh! I'm pleased, Dr Hope. Can I tell Mr Nash that his troubles will soon be over? He can remove to Bath."

"Mrs Porter," he said, looking anxiously around. "Whatever you do, don't say a word. Least of all to Mr Nash. It could undermine everything."

"Of course, Doctor. Not a word. You can rely on me," she said in a conspiratorial tone. "I'll tally up your dues until Friday."

Behind her the musicians in the gallery were tuning up. As she leaned over the table, making notes in her large leather-bound book, Marius could see Tofts tuning his mandolin. The musicians' gallery affords a splendid vantage point over the Walks, he noticed.

"Well, sir, I've totted up what you owe, and the payments made. As I see it there is nothing more to pay. So I'll be on my way."

With that, she moved swiftly to unsuspecting clients, who had missed the opportunity to evade her when she first appeared.

It was trying for Marius. Even though he did his best to give no indication of his inner disquiet. They were seated in the library at Rusthall. Russell was the last to arrive, and until that moment they had been chatting amiably with Captain Miles, the officer in charge of the detachment.

A man in his thirties, with a pronounced military bearing, the upright stance evident even when he was taking his ease on the sofa. A conventional face, thought Marius, blue eyes, straight nose, a handsome moustache. Clearly, someone who would engender respect on the parade ground and in battle.

As Marius' thoughts turned to the purpose of the meeting, Miles was responding to a comment from the Lord of The Manor.

"Yes, thank you for your hospitality, sir. All the men are well-billeted, and the horses stabled."

"Not at all, Captain," Conyers replied expansively. After the urgencies of the past few days, he was now relaxing. The militia about to play a prominent role.

After being introduced, the constable remarked. "Tell me, Captain, what is your regiment, the Thirteenth?"

"No, sir, the Tenth Dragoons. We originated in Hereforshire, and at the moment, until the regiment is allocated a new base, we are temporarily stationed at the garrison in Dover."

"Are you Heavy or Light, Captain?" enquired Russell. Marius was surprised the constable was knowledgeable about the military, a subject of which he knew little.

"Light, sir."

"Humphrey Gore's Lot, eh?" smiled the constable. "Built for speed."

"How do you mean, Mr Russell?" enquired Conyers.

Miles answered.

"What Mr Russell is referring to, Mr Conyers, is that the Light Dragoons do not carry much weaponry, no guns or powder, only sabres and small arms. We were originally formed for reconnaissance and scouting."

Conyers was clearly taken aback.

"Well, I must say, Captain, I'm disappointed. I expected a force fully armed and capable of routing these smuggling gangs."

Miles was unperturbed.

"There are thirty dragoons in my troop, Mr Conyers. All with sabre, lance, and short sword for close fighting. They are battle-hardy, having played a major part in keeping the Jacobites in order."

"Were you at Preston in "15, Captain?" enquired Conyers.

"A little before my time, sir," smiled Miles.

Shortly thereafter, Conyers commenced the briefing. He outlined the situation confronting the township for the captain. Stressing the rapid increase in contraband, which now appeared to be a device to cover the real purpose of the scheme. To deprive the freeholders of their titles to The Walks.

Marius noted the Lord of The Manor had readily adopted his theory. Conyers recounted all they had discovered, as well as the actions taken, thus far, to counter the conspiracy, including the details of the afternoon gathering at Clifford's bedside, which had produced agreement among the three freeholders to assign their shares to Lord Abergavenny.

"What is the precise role of my men in all this?" asked Captain Miles.

"Quite simple," commented Russell, picking up on Conyers' remarks. "The dragoons are here to apprehend the smugglers and to smash the chain of distribution. That is still our abiding concern. However, as Mr Conyers has said, we must also stop the sale of the remaining shares. The two activities are intertwined. So, tomorrow morning, the first requirement upon your men is to safeguard Lord Abergavenny on his journey to The Wells from Eridge."

Conyers resumed the briefing. Giving the dragoon captain a detailed expectation of what was needed: the timings and the locations of the smugglers' sites in the nearby forest and on the banks of the River Medway.

"Tomorrow morning, Dr Hope and I will accompany you and your force to the Eridge Estate. From there we shall escort Lord Abergavenny to the magistrate's offices in the town."

He looked around at those seated in the room.

"The constable, meanwhile, will take up position close to the magistrate's offices. I would suggest half a dozen dragoons accompany Mr Russell, Captain. In case matters get out of hand before we arrive."

"Very good, Mr Conyers. That can be arranged," responded Miles. "My only concern at the moment is that I expected Mr Fielding, The Southern Excise Controller, to have been present. Forgive me, sir, I am aware I report to you, but I understood he would be party to these discussions."

"You are perfectly correct, Captain," said Conyers, unperturbed by the soldier's remarks. "Unfortunately, he could not be present with us tonight. However, we shall meet with him tomorrow."

"After we have escorted his Lordship into the town, what are our next duties," enquired Miles.

"After that little matter has been concluded, Captain, we raid the warehouses storing the contraband. However, I should point out that we expect an assault on Abergavenny's carriage. We believe they will attempt to stop him reaching the magistrate's offices. Judging by their callous actions thus far, it could be bloody," declared Conyers.

"Several of my deputies will accompany your detachment, Captain," declared Russell. "Their job will be to take charge of any captives, to encourage them to reveal the names and whereabouts of their compatriots. If we time it right, it should be a fine old haul."

The rest of the evening was taken up with the minutiae of planning and organisation. When the group finally dispersed, it was close to midnight.

En route back to their lodgings, Dashwood turned to Marius. "You were quiet, tonight, Marius."

"I had nothing to contribute, Roger."

"Or, was it something else?"

Marius said nothing for a few minutes.

"You're right. I felt sad being at Rusthall without Beth's presence. I miss her, Roger. I sorely miss her."

As they rode into the stable yard at Ashenhurst House, Marius said. "I can't stay in The Wells any longer, Roger. I have made up my mind. I'm returning to London on the Tuesday coach."

CHAPTER SEVENTY THREE

"You've done well! With four and thirty men with arms we shall easily carry the day. No doubt, Abergavenny will be guarded, and that irritating doctor will probably be with him. I wager it is he who has organised the sale in Abergavenny's favour."

"What if they don't surrender, and there's fighting?"

"I don't want any bloodshed do you understand? That's why there are so many of you. Don't kill any of the local people. You may have to defend yourselves, but they should be quickly subdued, especially if you surprise them. The doctor doesn't matter. In fact, blood letting in that quarter would be welcome."

"Where do you suggest we take them?"

"I've given a lot of thought to that. Here's what I want you to do."

He unfolded a large square of paper.

Some twenty minutes later, he remarked. "Jordan, I want you to lead the attack. Take Abergavenny to the barn in Waterdowne Forest. We won't need it anymore."

"Have you forgotten? The Hawkhurst Gang are delivering a shipment on Friday. They'll want to be paid. Besides, it's a very lucrative business. Surely, we should continue working with them, after all it's easy money."

"Let me tell you something," said the gentleman. "It was only ever a device to draw attention away from the main purpose. Phillips hasn't enlightened you, but the contraband project is doomed. The militia are about to descend on The Wells, and that will be the end of it."

CHAPTER SEVENTY FOUR

It was twenty minutes after the hour of ten. Perfect timing, thought Marius, as they cantered along at the head of the column with Captain Miles. Riding beside Conyers, he noted the Lord of The Manor had an air of self-importance about him. Behind them, the metallic clinck of weaponry, the measured step of the horses, and the creaking of leather sounded reassuring.

He had been surprised by Roger Dashwood's absence. Rising early that morning, he had knocked at his door, but there had been no reply. Nor had he been in the breakfast room. Questioning a porter, he had been informed Mr Dashwood had ridden off earlier. At Rusthall Manor, Marius was puzzled to discover he was not there.

"Did you mention he was riding with us?" enquired Conyers.

"Well not in so many words. I naturally assumed he would."

"Perhaps he had a more pressing engagement."

Miles had been standing close by, and Marius had been intrigued to witness him remove his cocked hat and place an iron-framed skull cap on his head, fixing the strap under his chin. He noticed Marius' interest in the headgear.

"A soft hat is little defence against a ball or sabre thrust, Doctor."

As they approached the gates to the Eridge Estate, Captain Miles halted the troop.

"You said, sir, we should wait here for Lord Abergavenny's carriage," he announced, turning towards Conyers.

"If you would, Captain," declared The Lord of The Manor, turning to witness the dragoons forming up either side of the entrance. The precision, the stillness of both horse and rider giving them a formidable air.

"Dr Hope and I will ride up to the house and inform his Lordship we are in readiness."

They trotted up the drive towards the imposing building of Eridge Park, coming to a halt in front of the main entrance. A groom hurried across the gravel, at the same time one side of the double doors of the house opened. Conyers and Marius dismounted and walked towards the butler standing on the entrance steps. He looked enquiringly at them.

"Good morning, gentlemen. Is anything amiss? I thought you were meeting his Lordship at the Frant Lane entrance to the estate?"

Marius was stunned.

"I was quite clear! I said to Lord Abergavenny that Mr Conyers and I would meet him at the house. Then escort him to the guard waiting at the Eridge Road entrance gates!"

"But then you changed the arrangements and the time."

"I did no such thing," said Marius incredulously. His heart pounding, breath tight in his throat.

"The estate manager was quite specific, sir. He said that others were aware you planned to travel to The Wells by the Eridge Road. You now thought it best to alter the route, and make the journey along Frant Lane."

"Quick, man! When did he leave?" cried Conyers.

"At ten of the clock! You were to meet him at the gates," said the butler waveringly.

Marius ran and leapt on his horse, shouting to Conyers. "Get the dragoons!"

He galloped across the lawns, clods flying. Clearing a low hedge in a single stride, over a small ornamental wall and on to the track to Frant village.

At the estate gates Marius slid to a halt. There was no sign of the coach. Dismay overwhelmed him. His head sank. If they had taken Abergavenny the plan was in ruins. If they harmed him, it would be a disaster.

Marius drew a long breath. On impulse, he turned his horse in the direction of The Wells. Urging his mount into a gallop, he flew along the narrow roadway. Rounding a slight bend, he almost collided with the slow-moving vehicle, managing to squeeze through a narrow gap between the coach and the hedgerows.

"About time too, Hope!" called the baron from the window. "Where the deuce have you been?"

Marius reined in his horse and trotted back. Dismounting, he took a deep breath, and walked over to the coach.

"I told 'im we should wait! But would 'e listen!" called the coachman. "I said you'd told me not to leave the estate without the escort. It din't matter about the time."

Marius looked up, and smiled his appreciation.

"Well we're going to be late, thanks to you," said his Lordship. "I told him," Abergavenny jerked his chin towards the driver, "to get on with it. Even in the yard he took his time. When we got to the gates, and your people weren't there, I said we would go on our own. Damned impudence! He refused to budge! I told him he was dismissed. Still he wouldn't listen. In the end I declared his entire family would be run off the estate before he cracked the whip, and we moved off. Though at a such a confounded pace a snail could match."

"Lord Abergavenny, I didn't change the arrangements," declared Marius, standing at the open door.

"Bowes was adamant. Positive the meeting with the magistrate and freeholders was now arranged for half past ten of the clock."

"It was false, I'm afraid," murmured Marius, holding on to his temper with difficulty. "It seems you have someone working for you who is in the pay of others."

"God's Teeth, Hope! I shall dismiss him immediately!"

"In all probability, my Lord, he has probably gone already."

A thunder of hooves signalled the rapid closing of the dragoons. They wheeled about the coach. Conyers and Captain Miles dismounted, and came towards the vehicle.

"Thank God you caught up with him, Marius," cried Conyers. "Are you all right?" he said, addressing Abergavenny.

"Yes, thanks to my stubborn coachman, and the good doctor," responded his Lordship. "According to my driver, Dr Hope was emphatic we should not leave the safety of the park without the militia."

"I'm delighted the driver stuck to the doctor's prescription," said Conyers, grinning at Abergavenny's discomfiture.

"Well, we are in good time, shall we proceed?" humphed Abergavenny, changing the subject.

"If we do so, my Lord, I believe we shall most likely run into trouble," stated Marius quietly. "Let us get the opinion of Captain Miles. The coach has been deliberately diverted to another route. If it continues, it will surely be attacked along the way. For the moment, let us consider what lies ahead, what tactics you would adopt if you were the enemy."

Abergavenny's coachman was called from his box. With his local knowledge, he was best placed to offer advice. Miles listened attentively to what he had to say.

"This road to The Wells winds its way to the top of the "ill," said the driver, squinting as he contemplated the route.

"Either side there's scrub and bushes. It's narrer, 'cos there's only farm carts and the like use it. At the top, there's a sort of meeting point where a lane goes off to 'awkenbury, a village a mile distant. This is a flat area afore you go down the other side int" town."

"So where might we expect an ambush?" asked the captain.

"I reckons at the top o" the 'ill, sir," replied the driver, stroking his chin. "That's where I'd do it."

"What do you suggest, Miles?" enquired Conyers.

The dragoon officer turned to Abergavenny. "Is there any way a detachment of soldiers could skirt the lane, and come out at the hilltop?"

Abergavenny looked at his coachman.

"Yer could, sir, if yer cut across Waterdowne Forest to the west, and pick up the ridge. There's a track along the ridge, which'll bring yer back ter the crossing at the top."

"What I will do then, Mr Conyers, is send half the force through the forest to come out at the crest," declared Miles. "The others will accompany the coach. Do you and Dr Hope still wish to ride with us, or in the coach with Lord Abergavenny?"

"We'll ride with you, Captain," said Conyers. Marius would have been more circumspect. He had been given a weapon at Rusthall, but he was no swordsman. Now Conyers had settled the matter for him. It would appear unseemly to alter that decision.

The captain quickly selected twelve dragoons. With the coachman explaining the terrain, Miles briefed the sergeant leading the party. When the mounted group had disappeared quietly into the trees on the thickly-wooded slopes, he returned to the coach.

"We are moving off in fifteen minutes, gentlemen," he announced.

For Marius time passed slowly. He found himself with Conyers at the rear surrounded by dragoons, a position he found comforting. The convoy stood in silence. The riders unmoving. Just the occasional shift of hooves, the bobbing of heads, the snuffle of muzzles. When the order to mount was given, he was still taken by surprise. Captain Miles rode to the rear, nodded to Conyers. Then wheeling to the front, he gave the signal. The convoy was on the move.

CHAPTER SEVENTY FIVE

Jordan sat astride his horse with growing impatience. He had been told the coach and any outriders would broach the hill long before now. His lookouts still gave no signal of their approach. He was becoming anxious, though his men seemed not unduly concerned. They sat slouched in their saddles, chatting in low voices. When he gave the order to charge, Jordan had impressed upon them the need for an excess of noise with the minimum of violence. The aim was to capture the coach, and take it and its occupant deep into the forest. His Lordship would not be best pleased when held for at least three hours. They all had "kerchiefs around their necks, ready in a moment to hide their features. It would not be sensible to be recognised by any of Abergavenny's men.

A few of the band were re-checking their flintlocks, sharpening their swords. Indicative they were getting edgy.

"Are you sure they're coming, Mr Jordan?" asked one, glancing across at him.

"Course they are! Just be ready when they do."

One of the lookouts ran into the small clearing. "I can hear the sound of a coach and riders! They'll be here any minute!"

"Get ready, men. Move to the tree line by the lane! Remember, wait upon my word!" shouted Jordan, covering the lower half of his face.

CHAPTER SEVENTY SIX

The lane appeared to be levelling out. Hemmed in by dragoons, Marius could not make out if the convoy were close to the crest of the hill where the lane divided. Suddenly, a wild cry rang out. It was followed by the thundering of hooves. Riders burst from the trees brandishing weapons, a number of them discharging flintlocks. Marius caught sight of swords flashing in the morning sunlight. Horses whirled to meet the aggressors. The noise was fiercesome. Someone went down. Marius reached for his own sword, pulling it clear of the scabbard. The attack, though expected, was still frightening in its clamour and ferocity.

The dragoons bunched around Conyers and himself. The coach slewed to a halt. Then, Marius realised that there had been a similar assault on the convoy to the front. A dragoon at Marius' side fell across his saddle. His flank pieced by a sword thrust. They were outnumbered. It was difficult to ward off the attack. Marius entered the skirmish wielding his sabre, shouting wildly. A downward sweep of a blade caught at his sleeve.

At that moment, the rest of the detachment suddenly burst from the trees, bearing down on the marauders. They spared no quarter. The ambushers were decimated as the soldiers fell upon their attackers. It was over in a moment. Those still in the saddle riding blindly to escape the cut and thrust of the dragoons.

Marius sat on his horse, shocked at what he had witnessed. Though safe within the cordon around him, his heart was pounding furiously from a mixture of fear and exhilaration.

"Are you all right, Doctor?" enquired the captain, wheeling his horse alongside. Marius nodded, not immediately able to speak.

"Mr Conyers?" Marius looked at Conyers. He was clearly in shock, his face ashen. But he, too, nodded assent.

Marius saw a dragoon lying on the ground, and went quickly to his aid. However, it was clear the fallen soldier had suffered a mortal blow. His eyes already glazing as Marius undid his uniform jacket. With blood spurting from the deep gash in his chest, the dragoon's head fell slowly sideways.

"I'm sorry, Captain," said Marius, looking up at the mounted officer.

Miles turned towards the coach. As he approached, the door opened slowly, and Abergavenny stepped down. He was visibly shaken by the ambush, the tumult, and the dispassionate show of force used to repel the attack.

"My God, Captain! It's my good fortune I didn't continue on my own," murmured Abergavenny, in a hoarse voice. He turned to Marius. "Thank you, Doctor, for being insistent."

His driver dismounted from the box. "You all right, my Lord?"

Abergavenny clasped his hand tightly, and held it for some moments before releasing it.

"Are you in a position to continue, my Lord?" asked the captain quietly.

"I will be in a minute, Captain Miles," he said with a thin smile. "How many men have you lost?"

"One, sir. Young Franks. The rest suffered a few cuts and bruises, nothing serious." Abergavenny nodded.

"Captain," called Marius. "Can you spare one of your men? I want to go back to Eridge Park, to confront the estate manager. If you agree, I'll take Mr Franks' body with me."

"By all means, Doctor, when you're there, with his Lordship's permission, perhaps you could arrange for a cart to remove the other bodies?"

Marius looked around for the first time, realising that there were at least a dozen or so attackers motionless on the ground.

"Get my butler to organise it, Dr Hope," said Abergavenny grimly. Then added. "I trust you'll apprehend Bowes, if he hasn't already made good his escape."

The dragoon's body was laid across his saddle. Marius, accompanied by another soldier, turned back down the hill. He heard the order to mount up, and looking over his shoulder, watched the coach with its escort move slowly over the brow of the hill.

CHAPTER SEVENTY SEVEN

Jordan had urged his band forward, shouting commands, and yelling with every breath. But as they charged out the thicket to lay about the caravan, something prompted him to hold back. It may have been the overriding instinct for self-preservation, or perhaps, as the commander of his force, there was little need for him to enter the fray. There were more than enough for an easy victory. It was never clear in his mind why he did not join the headlong rush into the conflict.

When the contingent of dragoons swept past him, he knew all was up. Even before the brief, bloody battle was over, Jordan had departed the spot as fast as his horse could negotiate a path through the wooded hillside. He stopped at the barn to gather a few belongings, and a brief moment at his lodgings to collect the rest of his effects.

Shortly, thereafter, he rode out The Wells, heading towards London and his smithy in Chelsea. He would never visit the spa town again.

CHAPTER SEVENTY EIGHT

He was at the table he used as a desk to run the affairs of the estate. A diminutive figure, close to middle age. He wore sturdy breeches, and a heavy overshirt. Clothing suited to walking the farms, checking fields, pastures and woodland, as well as the indoor tasks of keeping books, written records and writing letters. His face, coarsened by the elements, was drawn with worry. Had he been exposed? Should he steal away now before he was accused?

Jordan had made it clear no one would be hurt during the mêlée. But would the finger of suspicion point at him? He had been promised more than he could earn in a season. He had grabbed at the chance. Perhaps a word with his Lordship's butler to discover what he had said to Hope? If it had been a bland remark, he may not need to upset the cosy position he enjoyed. Over the years, in addition to his salary, he had been able to divert not inconsiderable sums of money into his own pocket. Many of the ventures he had devised had paid handsomely. He continued to sit there, unable to decide. Records open and unattended, a quill pen nervously twisting in his fingers.

There was no knock. The door burst open. Bowes was drawing breath to berate the intruder. The cry died on his lips.

"I was told you would be here, Bowes!" cried Marius.

A dragoon entered behind him, a drawn sword in his hand.

"You said to Lord Abergavenny the arrangements had been changed. Who told you to give him false information?"

Bowes sat back in his chair, aghast. The quill still winding aimlessly in his fingers.

"I … er … I don't know what you mean," he stammered.

"But for the coachman's reluctance to drive his Lordship into The Wells, we might have had a bloodbath on our hands!" shouted Marius in fury. His mind still re-enacting the scene of the ambush.

Suddenly, Bowes knew all was lost. His head dropped.

"I was told by a messenger, who called at this office," he stammered. "He said he was from Mr Conyers. The meeting in the town had been brought forward. I simply passed the word on to his Lordship."

"I don't believe you, Bowes!" cried Marius in exasperation. "Who was this messenger? What were his credentials?"

"I ... I didn't ask his identity."

"Tell me, Bowes, what prompted you to tell his Lordship he should leave by the Frant Gate?" asked Marius, his tone low and menacing.

"I thought it might be safer."

"More dangerous, most likely."

Bowes was still turning the quill in his hand. Marius stared at it, engrossed in the motion of the pen, as it passed between the manager's shaking fingers. Something stirred in his memory. Another person, a similar act. Where? Why, was it so important?

He shifted his gaze from the quill, and looked directly into Bowes' eyes.

"I am not convinced of your explanation. This soldier will accompany you to the constable's office. As the officer of the law, he will deal with the matter of your deliberate misdirection, calculated to lead to your master's death."

Marius turned to the dragoon, and nodded. Taking up a length of rope, the soldier bound Bowes' arms, then led the hapless manager into the yard. Marius shut the door. Walking to his horse, he tried desperately to recollect why the quill had such significance.

At the constable's office a deputy took charge of Bowes, escorting him to a cell. Marius was about to leave the premises, when the door burst open to admit Maurice Conyers, and Mr Russell. Both were jubilant. All had gone well at the magistrate's. Although the titles had not been assigned to Lord Abergavenny.

"Why ever not?" enquired Marius anxiously.

"My dear fellow, in the end there was no need," declared Conyers. "But let us tell him the whole story, Mr Russell. Though, first, a little refreshment."

"I believe we have earned it, Mr Conyers," responded Russell.

Both were enjoying the moment.

"Now, Marius. Where were we?" said Conyers, taking a deep draught. "After leaving you at the top of the hill, without further incident we rode straight to the magistrate's offices. Mind you, everyone was alert to another raid. Fortunately, nothing untoward occurred." Conyers smiled at the recollection, and Russell took up the story.

"Our group arrived outside the offices a few minutes before eleven of the clock," recounted the constable. "We waited until the appointed hour. By this time a fine crowd had gathered. Few have seen a contingent of dragoons before. I even saw your musical friend, you know the one who plays in the gallery in the Walks. Though, on this occasion he was soberly dressed."

Conyers was keen to pick up the narrative.

"The hour had just finished striking when Abergavenny, the Captain with a clutch of dragoons and myself, went into the building."

The constable nodded his agreement.

Conyers, rubbing his hands together, said briskly. "Fines was busy in the outer office where we joined Mr Russell, Clifford, and his fellow freeholders. I then asked Fines if he would care to advise Mr Phillips of our presence."

Conyers lifted the mug briefly to his lips.

"The magistrate came to his office door, and Fines stood aside to let him enter. I have never seen anyone's face assume so many hues. There we all were, standing there as though nothing had happened. His jaw dropped. At first his face was ashen, then it reddened and finally changed to purple. I thought he was about to die on us. Didn't you, Russell?"

"He was quick, Mr Conyers," added the constable. "Mighty quick. He stepped back, and as we rushed forward, he pushed Fines into us and slammed and bolted the door."

"By the time we had broken it down, he'd gone. Though guess who was in the room, Marius?" asked Conyers, raising his eyebrows.

"Mr Brown."

For a moment Conyers was nonplussed. Then he went on. "Apparently, Brown's captors also fled when they realised we had the support of the militia. The upshot was that Brown sat down, and put his signature to all the registration forms Fines had prepared. Re-assigning all the shares and titles to their original owners. There was no need for Lord Abergavenny to acquire the remainder. All he did was counter-sign some legal document affirming that Brown was doing so of his own free will."

"Well, sir, I'm delighted. I truly am," said Marius, relaxing for the first time. Comforted there would be no more bloodshed.

A deputy came into Russell's office and asked him to sign the committal for Bowes. The constable moved to his desk, and dipped his quill pen in the inkpot. Marius noted idly he wrote with his left hand. Suddenly, he leaned forward.

"Mr Russell, I see you use your left hand. Holding the pen in that manner, could you possibly write in a more cursive style, sloping to the right?"

"Not easily, doctor. I would have to re-cut the quill," commented Russell, puzzled by the request.

"Humour me, Mr Russell, if you please. Don't worry about legibility. I just want to know if it's possible. I'll sharpen the quill to suit the hand."

Russell looked quizzically at Marius. Nevertheless, when the tip had been re-fashioned, he did his bidding. Dipping the quill into the ink, he put pen to paper, bending forward in concentration. The quill caught, ink spluttered across the page.

"Try again, Mr Russell," insisted Marius.

"What's the point, Marius?" asked Conyers.

"Bear with me, sir," exclaimed Marius. Taking the sharpening knife from the desk, he again spent a moment trimming the quill tip.

"Now, Mr Russell, if you please."

Russell stared at Marius. Then, once more, applied himself to the task. He moved the pen slowly, this time able to write more smoothly. Even so, it was impossible to attain the angle of script urged by Marius.

"I can't do it, Doctor. No one can write in the manner you are asking."

"You mean no one who writes with his left hand," declared Marius. "Thank you, Mr Russell. I think we are close to solving our mystery. Constable, gentlemen, would you care to accompany me to the Walks?"

CHAPTER SEVENTY NINE

Phillips was exhausted. Where was he to go? By now they would be looking for him at his home. He had lost everything. He heard himself sob: dread and anxiety in equal measure. He had taken his horse, stabled at the rear of the building, and galloped first towards Mount Ephraim. However, the dragoons would soon be upon him. Halting, he tried desperately to come to a decision.

He wheeled his mount in the direction of the Walks. He would have to give him money. The fellow had plenty. He could then make good his escape. Perhaps, even to France, until things died down. That was it. Don't ask, demand! Or he, Phillips, would disclose everything.

On Bishop's Down, close by the Walks, he left the horse tied to a branch in a nearby copse. Glancing frequently around for fear of pursuit, he made his way quickly towards the fellow's lodgings.

The half-glazed front door did not delay him. It was the work of a moment to break a glass pane, put his hand through the gap and free the catch. Anxiety lending him strength to force an entry. He mounted the stairs to the upper floors. No one was there. He moved to the top floor for a better vantage point. From a window overlooking the Upper Walk, he scanned the tables, and the company seated below.

There he was! At one of the tables. Somehow he had to draw his attention.

It was late in the afternoon, though warm, clouds were thickening on the horizon. Marius noticed the air was now quite still. Conyers, Russell, and his deputies had been on the point of leaving, when Captain Miles had arrived. Much to Marius' consternation, it had caused further delay.

Hurriedly, he had suggested the dragoon officer accompany them. Even so, it was another half of the hour before they rode the short distance to the Walks.

Retreating down the stairs to the first floor, Phillips remembered the balcony above the colonnade of shops. He could catch his eye from there. Opening the door, the hubbub of conversation, laughter, the tinkling of cups, the sound of music, rose to greet him. Phillips ducked down. Anyone looking up, and he might be seen. He was only visible to the musicians. From their eyrie, he was in plain view.

Along the verandah, he saw an opening, which conceivably housed a staircase to below. Moving cautiously to avoid bringing attention to himself, he came to the gap and a flight of steps. Descending with the same care, Phillips emerged between the shops.

Luck was with him. A serving girl carrying a tray, was making her way through the tables. He called to her softly. Putting a coin in her hand, he pointed out the gentleman, and gave her a brief message.

He returned quickly to the balcony, stepped through the door and shut out the world below. Realising he might need additional persuasion, Phillips began searching for the pistol he had once seen in the fellow's possession.

Halfway to the Walks it began to rain. Clouds were darkening, closing over the township. It was a lowering sky, with all the signs of an impending storm.

They left their horses with the ostler in charge of the coaches and carriages in the Lower Walk, and headed purposefully through the throng. The rain began to fall more insistently. Around them, drivers and servants hastily unfolded seat protectors, tonneau covers and carriage hoods.

Marius, who was leading, stopped suddenly on the top step to the Upper Walk. Open to the elements, the area in front of Smith's Coffee House had been rapidly vacated. She was there, alone at a table under the colonnade.

Marius turned to the others. "I suggest I go alone, to avoid overwhelming her."

It was quickly agreed. Conyers, Russell and Miles moved away, whilst Marius walked towards her.

"Good afternoon, Mrs Fielding," he said casually. "Do you mind if I join you?"

"Please do, Dr Hope. Suddenly, it has turned most inclement."

"Your husband is normally with you at this hour, is he not, Mrs Fielding?"

"Yes. He has been called away this very moment. Though, I imagine he will return shortly."

"He is a very busy man with this smuggling epidemic making the Excise Commission's work so difficult," Marius remarked. "Although I would have thought he might be drawn away from The Wells more frequently than seems to be the case."

She looked startled. "Well, I'm sure he is doing his best, Doctor."

"When do you expect to return to London, Mrs Fielding?" enquired Marius, gazing intently into her face.

Her eyes took on a look of uncertainty. Her eyelids fluttered, and she turned her head from his gaze.

"I ... I really can't say. It's up to my husband."

Marius continued relentlessly. "I understood from Customs House that Mr Fielding, was expected back soon. What has detained him, I wonder?"

She was clearly flustered. Her cheeks reddened. Again she turned away to hide her bewilderment.

"What hand does your husband write with, Mrs Fielding?"

"Oh! ... the right." She stopped, alarmed at what she had said. "No ... No, I'm wrong," she said agonisingly. "It's the left. Yes, it's the left!"

Marius felt into an inner pocket, and removed his hand. He held it, clenched tight before her. Slowly, he uncurled his fingers. There, in the palm of his hand, was a button.

"Do you recognise this, Mrs Fielding?"

She sat absolutely still. Scarcely breathing, the colour draining from her face. Her body sagged, eyes filled. Then, she emitted a shrill, keening scream that echoed the length of the Walks. It went on endlessly, growing in intensity. Suddenly, she collapsed across the table. Those around her were transfixed. Conyers, nearby, was frozen in his seat. The constable and the dragoon officer rushed to Marius' side.

"What on earth did you say to her, Doctor?" cried Russell, lifting the woman gently back into her chair. She was in a dead faint.

"I believe I have just made her aware, Constable, that her husband is dead."

"What do you mean? Has Fielding just died?"

"No, Mr Russell, he was murdered some weeks ago," said Marius. "The man accompanying this woman is an impostor, and a dangerous one at that."

Gently patting her cheek, giving her sips of water brought by a serving girl, Marius gradually revived the distraught woman.

"Mrs Fielding, let me help you back to your lodgings. I believe they are close by, are they not?"

The woman's eyes opened. "If you please, Doctor," she whispered. Then they opened wide. "My God, he is there!"

"What do you mean?"

"That man, that terrible man, is there!"

Conyers had joined them.

"Where? In your lodgings, Mrs Fielding?"

She nodded. Her face portraying the ordeal she was suffering.

"Where are you staying? Tell me quickly!"

"Above here Doctor! Number forty-eight! Go up through there." She pointed to an opening. "Towards Bishops Down. The main door is the other side of this row of buildings."

"Stay with her, Mr Conyers," cried Marius. "Come on!" he called to Miles and Russell. He led them along the narrow passage under the colonnade. Turning up the steps leading to the entrance, the door was ajar. Pushing it open, they raced through a small reception area and found themselves in a servant's room.

Phillips was there, crumpled in a corner. Terror etched on his face. He was dead, one hand clutching at a bone-handled knife that had been plunged into his chest. The other tight round a silk handkerchief. Marius was momentarily shocked. The constable looked over his shoulder.

"Is it Fielding?"

"No, it's the magistrate!"

While Marius glanced quickly round, Miles headed for the staircase on the far side, Russell followed him. The three of them reached the next floor and dashed into a spacious salon overlooking the Upper Walk. Suddenly, they heard the distant staccato steps of someone descending from the upper storey. Shoes beating a rapid tattoo on bare wood echoed through the silence.

Fielding appeared before them, motionless on the last tread of the stairs. His hands clasping a small valise to his chest.

"What do you want?" he cried.

The constable's voice was loud in Marius' ear. "To apprehend you, sir, for murder and conspiracy!"

A desperate look suffused his face.

"Stay away from me!"

Throwing the valise at Miles, he rushed for the door leading onto the balcony. He was through, twisting towards the stairwell to escape the grasping hands of the dragoon officer. The narrow walkway, now wet with rain, would have been hazardous for someone merely walking. Turning quickly on such a surface was courting danger. His well-made shoes, ornamented with a lion's head buckle, were highly polished, the soles smooth. Pivoting on his right foot provided little purchase. He continued his forward momentum.

Pitching against the guardrail, his weight and height conspired against him. Even clutching at the support only slowed the inevitable. With a cry of desperation, Fielding slowly cart-wheeled over the ornate cast-iron barrier, to crash sickeningly onto the empty tables below.

Marius and Russell stood beside Miles in the heavy rain. Fielding was spread-eagled across scattered tables and chairs. No one near him. The rain beating down on the broken body.

"I must go down to him," declared Marius shakily. He moved quickly through the house, along the passage, and out into the Upper Walk. He was bending intently over Fielding when the others joined him.

"Is he dead?" asked Conyers.

"Not yet. But I don't hold out much hope," he murmured, examining the still form. "There's a chair leg impaled in his gut. I can't move him."

Fielding's eyes fluttered, then opened.

Recognition dawned as he saw Marius leaning over him.

A crooked smile. "Well, Doctor." He coughed, catching his breath. "I didn't expect our confrontation to end like this."

Marius took off his frock coat, covering Fielding as the rain beat down across his face.

"Why do you show me concern?" asked Fielding. "I'm a dying man. You've won the day."

He suffered a prolonged bout of coughing. Blood spilled from his mouth.

"Why did you contrive such a plot, Mr Fielding?" asked Marius, wiping the blood gently away.

"Haven't you guessed? You seem to have got everything else right. My real name is Woods. I work for Jansons. We wanted the Walks for ourselves, and I devised a way of getting them."

"Did you set up the smuggling?"

"Of course, I did. And it went well," said Fielding, his features now contorting with pain. He gasped, "Except you worked out what I was doing."

"Did you kill the Lovedays?"

"No … I just encouraged their demise."

He was fading, eyes dimming.

"Who did kill them?"

The response was slower, it took more effort. Fielding's face was now a mask of agony. "Can't you guess? He was always under your nose," grimaced Fielding. He coughed raspingly. Lungs filling, breathing increasingly difficult.

"Or should I say, above your nose, Doctor," he said in a painful laugh, that turned suddenly to a gurgle as a great gout of blood issued from his mouth. His head fell limply to one side. Fielding was dead.

"What did he mean, "Above your nose"?" enquired Conyers.

"I can't think. We had better talk with Mrs Fielding."

The lady had been helped back to the lodgings, and was now reclining on a daybed.

"Can I get you anything, Mrs Fielding?" enquired Marius. "A soothing tisane, a little laudanum?"

"Nothing, doctor. I shall rest." She lay there with her eyes closed, trying to shut out the reality of all she had endured. Realisation that her husband would never again be with her.

"Tell me, Dr Hope, did he suffer terribly?"

"I don't think for a moment, Mrs Fielding."

She nodded slowly.

"May I ask you one or two questions, Mrs Fielding?"

"If you must, Doctor."

"When did you discover the fellow was not your husband?"

"The day I arrived by the coach from London," she said in a low voice. "I was met by someone employed by my husband. Or so I thought. He escorted me to these rooms, and Mr Woods came in, and proceeded to tell me." She stifled a sob. "Proceeded to tell me that Robert was in his clutches. I was to act out this charade, with this man pretending to be my husband. If I did so, Robert would be released, unharmed."

She burst into tears.

Marius turned away and walked over to the window. He stared idly across the Walks. The musicians had finished, and were collecting up their instruments and sheet music. Tofts was among them. Not so brightly dressed, as the constable had observed. In fact, compared with previous occasions, he seemed to merge into the background of the gallery. His mind turned again to Fielding's – no Woods' – dying comment, "Above your nose, Doctor!'"

Suddenly, it all made sense!

There was the cold-blooded killer of the Lovedays! Responsible for the callous threats to the freeholders, Clifford's attacker! Bennett's murderer! There he was, calmly packing away his mandolin. He had the perfect view of all that was happening in the Walks. Able to liaise with Woods, to do his bidding with no one aware of his close involvement in the scheme. But for Woods' deathbed remark, he would have gone unnoticed, slipping clean away.

"I know who the killer is!" shouted Marius. "Quick, follow me!"

Captain Miles was the first to react. As they ran down the front steps of the house, Russell and his deputies joined the chase. They raced through the passageway, emerging in a rush into the Upper Walk.

Tofts saw them. In an instant realising they were on to him. He gathered up his beloved instrument, darted down the gallery steps, and turning from his pursuers sprinted along the Lower Walk.

Past the fish market, the stalls, and on towards the Well. He raced through puddles, colliding with those scurrying for shelter in the torrential rain. Marius was not gaining. Miles was suddenly at his elbow, then passing him. His military headgear gone, together with his sword belt. The constable was nowhere to be seen in the swirling downpour. Across the bridge by the church. Marius was now ten yards or so behind the dragoon, gasping for breath, his legs tiring.

Up the narrow lane behind the Angel Inn they ran. Marius could see that Tofts was slowing. Miles now less that than a few yards from him. The wind blew a heavy shower directly at Tofts. Though his step faltered, he did not stop. Miles was shortening the distance between them rapidly, seemingly unhampered by the driving rain.

Marius kept going, but his strength was fast ebbing away. Ahead, he could see the opening onto the upward slope of Mount Sion. He prayed the chase would not take that direction.

Miles was closing. A matter of an outstretched arm, as the pair burst from the entrance to the lane obscured by overgrown trees and shrubbery.

Tofts was still running hard. Looking desperately over his shoulder. It would have made little difference. His velocity propelled him forward, even though his brain was now telling him to stop, change course, put out his hands.

He had little chance. Miles was luckier. He managed to alter his pursuit, as the coach from London slithered down the hill. The driver and his mate both pulling hard on the brake, but unable to slow its downward progress.

Tofts went under the horses' hooves and the wheels. The coach pulled sideways, almost pitched over. Miraculously, it righted itself to continue its snake-like path to the bottom of the slope in front of the Inn.

Tofts was dead when they reached him. There was nothing Marius could do. The body was broken, clothes torn and shredded. The mandolin, which Tofts had held onto throughout the chase, now a thousand splinters. Inside his tattered jerkin, were several bone-handled knives.

CHAPTER EIGHTY

Marius ate a lonely breakfast.

He was worried about Roger Dashwood. No one could account for his disappearance. All they could say was he had taken a horse from the stables, and had not been seen since. When I make my statement to the constable, I shall insist he discovers his whereabouts before I leave, determined Marius

He had dined alone the previous evening. In many respects, he had welcomed the solitude. Though, not as in former times, when he had consciously shunned others. On this occasion it had allowed him to marshal his thoughts. To review events, not just of the day, but since he had first arrived in The Wells.

Marius remembered, vividly, his conversations with Mrs Johnson. He still felt aggrieved there had been no firm resolution in the manner of her death.

In the time he had been away from the hospital, much had happened. He had been assaulted, fired upon, and involved in combat. He had faced fear, stooped to cunning, and, surprisingly, been instrumental in foiling a villainous plot.

All of which had made a significant impression on the once-retiring doctor. His mind also turned to the joyous moments spent in the spa town. Recognising that meeting Beth had been the most blissful of all. Now, on the point of leaving, he realised that he had learned much these past weeks. About other people, and notably, about himself.

He finished his meal, and sat for a time in the empty dining room. He had come to accept he was no longer the diffident fellow who had once shied away from confrontation. His resolve was much stronger. The one aspect he had yet to come to terms with was the loss of Beth. Not a forward person, conceivably she had not been fully aware of his growing affection. Now it was too late. She had gone from his life.

He rose from the table, committed to returning to London. In the future, he would be more able to deal with the bureaucratic, small-minded people he would encounter at St Bartholomew's Hospital. Regardless of them, he was determined to become the physician who would give his all, not only for those with the wealth to afford it, but those with nothing more to offer than their gratitude.

Strolling down the hill, he passed the scene so etched in his mind the preceding day. Of Tofts tumbled like a rag doll under the coach. He shuddered at the recollection. Linus Woods, for that was his full name, had much to answer for.

The valise he had thrown at Captain Miles had been a treasure trove of information. Woods had been meticulous in noting every meeting, transaction, act of aggression, even murder.

Returning to Woods' lodgings, the constable and Marius had sifted through the travelling case. In a side pocket had been nearly twenty thousand pounds. In another, a list of the freeholders' names, their title deeds equating to their share holdings, and when they had been purchased. In the body of the case, Russell had found the smugglers' routes; details of the meetings with the Hawkhurst Gang; the deed for the building in East Peckham; and the details of the barn in Waterdowne Forest.

"Acquired when he wanted to increase the distribution of the contraband," commented Russell. "And it carries Bowes' signature!"

The other items included a list of the occasions when threats and acts of violence had been carried out. Prominent were the references to the deaths of the Lovedays in the fire, of William Bennett on the racecourse.

Marius had also read through the papers, and come across a carefully annotated sheet which identified the involvement of Phillips, Jordan, and Tofts. It also referred, obliquely, to an informant aiding the magistrate. An unwelcome surprise was the naming of Arthur Marshal, the Riding Officer from Newhaven, in the conspiracy. Eventually, the documents had been replaced in the valise, and taken for evidence by the constable.

"We have more than enough proof for the courts to act against Jansons, the company hoping to gain from this little plot, Doctor," Russell had declared. "And with your testimony, there will most certainly be a conviction."

"Unless, Constable, Linus Woods was working for himself," Marius had added. "Perhaps he had an option on the shares they own. That will need investigating."

"Well, as far as I'm concerned," Russell said. "The case is closed. The only remaining question I have, is how did you know that Fielding, or should I say Woods, was behind the whole affair?"

Marius grinned at the constable. "Do you recall that meeting I attended at Rusthall when the Principal Minister was present? Woods sat opposite me at the table, writing occasionally, but more often doodling with his quill pen. The one thing I observed was he had the pen in his left hand."

"So that was it! That's why you asked me to write in a different manner."

"When I was in London a week or so ago, I went to Customs House. I caught a glimpse of the notes prepared by Fielding concerning his tour of the southern coast. He wrote in a broad, flourishing hand with a sloping bias. What I wanted to see, Mr Russell, was if a left-handed person could write with a quill pen at a similar angle. And the answer we now know ... he could not."

The warehouses would have been raided by now, thought Marius as he neared the constable's offices. Accompanied by several deputies, Captain Miles had planned the seizure of goods and smugglers at both stores. Starting with the barn in Waterdowne Forest, and thereafter the warehouse in East Peckham. He wondered how successful he had been.

As Marius arrived at the entrance, Miles rode up. He waited for the dragoon officer to dismount.

"So, Captain Miles, were you successful?"

"Moderately, Doctor," said the officer with a grin. "We took possession of a great quantity of goods – wines, spirits, tobacco, lace, and so on. But not many smugglers, I'm afraid."

Russell greeted them in the outer room, and asked the same question.

Miles explained. "It would appear a shipment of goods had just arrived at the barn close to The Wells. When we fetched up, a fierce fight was in progress."

The constable looked puzzled.

"It would seem payment had been demanded. I was told this by one of the captives. When no money was forthcoming, he found himself, along with his fellows, on the receiving end of a brutal attack. In fact, our intervention was more welcome than I could have imagined."

"Who was attacking whom?" asked Marius.

"It seems the Hawkhurst Gang, there were about thirty of them, brought laden packhorses from East Peckham," explained Miles. "After unloading, they asked for the outstanding payment. When they didn't receive their due, the gang went beserk. It's as well we arrived when we did. The trouble was those being attacked ran to us for help. In the process, most of the gang escaped. Though, we rounded up those working at the barn."

"What about your visit to East Peckham, Captain?" enquired Russell.

"The gang had gone there directly, Constable," said Miles. "So, as you might expect, we found an almost empty store. They'd taken what they could carry, and made off."

"Actually, Constable," commented Marius. "It works out rather well. None of the smuggling gangs will work with anyone from The Wells any more, and they certainly won't use the warehouses now they are known."

"I suppose you are right, Doctor," said Mr Russell reflectively. "Still, it would have been a feather in our caps to have apprehended the ringleaders of the gangs."

"They are too wily ever to be captured, Mr Russell," stated the dragoon officer. "They avoid the actual work of delivery and supply. They are more involved in the money side."

"Anyway, Captain, congratulations!" said Russell. "It follows a particularly fine job done yesterday." He added. "Now, I would like both of you to come into my office."

CHAPTER EIGHTY ONE

"Hello, Marius."

"Roger! What are you doing here?"

Dashwood grinned, and looked towards Russell. "I have a tale to tell, Marius, that even you might enjoy."

Marius looked puzzled. He turned to Russell. "Do you know what he is talking about?"

"Indeed, I do, Dr Hope. Sit down for a moment, if you will."

Marius and Captain Miles seated themselves. Roger stood by the window.

"Marius, you recall I was keen to discover more about Mr Johnson's love nest. You were much occupied with all that was happening here. I couldn't help much. So, I had a word with the constable, and he provided me with a deputy as an escort."

He paused, adding a moment of theatre to his story.

"Come on, Roger! Tell me what you have been up to!" exclaimed Marius, in exasperation.

His friend smiled broadly. "We rode for several hours, stopping at the inn in Tonbridge to enquire if they had seen Johnson recently. They hadn't, and as he wasn't in The Wells, I was concerned he might be there."

"Where?"

"At East Farleigh. Where I last saw him. I thought to have a word with the woman in the cottage. To learn how long Johnson had been consorting with her. The deputy was with me, so we could question her officially."

"So, that's where you went! You might have told me! I was worried when you were gone from the lodging house."

"I didn't want to say anything, in case you were adamant I accompany you to Eridge. As an inexperienced swordsman, I could have contributed little."

"Well, you could have left a note!"

"Come, Dr Hope. Let him finish his tale," interrupted Russell.

Marius frowned, but remained silent.

"As I was saying, the deputy and I went on to East Farleigh. Arriving in the afternoon, we skirted the village to avoid being seen, and approached the cottage along the riverbank. Fortunately, it is situated this side of the bridge."

Roger was clearly enjoying himself. He looked intently into Marius' face.

"I could see no sign of a horse in the outbuilding, and I presumed Johnson wasn't there. So, we marched straight up to the door, and knocked."

He took out his pipe, as he so often did on occasions when about to say something profound. He took his time, tamping down the tobacco in the bowl, lighting it, and inhaling swiftly to ensure it caught. Finally, he turned to Marius.

"Guess who opened the door?"

"Johnson?"

"No. Miss Roper! Johnson was standing behind her!"

"My God! Miss Roper! Do you mean he was consorting with his niece?"

Roger nodded.

"What happened?"

"I said something like, "Arrest these two people, deputy". Actually, they were as shocked as I was. The deputy took Johnson by the shoulder and held onto him. Miss Roper burst into tears and slumped down onto a stool with her head in her hands."

"Well I'm damned, Roger!"

"What is more, Marius, Miss Roper shouted "I knew we wouldn't get away with it.", and promptly declared, "It was all his idea!" Johnson shouted. "Shut up, you fool, you'll get us both hanged!""

"When I told her that she had better tell me the complete truth, she poured her heart out. It seems Johnson was enamoured of Miss Emily Roper. When his wife joined them, she soon came to suspect that his considerations were more than well-intentioned. They had several arguments. That's when he suggested to Miss Roper that they went away together.

"According to her, that was out of the question, for Mr Johnson was already married. The fire was a complete surprise to Emily Roper, she says. Johnson told her what had happened, he said everyone would be suspicious of their relationship, and they'd best leave. That's how they came to be staying in East Farleigh."

"I believe they are as guilty as each other," opined Marius.

Russell took up the story.

"They journeyed back as far as Tonbridge, and Mr Johnson and Miss Roper were placed in custody by Bridger. They arrived here, in The Wells, early this morning. The two of them are now firmly locked in our cells."

"Well done, Roger! So the fire at the Johnson's house was deliberate. Mrs Johnson was murdered."

"I only confirmed what you have been telling us all along, Marius."

"Then who was the person in the fire if Miss Roper is alive, Mr Russell?" questioned Marius, recalling the other body.

"Do you remember the couple from Woodsgate Corner enquiring after their daughter?   She was the maidservant working for the Johnsons, and the other body we found in the burned-out house. They callously murdered her."

CHAPTER EIGHTY TWO

Having risen early, he had breakfasted and taken a short stroll. The air was fresh. With a light wind blowing away the few remaining clouds, it promised to be a fine day. Not too warm, which would suit Marius on the coach journey.

The constable was travelling with him. In such a notable conspiracy, with the attendant murders, he would be reporting directly to the Justice in the capital. Marius would be giving his written account to Walpole, to satisfy the Principal Minister's interest and involvement in the affair.

After all that had taken place, the weekend had been something of an anticlimax. On the occasions he had dined with Roger Dashwood, he had repeatedly been asked if he would ever return to The Wells. Marius thought it unlikely, his mind now fixed firmly on resuming his work at the hospital.

"I might have been tempted, Roger. Only you know what might have been. Incidentally, I had another interesting meeting with The Master of Ceremonies. Mrs Porter told him what has been going on, and the outcome. Again, he offered to help me set up a practice in the town."

"What was your reply?"

"I said I was committed to St Bartholomew's."

"Pity. I could envisage you as a country doctor. Much more rewarding than visiting bed after bed in a miserable ward."

Marius had smiled at his friend's comment. Once it might have been. Now the town held little for him. Returning to his lodgings, he had collected his valise and carrying case. Roger was waiting for him in the hall.

"I'll walk to the coach with you, Marius. Let me take one of those." He picked up the carrying case.

They stood, companionably, by the bowling green. Shortly thereafter, they were joined by the constable.

"Good morning, Doctor, Mr Dashwood. Well, it's a little windy, but looks a fine day for a coach journey."

The baggage cart rumbled up the hill to the top of Mount Sion. The horses' flanks heaving after their exertion. The heavier baggage was passed to the driver, who stowed it carefully among the other suitcases and parcels.

"I'm not surrendering this one. I've prepared a detailed report," said Russell, patting the bag in his hand.

Chatting amiably, the trio formed an inward-facing group against the gusting breeze. Other passengers came straggling up the hill. Deep in conversation, Marius caught the sound of the approaching coach.

Suddenly, a voice said: "Marius, I see you are ready to leave."

Mr Conyers was at his side. He nodded to the others.

"Tell me, Marius, have you written your summary for the Principal Minister?" Conyers enquired.

"Like the Constable, sir, I too have prepared detailed notes for Sir Robert on the whole affair."

"Good! Good! Then you can pass them to me."

Marius stared at Conyers, uncomprehendingly. At the same time noticing smiles on the others' faces.

"Why on earth should I do that?"

"As the Lord of The Manor I shall deliver your report to Walpole myself. After all, I was responsible for overseeing the efforts to thwart the conspiracy. I shall take your place in the coach."

Marius's face reddened. Annoyed at the peremptory attitude so openly displayed by the Lord of The Manor.

"I don't think so, sir!"

"Marius," said Roger softy. "I suggest you reconsider. Look behind you to the carriage."

Marius turned. His heart leapt. He thrust the carrying case into Conyers' hands. He called. "Fetch my luggage from the baggage cart, Roger!"

Abandoning them all, he ran towards the carriage. As Beth stepped down to greet him, he swept her up and held her tightly in his arms.

AUTHOR'S NOTES

In the eighteenth century, The Wells *(Royal Tunbridge Wells as it is now known)* was a serious rival to Bath, the acclaimed spa town. Both were presided over by Richard "Beau" Nash. The Master of Ceremonies took The Wells under his wing, creating a transient society throughout the summer months known widely as "Mr Nash's Company". Its members observed strict rules in keeping to a weekly timetable of events, with gambling and balls held in the Assembly Rooms. What is more, the carefully constructed table of charges for all the many activities was rigorously applied.

Their collection was the province of Mrs Sarah Porter, a harridan employed by Nash, who was quite unabashed at approaching anyone, from nobleman to commoner, for their "dues".

The inspiration for the spa town came from a discovery in 1606 by Dudley, the third Baron North. Ill from consumption, he had visited his long-standing friend, Lord Bergavenny *(later Abergavenny)*. However, the fresh, country air did little to improve his well-being and it was decided he should return to London to put his affairs in order.

No great distance from Bergavenny's estate, North stopped by a spring to slake his thirst. Surprised that the taste and appearance were much like those of continental spa waters, containers were brought, and he journeyed on to London with a liberal quantity.

Improved in body and mind, and much taken by his discovery, North returned regularly to drink from the spring. His maladies abated, and he enjoyed rude health unto his eighty-fifth year. Such was his enthusiasm, thereafter a steady flow of travellers came to take the waters at The Wells.

Marius Hope, the central character, and his companion, Roger Dashwood are creatures of my imagination. Though, the relatives of the latter, Samuel and Sir Francis Dashwood, were holders of the title, Lords of The Manor of Rusthall. A role they fulfilled jointly until 1720.

Their successor, Maurice Conyers, was a builder prior to coming to The Wells; and this instinct for property construction and development may well have provoked the dissension between the freeholders and himself after the lease for the Walks (*The Pantiles*) expired in 1732.

As records show, this resulted in a protracted dispute between the two parties. The freeholders were not united. Each with differing views on what best be done with the site. Some seeking to limit expansion; others keen to enlarge the area; yet more looking for a generous uplift in the rents from the existing buildings, and handsome compensation for continued loss of grazing rights.

In opposition, the Lord of The Manor, resolute in his determination to acquire the lion's share of any division of the titles. Perhaps, it was because the township was growing in popularity, that the government of the day eventually stepped in to force an outcome to the dispute.

It was finally resolved when Parliament introduced *The Rusthall Manor Act of 1739*. This was a novel creation. It divided the Upper Walk into three lots. Two allocated to the Lord of The Manor; one to the freeholders. In the lottery, the freeholders drew the middle section of the Upper Walk – *(At the time, from the Great Gaming Room to the Flat House. This comprises numbers 18 – 44 in the present-day Pantiles)*

Importantly, the Act re-affirmed the integrity of The Walks and the adjacent common land. The area forever to remain "always open and free for the public use and benefit of the nobility and gentry, and other persons resorting to or frequenting The Wells".

One of the major title holders, Lord Abergavenny, commissioned John Bowra, a draughtsman and surveyor *(also leader of the notorious Groombridge Gang of smugglers)* to produce a detailed plan of the Upper Walk. This was completed in 1738, and was the basis upon which the Upper Walk was subsequently apportioned.

Smuggling was a major industry in the south-east during the eighteenth century, reaching its peak between 1730 and 1750. There were numerous gangs, of which the most infamous was the Hawkhurst Gang. Many of the smugglers referred to were alive and extremely active during the period referred to in this work

Moreover, the sums of money employed were truly staggering. It was nothing for a substantial shipment to cost upwards of fifty thousand pounds. Today, representing millions of pounds.

It was also true that the Excise was sorely stretched. There were few Riding Officers to patrol the coastline; and hardly any courageous enough to interfere in a landing of contraband, which frequently involved hundreds of men, and equal numbers of packhorses.

The Wells had considerable appeal to London's leisured classes. Although Bath was noted for its heated spa, the cold waters of The Wells were thought to have similar curative powers; and the town was invitingly closer to London than its counterpart in Somerset. However, as is true for most spas, it fast became a resort rather than a centre for one's wellbeing.

Sir Robert Walpole's mistress, Mrs Skerritt, had a weak constitution, and was often to be seen in The Wells. Thus, encouraging the Principal Minister to make regular visits to the spa town. Before moving to Downing Street as its first incumbent, Walpole lived in a splendid house in the grounds of the Chelsea Hospital. For his services as hospital paymaster, he was allowed to reside there free of charge.

John Castaing was a well-known share trader, and was the first to record dealings in his weekly publication, *The Course of Exchange*. Thomas Loggan, the artist referred to in the book, is not widely known in British art circles, although he produced a number of drawings and watercolours of and around The Wells. One of his more notable works was the portrayal of the many characters parading in the Upper Walk in the mid-18th century. These included Mrs Elizabeth Chudley – Duchess of Kingston, Dr Johnson, Pitt – Earl of Chatham, Lord Lytteton, David Garrick, and Beau Nash.

Loggan was a dwarf, who used a hut located at the south-west end of the Walks as his studio. Despite being hampered physically, he enjoyed a steady trade; and, when the company was in residence, was noted for his painting of fans for gentlewomen.

Although synonymous with the tessellated wood mosaic, the first Tunbridge Ware was undecorated turnery. Later, these wooden artefacts featured various patterns, or were painted to represent oriental lacquer work. Initially, a sideline for woodworkers in neighbouring communities, the interest in the bowls and boxes grew to the extent that enterprising manufacturers in London began making such items. But, the output of two notable specialists gradually dominated the production of Tunbridge Ware - The Wise Family in Tonbridge, and the Burrows in The Wells.

A form of marquetry decoration, depicting birds and butterflies, was introduced in 1762. However, the style of Tunbridge Ware, known so well today, which is based on the twin techniques of stickware and half-square mosaic, was introduced by James Burrows in 1830.

Patrick Gooch, 2012

The First Blast of the Trumpet

The Knox Trilogy
Book One

Marie Macpherson

Praise for The First Blast of the Trumpet

"Marie Macpherson's well-researched novel captures the period which led up to the Reformation in Scotland, in which decay and despotism led eventually to a new regime. She leaves the reader much better informed about the rivalries between the Scots nobility, and the way in which they used the late medieval church as a power base to consolidate their hold on power. In addition, she skilfully escapes the constraints of the known facts to give her readers an intriguing fictional tale of the early life of John Knox. The violence and brutality of life in sixteenth century Scotland is well captured, along with the struggles among the vying dynasties to supplant a weak monarchy. Her romances are earthy rather than ethereal, her nobles far short of heroic and the result is a book which portrays the main players in Scotland's Reformation as flawed human beings rather than the goodies and baddies which partisan history has often made them."

---**Rev Stewart Lamont**, *author of "The Swordbearer: John Knox and the European Reformation"*

"In this novel, set in one of the most turbulent periods of Scottish (and English) history, much historical, ethnological and linguistic research is in evidence, which - importantly - Marie Macpherson delivers with a commendable lightness of touch. Descriptions of contemporary superstitions, medicinal cures, and religious practices are impressively handled and closely linked to an engrossing plot and finely drawn, convincing characterisation. The over-riding theme of the novel is Keep Tryst and all the central characters are confronted with the issue of fidelity of some kind, with its breaching or betrayal resulting in an acute sense of loss and/or guilt. The novel well documents the corruption among church officialdom and the blatant misogyny of many of those in positions of power, yet the author handles these issues sensitively. I enjoyed this book enormously and would be more than happy to read it a second time. I'm sure such an accomplished debut novel will enjoy considerable success."

---**Charles Jones FRSE**, *Emeritus Forbes Professor of English Language, University of Edinburgh*

"With style and verve Marie Macpherson whirls us into the world of sixteenth-century Scotland: its sights and smells, sexual attraction, childbirth and death, and of course the ever looming threat of religious strife. Few are the known facts of John Knox's first thirty and more years, but this vivid creation of a fictional life for him not only entertains but raises many questions in the reader's mind about the character and motives of a dominating figure in Scottish history."

--- **Dr Rosalind Marshall**, *Fellow of the Royal Society of Literature, research associate of the Oxford Dictionary of National Biography, to which she has contributed more than fifty articles, and author of biographies of Mary, Queen of Scots, Mary of Guise, John Knox, Elizabeth I and Bonnie Prince Charlie.*

I

Hallowe'en

The night it is good Hallowe'en
When fairy folk will ride;
And they that wad their true-love win
At Miles Cross they maun bide.
The Ballad of Tam Linn, Traditional

Hailes Castle, Scotland, 1511

"There's no rhyme nor reason to it. Your destiny is already laid doon.'

Hunkered down on the hearth, Betsy jiggled the glowing embers with a poker and then carefully criss-crossed dry hazel branches on top. Huddled together on the settle, the three girls drew back as the fire burst into life, the crackling flames spitting out fiery sprites that frolicked their way up the chimney. Betsy wiped the slather of sweat from her flushed face and scrambled up to plonk herself down beside them by the ingleneuk.

"Doom-laden?" Elisabeth queried, her head dirling at the thought. "So where's the use in making a wish?'

"Wishes – and hopes and dreams," Betsy added, "are what keep us going. You make a wish in the hope that it'll come true, but you'll never flee your fate. Now then, my jaggy thistle, when the flames die down, cast your nut into the fire and wish on it," she instructed. "And mind, be wary what you wish for."

Elisabeth delved her hand into the basket and pulled out two nuts coupled together. "Ah, a St John's nut." Betsy nodded slowly. "That's a good omen."

"That my wish will come true?" Her ferny green eyes glinted in the firelight.

"Nay, lass, but it'll guard you against the evil eye. Don't fling it, but keep it safe as a charm against witches."

With a doubtful glance at her nurse, Elisabeth slipped the enchanted nut into the pocket of her breeches and chose again. "I will never marry," she began, pausing to savour the astonished gasps before throwing her nut onto the red-hot embers, "unless for love.'

"Don't be all blaw and bluster, Lisbeth my lass. It's a wish you've to make, not a deal with the devil. And in secret, otherwise it'll no come true," Betsy warned.

"Then I'll make it come true," Elisabeth retorted.

Betsy shook her head. "You'll have no say in the matter. You maun dree your weird, as the auld saying goes." Then, seeing Elisabeth's quizzical frown, she added, "You must endure your destiny, my jaggy thistle. And never, ever tempt fate by having too great a conceit of yourself. Forbye, if you marry for love, you'll work for silver."

"We'll see," Elisabeth replied, quietly determined that she wouldn't share the lot of those lasses, sacrificed at the altar for the sake of family alliances and financial gain. Leaning forward, her brows drawn tightly together, she glared at the hazelnut, willing it to do her bidding. The nut twitched around the embers before splitting open and spitting out its kernel.

"Sakes me!" Betsy muttered.

"What does it bode?" Elisabeth tugged impatiently at Betsy's sleeve.

"That your peerie heid and nippy tongue will lead you into bother, my lass," Betsy cautioned.

"And that no man will touch a jaggy thistle such as you."

Elisabeth twisted round ready to repay Kate's stinging remark with a sharp nip, but a dunt in the arm from Meg stopped her.

"Even the briar rose has thorns, mind," Elisabeth snapped instead. "Bonnie you may be, but blithe you're not."

"Tsk, tsk," Betsy chided. It made her heart sore to hear her three wee orphans, her bonnie flowers of the forest, bickering. She shook her head as her jaggy thistle, the sharp-witted, spiky-tongued Lisbeth lashed out at fair-haired, pink-cheeked Kate who, like a pawkie kitten, kept her claws hidden until provoked.

Ignoring their squabble, Meg leant forward and cupped her chin in her hands to gaze wistfully into the fire. She lowered her hazelnut gently into the embers where it sizzled and sputtered, before slowly fizzling out.

"Oh, dearie me," she moaned, sucking her top lip over her teeth to stem the tears.

"Don't you fret, my fairy flower." Betsy patted her knee. "That's a sign of a quiet, peaceful life."

"Is it Betsy? Truly?" Meg's watery blue eyes – the shade of the fragile harebell – glistened with grateful tears. Fey, frail Meg had no desire to marry but secretly craved the contemplative life of a nun, sheltered from the hurly-burly of the world behind a protective wall. Let not matrimony and maternity be my destiny, she prayed.

"My turn now." Kate had been rummaging through the basket, picking over the nuts until finding one to her liking. Smooth, flawless and perfectly round.

"We ken fine what you'll wish for," Elisabeth taunted. "And since it's no secret, it'll no be granted."

Kate's eyes blazed in the firelight. "Make her stop, Betsy."

While Elisabeth and Meg were daughters of the late Patrick, 2nd Earl of Bothwell, Kate's parentage was vague. An orphan of one of the minor scions of the family –

though tongues wagged that she was a love-child – the "lass with the gowden hair" had been taken in by the earl and brought up with his own daughters at Hailes Castle.

Pernickety and petulant, and endlessly teased by Elisabeth for being a gowk, the cuckoo in their nest, Kate aspired to improve her lowly position through marriage. But, knowing that Kate had set her heart on their brother, Adam, the young Earl of Bothwell, Elisabeth had set her teeth against it.

Taking her time, Kate inspected the bed of embers before deciding where to place her nut. They all bent forward to watch as it hopped and skipped about, before being spat out to land on the hearth. Instinctively they drew their feet back.

"You'll have to throw it back in at once for your wish to come true."

Betsy glowered at Elisabeth, but was too late to stop Kate who'd already picked up the sizzling nut. And dropped it again with a piercing yelp of pain.

"Cuckoo! Cuckoo! Feardie-gowk!" Elisabeth goaded her.

"Sticks and stones may break my bones, but names will never hurt me," Kate recited and sucked on her smarting fingertips to soothe them.

"You were the clumsy kittok for dropping the nut and now your wish is forfeit."

"I don't believe you. You're only saying that because you don't want me to marry Adam. Well, you'll see. I'm no common kittok. I shall be a great lady one day. I shall be the Countess of Bothwell." She flicked back her golden hair and glared at her tormentor.

"Over my dead body, brazen besom," Elisabeth muttered under her breath. She couldn't abide the thought of her cousin becoming her brother's wife and a titled lady, for she suspected that, beneath her simpering mannerisms and ladylike demeanour, skulked a scheming wench.

"While no-one will waste a glance on a rapscallion like you," Kate was saying, "a gilpie no a girl." She tilted her head to look down her snub nose at Elisabeth, clad in her brother's cast-off riding breeches, her copper hair tousled and unkempt.

Seeing her jaggy thistle about to snap, Betsy clamped her hand across her mouth. Only when Elisabeth nodded, to indicate that she'd keep her mouth shut, did Betsy let go.

"Wheesht, wheesht, my fairest flowers," she crooned, "this is no a night for bickering."

"These daft games are tiresome." Kate stood up abruptly and wrapped her shawl tightly around her shoulders. "I'm away to bed."

"Afore the witching hour? On your own?"

Elisabeth's deep menacing growl had the intended effect. Kate glanced round, horror-stricken by the sinister shadows cast by the flickering tallow candles, before stammering, "Well, why not? I ... I ... '

"There's no telling who or what you'll meet on Hallows Eve," Elisabeth continued in her spooky voice, fluttering her fingers in front of Kate's anxious face. "When ghosts and ghouls and boglemen walk the earth."

"Don't you be scaring the living daylights out of her," Betsy chided. "Don't fret, Kate, you'll meet your match soon enough. Come, now, and sing us the *Ballad of True Thomas.*" She leant forward to stoke the fire with more logs. "Coorie in my bonnie lassies, and listen.'

With a hostile glare at her cousin, Kate tossed her fair curls and began crooning softly in her linnet-sweet voice, which, though she'd die rather than admit it, Elisabeth loved to hear.

> "True Thomas he pull'd off his cap,
> And louted low down to his knee.
> All hail, thou mighty Queen of Heaven!
> For thy peer on earth I never did see.'

The girls listened spellbound to the legend of Thomas the Rhymer, lured by the Queen of Fairies to Elfland where he disappeared for seven long years, although it felt like only three days to him. Before he left, she gave him two gifts: a tongue that never lied and the power to see into the future.

"Betsy, have you the second sight?" Meg asked, her whisper breaking the mortcloth of silence that had fallen over them after Kate's eldritch song. Betsy Learmont came from an old border family descended, so she told them, from this very Thomas of Earldoune, half minstrel, half magician, famed and feared for his sorceries. Betsy stared into the fire for a few moments before answering.

"I jalouse we all have in some way or other. We've all been given a sixth sense, a third eye, some cry it, that sees beyond the veil, but more often than not, most folk pay it scant heed. For where's the use in being able to peer through the dark veil smooring the future with no power to change it? And those who are truly foresighted would say it's more of a curse than a blessing.

"But at certain times of the year, like tonight, All Hallows" Eve – or *Samhain* as the auld, Celtic religion cries it – the thin veil between this world and the next is drawn back. Nay," she said, shaking her head at Meg's raised eyebrows, "not your Christian paradise. Nor thon limbo where the souls of unbaptised bairns and pagans linger for eternity, but the twilight world between heaven and earth where the fairy folk and the unquiet dead dwell.'

"The unquiet dead?" Meg murmured.

"Wheesht!" Betsy put a warning finger to her lips, for to mention them risked rousing them. She lowered her voice to a faint whisper. "The restless spirits of folk that have been murdered or have taken their own lives, who roam the earth, looking for unwary bodies of the living to possess." Her chilling words sent a shiver through Meg. "On this night our own spirits can leave our bodies, too. That's why you're able to see the spectre of the man you'll marry."

The blustery wind soughed down the chimney, gusting smoke into the chamber and rattling the shutters. The cold draught at their backs sent shivers skittering down their spines. The girls drew their thick woollen shawls more securely over their heads and huddled in closer together. As the mirk and midnight hour approached, Betsy set about making hot pint. She plunged the scorching poker into a kettle of spiced ale sweetened with honey until the toddy sizzled and simmered merrily, rising to the top in a smooth, creamy froth.

"This will give you good cheer and good heart," she promised.

While they blew on their courage-giving draught to cool it down, Betsy scraped some soot from inside the chimney to rub on their faces as a disguise to fool the malevolent spirits of the unquiet dead. It was nearly time to ring the stooks.

"I'll just bide here by the fire." Kate shivered. "It's far too cold and dark to be wandering about."

"You mean you're too feart. And what will Adam think when he hears the future Countess of Bothwell is a feardie gowk?'

Ignoring Elisabeth's taunt, Kate smeared her pink cheeks with soot and then wiped her clarty hands on Elisabeth's breeches. Betsy deftly stepped in between to foil any reprisal from the jaggy thistle and handed them each a branch from the fairy tree.

"These rowan twigs will ward off evil spirits. Hold on to them for dear life. Or else." She lit the taper in the neep lantern and passed it to Elisabeth. Its ghoulish grin of jagged teeth glowing in the dark would scare the living never mind the undead.

"Now, mind and go widdershins round the stooks," Betsy said, before adding, "and beware of tumbling into thon ditch, my jaggy thistle."

The snell blast as they stepped out from the shelter of the castle walls caught their breath. Hearing the wind whistling and howling like a carlin through the trees, the girls hesitated. Top-heavy pines swayed back and forth in the wind, threatening to fall over and crash down on them. Trees stripped of their leaves were transformed into blackened skeletons with gnarled, wizened fingers pointing in menace. Leaves whirled and reeled madly like hobgoblins at Auld Clootie's ball. Clouds scudded past the furtive moon, casting unearthly shadows. Striving to make no sound that would alert evil spirits, the girls stepped lightly, but the crisp, dry leaves crackled and crunched underfoot.

By the glimmer of the neep lantern they skirted round the ditch filled with fallen leaves until they came to the crossing point. In the cornfield, the harvest straw gathered into sheaves stood like rows of drunken men leaning into each other for support. Kate hung tightly to Meg but kept looking round, convinced that they were being followed.

"Aagh! What's that?" She stopped to brandish her rowan switch.

"Wheesht! You'll wake the unquiet dead with your screeching," Elisabeth growled.

"Look over there." Kate was pointing with her twig. "Isn't thon a bogleman?"

All three huddled together to peer at the eerie shape frantically waving its tattered limbs as if in warning.

"Thon's a pease-bogle, you daft gowk," Elisabeth sneered as the scarecrow keeled over in the strong wind.

Stopping beside the nearest haystack, they bickered about which way to circle it.

"Betsy said mind and go widdershins," Meg said, her teeth chittering.

"The devil's way? Against the sun? Will that no bring bad luck?" Kate shivered.

Meg shrugged her shoulders. "Not at Hallowe'en. For this is the witches" night and we'll vex Auld Nick mair if we go sunwise, says Betsy. Now shut your een and hold your arms out in front. Circle three times and on the third turn your sweetheart's spectre will appear.'

"I … I… I'm no sure I want to do this." Kate was looking round, still certain that some malevolent spirit was stalking them.

"We'll do it together," Elisabeth suggested, for she, too, was feeling uneasy.

Having no wish for a spouse in any form – body or spirit – Meg held the lantern while the two girls, eyes tight shut and arms stretched out like sleepwalkers, began to circle the stook. Willing herself to see the image of the one she loved, Elisabeth squeezed her eyelids tight against her eyeballs until colours flashed and flared in her head.

As they came round for the third time, leaves disturbed by a field mouse or vole rustled nearby. An owl or bat whooshed past her, and then a high-pitched scream rang out, chilling her blood. In the shadows of the trees, Elisabeth could make out two shapes stumbling across the cornfield towards them. As they loomed nearer, she drew back, alarmed to see two bogles, the whites of their eyes gleaming in blackened faces.

"Beware the unquiet dead!" a menacing voice rumbled.

"Or the quiet undead!" another echoed.

When one of the ghouls darted forward to reel her in, Elisabeth turned tail. She flung aside her rowan switch and stumbled over divots towards the ditch.

Suddenly the burn bubbled up and a torrent swept her off her feet. As she was tossed and spun in the murky water, shadowy figures whirled around her. She tried to grab hold of a hand but the rotting flesh fell away from the fingers. A severed head spun towards her, its fronds of hair streaming out behind, its face stripped of flesh. With greenish-black pus gushing through the empty eye sockets and its jaws locked in an eternal grimace, the skull leered at her. The burn water thickened and darkened to blood red, brimming into her lungs. As the whooshing sound in her ears died down, she opened her mouth to gulp down air. From far away she heard an unearthly voice murmur, "She's coming to herself."

When arms lifted her up and propped her against a dyke, Elisabeth snorted to clear the stench of decaying leaves in her nostrils, but as she wiped the glaur from her eyes she let out a yelp. Behind the neep lantern with its jagged teeth, another ghastly head, with soot-stained mouth and bone white teeth, was yawning wide. She jolted backwards but, as she jerked forwards, her forehead whacked the fiend's nose with a loud crack.

"Ouch!" The bogle's hand darted to its face. "*Nemo me impune lacessit.* You're well named, my jaggy thistle. Who'd dare meddle with you? Your snite is worse than your bite. And there was I, ready to bewitch you with a kiss," he mumbled, dabbing at the streaks of sooty blood trickling from his nose. "Pity."

"She hasn't broken anything." Meg had knelt down in the glaur to massage her sister's ankles with fingers cold as the grave.

"What about me?" the ghoul wailed. "Not only my nose but my poor heart is sore."

"She's well enough if she can skelp him like that," Kate hissed, but, seeing the other bogleman approach, she widened doe eyes at him. "Forbye, this spanking wind is whipping the skin off my cheeks," she whimpered.

"Come, then, afore it flays the hide off you." The fiendish Earl of Bothwell was holding out one crooked arm to Kate who, needing no further coaxing, linked her arm through his. But when he offered his other arm to Meg, whose very bones were trembling with cold, Kate's face darkened to a glower. Meanwhile the other ghoul was helping Elisabeth to her feet.

"You ... you ... scared me half to death, Davie Lindsay," she scolded.

"Better not let the cold kill the other half then."

Lindsay pulled her into the shelter of his cloak but the acrid smell of soot from his blackened face began to prickle her nostrils. As she screwed up her nose to stifle a sneeze, he pressed his finger hard against her top lip.

"Squeezing is better than sneezing, my jaggy thistle. And kissing can wait. But keep in mind whose spirit you've seen tonight, otherwise the devil knows who you'll marry."